THOSE BEAUTIFUL EYES

THOSE BEAUTIFUL EYES

A NOVEL OF 2700 B.C.
AND THE PRESENT DAY

Ann Cowart Lutzky

Writers Club Press
San Jose New York Lincoln Shanghai

Those Beautiful Eyes
A Novel of 2700 B.C. and the Present Day

Writers Club Press
an imprint of iUniverse.com, Inc.

For information address:
iUniverse.com, Inc.
5220 S 16th, Ste. 200
Lincoln, NE 68512
www.iuniverse.com

ISBN: 0-595-20221-7

Printed in the United States of America

To Henry, Anna, Aaron, Jim W., Virginia and Jim A.

Epigraph

"If a diver is to secure pearls, he must descend to the bottom of the sea, braving all dangers of jagged coral and vicious sharks. So man must face the perils of worldly passions if he is to secure the precious pearl of Enlightenment. He must first be lost among the mountainous crags..."

—*The Teaching of Buddha* by Bukkyo Dendo Kyokai

Preface

In 1969 my husband and I departed from the only place where I had ever lived—the San Francisco Bay Area—to begin two years residence in a traditional village of ancient culture. Those years are the inspiration for this book.

When we arrived as Peace Corps volunteers in the village of Gbongayja, I was twenty-two. With a newly acquired degree in philosophy from Berkeley and a brand new marriage, I had questions about what sort of married woman I would be. I loved to ask anything that related to this topic, and my village neighbors loved to be asked, philosophizing far into the night. But their daily lives told me even more than what they said.

I learned to revere their ideals of strength and beauty; and to try, like them, to deepen my serenity in times of pain or trouble. Those years cast their light upon the patterns of my marriage, of motherhood, of work and friendship in all the years that followed.

That centuries-old village is no more; three years ago it was destroyed, eradicated in war. My book arose from powerful emotional bonds with that lost village consciousness as well as with modern life— with the perplexities of passion and commitment, betrayal, loss, and love which haunted men and women in that older world, as they do in this. I feel a need to share the awareness I have been given.

Those Beautiful Eyes is an intimate experience of the sexual and spiritual forces at play in both ancient and modern worlds. The story is a family saga that winds back and forth between one woman's life in a land of 2700 B.C. (chosen for its aspect as a relatively universal seminal civilization) and the lives of her descendants, a man and a woman of the San Francisco East Bay.

Writing this book incorporated several years of research on Mesopotamian and Indus Valley culture, and on world mythology and archetypes. Sensual and emotional nuances of pre-industrial life are enhanced both by my years in the village of the Vai, a trader people of equatorial West Africa; and by visits to ancient cities and villages in 33 countries. Subtleties of modern locations, in the Bay Area and in Mexico, Europe, Morocco, Uganda and Liberia, come from life. The multiethnic history of the main male character is loosely based on my own family.

The city of Orom and the village of Fa-Orszag are both fictional. Their cultures are derived from a synthesis of what is presently known of the cultures and literature of the 2700 B.C. societies east, in Mesopotamia, and west, in the Indus Valley. Orom and Fa-Orszag are located between these two.

Since completing my manuscript, I have experienced numerous interesting confirmations of the integrity of this synthesis: one example of these occurred when my husband called my attention to a newspaper article about a city which had recently been unearthed in the general location of my imagined city of Orom. When I read the description of the supposed culture of this unknown people, I found an amazingly close approximation to my description of Orom; it was almost word for word in some sentences. Another example took place when I came upon a book containing a poem of an actual Sumerian priestess who, like my character Anarisha, had recorded her life in journal-type tablets. This woman had used the same adjective in the same unusual metaphor as did Anarisha, to describe the situation of being uprooted from her home. The difference was that this woman's situation was the converse of my character's; the real priestess was exiled from her temple and forced into ordinary life while Anarisha was uprooted from ordinary life and forced into a temple.

The character Anarisha was, and is, quite real to me; sometimes her voice was so strong in my mind that it would compel me to go back and intuitively rewrite a chapter or conversation that had previously made sense in an entirely different way. I would "hear" her protesting "that isn't how it happened, that isn't what we said!" I believe she is a voice of the unconscious perhaps, of ancient poems and scriptures, of ancestral memories, if that is possible, of women I knew in Africa.

The imaginary *Twenty-One Hymns of Orom*, from which several chapter epigraphs are "taken" is derived from numerous songs, chants, epics, images and concepts, primarily from early Vedic and Sumerian sources.

Contents

Acknowledgements xvii

Prologue...xix

Part I: Does Anybody Know What Time It Is? 1

   1. *Anarisha's Husband* 3

   2. *Anarisha: My Life* 7

   3. *Approximately Five Thousand Years Later* 16

   4. *Gilgamesh—the Interview Concludes* 29

   5. *Memories of a Greek Island*.....................................39

   6. *In the Days of the Sumerians*...................................50

   7. *War with Heaven*..58

   8. *Betrayal*..62

   9. *Bondage*...67

  10. *Visions*...71

Part II: Woman of The Water 75

   1. *Maria Ananin* 77

   2. *Mythology* 82

   3. *Simbaya Brings Broth*..88

   4. *A Brief and Splendid Era* 91

   5. *A Rare and Precious Jewel*......................................93

   6. *Dinner and a Movie*...96

   7. *Spring of '63* 105

   8. *All in Perspective* 112

   9. *Gudea the Scribe* 119

10   High School Graduation 124
11. Marsh Birds at Twilight 128
12. The Gates of Orom 130
13. A Slave 138
14. To Guadalajara 143
15. Paris 150
16. Gardenias versus Pigs 158
17. The Slave Holders................................171
18. Anarisha's Dance 175

Part III: Mystery 185
1.   The White Robe and the Tree 187
2.   Fascination 193
3.   Invasion..199
4.   A Fertility Rite 204
5.   Mystery 208
6.   The Curse of Guilt 219
7.   A Letter from Venice Beach 222
8.   A Camera 225
9.   A Rainy Night in November 227
10. Coronado 229
11. Near Descent 233
12. Desperate Move 238
13. A Healing..241

Part IV: Travels through Time and Space 253
1.   The Morning Flute and the Morning Fire 255
2.   In a Bookshop of Nayarit 259
3.   Far from the USA................................270
4.   A Generation Gap 273
5.   A Singular Circumstance in the City of Orom ...276
6.   The Winter of Love..............................280
7.   On an African Riverboat 285

8. Morocco 290
9. Memories of a Marriage 295
10. The Greek Island: a Second Encounter.................298
11. Back to Berkeley...305
12. Maria and San Francisco 314
13. Meanwhile in the Suburbs 319

Part V: Inanna and Dumuzi 323
1. Let It Flow...325
2. The Rain Forest 328
3. Childhood Friends 330
4. Kama, the God of Love 342
5. She Opened the Door 348
6. The Journal of David Dagan 354
7. More from the Journal of David Dagan 362
8. Dear Maria 365
9. The Ohana Palace 368
10. The Ritual of Inanna's Descent 381
11. Brando 388
12. Ananin and Dagan 393
13. Inspiration...395
14. Anarisha's Information 398
15. On the Mountain and Beyond 402
16. In the Courtyard of the Temple of Inanna 415
17. Old Ties Still Binding...418
18. The Call 423

Epilogue: David and Michael 431
About the Author 439

Prologue

Anarisha

east of Sumeria, west of Mohenjo-Daro
circa 2700 B.C.

In a forest, in the very heart of the forest, in a place where the fragrance of wild ginger went beyond fragrance and became a state of being, a woman sat upon the earth. She drew her thighs up before her. Setting a moist clay tablet upon them, she grasped the tablet with one hand and her blue lapis stylus with the other. She began then to carefully chisel her lines. A stream of sunshine on the tablet gave a glow that caused her tiny pictograms to become warm and golden, favored of the morning, born of the light.

"Anarisha"—she deftly engraved the five graceful strokes of her own name into the sunlit table.

*   *   *

Michael

San Francisco
circa 2000 A.D.

He lay awake throughout a silent night. Now and then the long lonesome sound of a passing airplane smoothly covered the silence. The deep rumbling gave comfort somehow, an echo in the night sky of solitude on earth.

In the morning before rising, he reached down and dialed a number. He knew it well, even half-asleep. Every two months he called her. He listened to her message; but he never left his own. He heard something in her voice there. Desire? Was she waiting? He thought he could detect it—very subtle, in her breathing, in her speaking. In the timing. Was it he alone who thought that? Or was it clear to every caller, anyone who ever listened? All in his imagination? Had that been so when he had her? A false message, sent him as he touched her? In the timing of her movements, in the breathing of her skin? And now, within her voice mail, if he truly heard desire—so much time had gone by—was it there now for some other? Or was it always there for him?

As for himself, there was no question about it; he needed her. He'd needed her then and he needed her now. He put down the phone.

When he rose from bed and moved toward the bathroom, he felt the resignation. Resignation was always with him in the mornings of those days. Heavy, oppressive, like the stiffness in his back; it was part of him. He told himself to focus on strength. Go deeper for greater strength. A familiar image, Michelangelo's *David,* came with the focusing. David the King: passionate, aware, sometimes suffering, sometimes in ecstasy. Confused. But strong as living stone, holding onto something holy. He stayed with that image. It was a crutch that fit comfortably. It gave balance; it helped. He felt energy come.

Michael glanced at the mirror as he went toward the shower, and he liked what he saw. He was clearly tired, but the reflection closely mimicked the image in his mind. He began to whistle, purposefully. The song was upbeat, a favorite from the seventies: "Does Anybody Really Know What Time It Is?" Chicago Transit Authority. Great band. Great song. It would do him good to sing it out loud.

When he walked into the kitchen he was singing. His son Aaron, scrubbing a coffee mug, turned to give a smile and an upward nod. The young man, a merchant seaman, was with him for the week.

"Morning, Aaron!" Michael's voice was cheerful. "Well, looks like I'm late again." He changed his song now, without thinking, and resumed his whistling. "Beautiful Maria of My Soul" was the new choice for life's soundtrack. He could almost hear the trumpet as he spread cream cheese on a bagel.

For the remainder of the day, his thoughts would not fall upon his wishes or his memories. He sought only the present; not a fantasy of future, not a legend of his past. His time with her, and all that came before it, was over. Finished. Parts were clear, but most was murky. What good to dwell on it? You couldn't rewind life. He had business to take care of—two appointments, phone replies and e-mail, editing, and more…Some questions, though, persisted. Why always the voice mail? *Six months, and she's never come to answer.* Was she screening every call now? *From me?* He wondered. Or, so unlike his usual thinking—less well founded, far less rational—the question that persisted: *Does she really still exist?*

But by day's end he was all right. He joked with his son at dinner; they watched a video together; then Aaron left to meet a friend. As Michael finished his evening coffee, pleasant thoughts moved from here to there. Soon the train of thought was racing—a revelation, an inspiration, a sudden rush of new ideas.

Another woman filled his mind now, a woman he'd heard of years before. He moved quickly to set up the computer, as thoughts came fast and strong; he had to get them down before they passed away.

He sat cross-legged on the carpet, his back against the side of his sofa, the warm, quietly humming laptop balanced comfortably on his thighs. He stared at the glow of the blank screen as he ran dialogue through his mind. Feeling calmly expectant that something crucial was about to be fulfilled, he inhaled deeply, then nimbly struck his fingers upon the keys.

"Anarisha"—he clicked the mouse to center the title of his newest screenplay.

Part I

Does Anybody Know What Time It Is?

1

Anarisha's Husband

in a fertile valley, east of Sumeria, west of Mohenjo-Daro; a medium sized farming village named Fa-Orszag
2721 B.C.

Anurei of Fa-Orszag, eldest son of Erishoul and of Hita, wise father of Saraswati and of Endo, ever-fulfilling husband of the middle daughter of Astara and Oresh, was a coppersmith. He worked with copper, or sometimes obsidian or silver. And once he even worked with gold.

The coppersmith's bench was set far back from the road, near to the center of the village. It was hard for people to miss him. Sheltered by thatch but without walls, his workshop was as open as their outdoor kitchen plazas. Often it was Anurei, with his brightly even smile and his firm warm handshake, who would give the first welcome as the drowsy villagers set out to greet their neighbors in the mists of early dawn.

The people came to Anurei for more than the fine quality of his workmanship. They came to him for consolation and for advice—though he was not old—for his stories, and for his easy laughter as well. Generous and strong, he was only slightly restrained by a weak knee that made walking troublesome but not impossible. This was a man who thrived on being surrounded by others, who nourished his spirit with their intimacies, and who let their joking be his music while the feel of their eyes upon his work was the inspiration for perfection in his craft.

The high respect in which the coppersmith was held came from both his work and his good nature, and it came, too, from his position as the husband of Anarisha. For the wife of Anurei was a woman who was quietly desired, not only by the men—and a few of the women—of that village, but by the people of all the villages with which connection was maintained. His was a woman who, nevertheless, because of some unusual inward pull of her own nature, did not show knowledge of the neighbors' fantasies, clinging fantasies which perpetually stirred behind her, like dust upon the path on which she placed her feet. This apparent oblivion of the wife much increased the esteem in which the husband was already held.

It was Anurei the coppersmith who created the famous story; a controversial fable that would be passed down for generations in Fa-Orszag, of the jealous married mouse. As first he told it, to a small gathering at twilight in the plaza of his workshop, the tale began like this:

"My friends, our conversation this evening reminds me of a story," he said, as he always said, "of a similar circumstance. From a time long gone. When a pair of little field mice lived, with many relatives and friends, in tiny nests on the outskirts of our town. But, first let me say—I want you to know—it was not so easy for that mouse couple, nor for their kin! For the human ones of Fa-Orszag were so thrifty and so wise in that time, that hardly a crumb was wasted for the mouse clan to feed upon! Every night the little mouse husband would search for food, foraging about for many double-hours. But one evening he returned to his nest much earlier than usual, elated and very proud. For he had discovered an uncovered pot of grain in the storehouse of the human ones," and the coppersmith paused then, to wink at a certain forgetful child in the cluster of his listeners. "The mouse was happy, indeed! However, upon entering his own house, this mouse man made a second discovery, one which sent his emotions plunging as far down as his first discovery had lifted them up. For he came upon his dearly beloved wife lying in the nest with another mouse!

"The mouse husband immediately slunk off and sat himself down to collect his thoughts. 'I shall proceed in stealth,' muttered the mouse to himself, 'for that is how I best accomplish all my tasks.' And an idea began to take shape in his crafty little mind..."

When the coppersmith would conclude this particular fable, it was with an inquisitive smile and a gaze at his listeners that would pass momentarily into the eyes of many of them. Then somebody would clear a throat and somebody would cough and maybe somebody would shrug their shoulders, and they all would resume the banter which had been going on before the tale began.

How ironic it was that Anurei the coppersmith, who had given much thought to the ugliness and pitfalls both of betrayal and of jealousy, was fated himself to be forever miscast in the role of betrayed, and jealous, husband. For another storyteller pulled Anurei straight into the middle of his own tale. The newer telling was based on a cruel falsity, a rumor that was spreading then of Anurei's wife, Anarisha, and a handsome stranger in the town. Years later all was passed down in a yet more altered form; a story of a goddess, a lover, a husband (also a lame metal smith!) and a clever trap. But that final tale was imagined, of course, after both Anarisha and Anurei, as well as all the talebearers, had long since finished those lives of an earlier time and a younger earth.

*   *   *

Anurei was out of the village making necessary trade for obsidian, cautiously traveling by donkey-cart in that time of spreading war and hostilities, when his wife became the prey of the evil jaws of gossip.

In the beginning the talk was favorable. Throughout the village it was said of Anarisha that she was confined to her bed with an affliction which only occurred in the lives of holy ones. Since she was already set apart from the others by an extreme clear beauty and by her gentle spirit, as well as by her rare ability to read and to inscribe, it made sense to many of the people to suppose a likely sacredness. Furthermore, many had seen the much-revered elder, Agghia, enter and depart through Anarisha's door. It was said that all who loved Anarisha were receiving requests from Agghia herself not to visit that bedside while the ill one yet reclined. But among those friends who were given this strange taboo, there was one person who was skeptical, even of Ma Agghia. For this was one who held suspicion toward all things. It was this woman who, in voicing her misgivings, created the harsher version of what was so, a version which those who cared not for Anarisha, with her aggravating beauty, accepted as intriguing and reasonable. And worth passing on. Thus it was that the story traveled, from one to another, that Anurei's wife was lying in bed for six days and six nights with the man called Aris, a strong and handsome warrior who was recently seen to pass through town. At the time, neither Anurei the coppersmith nor his children were staying in the home. It was said that the witch Agghia was shooing people from Anarisha's door.

With one vigorous swoop the reputations of two women were cast beneath the *huluppu* tree to await the judgment of the village, a judgment that could be in some cases as hard and cold as the obsidian with which Anurei the coppersmith sometimes plied his craft.

2

Anarisha: My Life

circa 2700 B.C.

My tale has no beginning. For I sing the everlasting, the coupling of emptiness and that which enters emptiness to fill the void; a song of shadowed nights and golden mornings. Yet like an ephemeral seed of the marshlands, I shall fly downward and alight, to float upon the clear-and-murky river of memory that calls itself "my life." May holy Inanna and Enki; great Utu and Anu, and every God unmentioned, find welcome as I tell.

*   *   *

A bird I loved, a bird who lived in the father tree of my household, who sang of joy and of life, was singing too loudly.

I sent silent messages toward him, begging him to celebrate more softly. But that scarlet bird, as usual, was overcome with beauty; I could not blame him when he persistently ignored my requests.

It was the season of my only illness; perhaps it was the seventh day. I remember that on that day I was becoming more capable of thought. The pain was much less. On the first day I had been so uncomfortably filled with heat that I stretched out upon the cool clay of my floor, and that did not help. I ached everywhere, and the light around me veiled all things in a hazy, secret-keeping cover. By the seventh day I still ached, but less. It was interesting that I could reach the age of twenty-two years and never know disease. I understood now what others were talking of; how much I had assumed before!

My thoughts were, of course, feverish. I watched the beetles on my wall. They seemed to be aware, intelligent. They always had seemed so, to me. They were *safafi* (the "whisperers") big ones. I had observed their kind all my life, especially in my childhood, when I would become thoroughly absorbed in the world of those creatures. Except for my mother and I, my family was united in their disgust of them and destroyed them without hesitation. But I have never found it possible to kill anything. I regarded the safafi as something akin to my toys, not to be mishandled any more than I would my stick doll, with whom it was only natural to be loving and careful. The safafi, and all the other small ones—the ants, the butterflies, the spiders; as much as the birds and the cats; the pigs, the goats—those big ones; or the quiet ones—the vines and the grasses, the simple shrubs and the great good trees, the splashing water and the strong everlasting mountains: I was certain that all creation prefers kindness.

I sometimes imagined that the safafi could sense my thoughts and that I could sense theirs. I perceived that it was I who instructed them on those occasions when they would change their direction and, all in a straight line, turn perpendicular to where they had first been heading. And I imagined that when they formed their long and purposeful safafi columns that they were delineating, in their own unique cuneiform, some sort of instruction for me to follow. Which I would attempt to guess and to comply.

I have to admit that as I lay there on that seventh day, I felt annoyed by their presence. The fact that they were in my home at all was an indication of my illness. I would have shooed them out the door had I been myself! And they pointed, also, to my solitude, that no one was with me to give me any help.

I was hopeful that the solitude would soon be finished. I recalled being told that someone would visit in the afternoon. But I was often sleeping, often dreaming; I had no certainty for what was or was not so.

How I missed my children! My sister had taken them, quickly swooping them up on the first day of my fever. Ninta was, I hoped, giving effort to invoking the Invisible. My babies would then be strong, more able to defeat the bad spirit which had overcome their mother, so that it entered not into them. Ninta had no doubt given them medicine teas as well, to call forth spirits of herbs which would join my children in their strength.

It was the war; that was the reason that I lay upon my bed. I had, in truth, known for some time that I was moving in the direction of disease. Though we were not in danger of direct attack, I was deeply disturbed. I felt for the first time in many seasons that the joy-of-life was departing from me. And of course that had always been my main protection.

The war was clearly disturbing to us all. We knew there were certain households right in the village who would be losing sons and daughters. In the Egyab area of Fa-Orszag several families were already sending their own to join the fight. The Egyab people were different from the rest of us. In many ways. They believed that making war for a justified cause was not only honorable, but even necessary. They recognized no other process for settling large disputes. They were proud when their children lost their lives in such a war! Their elders knew nearly nothing of the science of negotiation, nor had they developed the art of palaver, not even to the level that a small child could understand. They did not meditate upon the sacred breath and they took great pride in what they owned. Also, they loved privacy and kept to themselves. Yet many of their children were adventurous, marrying outside of our village, even outside of the valley of the Nyuegat, and seldom returning to visit their kin.

It was among such peoples that the war was gaining momentum. What could the rest of us do when there were peoples for whom the customs of human friendship were not important enough to be either revered or studied or taught to the little ones to uphold?

They claimed we needed their protection. Protection from a distant king whom we had never seen, a man called "Gilgamesh."

But it was not the Egyab of Fa-Orszag who started those conflicts. I have always enjoyed my life with the lively Egyab people, in truth, and my heart yet pains for the losses which they came to know in that war. Of what use or good can it be to judge the ways of ones born in this life as Egyab? All the stars have their paths. And all the children of stars.

In the days just before my illness, the war upset me for a reason that I had yet to see with clarity. I knew that I found war incomprehensible, and that it therefore unsettled my moods. And I knew that I was grieving for our neighbors in the villages who were fighting. But these were not the elements of the crisis that caused me to lose my habitual joy, and my good health.

It was a thing more personal. A strange factor, it was similar to my connection with the safafi bugs. Somehow I was sensing that it was I, Anarisha of Fa-Orszag, who was responsible! My thoughts, my habits, my actions, something—or perhaps all—of myself was responsible for continuing that war. I knew this way of thinking was a kind of foolishness. And I made myself ill in the body worrying about this folly in my thoughts.

*   *   *

A few years before, in the home of Amaressa, also of Fa-Orszag, I had drunk of the red *lakuna,* the dilution of which would alter certain circumstances, thereby allowing me to conceive my children. I had then eighteen years, two years in the bed of marriage, and I was desperate. Gratefully, I soon did bring forth my firstborn. But I know now, assuredly, that it was not the lakuna alone which gave me that gift.

However, the lakuna was evidently potent and causative in another way. I had no sooner swallowed that blood-red medicine than the world began to change. It became even more mysterious and beautiful than it appeared to me before. The trees were more alive, more clearly full of spirit, more intimately engaging. I felt a bliss come to me, reaching from the bright green leaves and the glowing fruits. Our river, where we wash and bathe, became more sparkling, full of a more peaceful delight. I laughed so hard that tears were moving down my cheeks and I was afraid the laughter would cease not. I felt such a great relief to see that the world was as it was.

But Jesremy, my age-mate, was there, with his wife, walking on the path when I returned from the river. He was aware that I had taken the lakuna—how I never learned. Jesremy had always wanted me. And wanted me to want him back, from the time when we were children.

"Over here—look at this, Anarisha!" he called to me. He stooped and pointed to the ground, and I ceased perceiving my world and saw, instead, his. I saw how all things are streaming together: the pebbles, the shine on the pebbles, the earth, the roots, the vines.

I was not prepared to see as he did. At first I was filled with fascination. But then we came to the part of the forest where the *bishuti* trees grow. Tall and straight, leafy, but no branches. Just thick sticks, stems and leaves—one after another, after another, after another.

It went on so. I felt the repetition inside of life and I turned dizzy, and thought I could not endure, though I had always liked the bishuti until then. I became nauseous and terribly gloomy in the grove. I will never forget; it was a mood without hope. And such awful thoughts coming with the feelings! I began to believe that it was I who had created everything: the endless bishuti, Jesremy and Koa his wife, the forest, everything, the whole streaming world before me. I began to think that I had dreamt it all up. Me—Anarisha! And I knew not that any of this world was of substance.

I felt alone, shaking and gloom-conquered. And I feared the mood would never end, like the bishuti. I kept walking. Jesremy was there, yet, and his wife, and Amaressa, also. But I saw my Anurei in the distance, sitting under the huluppu tree, the grandfather tree of Fa-Orszag.

He was working on his pipe. He looked so beautiful and kind. I went to him and it came to me to ask him questions, questions about love—good, wholesome matters. He answered me gently; such purity was in his eyes, such truth. I knew he was more than just my own creation and, for the second time that day, I knew relief. From that hour forth I spoke no more with Jesremy.

My ordeal was ended, and I was nearly serene in a season or so, until the wartime.

The babies, as I said, came soon.

*   *   *

I lay sleeping and waking again. When awake, I could see an azure air moving through the dust about the room. When I slept, I could see it still. Shapes within its waving ethers appeared and disappeared, then reappeared before me.

There came a moment when I felt I was awake, but the shapes I saw were not my room. Not my home. So this is again a dream, it must be sleep, I thought. I watched, and that which I saw was not like any dream.

An odd place. A tremendous village storehouse. Or some place like a date and barley storehouse. A man, a boy…meaningless behavior, odd thoughts and conversation, shadows moving, slowly drifting…ghosts gaze at objects hanging on walls.

I see a woman's face upon a wall…her smile, her eyes, upon a wall; I sense those eyes might be my own.

*   *   *

The Louvre Museum, Paris
1954 A.D.

"Now you will see, if you just stand right about there, Michael, and then you move over here, her eyes will follow you."

A middle-aged man places his hands on a boy's shoulders to direct him where he's pointed. The boy looks up, then instantly pulls away.

David Dagan looks down, into the eyes of a stranger. The boy is not his son!

"Pardonez-moi, s'il vous plait, mon ami!" David bows formally to the annoyed child, then spins around. "Now, where did that rascal of mine go this time?"

For nearly a quarter of an hour Monsieur Dagan scurries from room to room, floor to floor, becoming even a little anxious, searching the never-ending Louvre for his nine-year-old. "Could it be he'd leave the building? The kid digs Monet, I do know that…is it possible he would have…but over there, that child over there—could that be Michael?"

The boy is squatting on the floor, looking upward at the contents of a glass encased exhibit. He stares fixedly at a small black statue, an ancient Egyptian figure about half a meter high.

The boy is unaware of his father's approach from behind, and for a moment David glances at the face of the statue. Irritable gratitude at finding his wayward son changes to interest. It is uncanny, the face of the noble Egyptian of so long ago; it seems an amazing though more mature duplicate of the face of young Michael Dagan!

David reads the French description and moves on to the English: "Block statue of the Chief-Temple-Singer, Pehutbit, son of Chief-Singer Irefaa-en-Neith and Astakhbit; Dynasty 26, 664–525 B.C.; black basalt." The handsome chief-singer has a slight smile, the dreamy expression of a young man patiently posing for his portrait, his mind on something or someone not present. A girlfriend, perhaps? Or maybe 'Pehutbit' was recalling the antics of his little brother or sister? David has seen that same reflective look on his

Michael's face. He sees it there now, as he bends and thrusts his own face beside his son's.

"So my man!! That's what you've been up to all this time!"

The boy's head turns with a startled jerk.

"Oh—Dad!" Michael's eyes rest on the friendly, crinkled eyes of his father, then return to the statue, "Yeah, I've been here for a while."

"You seem to admire Egyptian sculpture quite a bit."

"Oh, yeah, sure. But it's not that. I mean, I like the Egyptian stuff, but this one here—this is different—I just kind of have a funny feeling. Like I know the guy or something," the boy laughs.

"Hmm—Like maybe you just met him over at Ramses' place? Or—wait now—was it Tut's barbecue last weekend?" David scratches his head and mimics a puzzled frown.

"Very funny, Dad. But doesn't he look like somebody we know?"

"Well, yes, I suppose he does look familiar. I guess people haven't changed all that much. But, c'mon, Mikey, let's go! I'm ready for a soda pop! How about you?"

The boy nods absent-mindedly.

"Only, first, let's go back to where you deserted me. I want to show you a thing or two about the Mona Lisa." David grabs his son's hand and pulls him to his feet, taking one last glance at the sculpture. 'Looks like Mike had a double back there, a couple thousand years or so…the Chief Singer, it says. And the son of a Chief-Singer!' The face of the young Egyptian suggests an aware, well-evolved, good-natured fellow, 'just like my Michael,' thinks David Dagan.

*　　　　*   *　*   *　*

I awoke. It was a long sleep; already it was dusk. A noisy time, a time of people calling to one another, the birds calling, the clatter of pots and bowls, the shouts of children. These sounds that I heard every day of my life were becoming sharper. They intruded inside me.

As far as I knew, no one had come to look in on me. I felt the fever growing stronger. I knew my people must be praying for me, but I was bewildered that not one of them had brought me any food. Not even any drink. I still knew no hunger, but I did have thirst. My sister, or maybe it was a friend, had come with tea in the morning. An oddly flavored tea it was, or perhaps my illness caused that perception. The tea was long-since finished.

I supposed they thought I slept all day, as I had the day before. But that was no cause for keeping their distance. I told myself to bear patience. My people would not forever forget me.

I distracted myself by reviewing the words and sights of my vivid yet senseless dream. Many days afterward, when my husband returned, we discussed what the dream might have meant. Anurei's opinions were wise and interesting as always, but on that particular occasion his theories were not at all correct. I say this now, because years later I came to learn the true meaning of the apparition. I came to know nearly everything of that serious little "Michael" child who appeared within my fever, behind my closed and burning eyes.

3

Approximately Five Thousand Years Later

a Victorian flat in San Francisco
1994 A.D.

"How good it is to rein the mind,
Which is unruly, capricious, rushing wherever it pleases.
The mind so harnessed will bring one happiness."
—the *Dhammapada*, translated by Ananda Matreya,
with Ruth Kramer

Michael Dagan entered his living room slowly, balancing a full, steaming cup of homemade *chai* tea. The aroma was soothing. The tea would be delicious, blended in mindful compliance with the family recipe of his childhood friend, Valmiki. Valmiki Narada, now a disarmingly perceptive psychology professor, was, to Michael's regret, at that moment on a plane somewhere above the Atlantic.

Michael placed the hot cup upon a coaster on his coffee table. Then he eased into his armchair, trying to relax. But he glanced warily at the bespectacled young woman—and told himself not to think "girl"— who sat across his table, fiddling with her tape cassettes.

He had been trying all morning to reduce the emotions surrounding this interview. But his equilibrium was faltering. Even the fact that the woman was sitting there with a cup of coffee, having refused his *masala chai* as "too spicy," seemed almost a personal affront. His forehead and his palms were beginning to sweat, joined in self-betraying witness to his lack of serenity.

The interview was to appear in the Sunday supplement of the *San Francisco Chronicle*. It would be his primary, if not only, opportunity to tantalize the entire Bay Area with the idea of his "catalyst," as he had come to think of his film, the project which had consumed the last twenty-six months of his life.

Unfortunately, he suspected, his chief asset for maneuvering through the interview was at this moment failing him. The alleged "mesmerizing charisma," or some such thing, for which people were lately praising him—flattering him even to his face, to his inner confusion—probably had deteriorated. Either deteriorated, or perhaps, if he actually did possess it, become a detriment. An obstruction that would set him apart from this somber faced interviewer. And hence her readers. He was not sensing that any hint of personal magnetism would necessarily sway this woman. In fact, she just might be the type to bend over backward to prove she was not enthralled.

Just go with patience, he told himself. *Be thoughtful, kind. And keep a clear mind.* He repeated to himself some words which he often considered, words from his favorite translation of the Dhammapada: "*Whatsoever, after due examination and analysis, you find to be conducive to the good, the benefit, the welfare of all beings—that doctrine believe and cling to and take as your guide.*" He cheered himself with the memory of yesterday's satisfying debate with Valmiki over the nuances of those words.

The maxim certainly applied to his work. *I'll let my concept speak for itself,* he thought as the woman looked up from her equipment.

*   *   *

Deborah Anderson let her eyes rest on Michael Dagan just long enough for one last quick appraisal. *He's been totally courteous so far,* she thought. But reserved, she might even say cold. At the same time, she perceived an underlying energy, a quickness that seemed to include an observant awareness of herself. He made her feel on the alert. She hastily smoothed her dark-green woolen skirt over her knees. Then she looked directly into his eyes.

"To start off, Michael, I want to ask you to tell me a little bit about your personal background," she was polite herself, but took care to place some distance in her own inflection.

He nodded. "Fine, Deborah, go ahead."

"Then we'll move on to the history behind your work. Finally we'll get down to substance. Your *Gilgamesh*."

"All right. Sounds fine to me."

"Before we begin, though, do you have any questions? Guidelines? Any restrictions, maybe, that you want to discuss?"

He hesitated. "Uh, no…well, I mean, yes…come to think of it. I mean, obviously, I would like the business of the…the disappearance of…of Maria Ananin…to be avoided. Because not only would that be harmful, not at all conducive to what I'm trying to accomplish, but, to be frank, Deborah, it's a matter which is completely irrelevant. To the topic of this interview. And I—"

"Maria Ananin? Oh, but I don't really think we can avoid discussing Maria!" Deborah smiled. "Some mention will be expected. It won't be necessary to mention your wife, though. Your estranged wife. Rosie, that's her name, isn't it? Or anyone else. But Maria Ananin? She's the one topic that will simply be expected!"

"And must we do the expected, Deborah?" An inescapable apprehension turned the delivery of his words from the casual ease he intended into a moody rebelliousness.

He rose from his armchair and went over to the CD player. The beautiful Mozart arias of Kiri Te Kanawa that always made him feel so peaceful were actually beginning to grate a little on his nerves.

Deborah Anderson pushed a wayward strand of strawberry-blonde hair from her forehead and watched as Michael Dagan turned off his music and returned to his seat. She couldn't help notice, as she later told her housemate, that the man did have a striking elegance about him. Elegance was evident in every movement of his slender and "definitely buff" physique, as she later reported, if not in his clothing. But blue jeans and light blue button-down shirt, however well pressed, were surprisingly ordinary. Unimaginative, she thought, for a creative man, a man in his position.

Michael thought he could see a faint line of critical judgment fixing itself upon the woman's face. He detected, also, a hostility that was beginning to expand inside himself. He tried his best to calm it. Not only would it be calamitous for the interview, but a hostile mood was a useless, energy-consuming intrusion. Personal hostility was not to be admitted. He needed to dissolve it now, fade it out, a finished scene.

As he settled into his chair, he made a last ditch effort to avoid an attitude towards this woman. He put his mind to her machine, an inexpensive and very basic Sony.

Deborah took a sip of her coffee. Her hand was shaking, just slightly; probably the motion was perceptible only to herself. But she put the cup down quickly. She absolutely did not want Michael Dagan to think that he was making her nervous.

"All right, then, Michael," she said, "We're ready to begin." She clicked on the recorder. "Tell me a little bit about your childhood." Now she was smiling again, "Who is Michael Dagan, really?"

Something in the phrasing of the question, in the sophomoric knowing-everything-worth-knowing lilt he perceived in her tone, pushed him, finally, over the edge of his composure and into true annoyance and ill ease—still controlled, but there, complete. In a thin, nonresonating voice which barely covered his impatience, and which he had not heard come out of his mouth for a very long time, he opened the interview. The words tumbled out over themselves. They missed the degree of careful thought he had intended, nearly gaining, instead, their own direction and momentum. For no deliberate reason, he began the conversation with the troubling topic of his father.

"Well, Deborah, to answer your question, to go back to the beginning, I guess I could trace my motivations, and my interest in film, to a particular place and time. It was in childhood, when my Dad had left us. I lived with my Mom and my sisters. I was the eldest, the one who looked after things. My two sisters were great kids, but they were very young. During the time I'm thinking of. I was only eight or nine, myself. But I was the one who worried about leaving the lights on, wasting the water, turning off the oven. Things like that. I even braided my sisters' hair. And tried not to make us late for school."

He glanced down then—something at his leg; it was his cat he felt there, come to rub against him. He leaned down and scratched the forehead of the small black creature. Brando had appeared from a nap place somewhere in the room. It seemed the cat felt sympathy for its master. Michael took a deep breath.

"And were you ever late?" prodded Deborah.

"Ah, yes. A lot. And then we'd all be in trouble." He paused, smiling ruefully, remembering. After the rushing start, he turned inward, absent-mindedly petting the cat.

He knew he had never completely dealt with the memories from those days. The frequent beatings of the *rattan,* the principal's bamboo stick. And the deeper pain of watching the striking of his sisters. Nor had he forgotten the song the entire school would sing to the three of them, they were so late so often. "A lollar a dollar, you ten o'clock scholar, why do you come too late? Last week you came at six o'clock, today you come at eight*!*" More than anything else, the lack of sense in the words of the song had bothered him; he knew the principal had taught it all wrong. That used to get to him, that and the fact that it was their fate to have Kamara for their principal. Mr. Kamara was the one and only exception to the rule that nobody gave a damn about time; nobody even perceived it! Not in that nature-based land, that land of his childhood, where virtually no one possessed a watch...

"To this day I guess I'm over-concerned with time." He glanced at Deborah and shrugged. "But anyway, I was in trouble a lot for other reasons. Maybe because there were too many places to go that were far more interesting than school. Still, why the principal and I didn't get along, I'm not so sure what that was all about, frankly."

He paused, yet again, wondering what all this was about, right now. He guessed he was stumbling down this old, negative track out of the absolute necessity to achieve this woman's empathy. Which, judging from her expression, he wasn't about to get. But it wasn't Deborah Anderson's fault. He was uncomfortable talking about himself. And he wasn't speaking according to plan. He would redirect, slant everything more positively...

"My mother used to give me money to take my sisters out for dinner in those days. To 'Oscar's,' that was the name of the restaurant. It was on a high cliff, overlooking the ocean. In Monrovia. We lived on the outskirts of the capital, in a district called Sinkor. Did I say we're talking about West Africa, Deborah? Liberia, West Africa. On the equator, by the sea."

The young woman took a sip of her coffee. Reflexively, she gave a quick glance to his hallway, to the African masks near the front door. Mahogany, she guessed. There were three masks: a cow-like creature with horns, and two human faces. The masks were the only decoration she could see in his flat. His taste surprised her—it was so simple. Amazingly undeveloped, she thought.

"Sinkor was a sort of suburb of Monrovia. Western-type houses between small stretches of rain forest. Red earth and swamps. People were very friendly. And full of—of something—full of what? Of life.

And, many of them, full of wisdom, I'd call it, looking back. I guess there were the usual basic types as anywhere, but with equatorial, rain forest moods, not the moods of this city. Not like San Francisco, not a people unconsciously pushing against a cold wind. A warm easygoing people, of high bush and hot humidity. In a tropical land, by a warm sea…" His eyes deferred to Deborah's, but she had no comment or question. She waited, and he waited, then he went on.

"There were two or three villages in the Sinkor area. They dated back to the days before the city started to spread. I would walk almost every-day to see friends in one of those villages. My mother and sisters and I, we all would walk there together.

"But my sisters and I would take the bus to Oscar's. The 'money bus,' people called it. We loved that, all three of us, riding the money bus to town. The buses were fun to look at, brightly colored, with proverbs and admonitions painted on the sides. Like, oh, for example, 'You never try, you never know,' or—this was a good one—'Out beyond notions of wrongdoing or rightdoing, there is a field—will you come join me there?'"

He gave her a look, and Deborah's eyebrows went up.

"Rumi? Isn't that Rumi?!" She was incredulous. "They put stuff like that—quotations from Rumi—on buses in West Africa?"

"Well, sure, Deborah. Many families are Muslims there." He smiled, "So you know Rumi?" His eyes were sparkling now. Deborah wondered if he was putting her on. Hitting on her, flirting sort of, maybe, with that quote. If he was the sort of man to do that. Or was he just relating what he recalled? Of course she would decide later what to edit.

"They always played music on the money-buses. Every driver had a phonograph. You'd hear "Hound Dog," the Big Mama Thornton version, that was before Elvis, and they played a lot of B.B. King. We loved B.B. King. It felt like the whole bus was dancing, moving along over the potholes. Passengers would sing along. Give it all they'd got, some of them. And some, they'd be making observations, sharp comments about the people they saw through the bus window, or about somebody right there on the bus. Or about life in general. My friend, Alhassan, who was five or six years older than me, used to ride with me sometimes. He loved to go into his imitation of my American accent, he was pretty good at it, but he looked exactly like what he was—a boy from the village. Once we were sitting next to this old lady and he started doing that—doing his American imitation. He pretended he was all excited, and started pointing out the window and yelling about a girl with a tray of oranges on her head—like he'd never seen such a sight before in his life! The old lady next to him, a nice old lady she was—she got all excited, too. And she started pointing, herself, calling out well-known places—the market, the post office, the Montserrado River. Then she asked him if she could show him around Sinkor—which is where he'd lived all his life! But he said he had to meet his brother at the embassy. I kept holding back from laughing, then finally we got off and we both laughed our heads off.

"Out in Sinkor, more up country, and even in the city, the chickens, or goats, would be riding on the seat next to you. Sometimes the chickens would give you a little piece of their minds, too. But usually the chickens were the quiet ones…"

Deborah thought she detected a sadness, just then, coming into his eyes. But he went on, sounding cheerful and matter-of-fact.

"Anyway, to get back to Oscar's, my mother didn't like to cook much, or even know how to cook, really. She was accustomed to servants, her whole life. Maids, cooks, gardeners, drivers—the works. But when my Dad went away, so did the servants.

"Oscar's was the place to be in Monrovia. Even the president ate there. And it was the restaurant Mom knew best. So she always sent us to Oscar's. When I got a little older I realized that she'd never given me anywhere near the amount we needed to pay for it all. All those fancy lobster dinners. I used to think they charged part of it to some account she had with them or something; even at that age a kid knows what's happening, sort of. I figured maybe she was paying the balance later. But actually the people were just giving us all those broiled lobsters and fondues—we used to order fondues, so we could have the little fire on our table. And they gave us our 'Shirley Temples,' and the sherbets and the chocolate mousse desserts, and the high life music of their orchestra. They 'dashed' us everything, as they say in that part of the world; it all was nearly free. Out of affection for her, and respect for him, for the memory of him. My father, I mean. And, I suppose, also out of expectation of his coming back. He'd been what people called a 'Big Man' in Liberia. He still sent her money, but apparently it was barely enough to cover rent and pay for our school. Possibly he wasn't doing so well, then, I don't really know. All I can say is, I know him now to be a decent enough guy…"

He stopped, then, as if he'd said all there was to say, probably more than he wanted to say. Deborah waited until she realized he'd escaped once more to reverie.

"But, Michael, how did a childhood in Africa actually impact your career?" her voice was louder, pushing.

The sunlight of early afternoon was altering the room. He stared at the fiery radiance of light on the black fur of his cat; the cat lay sleeping in the sunlit center of a flow of slowly dancing dust.

He looked back at Deborah. The light fell, also, on her hair.

"My mother kept us home from school a lot in Liberia. We'd go to the beach; we lived near the beach. Or we'd go to a movie in the city. I guess it happened when she was feeling down, she wanted us to be with her," he smiled slightly, "so she'd give us a day off from school. I suppose I'd be a different person right now, in some other profession, if my mother could have had some Prozac. But her Prozac was the movies. We used to see Indian films. They showed them a lot in Monrovia. Fantastic films—funny, adventurous, and tragic, all in one movie. Music, dancing, drama. And they went on forever. We watched more than our share of movies. It was our real education. That was an influence, that and the rain forest, just behind our house. Also, indirectly, there was something else in West Africa. It affected how I see things. The obvious and visible suffering, the poverty, the hunger. And an image, when I was a child, of certain people—family friends and some of the neighbors—hardworking people who would never be anything but poverty-stricken, for the simple reason that they were so completely generous and kind. And, of course, the opposite image, too. People who had plenty, because they were so mean. You got to know everybody's character, everybody's business. It was all right out there, in your face."

Deborah played with her cassette containers, adeptly tearing off the wrappings with a long, well-manicured fingernail. She heard a breath, a suggestion of a sigh, and she wondered what he was thinking. She said nothing, and he went on.

"All this I'm talking about, it was just one little era. It suddenly came to its permanent conclusion. My Dad broke up with his girlfriend in California.

"I guess he was nostalgic, or guilty—whatever—he came back to West Africa for all of us and took us to Paris with him. Then, eventually, to the States. I never saw Liberia again. Now I imagine it's just about destroyed—the life I remember. Destroyed by the war, I mean."

She looked at him blankly. *My god the guy has beautiful eyes*, she thought, in spite of herself.

She didn't know anything about a war in Liberia. She tried, quickly and furtively, to examine his features more closely as she spoke. "You didn't mention," she said, "exactly what was your family doing in Africa, anyway? Was your mother Liberian? Were you born there, Michael?"

"No my mother wasn't Liberian. Though she did fit in very easily. My Mom was from the Philippines. She grew up, also, in Hawaii. She was part Filipina, part Spanish, part Welsh-American. My Dad was American, Jewish American…"

He hesitated. "I look a little like West Africa, Deborah, because that's where I'm from." He was straightforward, patient now. "It's the way I carry myself, maybe. There were a few other people from the States around, but we barely knew them. My Dad was away, you understand. And my coloring," he went on, "as for that, the people in the highlands of the Philippines, my grandfather's people, they can be somewhat dark."

"Oh, yes, I see." She'd heard something in his voice, something instructive and fatherly, or rather, perhaps, an older brother's solicitude. It left her feeling intrusive, with nothing fit to say. Nevertheless, she pushed on.

"But, Michael, tell me, how in the world did your father and mother come to be living in West Africa?"

"Well…" He frowned as he took his glasses from his pocket and Deborah tried to dismiss a thought that her questions were giving the man a headache.

"My father started out as a lawyer. Gradually he got more and more involved with his investments. He ended up in all sorts of ventures, or adventures, you could call them, all over the planet. He met my Mom in Honolulu, when she was eighteen. He brought her to Liberia. He'd invested in a mine there, a diamond mine in the Bomi Hills. He wanted direct hands-on involvement—with the diamonds, I mean.

"He was older than she was. But not all that old, really. And yes, I was born in Liberia. In one of the villages. My mother's best friend, Ma Kolana—she was like an aunt to my sisters and me—Ma Kolana was the midwife at my birth, at all our births. I even helped her with my youngest sister.

"My Dad eventually brought us to California. To Coronado. And then north, to the suburbs—Castro Valley. Because of another girl-friend of his, as it turned out. Not long after we'd settled there—in Castro Valley—he left my mother once more. This time for good. But by then he was well off again. And also he and Mom had learned how to be friends, with the help of a therapist. For the sake of us kids, I sup-pose. So she ended up with a lot of financial support from him. Later she made some good investments herself, all on her own." He paused and Deborah thought she heard a low chuckle. *Why the hell am I going on this way?* he asked himself. But he went on, driven compulsively, at least for the moment, more by memories than intent.

"In California, nobody knew what kind of slot to put me or my sisters into. I know that now, looking back. We were always feeling somehow a little different. We were somewhat shy there, in Castro Valley. Everyone was white, Protestant, Republican, you understand. Practically none of the other kids had ever lived outside of northern California. The state had fewer newcomers in those days; it wasn't like now.

"But once, at a party, somebody was talking about being different, and it seemed like everybody felt that way. At the time I wasn't even connecting my own discomfort with my different roots, where I'd come from, my mixed race, none of that stuff, clueless as that may sound. But it was the fifties, early sixties. Mostly, I just thought I was shy.

"When I graduated from high school, I didn't know what to do next. I remember the week after graduation sitting on this friend's front steps, smoking her cigarettes, one after another after another, which wasn't usual; I didn't smoke. But I was confused and nervous about what to do with my life."

He drummed his fingers on the table and took several sips of his chai. Deborah looked him over once again—the tall, dark and handsome, but not completely calm and collected rising star sitting before her. She smiled to herself. All her fears at meeting this local luminary had entirely vanished.

You're a little confused and nervous right now, Michael Dagan, aren't you? she thought, as she enjoyed a pleasant rush of relief and a feeling of rather maternal affection.

It wasn't true, what someone at work had told her. He was not a "dead-ringer" for the actor who played Superman, on "Lois and Clark." But his features were, she had to admit, somewhat similar. Not his "café latté" complexion, though. Nor his hair, which was abundant and included some silver mixed with the black. And not those hollows and wrinkles in his face. Maybe he was more like "Clark" fifteen years from now. Still, he did appear, at moments, rather young. And earnest, in the way of some younger men, men of her own age.

She was surprised at how much he was telling her. She'd been briefed he could be a frustratingly private person. And yet, she thought, with a little flash of pride, he seemed to be telling her everything. She thought of what he'd said about his mother, and his dad.

She could see him in her imagination—a cute little kid—and two tiny sisters, sitting by themselves in a ritzy tropical restaurant, legs dangling from their chairs, large brown eyes fastened on the flames of a simmering fondue...

4

Gilgamesh—
the Interview Concludes

"An empty pageant; a stage play; flocks of sheep, herds of cattle; a tussle of spear men; a bone flung among a pack of curs; a crumb tossed into a pond of fish; ants, loaded and laboring; mice, scared and scampering; puppets, jerking on their strings—that is life. In the midst of it all you must take your stand, good-temperedly and without disdain, yet always aware that a man's worth is no greater than the worth of his ambitions."
—Marcus Aurelius, Emperor of the Western World, 161–180 A.D.
from his *Meditations, Book VII*

About half an hour later…

"Oh, sure, Deborah, yes, of course." Michael was half smiling.

"Tell me about them."

"Well…there were hundreds of films. Maybe more. But the most influential of all? Well, that would be two. Those two are enough to balance everything else put together. Their influence isn't actually technical. A little might be overt, sure, but mostly it's subliminal, osmotic. Sort of like what you get when you're with a friend who's on something you once used to—what I mean is, those two films bring me to a way of seeing things, a vision I once had myself. Back in the seventies. You understand? And that's been very useful."

"Now you've got me curious, Michael. Just what two films are you talking about?"

"Jean Cocteau's *Beauty and The Beast*. And *Black Orpheus,* Renoir's *Black Orpheus*. As far as I'm concerned those two are the most deeply beautiful films ever made. I've got some other favorites, though—for example, Pagnol's *The Baker's Wife* is incredible, and *The Kiss of The Spider Woman*, you know, from the novel by Manuel Puig, one of my favor—"

"Wait, wait, hold on, Michael! I want to hear more about those first two!"

"Are you familiar with them, Deborah?"

"Well, I've—"

"Do you like the surreal? Surrealism with soul. An unusual combination, isn't it? Both those films have got it. And an unforgettable background score for *Orpheus*...I remember, when someone told me a while ago that Disney was considering a *Gilgamesh,* my first response was dismay—but then I felt a little elation, you know, because Disney did that version of *Beauty and the Beast*. The difference is that nobody's heard of me, and of course nobody's heard of my *Gilgamesh*. Not yet, anyway. But the whole world knew Cocteau's film, way before Disney's cartoon came out."

"Well, to tell the truth, Michael, I've seen critiques of the Cocteau, but I don't really know it very—"

"Oh is that so? I suppose a lot of people don't know it, these days. I guess I'm dating myself. But it had a following back in the sixties, in Berkeley, that's when I first came across it. You might like to rent the video. Or, call the Pacific Film Archive. They—"

"But I was about to say, Michael—what you just told me—you're totally wrong, you know, that nobody's heard of you. Like, everybody, at least in the Bay Area, everybody talks about your films. Especially the *Dance of Life*. Really, Michael, you're so almost famous!"

He smiled. *And you're 'so' still a kid*, he thought. *But not a bad kid, actually…*Odd, though, a film writer for the *Chronicle* and she never saw Cocteau's masterpiece?…*Oh, well, too many great films, too many these days to see them all; why judge her?…*

There was a long silence. He waited while Deborah Anderson, changing a cassette, wondered, *Now where can I take this from here?*

And just then, observing her, it came to him, sharp and sudden, the panic. Deborah could very easily—any second now, in fact—bring up Maria Ananin. His fear was not rational; he didn't fully understand it. Why, after all, should it seem unacceptable to him to discuss Maria? In any case, he would need to be quick with this woman, somehow beat her time.

And yet, even in his panic, he could not prevent his mind from lingering for just a moment where it most preferred to be, habitually.

Maria, he thought, *where in the world did you go, anyway? Where did you go?*

Where in the name of heaven did she go?…

*   *   *

Michael glanced at his watch. Not much time left. Deborah had quizzed him on almost every remotely relevant minutiae possible. But, incredibly, she had not mentioned Maria Ananin, had not even attempted a lead-in to bringing up the name. Astonished relief from this thought led to the first sense of peace he had known since the day began.

He was amazed at his good luck in detouring Deborah from the most tied-in topics. Most crucially, there was no reference so far to Maria's role in his film. The role of the fertility goddess Inanna. And with a woman reporter yet! He was beginning to feel grateful that it was Deborah Anderson who was given this assignment. A nice girl who apparently had both feet on the ground. A rare Bay Area woman with less interest in "goddesses" than he had himself. Or, more likely, she was simply, respectfully, bowing to his preliminary request.

Deborah, waiting for the reply to her latest question, looked up and saw that she had lost the man's attention. She, too, had gone inward. She rephrased: "And why did you say what you just did, Michael? Tell me what it is, exactly, that leads you to see these clues you're talking about? You say clues are there, in the Gilgamesh story—but we're talking about the first written epic ever. Isn't that so? From Sumeria—wasn't that the first civilization?! You honestly see things in that ancient story that are relevant solutions to our present environmental—"

"Well, no, Deborah, no, actually I don't. You're carrying it a little too far, there. And in a misleading direction, in fact. No, 'solutions' are not my area. What I do see in the epic are motifs—motifs that point to a useful way to *focus*, that's all. A way to see the problem more clearly. Which is what must happen first. Before we can truly solve anything of great significance.

"See, in the *Gilgamesh* project I'm focusing on a vision. A universal perception that could cause catharsis. In a threshold quantity of humanity! In order to achieve the will—the motivated energy—which is still the main thing lacking.

"Only with a passionate, universal motivation can humanity change sufficiently. To preserve the life of our planet, I mean. And we can first achieve the effective focus, I believe, by using a wide-angle lens. Not just observing our own little high tech episode on earth, our own narrow view. But rather by looking at the wide historical picture. And I don't even mean just the industrial period—I'm talking about looking at the entire history of civilization. Beginning with Sumeria. Looking at that emotionally, and very deeply. In other words, with our minds in the surreal…"

His voice had lost its earlier impatience. It took on, now, its normal calm. A harmonious bass, with a compelling quality that years before had carried him, shy though he thought he was, through "Love Me Tender" and "Heartbreak Hotel" at several high school parties. With an unrestrained conviction he spoke, as he glimpsed the end of his tunnel. He was just about home free.

"The situation in ancient Sumeria, at the birth of civilization, is congruent, Deborah, intriguingly congruent, with what we have today—in civilization's "old age." The Sumerians, some of them, were profoundly aware that the greedy and the powerful of their world were planning to not only use wild nature, but to completely destroy the wildness. Those kings did not cherish, did not want, the free wild life to thrive on earth!

"Their world had developed agriculture, had domesticated meat. Now the leaders wanted the destruction of the wildness. The uncontrolled and formidable wildness. Partly out of fear they desired its destruction, partly out of arrogance. And partly from an immense desire to dominate. So much ignorant desire! If only they had known the forest intimately. They might have had the wisdom to care.

"It was not only beautiful cedar furnishings that those Sumerian kings were beginning to demand. 'I am committed to this enterprise: to climb the mountain, to cut down the cedar and leave behind me an enduring name...' That's the translation of the Sumerian text of Gilgamesh's statement! From nearly five thousand years ago!

"Gilgamesh was the mover and shaker in his world. All the leaders and investors of all the multinationals, all rolled up into one man. Not that the numbers have changed that much, though, you know. We still have the situation that three or four human beings possess more wealth than nearly half the world's population. Did you know that, Deborah?

"So, anyway, now...in the epic that Sumerian poet-philosophers created, they present this 'hero,' Gilgamesh. The legendary king of Uruk, or 'Erech,' if you like. People are in awe of the man—a god-man, they call him. They depend on him. They fear him. He protects them. And he demands their women. Every bride in the city, on the night before her wedding, is required to lie with Gilgamesh. *Jus primer noctis*—an ancient custom, even in his time.

"Gilgamesh stands alone. But he finds one friend, one peer in virility. This is Enkidu—significantly, a man who once was one with nature. Enkidu is a newly civilized wild man—a Mowgli, a Tarzan—a man raised by the animals of the forest. Through sophisticated manipulation, with the help of a courtesan, Enkidu becomes civilized, and friend to Gilgamesh.

"After meeting, and immediately clobbering each other—in the earliest bonding battle in recorded history—Gilgamesh and Enkidu set out to kill a monstrous enemy together. Their enemy is none other than Huwawa, the Great One of the Forest.

"The *forest!* Do you see it, Deborah? The forest, which noncivilized peoples, even to this day, cherish and hold sacred! The forest, which we present civilized ones, of five thousand years later, at least some of us, are at last beginning to know is essential to human well-being, in fact to our existence.

"We are seeing this only now, as we approach the finish of the destruction which was begun intentionally, something like three hundred generations ago. By such as Gilgamesh. And by the tendencies of *yang*-dominated civilization that he and others like him—" But suddenly he stopped, with a low, barely audible intake of breath—Deborah wasn't even sure she'd heard it. He rushed to move on, before she could ponder what he'd just said, so mindlessly. For he had nearly introduced—like a complete fool, he later told himself—exactly what he had so efficiently avoided for over two hours. The goddess.

He began to cough. Loud, prolonged, and intentionally annoying, the coughing fit distracted his interviewer. And he was lucky; she missed her cue.

"Excuse me, Deborah. A little something in my throat. Maybe too much talking. But, anyway now, as I was saying…the problems came from an imbalance. An entrapping tendency—it's with us yet today.

"The individual Gilgamesh actually did live, and die, thousands of years ago. But as for Huwawa—contrary to the epic—he has not been finished off. There still is time for the Spirit of the Forest. And time for ordinary, 'unheroic' humanity. Time to claim the victory. But only if we act, and act now. We can't be late! I propose, Deborah, that—"

"Your old obsession, isn't it Michael?"

"Pardon me?"

"You know, Michael—'We can't be late.' Your need to be on time. Your school days in Africa? Your principal?"

"Oh, yeah. Yeah, I see what you're getting at. Sure, maybe so." *The kid's been listening.* He looked her in the eyes, which at that instant were rather solemn. Then he smiled. And suddenly all the composure, all the upper-handed confidence that Deborah Anderson had been gathering all day, was instantly shattered by his radiantly affirming smile.

She moistened her lips with her tongue, passed her hand over her hair and recrossed her legs, nearly all at once. He watched her for a moment and then continued.

"There is right now just enough time for the forest. Enough time for the children of the forest, the multitudes of ordinary humanity—the less greedy, the less proud, the less controlling—to be the final conquerors—"

"Oh, but, wait just a minute now, Michael! Aren't you looking at most of humanity through rather rosy colored—"

"If, that is—please excuse me Deborah—if we can find it in ourselves to be as children of the forest. Gentle, innocent, and strong. Stronger than greed; stronger than we've been for the last five thousand years. That which the great teachers—the Buddhas, the Rabbis, the Masters and Avatars, the 'Realized Ones'—have always told us that we can be!

"And does that really seem so outrageous to you, Deborah? We may be thoroughly acculturated to our civilized ways—but what is it that is still truly there, there in our DNA, in our genes? By nature we are the strong and gentle children of the forest—of the mountains, of the grasslands, of the seas. We are fundamentally of the earth. Disguising earth beneath our pavements and ourselves within our costumes and contraptions, and finally these days, within our cyberspace: none of all that changes who we really are, does it? Not in the least. After all, aren't our genes, even today, only infinitesimally variant from Cro-Magnon's?"

"But Mi—"

"No, please, Deborah. Let me finish. I just want to say that I believe the time has come to expose the play-acting mimicry we call civilized culture. Mimicry—learned behavior—it's a primate trait that has gone way, way out of balance, for the good of the species. As aspects of nature sometimes do. Learned behavior now overpowers our deeper, more instinctual wisdom. It's clear that the time has come to read-just—another natural tendency, fortunately. It's time to 'be all that we can be,' in the true, peaceful sense of those words. Time to recapture the wisdom."

"And just what does that mean to you, Michael? Are you suggesting that we all leave home and go eat locusts and wild honey?"

"No, Deborah. Not exactly. I'm simply suggesting that we all go out and see my film!!"

Deborah smiled, and Michael laughed. It was a soft and low, but gen-uinely joyful laugh.

"When the editing's completed, which it almost is. And then, from that, as I say, a dramatic catharsis—Hey!—Whoa! Brando!—What the hell are you doing, man?!"

The cat was on the table. Having not eaten for the entire duration of the interview, the animal had grown very tired of rubbing up against the legs of his master. And tired of getting no response. Suddenly he had leaped up, up on to the table, swishing his tail over Deborah's half full cup of coffee. She grabbed for the cup, but she knocked it herself, spilling coffee on her notes, and a little on the table.

"Oh my god!" she laughed. "Your cat could use a bit of 'learned behavior,' himself!"

Michael laughed too, and apologized for his pet. Then he went to the kitchen for a towel. The ice at last was broken. But the interview was done.

*   *   **

As Deborah Anderson was thanking Michael Dagan and about to say her good-bye, she found it impossible to resist an urge which had been pushing at her for at least the last half-hour. On impulse, with hardly any analyzing, she announced that she'd like to have him over to her place for dinner.

"—to get to know each other a little better," she explained.

He tried not to appear startled. He thanked her, then glancing into her guarded, though young and expectant eyes, he gently said that he regretted it very much, but he had a new friend he was seeing…he was very sorry, but his friend probably would not understand that kind of an arrangement…

He accompanied Deborah to his door and gave her a warm hand-shake good-bye.

So much for my own 'instinctual wisdom,' thought the embarrassed young journalist as she headed down the stairs.

*   *   **

While he carried his cups and wet dishtowel to the kitchen, Michael Dagan pondered the dishonesty of the excuse he'd just made. White lies, he told himself, were once in awhile necessary. Beneficial for everyone concerned. There was no one, in fact. No new friend. No old friend. No Rosie. And no Maria.

Then once again, as it so often did, a persistent memory drifted through his mind, like a fragment of a song that refused to go away. Once again, he was standing on a road, by the sea. It was morning, on a magical Aegean island—Paros, Greece. It was early spring, nineteen-seventy one. And the sun was extraordinarily bright...

He was back in the time when everything, all of it with Maria, as far as he could tell, had really first begun.

5

Memories of a Greek Island

The World, from the American perspective
1971 A.D.

U.S. conducts large-scale bombing raids in N. Vietnam...Lt. Wm. Calley, Jr., found guilty of murder in My Lai massacre...*The Bell Jar* by Sylvia Plath, published...violence in Ireland; Britain institutes internment without trial...China hosts U.S. table tennis team, begins era of *détente*...women attain right to vote in Switzerland...Rome reaffirms the role of celibacy...cigarette ads banned from U.S. television...India (assisting Bengali rebels) and Pakistan go to war...cyclone and tidal wave kill 10,000 Bengali...federal and state aid to parochial schools ruled unconstitutional...Bill Graham closes Fillmores East and West...USSR soft-lands a space capsule on Mars...Ten guards and thirty-two prisoners killed at Attica prison after five-day uprising....Charles Manson found guilty of Sharon Tate murder...U.S. explodes hydrogen bomb beneath Amchitka Island...Dr. Choh Hao Li, at the University of California, synthesizes hormone that controls human growth...Billie Jean King becomes first woman athlete to win $100,000 in a single year...Hank Aaron hits his 600th career home run...Igor Stravinsky, Louis Armstrong, Whitney Young, Gabrielle (Coco) Chanel, Harold

Lloyd, Francois Duvalier and Paul Terry (creator of Mighty Mouse) complete their time on earth.
—derived from *The Timetables of History, The Third Revised Edition*

Paros, Greece
1971 A.D.

A single bright star kept company with a full moon between the highest hilltops of an island silhouette.

It was the twilight hour of a windy spring day on the Aegean. The ever-changing sea, reveling since dawn in passionate god-like power, now, at day's end, transformed itself to child-size waves, playing innocently upon the shores of a pretty island. In that wondrously becalmed twilight, against the last fleeting traces of a rose and golden sunset, the passenger ship "Phryne" appeared on the horizon. Belatedly the ferry-boat came, to the destination of her seven hundred and thirty-second voyage to Paros, Greece.

The great and beautiful, though aged, vessel had been christened nearly twenty years before. She was given the name of an ancient super-star courtesan, a beautiful woman whose spirit might very well linger with us to this day—thanks to the fantasies of well-informed art historians who know that it was the gorgeous Phryne who posed for Praxiteles when he sculpted; Phryne's face and Phryne's body we encounter in that master's famous Aphrodite, *the quintessential goddess of our Post-Grecian psyches. Thanks, also, perhaps, to an occasional ambitiously sensual teen-age girl who, browsing well-worn pages in some antique shop or used book store, finds lasting inspiration in Victorian references to Phryne's geisha-like career. Or thanks, yet again, to the healthy memories of a sizable number of not necessarily inspired, but erotically well-educated Europeans, of various motivations, ages and sex...*

At the moment when the ship which bore the name of this legendary hetaera *at last came into port, deep sighs poured forth, drifting both from above and within the vessel's bowels. The Phryne had just completed a prolonged and tumultuous episode of her career as ferry between Piraeus and the islands of the Cyclades. Arriving at the port of the island of Paros, her passengers were yet a little shaken. All were relieved to conclude the dangerously stormy affair.*

So it was that in not quite normal condition—whatever that may have been in nineteen seventy-one—twenty-six year old Michael Dagan found himself stepping exhaustedly up onto the Parosian pier, helping his pale and dazed young wife up with him to his side. He balanced their disorientation with effort, sea-storm nausea still exerting its effect.

Immediately, an old man approached the couple.

Without hesitation, Michael accepted this weathered Parosian's offer to help them with their bags. Then, in limited pigeon-Greek, the younger man made a request for the elder to guide them to the closest decent hotel that the man could recommend. Cold and tired, the couple trailed the silent stranger along the dock, through the mists of the island's March evening, barely taking in the shadowy beauty of the Cycledian wharf. They passed through a doorway into an unlit stairwell and on up to the foyer of the second floor, where a second aged gentleman kept his desk. A large green parrot, kept in a hanging cage beside the desk, squawked angrily as Michael shouted to the seated man, who seemed unable to clearly hear.

"I didn't know there were parrots in Greece," Rosie Dagan whispered when the man looked downward to examine his ledger.

In spite of everything, Michael laughed. He hadn't laughed in a long time. "Maybe they import them, Rosie," he said softly to his wife, "just like Californians do."

It had been, in the first place, yet another elder, Michael's anxiously concerned father, who suggested (and cajoled and begged and pleaded, and then finally demanded) that the young couple make this journey to Paros. "Paradise" it translated. David Dagan had stepped foot upon the shores of the island long ago, practically in his own youth. And still he cherished the memories. Memories which caused him to think that if there was one single thing on earth that could gently, yet forcefully, awaken Michael and

Rosie from the enduring trance under which they both seemed to walk blindly "toward a bottomless pit," as David phrased it to his fourth wife, "of guilt-infested immobility and despair," it was that very special island of the Greek Cyclades.

Paros was, indeed, a little jewel of an island, sparkling and pure and strong. Famous since even before Homer for its marble, it had nevertheless remained untrammeled. Inexplicably, it did not draw the crowds that toured the other islands of its chain. It attracted, instead, as late as the fifties, the era when David had come, a modest number of travelers. Nonconformist types who returned home to tell their friends of the alluring Greek island they had "discovered." Where there "were hardly any tourists" and the only crime in the last hundred years was "the theft of a single violin." Or, becoming seduced into further hyperbole by the rhythms of their own praises: the weather was "never anything but perfect." But what David Dagan said in nineteen seventy-one to his son and daughter-in-law, as he handed them a paperback Odyssey with airline tickets to Athens tucked inside, was simply, "The more joy you give yourselves, the more joy you'll have to give to others. Here, you kids, take this! Be joyful!"

These words of enlightened self interest would, David hoped, appeal to his son. They fit, after all, into the perspective that he himself had handed down—in both word and deed—when Michael was a boy. The wisdom should make sense, that was, if even Michael's most basic philosophical foundations had not been cruelly knocked out from under him. And that, unfortunately, David guessed, was a real possibility. He could not clearly see, one way or the other, though, what his son's condition fully implied. He could not yet define the lasting effects of that not-so-recent-anymore tragedy as it continued to ravage the souls and psyches of the young man and his wife, just as international tragedies continued to ravage the souls and psyches of much of humanity in that same sad year.

The trip had been a final, desperate inspiration. Two years and a half had passed now since the terrible day. And still David could not perceive a single sign that either Michael or Rosie was even beginning to adjust. He considered that he had no notion of what they were really feeling; he himself had not lost any of his children.

How could he demand of himself even a glimmer of an idea of what those two were going through? And their first and only child. What that must be like...unfathomable. Whatever Michael and Rosie were aching with, David acknowledged, could only be guessed at. He did suspect there was a lot of self-blame contaminating the young people's grief. The way he saw it, though, the baby's death was anything but their fault.

He himself was tormented by a deep and exhausting anguish. His grandson had lived but eleven months. And David had seen him only twice. The confusion and pain, the impact of the betrayal of the universe, were immense. Especially from the sudden manner in which the child was taken.

David Dagan was not, however, a man to lose himself in tragedy. Life went on, with its good and with its bad, and with a great deal in between.

It was in the spring of nineteen fifty-five that David had spent his own short idyllic, albeit illicit, interlude on Paros. With a delightful girl, an Australian girl whose name was Betsy, a girl that David would never forget. They had searched for seashells, and for marble, had explored the coast, the hills, a fishing village, and each other. At the conclusion of those three weeks, they had said their reluctant good-byes to the island, and to each other, she returning to her job in Cambridge and he to his wife and three children. His family was, at that time, awaiting his return from the latest "business trip" in a comfortable apartment in the eighth arrondissement of Paris, France.

As David recalled those days on the island, the potential became compelling. The spell of the mythical Greek sunlight on the little white houses and the green hills, the simplicity of nature and of human existence, those delights which had inspired such a fierce, free happiness in himself and in his lover, all would be strong medicines, he thought. They would do their work on his sorrowing son and daughter-in-law.

But, as for Michael and Rosie, though they accepted David's offer, they could not actually see what difference it would make where they were. No *place on earth would alter the darkness that they knew. Their gloom stretched out to cover the entire world and beyond, certain to extend even to unseen future dimensions, for both of them. But neither had the energy or the will to argue with Michael's father.*

✳   ✳   ✳

"The bed is too small," said Rosie. Michael glanced at the mattress and frowned. It appeared to be a double bed. They were, both of them, restless sleepers. In San Francisco, at home, they slept in a huge "California king-size" (and even that felt crowded). But they both were too tired to complain or to make demands for something else. They simply retrieved their suitcases and paid the old man.

They looked at each other vacantly. The moonlight through the window illuminated a lodging the size of a large bathroom, at most a dressing room, nearly void of furniture and decoration; not even a mirror was in sight. That barrenness, at least, felt right.

"Let's go to sleep," said Michael.

✳   ✳   ✳

The first morning on the island Michael slept until ten. He was accustomed to sleeping late in those days, whenever, in fact, he didn't have to be at work.

Rosie was still sleeping when he rose from the narrow, cramping mattress. He decided to write her a short note and slip out to get a cup of coffee, maybe even a breakfast, without disturbing her. He felt no desire or need to wait for her to waken. One of the many depressing aspects of the last couple of years, he reflected, was the fact that he and Rosie had not grown closer in their shared sadness, but, rather, only farther apart.

It wasn't an obvious thing, their distance, it wasn't that they even fought that much, they simply couldn't find any comfort in each other. This distressed him, as far as he could be distressed within an all-pervasive despair.

But he had become used to the feeling (which on that morning turned into a thought) that he and Rosie, even in their mutual agony, did not understand each other. He thought of their life at home, of the evenings. She in the bedroom, diverted by Johnny Carson; he in the den, seeking different comfort with The Doors.

He should have been prepared, at least a little, by such thoughts, and a few other new insights, which followed, for that which happened next. But he did not pursue his contemplations far enough down any pathway to reach the revelation that this morning was already unusual, the first time in he-didn't-know-how-long that he had given any thought whatsoever to the state of affairs between himself and his wife.

He went down the windowless stairwell. It was almost as dark as the night before. Only on the second floor, in the foyer, did a small window shed a little shaft of sunlight, on the desk and the caged parrot, and on the old man, who was already sitting upon his stool. Michael tried to remember how to say good morning in Greek, when he realized that this person was not the old man at all, but a very striking-looking younger fellow. Yet the man did bear a strong resemblance to the older concierge of the night before. To such a degree, apparently, as to play tricks on the eyes.

Maybe his son, thought Michael.

The man smiled up at him, beaming, and raised his hand, which was loosely grasping what appeared to be a bouquet of wildflowers. Michael felt an eerie thrill of a moment of deja vu pass through him.

Then, before he could say "Kalimera" in his hesitant Greek, the young Parosian, himself, said "Good Morning, Michael," in clear and confident English. He spoke in a low, drawling manner, intimately, as if he were a long-lost friend.

"Good Morning," answered Michael, wondering if the older man had told this younger guy his name or if he knew it from the guest list. He supposed it was possible that Rosie and he were the only guests.

He continued on down the dark stairway, musing. But when he opened the door and stepped outside, his confusion ceased. He was astonished— the light upon the whitewashed walls of the town was so powerfully bright.

It was necessary to return up the stairs for sunglasses. He hurried with an uncustomary speed, not only to avoid waking Rosie, but to be back in that extraordinary brightness. As he passed the foyer and glanced again toward the desk, he was surprised to see that now it was not the young man who sat there; this time it really was the older guy. He saw, too, that the parrot was missing from its cage. The old man, yet parrotless, was there when Michael came rushing back down. For his entire stay on Paros, in fact, he never saw the younger fellow again, nor was there any parrot.

But he did not inquire into those mysteries. There were other, more pressing matters to pursue.

For a second time, wiping his lenses on his shirt, he stepped out of the hotel and into the radiance of the island.

What happened next became a lasting memory. The experience was unique in all his life. During that one profound moment his mood changed, shifted instantly. A mood that had been with him for an eternity of days, months and even years, just seemed to crack and break, disintegrating in the cool, magical brightness of the morning air.

Occasionally in San Francisco he had imagined that, conceivably, one day he would begin to heal from the perpetual feeling of loss. But he had believed, had known without analyzing it, that if deliverance at last came, it would not come in any way except very, very gradually. What was happening to him now, however, was so immediate and intense, it did not even allow for any questions. He simply enjoyed his expanding astonishment.

He seemed to have been suddenly pulled into new awareness. As if, he wrote years later in correspondence, "as if I were a newborn child, entering earth through a dark and seemingly infinite yin passageway that never forewarned the coming balance of a world that also included yang." ("You saw it all in such a strange mirror-image metaphor" had been the puzzling reply.)

He looked down the road, towards the Aegean Sea. Bright and sparkling, it at once both soothed and excited. A powerful expectation gathered momentum inside him, like the rising waves of the ocean that surged before his eyes.

The road ahead was empty, except for one lone figure walking in his direction, one small point of interest in the light.

As the figure drew closer and he could see that it was a woman, some lines from Homer, recently reread, surfaced in his mind. "'Athena did not fail to see him go; at once she approached, in the form of a woman, a fine tall woman…'" He mumbled the last few words out loud.

It was when the figure drew sufficiently close so that he could see her face—her questioning yet peaceful expression—that his astonishment and expectation exploded. They came together crashing, like the morning sea upon the island sands. For he saw that the woman coming toward him was not only very pretty, she was someone that he knew.

He took a long, deep breath.

"Maria Ananin!" he called. "What in the world are you doing here?"

And, as he would forever remember, even while he was asking the question, he sensed its answer come quite clearly. In spite of the fact that he was only barely acquainted with this woman, he knew, with unaccountable certainty, exactly what it was that she was doing there. He knew that of all the people in the world, this was the one who should now approach and stand beside him. She was coming, he knew, to share in the mystery of the disappearance of despair.

She stood there facing him, wide-eyed and silent. But he, who for so many months had been silent, found himself speaking, "Someone told me that the Greek light is magic," he heard himself say, "It seems to make everything…" He searched for the right word, and found it, just as she did: "timeless!" said Michael Dagan and Maria Ananin, together. And then, late twentieth century Americans that they were, they laughed in discomfort at the coincidence.

It was not the first time, nor the last, that such a declaration was made on the island of Paros, nor on the other islands of the Cyclades—his own father, in fact, once uttered nearly the same sentence. But, nevertheless, as if the pronouncement had been a uniquely brilliant incantation, time heeded and stood still. Michael and Maria stood there in its stillness, while each absorbed the beauty of the other as if it was essential.

Eventually they turned toward the beauty of the sea.

Later, an eternity later, Michael thought of Rosie.

But the woman at his side continued to watch the sunlight as it played upon the sea. The Sea and the Sunlight; with an emotion of reverence brightened by release, she thought of the thousands of centuries in which those two ageless Parents of all Life had thus been making love.

*   *   *

As Deborah Anderson set her tape recorder on the sidewalk and unlocked the door of her Honda Civic, she, too, remembered Maria Ananin.

"My god—I'm an idiot! How in the world did I forget her? He confused me, that's what it was! First he was cold. Then he was warm. Then he was cold again. Confident, vulnerable, confident! Self-revelations, privacy. Everywhere opposite messages, contradictions! God, he rattled me—and I thought he was the one who was confused! I didn't ask one single thing about her! I should go back in there right this minute!

"But of course, I can't... Shit!!! I can't believe it! How could I forget Maria Ananin?!"

*   *   *

The next morning, however, Deborah was less bothered with self-recriminations. She would call Michael Dagan and request just the most cursory discussion of Ananin. Over the phone, as a personal favor, "to save my professional reputation." He was basically a nice man; he would have to understand. And though she still greatly bewailed her bizarre omission of probably the most obvious essential of the Dagan interview, she began to console herself that nevertheless, she had chanced upon two provocative pieces of information. Not useful for the interview, but at least they'd be of interest to her friends.

Deborah Anderson, who prided herself on an accuracy of perception so dependable that certain types of friends and acquaintances were repeatedly telling her she must be "psychic," was positive that she had gained some knowledge simply by what she'd heard in his voice and seen in his eyes. When the man had, in that solitary reference to Ananin, rapidly pronounced the woman's name.

Deborah felt fairly certain that, number one, the filmmaker was in love with his leading lady. And that, two, Dagan did not believe—as did some cult-like followers of his "environmental surrealism"—that Ananin's disappearance was due to the fact that she was a victim of violence, probably perpetrated by some insane male who'd identified the actress with her roles.

No, it was quite clear in his intonation, Deborah told herself, and later told her friends; Michael Dagan believed that Maria Ananin was still alive. "But, then, of course," she would add, "Michael Dagan is not exactly your complete expert on what's happening. He's an ambitious, anachronistic artifact. A leftover dreamer from the sixties, or maybe it's the early seventies, back when we were all in diapers. Like, he's stuck there, in a time when people thought they could actually save the world. No. Wait. He's not totally stuck there—I mean he's looking back much farther—to the days of the Sumerians!"

6

In the Days of the Sumerians

circa 2700 B.C.

I have clear memories from my childhood of the hour of dusk. When I was very young, dusk was the time to gather with my friends beneath the great huluppu tree. We would make our "dinner" there—from the big green huluppu leaves, the fragrant purple flowers, and the long red pods of seeds. We crushed the seeds and flowers for our porridge, which we served upon the leaves. We set our eating place and we became a family—a vexatious family, making palaver about everything, usually!

My friend Debela was always wanting to be the mother in this play. "I won't be your friend anymore;" this was her tool to bring us to submission. And it always worked. Simbaya and I were the children and Debela was our ma.

When I was older I could not join with them at dusk. I had to study tablet, to read and to inscribe. My friends mostly chatted together then, full of intrigues and virgin's insights. Yet also they continued, till they married, to play a little beneath the tree. I did not take part in that later play. My family wanted me to know tablet, and I wanted it, too. I studied every day with Elder Ummia, as the light of Utu passed to the netherworlds and the moon began to show. My studies brought me much pleasure, so much delight that I came to know more tablet than most any of the young ones, and most of our elders as well.

As I grew older, when I spoke with Debela I came to see that she had changed, that she was looking upward to me. I came to wonder if she recalled that a time had been when she was the one who was *ninhursag,* queen of the mountain, the one who told us what to do.

It was knowing tablet that made my life go smoothly. Tablet helped me think to be a good wife, a good mother, a good friend, to have patience, and not to anger. I have never been sorry for studying; it gave me some of my assurance and a lot of my joy, and it has answered many of my questions, thanks be to All the Anunnaki.

*　　　　*　　　　*

It was not long after dusk that Simbaya and Charis finally came to me with food and water. The look of concern in the faces of my friends caused me worry. Would this illness not be finished soon? Did they know more about it than I? Perhaps they were feigning their extreme concern because they had not come sooner; perhaps they thought that caring words and faces would balance their lack of deeds. Or possibly their expressions were authentic, and my own appearance truly disturbed them? I knew not which alternative to prefer.

I asked them how my little ones were getting on with Ninta. And they told me all was well. They said that Sonaté and the younger Charis had begun the complicated process of getting word to Anurei. I knew it was not possible for my husband to come home from making trade, but it was correct for him to know of my condition.

Simbaya swept the floor and Chari dusted the walls and shooed the bugs away. They brought me a wet cloth for my forehead and turned me over so they could rub my back with oils of herbs—*hamun,* the "harmony plant" and *sisa,* the "righter of wrongs." I was shivering then, so they massaged me vigorously and asked if I wanted them to stay. Of course I wanted them! Had I not spent the entire day in solitude?

But I had no will to converse. They could make themselves comfortable and talk with one another. I would listen and be grateful. They put my guest-mats beneath themselves and against the wall and they sat, chatting pleasantly. Once Chari went outside to the cook pot and returned with cooled sisa tea. It was better for me to have them there, and I even forgot my troubled self, listening to their talk. Perhaps because of fever, heightening my senses, it all became sharp memory, forever vivid in my mind.

They spoke of the lack of barley since the war, and told what they were doing to prevent wasting the little they still had. But word from our gardens and from the market place was that much was going well. No matter what happened in the matter of barley, we could expect to have enough to eat, with plenty of bulghur and dates in the village storehouse. Lettuce was growing by the waters, and oranges and lemons were ripe upon the trees.

"Never have I seen you so, Anarisha," Simbaya said to me after a time. I gave a small nod. "In former days, when the Anunnaki were heeded not, people might have said that someone was casting hatred upon you. No one wills disharmony, now, I suppose. Yet, at times I wonder." She looked to me and waited. I spoke not.

But Chari answered her, "It might be, Simbaya, that the war and its evil purposes begin to reach to Fa-Orszag."

Simbaya's eyes widened. "Chari, there was a time in our village when disturbing things truly did take place..." She hesitated. "My grandmother told me...the way it was, in this village when she was young. There is a story she told us; she told it often and I know it well:

"My Grandmother Anuyé and my Grandfather Tumal had made a trading journey to the north. They departed the village in the time of the Greater Harvest. They were away from Fa-Orszag for two seasons. When Grandmother at last returned, the people seemed not to be her own. They were much too grim, and they were quiet.

"She had thought that playful rejoicing would greet her on her return. But instead the people spoke little with her. She thought they were angry because she left them for too long. She heeded not that they spoke as little to one another, as little as they did to her.

"This went on for nearly one moon. Then one day she went to market, and when she returned she found that Fa-Orszag was as noisy and friendly as she had always known it. A neighbor ran up to her as she walked through town. He asked if she had heard the news.

"'A boy died this morning, Anuyé. In the old section,' the neighbor man, whose name was Nin, informed my grandma. 'And just before he passed, he made confession to us. Anuyé, that boy joined the Wanting Ones! Some time ago,' Nin explained, 'the Wanting Ones came to the boy, in the way they like to, at night. In his dreaming. *Join us*, they whispered, *and we will give you whatsoever you desire.*

"'*What must I do to join you*? the boy asked, thinking they would require a bit of hair, a piece of fingernail. *Give to us your small brother, a true sacrifice!* they whispered. *All right, very well, then, let it be so, as you say*, the boy replied. The next morning the little brother awoke with fever. That small child wasted away for many days, until he was too thin and too weak to move. We all saw him,' said Nin to my grandmother, 'he was right there in front of his house, lying under his family tree. His mother sat beside him, wasting also, with the agony of worry for her little one.

"'The older boy told us that when he saw his brother and his mother lying so, weak and dying, day after day, he began to lose all confidence, and to feel sorry for the thing that he had done. Finally one night he returned to the Wanting Ones, again in his dream. *I can not give my little brother to you*, he told them. *Well then, so be it*, they replied, *but you will have to give us, in that case, yourself. For you must understand, we have already allowed you the thing you bargained for, exactly what you wanted: the high respect of all the people of Fa-Orszag. Has that not been so, good friend, during these many days*? And the boy answered, *Yes, it has, it has been so, but I can not give you the life of my little brother!* After that, and we are all here witnesses,' declared Nin, 'the little brother quickly regained his health. And the big brother grew ill in his stead! This very morning, Anuyé,' exclaimed Nin to my grandmother, 'after this foolish, unfortunate one spoke his confession, and breathed his final remorseful breath, our village was cleansed. We all have seen the passing of that wicked monster, Gloom, who has dwelt amongst us for all these many days. So, now, tell me, Anuyé, how was your journey? And why did you leave us and make us miss you for so long?'

"And my grandmother told us that she could clearly see that everything which her neighbor had spoken was so," Simbaya concluded.

"But do you yourself believe all that?" asked Charis.

"This I heard many times at my grandmother's feet." replied Simbaya. "Yes, of course, I believe it."

"Well, 'the seed of belief brings forth the fruit of truth,' as my father used to say," declared Chari. "'Whatsoever a person believes becomes true, for that one.' And that is why," she added, "I, myself, put my thoughts to An, the Upholder of All that is Good."

"Perhaps you are right," said Simbaya, "but, Chari, tell me, how do you know, always, what is good?"

I remember that much of the conversation, but about then I drifted into sleep. That night I dreamt that I had run out of peppers. I went to buy more, but the market also was finished with peppers. "There seems to be no more peppers," I complained to one of the women of the market. "Yes, that is true," she answered. "I do believe that this world is coming to its end."

*   *   *

The next morning I was no stronger. I still had no desire to eat, but I was glad for the barley and honey tea that Simbaya brought me. Glad, and also thankful, for barley was so scarce. Simbaya was a kind friend; I had been foolish the day before, to imagine that she and Chari were neglectful of me.

Simbaya had been a graceful child, easy in play and easy to join with in tasks. I always felt harmonious when I was in her company; when we parted I held no regrets that I had said or done a wrong thing.

Simbaya knew what it was to be sick, she had been ill many times and her head often ached. Now that I was ill, myself, I felt a rush of empathy for Simbaya's troubles. I puzzled over why she was given so many of them. And the bed of marriage had provided no haven, in truth.

Her husband, Nergal, chose her for her sweet nature of easy accommodation, I suspected. But Nergal cared not about my friend. He saw not who this Simbaya was, and he had no patience for either her sickness or her perpetual questioning. For never was Simbaya able to make a ready choice. She believed that her husband, or her friends, or even her little ones, knew more about what was right for her than did she herself. But I always tried to encourage her; I knew she had hopes that one day she would see to find clear answers for herself.

On that eighth day Simbaya brought me her tea and then quickly departed. I did not see anyone again for two days, though tea or water was left me when I slept. Those were not days of high fever, yet I was weak, often nauseous, and miserable. I understood not what had come upon me and I began to feel a scarcity of love for the first time in my life. Morbid thoughts about the war and about myself played through the fogginess of my poor mind. I contemplated, repeatedly, the story Simbaya had told about the little child who was made sick through the selfish craving of his elder brother. I wished she had never told it.

Then Agghia came to me. She was Chari's mother's aunt and I had known her all my life, though I had not known her well.

"I have come, Anarisha," she greeted me simply, without ceremony. "I have learned that you dwell not easily in the body." She set by my side the cup of tea she had made me.

"That is so, Ma," I replied.

"I have known it for some time. I have had dreams about you, Anarisha. Many dreams, both in the day and in the night. And I have advised the people to come not to your door."

"Come not to my door? What do you speak, Ma Agghia?" I felt a sudden alarm, and the strength of it brought me upright to a sitting position on my mat.

"It is good that you remain alone," she said softly. "This sickness that you have, it has come on the wind; it is of Enlil. You are near to a change, daughter. Not a small change. An auspicious matter shall now take place."

"What are you speaking, Ma?" I whispered, weaker with her words. "I ask not for any changes. The Anunnaki allow me to dwell in happiness. My life is harmonious, thanks be to An. I ask not for change. I have love in the family, thanks be to An. I want no changes, Ma!" I was beginning to have a spinning feeling that Agghia herself was a dream, a dream that I could not long abide.

She fixed her eyes firmly on my own. "Your life, which so pleases you, has been moving always toward this day. It is for this hour, Anarisha, and what it portends, that you have been given life."

"Please, Ma Agghia, explain what you are saying. I can not take in your words, they are making me more ill!" I protested with all my diminished force.

"Listen, daughter! Your sickness, it is not a sickness! It is a healing. The rain is washing away the dust. You saw not clearly, Anarisha. Now you sweat away the decayed thinking that has made you look upside down and inside out."

I had heard of such illness. But, yet, I began to think, who is crazy, Ma Agghia or I?

I lay back down and she tried to reach me through her eyes. But I would have none of it. I looked her over in the silence. In truth, she was a wonderful looking woman. Her silver and black hair, long, shining and alive, had lost no glory with age. Her skin, as well, was vibrant, clear and fine, like *asimbabar*, the light of the new moon. Her broad face and deeply set eyes were full of the assurance and comfort of a good mother. Her lips were peaceful, but conveyed also vibrancy and strength. Her slenderness surpassed my own, and she was graceful, with the grace more of a girl than of a woman. When I looked at Agghia, I felt I could see not only the old one she was now, but all that she had been before.

She seemed at that moment somewhat saddened.

"I can see, Anarisha, that you receive not my words. You move not upon the sparkling river that runs deep. Perhaps you have not suffered enough to touch the depths wherein it flows. I have to confess to you that I never considered that this would be the case. I imagined that you would be receptive, that you would greet me joyfully, that you would already see glimmers of what I came to say. I hope that you will be ready with but a little more time to consider, rather than many seasons or years of life. But I am fully patient. I will go away. You need some time, child; how long it may be, I can not know." Then her voice grew lower: "May you become the fish *Rohita*; may you be found in the river that flows through the homeland of your soul. Love be with you always, Anarisha."

And with that unique farewell she was gone from the room.

She did not come again to me for many years. And by that time, of course, I had changed. I was, in truth, no longer Anarisha of Fa-Orszag.

When she was departed, I remembered her tea. I drank, and I discovered it to be the same tea that I had found at my bedside every morning. Only this brew was far stronger, highly potent with those flavors which I knew not. As before, the flavors soothed me. Soon I was deep in sleep.

7

War with Heaven

Fa-Orszag, the 'Tree-Land,"
circa 2700 B.C.

It was in the time when Anurei had returned from making trade, the time when Anarisha once again knew the clarity of good health, even as cloudy rumors gathered secretly against her, that the winds changed. A coldness came in from the north and people wrapped not one, but many cloths about their shoulders.

Their calm faces grew tight and hard as they braced themselves for the winds. These winds at first crept gently through the village, but then grew strong, unyielding as a demented enemy. The villagers were not accustomed to harsh climate in their world; it was the first such cold ever in Fa-Orszag, as far as they recalled, and in all the valley known as the Nyuegat. There were not even legends of such a trouble.

All was gray; the color of the heavens was altered in that time. Often an entire day would pass when the sky would not change to blue from dreary gray. Gray ethers veiled the face of Utu; neither sun of day nor stars of night were left unmasked.

The people began then to drink their beverages hot. Never had such a thing occurred, tea was taken cooled until that time. Some protested the new habit. Protection from cold had never been a needed custom. And although the people of Fa-Orszag were smoothly practical through all their waking hours, some minds just could not make a leap to plan defense against this new and unknown trouble, a trouble that some had named "The War with Heaven" and others called "The Season of Great Cold."

Instead, they bewailed and cursed the winds and made fires to the Anunnaki, begging Heaven to forever cease this trial. Each day the smoke rose heavenward, and Anarisha marveled with her children at the beauty of its tendrils in the cold damp morning air.

And it came to pass that this cold went on for the number of days that three full moons can shine—though no moon appeared in that time whatsoever. In the middle of those days, on about the thirtieth day of the War with Heaven, the people began to know discord. Within the families, and amongst the neighbors as well. Thoughts of a sort which had always been kept to oneself were now told forth, with lingering attempts at courtesy, it is true, but nevertheless the words were small-spirited, critical, and not thought out with care.

Thus began the retorts and the arguments. And the smoldering angers, far more common than before. Gossip grew constant as people lost face on hearing, for the first time, blunt insults aimed straightforward at themselves.

Scapegoating partnered up with gossip. So that one day Anarisha's friend, Charis, said to Simbaya, "Remember that tale your grandmother told you; the one about the boy whose secret evil brought gloom upon the town?" No one knew it then, but the village was beginning to shift itself, to move into a fine tuning of dark thinking that would ready it for the subtle treachery that would soon confuse them all.

*   *   *

It was two days after Anurei had returned from making trade; sixteen days since Anarisha had recovered from disease. In the late afternoon, two strangers, a pair of traders from the southwest, hitched their donkeys to a cottonwood in the meadow and walked into the town. The strangers were dressed in robes of a tightly woven, white flaxen cloth, robes which they had purchased from tradesmen more northern than themselves. For the two had heard of the cold that had overtaken the valley of the Nyuegat.

The tops of their heads were shaven, the sockets of their eyes were deep, their features large, and their expressions dignified and stoic. One man was short and stout, the other of average height and weight. There was nothing so very authoritative about them, until the shorter one began to speak. His voice was melodic, low and controlled, and the people of Fa-Orszag attended.

"We come seeking," said this trader to the group of men and women who were gathered in the meeting house, called there when the traders asked for " your most respected ones." The people were silent as they pondered the man's accent, and his statement. Finally a villager stood.

"For what are you looking?" this man inquired.

"We are seeking a certain woman," the trader replied. "We know of her from the teachings of our Temple. She is said to be of this land, of this valley. And the people of the southern villages have directed us to Fa-Orszag."

"What do you want of this one?" another man asked, instinctively protective of his neighbors and his kin.

"We mean her no harm," said the trader evenly. "We wish only to converse. We are looking for a woman who is said to possess a superlative beauty. A woman who men would dream of and not forget."

There was a long silence. "There may be such a woman here," said an old man at last. Some glanced at the old one apprehensively.

This time the taller trader spoke up. "Is this a virtuous woman, grandfather?" he asked, trying, but failing, to keep his voice from betraying the excitement that began to pound in his heart.

"She is a good woman," the old one nodded.

"Is she a virgin?" asked the shorter trader.

"No, no. The woman is married. She is a mother."

"This woman—you tell us she is virtuous. How are you so certain that she has always been faithful?"

There was again silence. How did anyone know such a thing with certainty?

"I am her husband," Anurei broke the thick silence with his calm, soft voice. Many were already glancing his way, the others turned. No one objected or said a thing, but the taller trader sucked in his breath.

"Ah, yes, I see," he said. Then Anarisha, who was among the group of 'respected ones,' also made a small gasp. Her eyes opened wide as she looked first at her husband and then at the rest. Then she surprised even herself by rising and running out the door of the meeting house and through the village to her home. They all turned and gazed upon the fleeing figure. Her head-tie fell to the ground and her long copper-black hair came streaming behind her as she ran.

The traders concluded the meeting then, declaring that they wished to remain for a night and a day, to talk with the people of Fa-Orszag, one by one. The people offered the foreigners their new beverage, a heated tea of cinnamon and cloves, and they offered them their juice of the *soma* plant, from which to breathe and refresh their souls. The traders were given mats and cloths, and the use of the meeting house to spend the night.

The meeting ended with joking and smiling conversation, though most continued to feel an inward apprehension. Anurei stayed until the end, listening to everything, but he spoke not a word, not even when approached.

8

Betrayal

In the morning, yet another cold morning, the strangers mingled with the people. They were seen to spend much of the dawn time with the coppersmith. Anurei did not look pleased. The strangers went on to talk with others; it seemed they spoke with nearly every man and woman in Fa-Orszag.

When they came at last to Anarisha, she was sweeping leaves from before her doorway. The shorter man inquired, "How are you in the body this day, Respected Woman?" Beneath her married woman's head cloth he could see the innocent eyes of a thoughtful and very pretty child.

"There is no dust on Heaven" she replied in the manner of her people. She ceased sweeping and stood supporting herself on her bishuti broom. Her little son and daughter watched from the open door, and three chickens searched for grains about her feet.

She had felt such a strangeness since the night before. It was as though a formal declaration of desire had been made for her at the meeting house, by the entire village. And while this seemed to be some sort of dream, it was at the same time a thing that she knew had been hovering about her for nearly all her life, perpetually pushed away by her own mind for the sake of her own good.

"And you, how are you in the body, Respected Guests of Fa-Orszag?" she asked the men.

"There is no dust on Inanna," they replied as one.

And hearing this odd alteration of the village greeting, she felt a shiver pass through her. But she responded calmly. "So life is," she clearly pronounced the usual response.

"So life is," replied the traders.

They spoke no further with her. They simply looked her over, with a quick and subtle sureness that somehow managed to maintain respect. Then they nodded, almost imperceptibly, to each other.

As they walked away, the taller man, whose name was Kerem, said to the other, called Ursunabi, "You must realize, the husband will not agree to any price, whatever we may offer."

Ursunabi nodded thoughtfully. "We must approach this matter a bit differently than we had supposed, Kerem. The main door is locked, but I think I have found the key to a side one."

The traders had heard the gossip about Anarisha and the warrior. After assessing the talk, with the superior shrewdness which had made them successful businessmen in all the lands from Uruk to Mohenjo-Daro, they had come to the conclusion that the talk was all gossip and nothing more. But they saw now that this gossip would be useful.

They returned to the woman called Debela, the person most often sited as its source.

"Yes, I believe this is true," she replied slowly, but firmly to their questioning. "Anarisha and that Aris—yes I can surely imagine them together. There is something about her. You see, I do not trust her loyalty." Debela shook her head emphatically. It was true that she did not trust her old childhood friend, that one who had once been so agreeable but who had later gone down her own pathway, from the time when she was taught to use a stylus. Anarisha and, in truth, all of the people of Fa-Orszag, were not to be completely trusted, thought Debela.

Who knew the secrets of anyone, especially those of the self-possessed Anarisha? As for that man, Aris—a man like a handsome bull—of course a woman might have him if he offered! And once he glimpsed Anarisha he had no doubt offered! Besides, all the village was talking and confirming that the affair was so. *What does it matter if it was I who was first to guess the truth?* Debela asked herself.

After talking with Debela, the traders decided to wait for one more day before acting. They begged to meet again with the respected ones of the village. Anarisha did not attend, but Anurei was there, listening grimly as he chewed on a piece of *enten* nut.

The trader's speech was brief and to the point.

"We have learned much in your village of Fa-Orszag," began Ursunabi. "And we have found the woman to whom the learned have directed us. I will tell you now, people of Fa-Orszag: we have come to your village with the purpose of obtaining and carrying this woman. To our sacred city of Orom, which lies in the distant southwest. The people of that marvelous city—a city where, let me tell you, every day is a holy day, and where the citizens array themselves only in festive linen attire—we are seeking slaves to serve us. Slaves to enrich the spirit of the city; we want only the most favored of the lands."

There was a collective gasp and then a silence. The people of Fa-Orszag did not possess slaves. Nor did they sell any of their own into slavery. Nor had they been taken as slaves in war. Yet everyone had heard tales of the practice, mostly from traders, and from passing warriors, as well.

"We have learned, by talking with you people, that the woman known as Anarisha has been unfaithful. In this very season—" But the man did not continue, for Anurei, who was sitting in a squatting position near him, suddenly jumped to his feet, oblivious to the pain which this caused his infirm knee.

Seldom had those villagers seen such an anger, not from Anurei, who very nearly never angered, nor from anyone of their own. The muscles of his face, his entire body, the veins, his coloring—which changed from golden brown to pale yellow—all bespoke of a murderous emotion. It flashed from his eyes, like lightning, to the trader. Three men jumped up almost simultaneously and grabbed the young husband by the arms to hold him back. The trader fixed Anurei's eyes with his own steady gaze. "And I believe that it is this unfaithfulness of the woman called Anarisha," he continued, his voice loud and clear, "which is the cause of the War with Heaven, the coldness, here in the Nyuegat! Anarisha is, without doubt, a woman of power. But because she has not used her gift for the good of Anu, these cold winds have befallen the village of Fa-Orszag, indeed, the entire valley of the Nyuegat!"

From deep within Anurei's throat a guttural, almost growling, spasm of sound came forth as he attempted to break loose from his restraining friends. Two more men came to join those who held the muscular coppersmith, while the stranger continued. "We understand very clearly that it would be to the benefit of ourselves, and to our sacred city of Orom, to obtain this woman, she whose lack of faithfulness would not be of any import to us. Not in Orom. For, in powerful and lawful Orom, all of her behavior would be entirely under rule. And, at the same time," said Ursunabi, becoming even louder and more emphatic, "it would be of utmost benefit to the innocent and suffering people of Fa-Orszag to send this Anarisha from your midst. Of utmost, lasting benefit. To satisfy All Gods. And to thereby put to an end the time of trial and torment which you have been enduring so bravely and so long." He paused a moment. "And of benefit, as well, to insure your village against the ravages of war, ravages which threaten you much more dangerously, I am certain, than any of you are presently aware.

"With all of this in mind," his melodious tones grew lower so that now some strained to hear him, "I wish to let it be known that we bring with us the precious gold of Orom, to present to you in respectful offering—" But just then, as the trader reached for a leather pouch tied at his waist, Anurei made a heaving lurch forward, moving all the men about him, and even knocking one man to his knees. Then the coppersmith let forth a great gasp and also, himself, fell to the ground where he lay, with his hand clutching his heart, in a great still heap.

By the next day the matter was decided. The village agreed to accept two pieces of high quality gold, each about the size of a small fig, in exchange for Anarisha. They kept her that night in the meeting house, where, in fever once again, she gazed upon a now familiar figure—a boy whose name was "Michael," who ran and leaped and shouted while he played with other children in some strange and distant world.

*   *   *

The village, for the most part, excluding the friends and family of Anarisha, was very nearly exultant in acquiring the gold, and in having a hope kindled that the time of the coldness would soon be done. This exultation was tempered with the concern and sympathy that many felt for the much beloved coppersmith. Many there were, both women and men, and children, as well, who came to care for Anurei as he lay in voiceless suffering with his shocked and sickened heart.

But it was only Anurei himself, with the help of Heaven, who could heal the wound of bitterness which was made that day in his soul, and which silenced both his laughter and his stories for so many of the years that followed.

9

Bondage

Oh, Debela, Debela, I lamented, calling out like a woman in travail. How came you to this? I knew you, I loved you; hear me now. You were the proud one; proud like the Zu-bird was Debela of Fa-Orszag. You lacked in patience and you stood aside. But never did I possess the secret of your cruel and jealous heart. I saw not this unique hatred that only now creeps forth. Debela, you are a portion of my self. My age-mate, the constant playmate of my days gone by. Never was there Anarisha who knew not Debela. As never lived Debela who knew not my self, this one called Anarisha of Fa-Orszag.

But so life is, for thus does it come of the Invisible.

*   *   *

They led me from the village in the afternoon. One man on either side, each taking me by an arm. I began then to feel the shame, though I knew I had done no wrong.

We walked through the village of Fa-Orszag, and the faces of my people turned from me as we passed. Not one would regard me, only Charis and Simbaya who walked where I could see them, ahead and to my side. They carried my babies and they wept. The comfort which these two friends gave was great. I knew that there yet existed in this world a love and trust of companions, even if there were but two. And I knew that their love would be portioned to my children. This alone lightened the burden in my heart at that doom-filled moment.

I wondered where Ma Agghia and the two older holy ones were keeping themselves, for they were nowhere to be seen. Nor were my sisters. Nor was Debela.

I passed the trees of Fa-Orszag and in my heart I paid them a final reverence. I felt their strong and silent love reach out to me. I passed my husband's workshop and I could almost see him standing there, but he lay, I knew, upon our mat, unwaking. My longing for my husband and my babies screamed out inside me, but I gave the cry no voice. I bowed my head, looking down upon the fine-grained soil of my village, my home.

*   *   *

The two men were not rough to me. In truth, they were quite careful. But when we came to the outskirts of the village, where the wilderness begins, though the road goes on, they came to a halt before their two hitched donkeys. And then, with the exception of my sandals, they removed all my attire.

"You will not need these again, Anarisha," said Kerem, putting them into a sack on the side of his beast.

When the clothing was off, first one and then the other let their hands wander all about me. Then one trader held me by the arm, while the other moved away, so as to see. "She is fine, very fine. Like a temple carving of Orom," he said.

"Like a living daughter of Inanna," the other, with his hands again upon me, whispered. "So delicately, so perfectly she is made." He cupped my breasts in his palms, "Lush roundness…and you see…delicious harmony with shoulders and belly. Yes, we are indeed fortunate, my friend!"

"And the ass of her, Ursunabi, come 'round, come see! So ready! So full and sweet!"

"We shall market her privately, Kerem. Only the select shall receive invitation. We shall not display this treasure in the public market place!"

"As it should be. As it should be! Is it not? I have long supposed, since it was the teachings you received at the Temple, since the teachings initiated this whole venture… I thought there was no question, 'Abi…'"

"Yes, yes, I know, Kerem. You had good reason. But it seems that I have not possessed a faith so wonderful as your own, my friend. In truth, I knew not just what we were going to find. Ah, but to see is to believe!"

"And to touch is even better!" smiled Kerem, while his fingers shaped my loins.

They took a long piece of hemp from a sack then, and they tied my wrists and my belly. Then they continued for a time to pass over me with their hands and with their eyes. To my great surprise and to my shame, I began to know the sweetness. For they were gentle, and their appreciation was intense.

"Ah, yes! I believe this truly is the offering that the Temple has awaited," said Ursunabi, as he discovered that my nipples had grown firm and that my vulva was moist, "Yes, we shall auction her privately, and the old priestess shall come. And, O Kerem, we shall not settle for anything less than she is worth!" he again spoke in a whisper. One of the donkeys turned its head then to look upon us. With her great soft eyes she acknowledged me, as though she understood everything; I remember the moment clearly.

"Our fortunes are made, this day, 'Abi," said Kerem.

"Put her clothing back on." said Ursunabi, curtly, suddenly concerned. "I have come to my senses. How foolish to let you catch cold, dear Anarisha!"

When my clothing was on and the hemp retied, they loosened their donkeys and walked on, pulling the animals beside them. As before, I walked between the traders. Only now, instead of leading me by the arms, one trader held the leash of hemp, as if I were his animal. The other took me by the hand, as if I were his love.

As we journeyed, I put my mind to dignity, beautiful dignity. And I thought of peace, as my mother had taught me to do when in time of trouble. I thought not of Anurei, nor of my babies, and I did not see the road, nor what was to the right nor to the left, nor even that which passed before us straight ahead. I saw instead my mother, as she had once appeared, so long ago, when I was but a little girl and she was everything I yearned and hoped to be.

10

Visions

My mother was a small and serious woman. Even when I was a little child, she seemed so slight to me, I did not sense that she was larger than myself. She was as a breath, immaterial, composed of motion and of light.

I can still see her dancing in the firelight of evenings, on nights when intimates gather, and the drums and the lutes and the clapping hands of men go on until even the dawn has slept. She danced quickly and easily, as the flickers of the fire, spinning and gesturing with the grace of ecstasy and trance.

On the outskirts of the group, where the children watched, I would try my best to be her. And some nights I would forget myself, joining the women, dancing as if I too were an aspect of their unity and their wisdom and their power.

Or I would watch her movements of the day. Sweeping, her back bending from the hips, swishing the leaves with sparse gesture and abundant efficiency. Pounding the grain in unbroken rhythm. Tiny feathery woman of strength.

As she moved through our daily chores, guiding my sisters and me, watching us, she spoke but little. When she spoke it was, most often, to instruct. Her words could hold me inside them. They would caress me and at the same time pierce my heart. Rarely, but sometimes, they would make me laugh.

She taught us that there are four good ghosts who dance around and through the heavens with the Anunnaki, the village of gods. These ghosts come from the breath of the gods. And likewise they flow back, returning for the gods to breathe them in. The names of these spirits are Wisdom, Strength, Beauty and Love. Together they feed the heavenly Bliss, which forever courses through the Holy Ones as if it were their blood.

I craved my mother's shining tales of the four ghosts. In time, though she was often silent, I came to be filled with her stories. Thus did she nourish me when no longer I took her milk.

My mother died when I had twelve years. There was no trouble to find care for me. My father took his second wife, but my sisters and I were grown too much to need her help. My father was glad that old Ummia was teaching me tablet, it would continue my learning, and that, he said, was the path for me. Father greatly missed my mother and grieved for her until he himself sickened and died, not many seasons afterward.

My mother's death made a stronger love between us all. We lit a small fire each night and spoke with her inside ourselves, as she had told us to do for our grandparents and for the two baby brothers who died when they were yet at breast. Once a year we lit fires with all the village in honor of the dead. But we never talked of her again.

I, myself, missed her, but I grieved not. For as she lay unliving on her mat and the people sat encircled, drinking barley ale and chanting, just as they rose to dance the dance which helps departing spirits, I saw her spirit leave her body. It appeared as an image of her, and it spoke to me, with a strong, clear voice that was hers. I looked about me and the people were seating themselves again, behaving as though nothing had happened, though the chanting seemed to grow faster. And I knew that no one had seen what I saw, nor heard her voice.

She told me that she was happy, but that I was at an age where her death might do me harm. The only thing lacking in her happiness was the assurance that I would remain joyful for her. I obeyed and imagined all sorts of good for my mother in some other world. I knew no grief, for the words of her mouth and the voice of her throat were just as when she lived. They caressed me while they pierced my heart.

*   *   *

As I made the journey to Orom, I saw again my mother, giving comfort to me. But what I saw came not by the light of the sun, nor did it enter through the gateway of my eyes.

In the midst of the journey I also saw one other. I saw a little child. She was playing in a garden, making wishes, a girl child of another world. A unique little girl, of feature and of color which are never to be seen. Not in Fa-Orszag, nor in Orom, nor in any land of which I have heard tales.

Part II

Woman of The Water

1

Maria Ananin

east of San Francisco
1949 A.D.

> "The Young Woman of the Morning comes shining.
> O Holy Inanna,
> Your gaze is upon us.
> With light you appear, with love you appear.
> You meet us this day,
> You greet us this day,
> Smiling and singing and shining,
> Goddess of the Morning Star."
> —from the tablets of *The Twenty-One Hymns of Orom*

In later years when she recalled a certain luminous era of her life, the memory of the lovemaking would come to her most clearly.

Not just in her mind, nor even just her heart. Rather, it came as a deep warmth that filled all of her—mind, body, heart and soul—with an exquisite tranquillity that was at once blissful and almost unbearably sad. In the moments or hours when she thought of him, he whose presence had defined and flowed through that time, that place, and that self—who once had been her self—she would appear to sympathetic acquaintances, those who knew her only slightly, to be holding on to an old melancholy or a sorrow. But it wasn't sorrow she was carrying; it was something much more beautiful and whole.

Wholeness of being was not a quality that Maria Ananin had owned and lost and then claimed again. It did not seem that she had come into this world with a given set integrity. It was, instead, a little-while friend that played hide-and-seek with her from the start, coming and going—mostly going.

Nor had her beginnings held some precursor or hint, even, of he who would eventually bring to a climax and conclusion that elusive dance. There was no brother nor father who she would later notice as reminding her of him, not even slightly. Only, she remembered, there had been a foreshadowing of the magic...

*   *   *

Through the lace-curtained window, the sight of a robin beyond the sunlit grass: soft orange breast, soft brown wing and tail, little round head, the small plump creature upon a branch of light pink cherry blossoms. Echoing throughout life she would come upon impersonators of this image, in paintings or cards or books, common and pervasive as sunsets over hills or madonnas holding babies. But never again would there be such a bright green lawn, such joyous blossoms, such an eternally real bird, such a surreal time and place as East 28th St., Oakland, California, 1949.

For one thing, it had been there and then, when she was just a little girl, that the mysterious *Woman-of-the-Water* had come to visit her.

It had happened in her special secret place, the baby-tear fern garden beneath Grandma's back porch steps. The garden was a small shaded setting for play and happiness. Mossy and full of ferns, hidden from view, but accessible to rays of sunlight midst cool shade, it was a damp green world of stepping stones and earth, of life and leafiness. Its fragrance was unlike anything else that she knew, almost a taste; years later she would recognize that fragrance in rain forests. She liked to sit there in her special place with a little stone in her hand, and to become the stone, putting herself into it, wandering into the luscious, now immense, green wonderland. She was, as the stone, a tiny hungry jungle girl, moving through tall ferns and trees, searching for her meal.

On that particular, momentous morning she had found wonderful pretend fruits and nuts, wonderful foods that not only tasted good, but gave you magical powers: a tiny pretend yellow banana that allowed you to disappear; a lumpy, bumpy avocado that you could talk with; a tiny fig that granted three wishes.

The pretend avocado had made the suggestion that she should take off all her clothes, so as to be like a real jungle-girl of this land, because the people here were only allowed to wear leaves and flowers. She liked to take off her clothes and to see her round peachy body; it made her happy—so she did. She felt so good with them off. And it was such a sun-shiny warm morning. The feeling of her bare toes and her bottom in the baby-tears was scrumptious and perfect. She put her hand on her tummy to pet it; she already knew how good that felt.

Then she picked up the little green weed-bud that she called a "fig" and said to it, "Now it's time for you to grant me my wishes." She held the bud in one of her hands and continued to gently pet herself with the other. "My first wish is: I want Mommy to always hear whatever I tell her. The second is: I want a magic wand, to make everyone, and all the plants and animals, in the whole wide world, as happy as can be, forever. And my third wish is: I want a magic lady to appear, please, now!"

And then it happened. Though, in just a few days she would convince herself that she had fallen asleep at that very second and that it was only in her sleep that the magic had taken place. (She didn't know then that she was on the western coast of the western hemisphere, and that the most amazing circumstances can still occur in that region, from California to Chile, reaching a peak, some say, in Mexico.)

Out of her warm contentment, out of the baby-tear ferns, in a deeply shadowed spot which was always left damp and even wet from Grandma's latest watering, a drifting steam arose. It grew higher and thicker and wider, becoming a foaming waterfall in the air, hiding everything that was behind it or inside it within its mist. Before she saw anything else, there came out of the water a voice, a most loving, indescribable voice, a sweet and low woman's voice. *Maria, I am here. I am coming. To you, I am coming. Out of the water I am coming...*

Maria's hand stopped moving. Her body grew as still as her little stone. Only her heart moved, in big fast poundings. The water turned to steam again and drifted up into the air. And there, standing before her, was the Lady. Just like Maria, she was naked, covered only by her long and swirling hair. Her eyes sparkled with light, like stars in the night. She looked a little like Maria's mother, but she was even more beautiful than Mommy, in fact she was so beautiful that it seemed as though a low and musical hum was sounding from the sight. Maria almost could not stand to look in her direction. But she did look, she looked at her for a very long time, long enough to remember what she saw for her entire life.

Then the Lady disappeared, just like the water and its mist. Maria did not even think, for then, about her first two wishes.

*   *   *

There had been another sparkling day, perhaps it was the same year, the year that she was four. A summer Sunday afternoon, driving to Great-grandpa's...The shiny blue, brand-new Oldsmobile, so beloved of her father. The windows all rolled down; delicious summer scents in breezes of warm air...Her pretty mother, caught in a moment of gaiety, singing. "Come Away with Me, Lucille," and "In the Good Old Summertime." Maria sings, too, and so do Daddy and Grandma...

From their house on East 28th Street they drive by Highland Hospital with it's mysterious fairy tale palace structures rising up between tall alluring palms. Seen from the upstairs back porch at sunset time, the image always gives her a strange, clear, spreading feeling which she doesn't know, then, is called "reverence."

They arrive at Great-grandpa's, in the garden-growing, big-front-porch town of Piedmont. She runs from the car into a sunny realm of fruit trees. Great-grandpa grows plums, pears, cherries, apples, apricots and—best of all—figs. How exotic and glowing are the shapes, the colors, and the fragrances of fruit the year she is four!

Amongst the trees are paths lined with bright fragrant marigolds and tall grassy weeds in dark, richly pungent earth. Leading her family through it all is a very thin, very old man. He wears a baggy blue-gray shirt and faded baggy pants, with a slightly raggedy hat of straw. His face is full of tiny wrinkles, surrounding golden brown eyes and a shy smile. His ways are quiet, kind and tender, accepting her completely.

His thin arms lift her own small body up into the green leaves so that she can reach a ripe pear. Then he places her on the ground and takes her empty hand. Such a feeling, an all encompassing contented feeling, more wonderful than getting presents, spreads throughout her body, and spreads throughout the world.

Knowing that she has become a new somebody, someone far more special than the at-home Maria, she wants to stay forever with him, or come back as soon as she can. To the light that is shining through the green of his trees and the gold of his eyes and the shine of his fruit. He leads her into more trees. With a frail finger, he points to a plum tree. A mockingbird is singing on a branch.

2

Mythology

east of San Francisco
1950–1959 A.D.

> "When analytical psychology speaks of the primordial image or
> archetype…it is referring…to an inward image at work in the
> human psyche. The symbolic expression of this psychic phe-
> nomenon is to be found in the figures…through the whole of
> history…in the rites, myths, symbols of early man and also in the
> dreams, fantasies, and creative works of…our own day."
>
> —*The Great Mother*, by Erich Neuman

Nineteen-fifty: the year that the Wonder-Bread truck drove up to the
house next door and sent a hundred brightly colored balloons floating
up to the sky, the year her father bought the first television set in the
neighborhood. The song "Enjoy Yourself" is always on the radio, and
the "boys" have been home long enough to be fathers of kindergartners.

The old man is in bed, pulling her with little more than a gesture, to
his face. "Say good-bye to Great-grandpa, Maria," her grandmother
urges, "You likely won't see him again." The words barely seem to regis-
ter, yet they drift to the place where memories last forever.

She does see him once again, though, years and years later. It is a
snowy-covered mountainside. Everything is white, with a little green of

pine branches poking out here and there in the whiteness. She is climbing to the top, in the clouds and the snow. And there he is, seated in some kind of gnarling redwood chair in the center of the snowy meadow, beneath a tall pine at the top of the mountain. Pine branches are growing out of the chair; they make a frame around his face. He wears a coat of burgundy, trimmed with black. Why doesn't he look so gentle, as he used to, she wonders. But the place is majestic, beautiful.

*   *   *

Besides that solitary and very delayed sighting, she had grown up with one thing more that was of her great-grandfather. Something that was a kind of secret message waiting for her and her alone, offering the first fragments of mysteries that would confuse, seduce and obsess her for a good portion of the rest of her life.

Her great-grandfather's books resided in the long narrow antechamber that lead into her grandmother's level of the house. Her grandmother lived upstairs, coming downstairs for dinner, and sometimes for lunch, or even for breakfast, depending on how she and her daughter-in-law were coexisting at the time. Maria visited upstairs, lingering for many slowly moving hours. The two households were two kingdoms, occupying not only separate space, but separate customs and times as well. Maria and her mother and father lived below, in the same forward moving fifties that was everywhere. But the grandmother lived above, in her fascinating, sunlit afternoon world of rooms that kept forever the feeling of days that used to be.

Years before, newly married Olivia Melville Ananin, filled with a Colorado farm-girl's dreams of what a tasteful city home should be, had decorated her Oakland Mediterranean in the most artistic and comfortable manner that she could afford. Olivia was the bride of the owner of a chain of seventeen Bay Area "dime stores." She lived in comfort and security, but nevertheless she was no stranger to frugality, for Joseph

Ananin was a man who was careful with his nickels and his pennies, not to mention his dimes. Once her decorating reached completion, Olivia never altered anything, never bought new lampshades, or footstools, did not even up-date her curtains or her drapes. Not after that one single-minded shopping spree which began in 1926 and ended in 1934.

The three pictures of round, rosy-cheeked children who munched from cartons of brands of food that by 1950 still had not become extinct—cut from women's magazines where Olivia was first enchanted by them, and lovingly framed and hung on kitchen walls—had remained unexchanged for some twenty years, and would do so for many more. The deep-toned mahogany tables, faded egg-shell lace doilies, oriental rugs of burgundies and blues, potted palms, beaded lamps, tapestry wall-hangings and pillows, the RCA Victor Victrola— with the dog listening for "*his master's voice*" decaled on the side, the watercolors of dreamlike lakes that shared walls with dancing girls posed between Greek columns; all things melded together to create an exotic, yet intimate province. It was a home that never ceased to comfort Olivia, nor to caress the melancholic temperament of her quiet little grandchild.

Olivia's library in the entranceway, like everything else, was of that Oakland era; that Juanita Miller, Isadore Duncan "Athens of the West" first portion of the century. The library lay untouched by Olivia, except for when she dusted, and by everyone else in the family but for the little girl. For even before she could read, Maria had discovered riches in that so often sunlit room.

In one corner there stood an ancient pedal-operated sewing machine. Black and gilded with tiny multicolored flowers on chipped gold vines, it seemed a "spinning wheel," just like in *Sleeping Beauty*. In another corner, a radiantly alive chartreuse and red leafed begonia that looked and felt like velvet, growing in a giant, bright blue pot of clay. And, next to the bookshelves, the hidden delights of far-away places and once-upon lives within the photos of musty *National Geographics*, stacked in piles down on the floor.

As she learned to read, Maria decided whose books were whose: British romances of the 20's (*His Official Fiancée*) once were read by Grandma; the *Hardy Boys* and the *Books of Knowledge* belonged, of course, to the boy that was her Dad. Only the *Alice-In-Wonderland*, with its mysterious tale of descent to another world, eluded her. She never could figure out who it was the story belonged to; giving up, she claimed it for her own.

But it was Great-grandpa's books, which took a great deal of the space, that came to dominate everything. Eventually they very nearly glowed upon the shelves. In Maria's treasure room, Great-grandpa's books were, by childhood's end, the most highly valued jewels.

*   *   *

There was the set of small red and golden volumes called *The Secret of the Ages*, there was Madame Blavatsky's *The Secret Doctrine*, Plato's *Symposium*, and Rousseau's *Autobiography*; collections of Kierkegaard, of Heidigger, of Dostoyevsky, of Emerson and Thoreau; the Bhagavad Gita and the *Meditations of Marcus Aurelius*, a Bible and *The Lives of The Saints*. Volumes of Greek mythology included the *Iliad* and the *Odyssey*, in translations that sounded aged and true.

And that was what came to intrigue her, soon enough—even before she could understand the concept—the compelling antiquity of everything. For there was something powerful, yet soothing, about traveling to a far-off time, first in her grandmother's rooms, then in the mythology books, and finally in the heavier volumes. There was something that drew her, lured and enticed her, without fail.

Thus it was that she came to encounter unusual dimensions; places in the soul that mirrored older layers of the universe. That a childhood fascination with the ancient began to unveil the gods and goddesses, their enchanted lives in distant lands, in golden ages of radiance and health and natural grace. The infatuation was nurtured, it came to grow and to thrive. And eventually it bore its fruit. For by the time Maria Ananin had turned thirteen, Zeus and Hera and Isis and Osiris were more intimate than any classmates at school or the neighbors down the block.

The vigorously spirited maidens and goddesses of ancient Greece and Egypt and India, and of yet older worlds, became her models, not movie stars or older girls she knew. Running through the neighborhoods of East Oakland, years before "jogging" came to city streets, her golden-brown hair streaming behind her, she imagined she was, sometimes, sure-footed Artemis. Or the goddess-like, but mortal, Atalanta. Orpheus sang in her daydreams, not Elvis, and Benares was more real than Kansas City or New York.

And so it came to be at the age of fourteen, when a time had come that she was noticing serious glances from handsome men and boys as they gazed at her through windows of Thunderbirds or Triumphs, or served her root beer floats at A&W, or taught of Rimbaud and Beaudalaire at the front of her high school class, that Maria's mind would turn to thoughts of Apollo, or Rama or Sita. Or to Aphrodite.

And the boys and the men would never guess that this radiant girl whose smiling eyes returned their gaze as she walked or sat, or maybe ran full speed ahead of them, did not have either themselves or even herself completely on her mind. But was flirting, instead, with beings who had walked and run and traded glances thousands of years before—centuries before, in fact, that magical time of metamorphosis when legends of lives are transformed into myths.

Myths, those fantastic interpretations of parallel lives and visions, became the carrier ships for unfamiliar essences. It was myths that transported and delivered those ephemeral archetypes, safe and unharmed to the welcoming harbor in the heart of a California teenager. With no small consequence to herself. Or to her newer world.

But perhaps there was more to it than that, more complicated dynamics which prepared those shining never-to-be forgotten spirits for entrance to that place and that time, that "twentieth" century which, for many of its inhabitants, had become, in the language of myth—Sumerian myth—a "nether" world. An ambiguous netherworld composed of progress, it is true, but ravaged with suffering—with holocaust and with genocide and sophisticated torture; with poverty, pollution and confusion, with starvation and abuse; and, for many of its children, a nearly unrelieved despair.

To that new distant world the great spirits descended, clothed only in beauty while conquering time.

3

Simbaya Brings Broth

back in the village of Fa-Orszag
circa 2700 B.C.

The cold was becoming more difficult to endure. It took the form of a bone-stiffening dampness that came in the wind and had no mercy. Often a stronger gust attacked, and then a rainstorm, lasting several days. To go beyond the door of one's house was increasingly distressful.

Simbaya peeked out the doorway at the rain. Then she scurried through the heavy drizzle, over the puddled earth to the home of Anurei and his children, as quickly as she could while clutching and balancing a large bowl of warm barley broth upon her head.

Anurei was a little better, it seemed. She found him sitting now sometimes, not always lying upon his mat. Soon he might be up and about, she thought. But though his body was improving, what could be done, she wondered, about the anguish in his mind? She felt that the entire village was living in the mists of the monster Gloom, ever since Anarisha was taken. It was impossible to even imagine her own self ever recovering from the loss of that dearest friend.

So long it was now that Anarisha was taken from them. And good-natured Simbaya did not possess a single gloating consolation, only more sadness, in the knowledge that the time of the cold did not disappear as the traders had promised. The cold had only become so much the worse with the departure of that true, good woman.

Every day Simbaya carried an evening broth or stew to Anurei and the children, a portion of the supper that she made for her own household. Anurei's brother's wife and Anurei's sisters provided other meals. All through the day the children stayed with Anarisha's sisters. But in the evening, Simbaya found them huddled with their father. Little Saraswati was lethargic, yet every now and then she would forget herself in play. Endo, Simbaya thought, acted poorly, crying overmuch. Sometimes the child even thrashed himself about, falling purposefully, and making sounds as if he were a brittle vessel come crashing down to break upon the hardness of the ground.

Each night Simbaya spoke with the children and sometimes she sang. Soft quiet songs, nothing very lively. She could not bring herself to be lively, and the little ones did not seem to want it, either, though she wondered if someone happier than herself or their father might not have been more able to cheer them. Everything felt similar, she thought, to the time after her first little son, Siveh, had died, just before she began to bear the rest. This memory, alone, encouraged her longing that one day all of them would be stronger in carrying the sadness.

Anurei spoke not, neither to Simbaya nor to his children, which added to Simbaya's grief. "He must speak to his children, even if to no one else," she would tell her husband, who seemed to think that the matter was nothing of importance. And she would tell Anarisha's sister, who said only, "Give the man time, Simbaya. What else can we expect?"

*　　　　　*　　　　　*

"Here is your broth, Anurei; Endo, Saraswati. Tonight I have made barley, with onions and lemon!!"

"No, Ma Simba!" cried little Endo, "Go from here, Ma Simba! Endo hate broth!"

Simbaya looked sadly at the ground. Never would the child have been so rude when his mother was there.

"Hush, boy," said Anurei gruffly.

Simbaya looked up at Anurei's heavily bearded face. Those were the first words she had heard him speak in all the barren days. She left his house that night with a growing seed of hope. Perhaps one day a little good might come to them all once more.

*   *   *

At the edge of the village, under a tree

Ma Agghia opened her eyes and took her hands from her lap. She stretched her arms out behind her on her mat. Then she threw her head back and gazed up into the wet mist and the night wind, suddenly aware of the drops coming from the wet huluppu leaves above. It had been an exciting meditation and she smiled to herself with intense satisfaction. In truth, never did life cease to amaze her on those occasions when she was given the mercurial sight of the inner eye. And this evening the vision had been most vivid, most entrancing. Also it had brought relief. It was good to have some trusted assurance.

"Two double-hours," she told herself. "That is all it will take! When two double hours have passed, that will be enough. Then I shall return…But perhaps I'll make a visit at some time in the middle. Just to be sure that all goes well!"

A soaking wet little girl, a great-niece, sitting there patiently beside Agghia, heard the sound of those words. But she had no idea what her ever-mysterious old auntie was mumbling about.

4

A Brief and Splendid Era

the city of Orom, east of the Euphrates
circa 2700 B.C.

The celebrated city of Orom clothed itself with a bejeweled history, numinous as it was luminous. But there was one moment in that history which was eminently sparkling and fine.

Everywhere, in that time, all of the gods—the Anunnaki—were given homage and reverence. And each city honored, also, its own special divine one, its guardian goddess or its god. But Orom had god and goddess, both. Unlike all other cities of its world, Orom the Just, in that certain brief and splendid era, prided itself on receiving the protection of not just one guardian deity, but rather the protection of two.

That was a time when, throughout the lands known as the Nyuegat, as well as in the lands to the west, even as far as the Land between the Two Rivers, Father Enki (god of water, god of wisdom, god of semen and of time; he who guides the plow, the yoke and the oxen, he who makes the grain to grow in the furrowed field) was gaining universal respect for his accomplishments. He was, indeed, beginning to supplant Inanna, civilization's youthful version of the primeval Mother, to become the newly favored Beloved One of humankind.

In some cities, Enki sat already in his temple. Inanna's once impressive creations of gardens and of crafts, even her invention of agriculture itself, were no longer praised. In those cities, in song and dance and tablet, Inanna begged tearfully to the god, *"But Father Enki, where are my prerogatives?"** and he heeded not. In other cities, Inanna's influence, inherited from the Great Mother, though not as mature and deep as the Mother's, was able, by youthful erotic potency, to keep Enki worshiping at her feet.

Only in Orom, did Holy Inanna, Queen of Heaven and of Earth, respectfully share her city's reverence with the Great Father. Inanna and Enki were held in equal adoration as the divinities of that realm: the Goddess of Beauty, the Father of Time. For each a temple was built. In Orom, City of Fair Law and Justice, the male and the female were united in double-power. God and goddess directed their energies of fertility and war to lover or to spouse. But when the two guardians came to meet each other face-to-face, it was in pure familial love, composed of peaceful understanding and benevolent good will.

Such communion was a premature utopian fluke, with a certain hidden underside. It could not go on forever. Eventually the newly favored Enki overshadowed Inanna, even in Orom, in conformity with a pattern that was happening worldwide. But for a short time, in a fortuitous intersection of the ages, a divine *yin-yang* sharing of dominion balanced civilization behind the walls of that singular city-state.

It was in the prelude of this age that Anarisha—daughter of Oresh and of Astara, wife of Anurei, and mother of Endo and of Saraswati— was taken from her village of Fa-Orszag and carried to the venerable Temple of Inanna, in the heart of the sacred center of Orom. The Temple of Enki was, in that year, merely some tablets of ground plans, locked within a cedar chest of the archives of Inanna, Queen of Heaven and Goddess of the Morning Star.

---

* 'Where are my prerogatives?'—translated from the cuneiform, in *The Sumerians, Their History, Culture, and Character*, by Samuel Noah Kramer, University of Chicago Press

5

A Rare and Precious Jewel

on the journey between Fa-Orszag and Orom

Ursunabi and Kerem, conservative and efficient trader professionals, both, were born of old, well-established merchant families. They did not mishandle the woman they had acquired in the Nyuegat. They sustained, in fact, an unbroken courtesy towards her, conscientiously refraining from sensual indulgences as they made their journey, and in that way taking precaution against further alteration of her being. They acknowledged that their acquisition of this village housewife was, for her, a tragedy. And therefore they could not expect her to remain quite the same woman they had discovered in Fa-Orszag.

They carefully chose their words and actions. They would remold her into the finely crafted product they desired for presentation to Orom. They did not plan for that product to be precisely the freethinking young village wife and mother whom they had first encountered, nor did they want her to be a fearful, hostile, or otherwise damaged woman. What they wanted was a woman whom the priests would feel compelled to purchase, at almost any price; a rare and precious jewel. Partly this meant that they give a modicum of respect to the woman, keeping her much as they had found her—in good health and sound mind. But also it meant that they would change her, modifying her attitude, shaping her into an obedient slave, one who displayed the passive acceptance and deference of a slave, a slave par excellence. The nature of this balancing act was familiar to them, an "old story," but the degree of perfection to which they aspired, in this case, was an untried challenge.

They had, they believed, the many double-hours of their journey to accomplish the task.

*   *   *

As it happened, however, it was not until the journey had finished and they had at last reached the longed-for Gates of Orom that it was possible even to begin. For Anarisha was almost as though sleeping for the complete duration of the trip. She complied with everything, but said no word, and appeared to observe not a thing.

Finally, however, as they came to the outskirts of the city, they saw with immense relief that her soul was returning to fill her senses. Their joy in this made the traders even more kindly disposed toward the woman than had their natures and good sense.

Then Kerem reminded Ursunabi that they must concentrate immediately on preparing Anarisha for formal presentation, in the little time that now remained.

"It will be necessary to stretch the time," Ursunabi answered. "We will take her directly to my home, and there we will prepare her, until she is truly ready. I am not about to serve my guests a bread that is but partly baked."

"Even though the dough is tasty," amended Kerem.

"Delicious dough gives belly ache," said Ursunabi. "Finished bread fulfills."

"Truly the House of Ursunabi and the House of Kerem shall be fulfilled if we are diligent in this baking," said Kerem.

"Thanks be to Inanna," nodded Ursunabi solemnly, but then he broke into a genuine and charming little smile.

It was a smile which the woman, herself, did not observe. For Anarisha had left her body, with its five or six perceptions; she lived only in her mind, temporarily persuaded that she was once again a child.

6

Dinner and a Movie

east of San Francisco
1963 A.D.

Firelight flickered among the rose vines on the wallpaper and upon the polished oak wood floor of the apartment living room where Mr. Jean-Marc Romier's third year French class comfortably reclined amidst tapestried pillows on a Turkish rug. The high-school seniors, on their best behavior, quietly chatted while they relished their delicious dinners of tomato aspic, beef bourginonne, warm sourdough bread with garlic, potatoes au gratin and Napa Valley white wine. This impressive, *au moment* Bay Area meal had been planned and prepared by Mr. Romier's girl friend, Mei, now absent, and served by Mr. Romier himself.

Maria Ananin sat enraptured, even forgetting at times to eat, and feeling too shy to speak with her classmates, among whom she felt comfortable with only two, neither of whom was sitting very near. She gazed out the picture window which overlooked the lake. At twilight Lake Merritt was a large dark mirror. Sparkling in the center of the city of Oakland, the water reflected the necklace of apartment lights glowing above its shore. She later learned that for Jean Romier this sight invoked a feeling of Budapest, where once he had lived, long ago, in an apartment by the Danube.

The French teacher, who had just finished playing a section of Albeniz's Piano Concerto #1, rose from his piano bench and began to roam around the room. He smiled apologetically as he collected the wineglasses and the bottle of remaining lachryma Christi (1952). He did not intend any of his under-age students to sneak more than the allotted half glass which he himself had poured. Maria watched him move about. She sensed, without thought, the youthful relaxed elegance of the man and the refined taste and old-fashioned European coziness of his apartment.

She sat close to the heat of the fire, becoming warmer with the wine, and warmer still as she discovered that her teacher's thoughtful eyes were gazing down into her own.

It was May, 1963, the second to the last month of Maria's final year of French. In one month she would graduate. Then, soon, she would be moving away from home, attending the University at Berkeley, living in the dormitory with an unknown roommate, saying goodbye to her closest friends, and leaving Jean-Marc Romier forever.

Maria could barely remember what life had felt like when her first thought in the morning and her last at night had not held her French teacher. She had walked into first year French that day two years ago, and at the first taking in of his soft wavy brown hair, his slender form in a light gray suit, and his caring expression, she had felt an immediate, serenely pleasant interest in the teacher of that class. The interest had soon expanded as she experienced his gentle dignified manners, his spellbinding voice, and his special attitude, or so it seemed, towards herself. She progressed from fantasizing about dancing with him in a grassy, rocky, tree-filled place, or sitting across a table at a seaside restaurant, to actually looking up his phone number and address and learning his age (thirty-seven), the hour he arrived at school (7:30), and the time he went home (it varied). She knew that he sometimes liked to go to the popular ice cream parlor, Fenton's, not too far from his apartment—her best friend had seen him—that he drove a chocolate-brown Alfa Romeo, and that he liked to drink his coffee black.

She herself no longer lived in Oakland. Her mother, who had developed a chronic arthritis that quickly advanced to strong, lengthy intervals of pain, required a climate void of cool damp winds. The family had left Oakland for a new home in drier, suburban Castro Valley, just as Maria turned fifteen. It was six months since her grandmother Olivia had died, killed instantly by an automobile while returning from an afternoon of *Canasta* with a neighbor across the street.

Maria had begun her second year of high school at Castro Valley, somewhat aloof, bookish and dreamy, as she had been in Oakland, and even more quiet as a new girl. But a few close friends soon appeared to make life almost satisfying. She had little interest in the boys at school; they seemed so young, either unpredictably intimidating or awkwardly immature.

*   *   *

In that same year, just before Christmas vacation, Mr. Romier had introduced the class to existentialism. They read stories and essays by St. Exupery and Jean Paul Sartre. "One of the earliest forefathers of existentialism was the Russian novelist, Fyodor Dostoyevsky," declared Mr. Romier, in his entrancing story-telling cadence. "Dostoyevsky was concerned with many of the problems which the French existentialists later tackled. His works came, however, from a more orthodox perspective. He maintained that a belief in God is necessary to the wellbeing of man. Yet his writing also bridged into a time that became known as the 'Age of Reason.' He was an in-between man in an in-between era.

"Dostoyevsky, the son of a cruel father who was murdered by his own serfs, was himself a radical and a socialist. His life, which held many miseries, including epilepsy and imprisonment, led to a deep exploration of the subject of human suffering, and a criticism of the conditions of his day.

"In 1848, when Dostoyevsky had about twenty-seven years, there was a revolution which brought the end of the socialist circle to which he belonged. The next year its members were arrested. Fyodor Dostoyevsky was sentenced to death, and endured a horrible moment before the firing squad. He expected, of course, to be shot. Just imagine such a minute! This was a great, profoundly influential event in his life and it inspired great, profound thinking about human existence. The resulting ideas are basic to his novels, which are, as I said, the forerunners of French existentialism.

"The moment which followed his 'last moment,' was, obviously, not the firing of the guns. Instead there came an announcement of a reprieve. In place of death, he was sent to a hellish prisoner's life for eight years in Siberia. There he turned the compassion of his youth into a spiritual ideal of salvation through suffering." Mr. Romier smiled, "You might say Dostoyevsky was an incurable optimist!"

"If any of you are interested in some of the questions of existence, of *la vie et la morte* which the French were exploring, you might find Dostoyevsky's thinking to be an interesting counterpoint, or prelude, especially his brilliant exploration of atheism and organized religion— that is if you enjoy a good long read!"

Maria Ananin raised her hand, and as this occurred rarely, Mr. Romier ceased talking immediately and called her name. All heads turned. He called on her so quickly that he caught her in the middle of deciding how to word her question; she feared the question would sound as if she was trying to impress. "I, uh, never mind," she said, and looked down. All the class, including Mr. Romier, watched as the girl experienced a hot deep blush. The teacher mercifully hastened to return to his lecture.

But at the end of the hour, before she could escape, he was at her desk. "Maria," he said in his gentle, accented voice, "You know, I am so curious to know what it was you were going to ask me a little while ago. Would you mind if I ask you to tell me your question now?" Maria, surprised, but now more composed, was still reviewing, meticulously, how she might have chosen her words.

"I was just wondering," she said seriously, "about Dostoyevsky's novels—because, I've read…a lot of them." No need to say 'all.' "And I was just wondering—which book do you think gives the best answers to the questions, you know, like, is there a God, or a heaven, or a hell, and what are heaven and hell, anyway? And what kind of God would set things up like…" He laughed for some reason, but she did not feel embarrassed then, alone with him, she was feeling mainly peaceful. But at the same time she was slightly excited. She felt an elation in that moment, finding herself asking the mystery questions of her life to the very person in all the world for whom she had the most respect.

"You have read the novels of Dostoyevsky already, Maria?" The smile in his eyes had sobered and he looked sincerely curious.

"Yes, I've read them," she said shyly. "And I intend to read some of them again."

"I found them to be very deep, and difficult, even when I was twenty-five. And all those complex names!" he exclaimed, "But I have come to have a lot of admiration for Dostoyevsky." he added. Then there was a long, and, for Maria, uncomfortable silence.

"Which of his books do you think answers those questions of yours best?" he asked at last.

"I don't know, really, Mr.Romier. Maybe *The Idiot*. And *Brothers Karamazov*."

"And what answers do they give you?" He looked intensely expectant, almost as though she were the teacher, and he the student. She immediately felt a slight aggravation, as she usually did when a teacher turned a person's questions back to them.

"I asked you first," she said, trying to sound light and playful, but she found it nearly impossible to do that with him; the words came out serious, and childish.

He looked at her then, for a moment longer than she might have thought comfortable. But his look had nothing of critical or judging traces, in fact it seemed to be a look of love, and she later recalled it over and over again.

Now, in the apartment of his living room, she recognized that same expression as he looked down at her sitting there on his carpet, eating dinner with her classmates. She felt happy, but she could not guess what he was thinking, that she was undoubtedly the most enticingly beautiful girl that he had ever seen.

*   *   *

Back that day, in the classroom, he had finally stopped gazing at her. "Maria," he said, "do you know what I think? I think those are questions we all, even Dostoyevsky, spend lifetimes never answering. The process of asking and refining those questions is, I think, more beneficial in itself than guessing at what the answers might be, and then—as so many people do—grasping and holding on, for dear life, to the mere guess. Is there a God; is there a heaven? Those are mysteries, not for the knowing in the duration of this life." His voice was so low; it was almost as if he were talking to himself.

It seemed illogical to her that the effect of those words of incertitude was, at least for awhile, that she felt somehow comforted.

*   *   *

When the dinner was over the students put on their car-coats and jackets and departed into the night for the bus stop. There was a fifteen-minute wait and then they were on the bus to Berkeley. They got off the second bus on Telegraph, near Sather Gate, and walked past cafés, smoke shops and bookstores, into the campus of the University. Like most of them, Maria, although she'd soon be attending it, had not yet visited this, nor any other, college.

The campus was a surprise. It seemed much more than forty minutes, by freeway, from Castro Valley. It seemed, in fact, almost as if it were a foreign country. Maybe Mr. Romier's homeland. The warm spring air held the fragrance of night-blooming jasmine, and the old fashioned streetlights made her think of movie scenes of nineteenth century Paris, or maybe London or New York.

The class walked in pairs and clusters from Sather Gate to Wheeler Auditorium. They pretended they were already college students. Slightly awestruck, they passed the real Berkeley students and made jokes, attempting to adjust their suburban sense of cool. The teacher found himself at the side of Maria Ananin.

Then they saw their movie, *Le Rouge et Le Noir*. It was adapted from the novel by Stendahl, which they had reviewed and discussed all week in class. Maria was absorbed. She watched Danielle Darieux studiously. She had never seen an actress quite like her. She watched Gerarde Phillippe and temporarily forgot Jean-Marc Romier.

Except for old British movies on TV, this was the first foreign film she had ever seen, the first that was subtitled, the first realistic seduction. And the first adultery upon which her judgment did not pass. The rhythm and the poetry of the movie soon blended into her own being. And thus it was that the final touches were added, to a backdrop against which the scenes of her life would soon be played out. A foundation of taboos, constructed by society to hold good girls safely above the rabble, quietly disappeared, smoothly curtained by a new, expansive vista of freedom.

Eventually she would come, as so many of her generation, to heed new morals, morals of her own device. But such innovation awaited the death of John Kennedy and his "*Camelot*." And the consequent years of that complex decade. At the moment, on this spring evening of 1963, as she watched the pretty wife and the handsome tutor fall to the floor beside the woman's bed, ecstatically giving in to their powerful forbidden desire, she simply absorbed everything. She absorbed not only as a romantic seventeen year-old—and she was certainly that—but also as though newborn, inhaling the first energizing breath of life.

All the while, seated to the right of her, Jean-Marc Romier restrained himself from glancing sideways. He kept his eyes, without attention, on the movie. He had already seen it twice, once for pleasure, and once to confirm that it would be appropriate for his young students. Now the nearness of Maria Ananin dominated everything. Sitting there beside her, he was rapidly becoming uncomfortable, to the extreme.

He had long before acknowledged the potent fascination that this girl held for him. But he had easily dealt with any fantasies that wove their way into his thoughts or dreams. Fantasies were a natural, normal consequence he told himself, of his being a single normal human being and of having this quite stunning and innocent female student, who was, as could be expected in such situations, also the most intelligent person that he taught. A situation as old as the hills—or at least as the education of women. In fact, he surmised that—knowing himself—it was bound to happen at some time in his profession. He'd found it relatively simple to mold his feelings for the girl into wise fatherly regard, flavored with maybe a small amount of tenderness. It had not been, for him, a problem.

But now, however, this unrelenting physical proximity in the dark and quiet theater was another matter. He berated himself for the recklessness of seating himself beside her.

By the time the long film had moved into its ending scenes, Jean Romier was sure that he had made a turn in his life, was at that moment beginning to travel in a rather precarious direction. The pleasant thrill which came as he realized this confused him. His mind tried to steer back to its familiar control and well developed commonsense. But the chords of the film's erotic soundtrack persisted in the darkness. They mingled with something almost tangible that drifted from Maria's seat, which was undeniably much too near. At last, he excused himself and passed over her, down the aisle, out the door, and to the entrance of Wheeler Auditorium, where he lit a cigarette, and stood for some time. He had lit two more before he regained some of his uncomplicated acceptance of existence.

The movie finished almost exactly as he returned. The class arose to leave. Maria's face as she turned to her teacher seemed like a painting, exquisitely formed, and with the expression of a woman in a trance. "She is a woman, not the teen-aged kid…" he thought, influenced, no doubt, by *Gigi*, another movie he'd just seen, a few nights before, with his girlfriend.

The class boarded the bus and rode back to Oakland. Their cars and their parents' cars, some with parents inside, awaited them at Jean's apartment building, where they all said goodbye to each other, effusively and politely thanked their teacher, and returned back home to the suburbs.

7

Spring of '63

In the morning, Jean Romier fell asleep as the world awoke. In just one hour he was awake again, jolted by the buzzing of his doorbell.

At the door stood his girlfriend, Mei, looking clear-eyed and fresh and hopeful. Yet even in the presence of this congenial woman with whom he had shared, in many ways, the last two years, he could not quite guide his thoughts away from his seductive student and the night before. It was finally the sharp appetizing aroma of Mei's coffee, the frying bacon, the toasting bread, mingling with the metallic, but cozy odor of his heating system, which Mei turned on to make the old, cold apartment more comfortable (it was spring, but by the Bay) that brought his mind back to his senses. By the time that four loud and rather unruly friends had joined them at their breakfast, his thoughts were mostly on whether they all could make it in time to the Piedmont tennis courts that he'd reserved.

Maria, meanwhile, spent that weekend writing a term paper on *The Brothers Karamazov*, due in two weeks for her World Lit class. Dostoyevsky distracted her from thoughts of Mr. Romier and from the tugging of a new mood that had begun to come upon her in the daytime as well as in the night.

*　　　　　*　　　　　*

As the last week of May began, Jean-Marc found that he was in a constant struggle to subdue his obsessing. A man who had always told himself it was fundamental to follow the "passions of the heart," he also prided himself on being a man of reason and practicality. Now he was trapped in his own ambivalence; it made for weak, indeterminate inertia.

But on Wednesday morning he drank two cups of espresso and mustered some ambition. Using all the power of the Zen-like concentration that he had inherited from his father—an actor and a dancer—he focused on his lesson plans. He would make a powerful summer exit from the school; they would all remember him, a fantastically interesting and highly respected teacher of French. As if it were vital to the income and self-respect of the rest of his life, he prepared for each of his classes with the intense imagination of a creator of small artistic masterpieces. It was a good approach for awhile, and more than a few of his students experienced a growing admiration for this teacher whom they already considered a favorite. Some even developed a greater aptitude for French. One boy was so inspired, it turned out, that he majored in that subject and became a tax consultant in Quebec.

Even the faculty sensed that some sort of odd last-minute excitement was occurring in the French classes. They puzzled over this sudden burst of energy in Jean Romier at a time when they themselves were groggy with the lassitude of late spring and the siren calls of travel or of home.

But while Jean-Marc' sublimating activity seemed to be rescuing him from Maria, her response just turned everything inside out. His virtuoso performances only made her admiration increase, to the point where her cravings spilt over. Silently they infused his own.

On a warm June morning, when the East Bay breezes were laden with pollens that bore allergens and confusion, he awoke from a comfortless night to the decision to "let nature take its course." The fact that it was the last week of school, and that whatever would happen could thenceforth be safely private, was no doubt a factor. He was aware of that, as well as every other subtle and not so subtle implication, as he told himself at the time, to his career and to the other areas of his life. Such as Mei; for whom, he concluded, nothing need be revealed.

*   *   *

Maria, on that day, woke to find herself in a state of end-of-school-joy, fringed with giddiness. Her mother called her to the phone almost as soon as she awoke. The high feminine voice on the other end was rushing; it echoed Maria's excitement.

"Maria? I made an appointment to have your hair done on Thursday. With me! Four-thirty, The Village Salon. A 'D.A.' for me, and a 'Flip' for you. Okay? Spur of the moment, kind of. But you can make it, can't you, Maria?"

"Yeah, sure. Thanks Jo, that'll be—"

"Hopefully, we'll be done by six, then you can have dinner at my house and we'll go to graduation together, then you can spend the night. But, my god, Mar! Can you believe it's really happening?!"

"No, I can't. I feel like I'm dream—"

"I just can't believe it, Maria! I really just can't believe it—I was beginning to think high school was all there was to life, completely! Now it's all over! And it seems like it just started. But it still feels like it lasted forever, you know what I mean? Promise me you'll be my best friend forever, okay? And when we're little old ladies we'll have our tea and crumpets together!"

"Sure, Jo-Anne. But, Jo," she couldn't resist teasing, "do you actually know what a crumpet is?"

"Oh, Maria. Of course I do. It's a—some kind of a pudding, isn't it?"

"Where did you get that idea?"

"But it is, isn't it?"

"Jo-Anne, I bet you're thinking of 'compote.' But you don't even have the right definition for that one, either, you know."

"God, Maria, you're so, what's that word, you're so—if we weren't as close as we are—"

Maria laughed, as a thought came to trick her not very worldly friend. "A crumpet isn't a food, at all, Jo-Anne—you honestly didn't know you were using a word for prostitute?" She giggled.

"Prostitute?…Are you sure about that, Maria? Really?"

"Just imagine, Jo—us two old ladies having our tea and our prostitutes. But you must mean 'gigolos,' I think, maybe." Maria laughed again. "Yeah, why don't we make it 'gigolos,' instead?"

"Prostitutes, gigolos? Maria, I'm looking up 'crumpet' when I hang up—but you might as well tell me right now if you're putting me on!"

"Well, oh, all right, Jo-Anne, but only because it's the last week of school. A crumpet is sort of a muffin, sort of a cake. A strumpet is a prostitute, or to be more technical—"

"So! I knew I was right all along! I've always known what a crumpet is."

"Well, it's a food, yes, but it sure isn't a pudding. You didn't really know what you were talking about. You better watch yourself, Jo."

"Watch myself? You better watch your own self, Maria Ananin—you're the one with the dirty mind!"

"Dirty mind!?"

"Having tea and—and gigolos?"

"I didn't think that was dirty."

"You wouldn't, Maria."

She really means 'risqué,' thought Maria, who currently held that word as a favorite.

"I'm out of my mind with happiness!" Jo-Anne shrieked suddenly, changing the subject back to where it belonged. "I've been waiting all my life for this! Graduation!"

"Yeah, Jo, but, you know, it's going to be very sad, too. I'm going to miss some people, I—"

"You're going to miss people? How do you think I feel? I've been with these kids since kindergarten—and you practically just moved here! Besides, Mar, you hardly even speak to anyone, anyway!"

"Oh, is that what you think? All the same, I am going to miss a few people…"

"Well, maybe—but anyway, Maria, don't act like it's the end of the world! We'll see each other. And everyone will be swimming at the school all summer, or at Annette's. And there'll be parties. Reunions. And weddings! Donna's wedding, Karen's wedding…"

"Baby showers!"

"Funerals!"

"Funerals?! Oh, yeah, Jo, lots to look forward to!"

"You know what my Mom always says—'It all flies by so fast, after high school'—" "*The descent is much too deep. No, child, let her be.*"

"What? What was that, Jo? What did you say?"

Jo-Anne giggled. "'*No child, let her be!*' Ma-ri-a!" now she squealed uncontrollably, "You really thought that was me?" Jo-Anne was laughing too hard to stop. Maria waited.

"But, who in the world was it then?"

"It must have been our party-line. Did you forget my phone has a party line?…'The descent is much too deep'—You actually think I'd talk like that, Mar? Me? The girl who doesn't even know a crumpet from a—a—"

"—a strumpet. Well, yes, I guess I did think it was you—quoting your Mom or something. But what in the world did she—your party line—Oh, never mind, Jo, we're going to be late. I really gotta go now. See you at school!"

"O.K. But don't forget about our hair appointment! See you later, Maria!"

She put on her new white spaghetti-strap sundress and pulled her hair into a high ponytail. Ellen Ananin, sipping Sanka at the table, watched as her daughter prepared a bowl of bananas and Sugar Corn

Pops. Ellen noted, not for the first time, how her daughter seemed somehow a little like Audrey Hepburn, in *Roman Holiday*—not that Maria had similar features, there was just something…But as always, Ellen kept such an observation, which could go to a girl's head, safely to herself.

The doorbell was ringing. Maria grabbed her books, kissed her father goodbye, very gently hugged her mother, so as not to hurt the arthritic shoulders, and was out the door. Acutely attuned, as always to any sadness her self-contained mother was feeling, she called out "Love you, Mom!" without needing to see her mother's moist and yearning eyes.

She walked to school with two neighbor friends, Carol and Julie, all three in an almost drunken state of excitement. Julie, who normally smoked when she arrived at school (in the "D" wing "lavatory") did not wait for that this morning, but lit her first Salem in clear view of the neighbors. Maria and Carol, who never smoked, bummed cigarettes from Julie for themselves. They choked a little, but it felt right.

They were all soon in hysterics. For one thing there was Carol's perfect portrayal of Mr. Jay, their absentminded history teacher. Feeling cruel, Maria tried her best not to laugh. It was Mr. Jay who, one cloudy afternoon had come over to her desk and whispered, "You are especially beautiful when you're sad, Maria, but whatever, or whoever, it is, it's not worth it. Stay on the sunny side—you're lovely that way too."

But she was powerless to suppress anything this morning, and Carol's imitation was flawlessly correct.

Near the school they finally calmed themselves, gathered some public dignity, went to their classes and let the laziness of the now hot and dry valley morning overcome them.

*   *   *

The term papers were collected in World Lit. And then, to the dismay of all, Mrs. Bowers announced that she was going to pass some of the essays back, to be read aloud in class.

"I'd like to have the chance to hear your almost-graduate reactions before I react myself!" The teacher smiled as though she'd discovered a clever justification for another of her many inconsiderate surprises.

The tightness of Maria's stomach warned her that she was going to be one of the chosen, and, of course, she was. The morning's giddiness vanished. Her terrible shyness returned. It spread throughout her body as she thought about her essay, how strange and awkwardly passionate it was going to sound. To her classmates, whom she'd never guessed would be hearing what she wrote.

As her name was called, her throat turned dry, so dry that she found it necessary to ask permission to go to the water fountain, her voice croaking in a ridiculous whisper. In fact, somebody—a popular boy in the back row—did laugh. She felt then almost like crying. Completely oblivious that the boy had laughed only because he felt so much empathy for her situation, she sensed the familiar heat of embarrassment increase across her face as she began to read before the class:

"In the seventeenth century, a Russian Czar decided to tour Europe, an act which had not been attempted by Russian royalty since 1000 A.D...."

*   *   *

At the end of the hour, walking down the hall, she passed the boy who had embarrassed her. He touched her lightly on the arm as she passed.

"Hey, Maria, wait a second, O.K.? Listen—did you think I was laughing at you in there?"

"Well, it kind of seemed like it, I guess." She looked down at the books in his arms. Michael Dagan had never spoken to her before.

8

All in Perspective

Couldn't be better, he thought as his gaze swept from her long-lashed eyes and her dimples, which were deep though she wasn't smiling, to her tan shoulders showing beneath the thin straps of a white dress.

"I wasn't laughing at you, Maria," he said, his voice low and polite. "I was laughing 'with you.' You know, like they say...I mean, I was thinking how it would feel to be you—having to give that report all of a sudden like that. And your throat getting dry, and all, like it seemed to. So I kind of laughed. I couldn't help it—I felt bad for you, but at the same time I was so glad it was you up there. And not me. You know what I mean?" He looked at her directly again and waited.

"Oh, yes...I suppose so." Her voice was thoughtful. She was wondering if he'd seen that she nearly cried when he laughed. If that was why he was bothering to apologize. She hated her over-sensitivity.

"It wasn't anything to me, your laughing," she said. "I barely even heard you. I was just upset about giving the report." She tried to see in his eyes if he was believing what she said. She saw then that his eyes were warm and understanding, that they were dark, deep, unusual.

Then, suddenly, at that instant, completely out of the blue, she saw before her a startling image. It was as if a veil lifted, and the boy became another person. Not Michael Dagan, not the popular basketball player her friends were always gossiping about, but someone else, somebody from another time. It was David—the David in the Bible—when David was a shepherd boy! Or maybe it was some other shepherd, some ancient mid-eastern shepherd. *What a bizarre thing; lucky he can't read my mind!* she thought.

"Well, that's great," he was saying with a smile. "I didn't want you to think I was making fun of you. It wasn't like that. O.K., gotta go to Chemistry. See you around!"

"Yeah, see you around. And thanks," she added, in a calm voice. She was surprised at the way she felt now. No longer embarrassed, not flustered. In fact she could not remember when she had felt more self-assured. But the feeling left soon, not long after he disappeared through a doorway.

She did not see him again, not the two of them alone like that, not for nearly ten years. And then it was not "around," at least not around that California suburb, but rather on a seaside road of a beautiful Greek island, thousands of miles, and thousands of circumstances away.

They themselves would hardly be the same. The life-changing and even world-changing waters that would come to pass, under both their bridges, would completely wash away the perplexities of being seventeen and standing in the hall of 'B' building on the week before graduation, June of 1963.

*   *   *

Jean-Marc Romier was in the teacher's lounge at noon when Liz Bowers mentioned the "brilliant" report on Dostoyevsky that Maria Ananin had delivered to the class. Liz exclaimed over what a remarkable student the girl had been. Another teacher, Milton Jay, cleared his throat and agreed. There was a silence. Jean Romier kept his eyes on his potato salad and did not join the intense conversation that then developed. Within seven or eight minutes he quietly left the lounge, returning to his desk. At two-fifteen his next class, the senior French class, would meet, and he simply waited for that hour, having made a plan.

At last the seniors drifted into the room. Maria, sweaty and exhausted after a hot and stressful day, had long forgotten her free-spirited morning. But Jean was too excited and obsessed to see that his fantasy was neither cool nor collected. As far as he was concerned, and evidently, as far as the rest of the male faculty was concerned, this girl unfailingly moved in a graceful state of near-perfection.

He hurried through his lecture, a lecture devoid of the subtle pleasures or humor that he had invented in the last few weeks. Then he assigned a dry, uninspired grammar exercise, not bothering with his complicated lesson plan. He pushed his chair to the wall and sat in the late spring breezes of the open window, staring out at the green hills while the students wrote answers in their texts.

When the bell rang he was matter-of-fact as he dismissed them and then added, "Maria, would you please stay for a moment?"

Maria nodded and brushed back a strand of hair that had come loose from her ponytail. She set her books back down on her desk and looked up at him.

"Maria," he paused and fingered his pen, nervousness unexpectedly invading. He spoke rapidly. "Maria, I haven't mentioned this before to the class, but in my spare time I have an interest—an avocation—in which I am involved. It very much occupies me, in fact. I don't believe you have guessed that I like to spend my time painting and drawing? A little sculpting, too."

"Oh no, I didn't know that." She was surprised. As much as she thought about him, she had been unable to imagine what he did when he wasn't at school. Except for the piano playing she heard that one night, with the class in his apartment, she knew nearly nothing. But she wondered why he was telling her this.

"Currently," he went on, "I am involved with a—a painting of the fountain at the campus of the university—students like to gather and talk there, you know, and, for me it evokes the—um—*l' esprit des jours de la juenesse*—I guess I'm missing my own university days—and I'm trying to recapture those days. In my art. That's what art is for me, you see, a way to make more tangible *les memoires vielles*, the old memories, you know, to put them all in perspective—forgive me, Maria, I'm jumping back and forth with the language. It's incredible, after all this time— sometimes the English evades me, just for a moment. But then, you do know the French, don't you?" he smiled.

"In any case, I've been sketching the students as they come and go. But I need a more permanent model for my main figure. And, Maria, since you are about to become a Berkeley student yourself, and since we already know each other, I was hoping that you could spare a few days in the next few weeks…to be my model? All you'd have to do really is to sit and read a good book, maybe your Dostoyevsky, if you like." His eyes sparkled as a momentary merging of Maria Ananin and Dostoyevsky's femme fatale, Grushenka, flashed through his mind. "Some preliminary sketching could be done in privacy, at my apartment. And we'd also go to the fountain. Would you consider this for me?"

He looked at her politely, as though he were giving her a special homework assignment. He sounded so completely straightforward, so almost like his usual self, that the request seemed normal, though it did excite her, and she said, very easily, "Yes, that would be fine." His eyes changed slightly as he asked, "Would you need to get permission from your parents?" And because he was thirty-seven years old and she was only seventeen, she immediately replied, in the most mature tone that she could muster, "No, I wouldn't need to do that."

"All right, then, we're on." he said softly, but he was unable to prevent the exultation from vibrating in his voice. And hearing it clearly, she was filled with happiness herself.

*　　　　　*　　　　　*

When she arrived home she quickly slipped out of her sundress, changing to her black "Bermudas" and pale pink halter. With a bottle of nail polish of the same shade of pink, a glass of iced tea, a book, a tube of sun tan lotion, and her transistor radio, she went to the patio, into the sun. She set the polish in the shade, happily applied the lotion, relishing its scent of summer, took some sips of her tea, and settled into the chaise lounge to begin her book.

But first she examined the torn, threadbare fabric that covered the novel, running her fingers lightly over it. She had discovered this odd old volume on the shelves of an antique store on Castro Valley's main street, The Boulevard. A geometrical, foreign-looking design on the brown cloth cover had immediately caught her eye. Was that Hawaiian *tapa* or—what exactly was it? The book seemed to be, she decided, homemade, carefully homemade. It's pages were of a fragile paper, maybe rice paper? Most of the pages were typed, but a few were handwritten in ink. The shop owner had told her that he purchased this manuscript from the estate of a retired doctor in Sausalito. The collection contained, he said, many more rather extraordinary books and objects that might also interest her. But she had neither time nor money that December afternoon; she quickly glanced through and paid for only the one book.

Then she saved it, for several months, for the unbothered pleasure of summer reading. It wasn't quite summer, but the book was meant for a day like this day—hot, magical, and filled with promise. Shifting her body more comfortably on the cushion of the chaise lounge, she contentedly began to read.

Music was playing on her radio, a song that she liked, but she switched it off after reading just one page. She couldn't possibly take "Run-Around Sue" with her, not where she was going....

*   *   *

The Goddess of the Morning Star
Forward

The following material is adapted from a privately held collection of personal histories. These histories consist of several separate sections, translated from the pictograms of the original clay. The tablets are dated, approximately, 2500 to 2800 B.C.

Location is not clearly specified in the writings. It can be deduced from the content, however, and from the style of the cuneiform-like pictographs, that the writer lived east of the Sumerian territories, and west of the Saraswati River and the early Indus Valley civilization (currently known as Mohenjo-Daro and Harappa). The culture was neither Sumerian nor Dravidian, however, but seems to have been influenced by both of those greater civilizations, as well as the converse. Religion seems to have been a blend, with some significant uniquely characteristic mutations. The literature is astonishingly developed, inexplicably advanced for the first literate millennium, a millennium known mostly for its bookkeeping records.

Where and when the tablets were originally discovered is undetermined, though the site of a temple ruin is probable. It is likely that the tablets passed through many hands, in many places, before coming to the possession of an antique dealer in the vicinity of Baghdad. The tablets were purchased from that dealer by a Mexican collector of antiquities, sometime in the 1930's.

The pictographs remained undeciphered until 1958, when a member of the collector's family, with the assistance of three employees, completed this task. The memoirs were, at that time, translated into both Spanish and English. Currently the manuscripts remain unpublished and in the possession of two private individuals (residing in the vicinities of San Francisco and of Guadalajara). Unfortunately, the clay tablets, most of which remained intact until the completion of the process of translation, met with a tragic accident. The consequence was their irreparable destruction.

These memoirs represent a civilization and a people who, due to the limited record (with no related existing artifacts of substance) as yet remain unknown to but a handful of scholars. All that can currently be offered is an imprecise estimate of date and location of the material. But, having had their existence contemporaneous with the pinnacle of Sumerian civilization; with the early Indus Valley cities; with the bronze age in Bohemia; the reign of King Menes the Fighter, uniter of Upper and Lower Egypt; and with the great Originator-Emperor Shen Nunn of China; this unnamed people formed a society whose influence reciprocated with that of the creators of the earliest known literature. Certainly, as time went by, in Sumer, in India, then in Babylon, in Egypt and in Palestine, in China, and later in Greece and on through the cultures of the centuries, this eventually dissolved people infused not only their legends and the consequences of their lives, but their genes as well, even on to those ones who are the inheritors of the earth in this, our present age.

Note: The translators have taken the liberty of utilizing a small, second group of memoirs, retained with the primary collection, to synthesize a fictional biography-autobiography of the woman "Anarisha," as the subject of the main body was designated. The "B" group tablets were apparently inscribed by Anarisha herself, while the larger "A" group were the work of her contemporary, "Gudea," a temple priest of the city of "Orom," who knew this woman intimately for a period of several years. Gudea is mentioned frequently in the woman's own account.

Introduction

She engraved her life with sharp, clean strokes into the wet clay. When she had long been departed from this mortal province of objects and senses, and the memory of her would not weaken, he recorded his own version of who she had been. For a little less than five thousand years the tablets lay together in the earth, midst the decaying pieces of the temple that once had been their world...

9

Gudea the Scribe

the city of Orom (east of the Euphrates, west of Mohenjo-Daro, south of Fa-Orszag); in the palace of the king
circa 2700 B.C.

"In the beginning there was the sea, the *abzu*, the first sea. From the sea there formed the heaven and the earth, with their vault between. Within the vault of the heaven and the earth there lay the *lil*. The brightness of the lil became the sun, the moon and the stars.

"Father Enki was the lord of the abzu. Enki was lord of water, of semen, and of time. Of creation and fertility. Enki was ruler of the sea. He also ruled the land. He was lord of the netherworld, which contains the abzu. For Enki fought the *Kur*—'the future'—that unknown terror for whom the netherworld is named. And Father Enki was victorious. He won the title 'Lord of Kur.'

"Wise Enki had compassion for Inanna. It was Enki who rescued our beloved Goddess from the netherworld. He sent two messengers, the *kurgarra* and the *galatur*, to Ereshkigal, the terrible sister of Inanna.

"Those two clever creatures were successful. The galatur and the kurgarra gave sympathy to Ereshkigal; sympathy with her sad fate, for Ereshkigal was eternal goddess of the netherworld. They sympathized, as well, with her many aches and pains. 'Ohhh! My head! Ohhh! My stomach! Ohhh! My liver!'—such were the laments of Ereshkigal.

'Ohhh! Your head! Ohhh! Your stomach! Ohhh! Your liver!' responded the little galatur and kurgarra. Enki's messengers gave great sympathy, knowing that Ereshkigal would be abundantly pleased. And would release to them her sister.

"None but Enki cared that Ereshkigal had turned Inanna to a corpse, a corpse that was hanging on the wall! None but Enki thought it necessary to revive our Goddess of Love and Beauty from Her permanent extinction!"

*   *   *

Gudea, son of Adama the Baker, carefully placed his long and heavy tablet on the ground to the side of his right foot. Then he looked upward, into the disgruntled eyes of Diku, brother of Asimbabar, King of Orom. Diku was nearly squatting, his tiny wooden chair the same size as Gudea's own. The chair did not suit him.

"Well read, Gudea, well read!" declared Diku. "I do enjoy your soothing voice. And I see that you have been accomplishing your task. I want more, however, much more. My brother must not be shamed before the ambassadors of Eridu. He requires much more knowledge than what you have inscribed here." The imposingly large Diku daintily licked the crumbs of his mid-morning butter cake off of his fingers and rose from the annoying little stool.

"Gudea, I have it in mind that you should visit the house of Ashgab-Agal. Ashgab is a young leatherworker's official who leads a gathering of Enki worshipers. They meet each evening there, at Ashgab's home, just after dinner. I want you to become one of them. Then, later, perhaps in the next moon, there are several other *shuls* you can visit as well." The muscular and nervous nobleman now paced back and forth across the room, unknowingly synchronizing himself with the king's caged lion, who paced one floor below, in the courtyard, at that moment.

"It is, in truth, a matter of great foolishness that we are proceeding so hastily with the contracts for construction of Enki's temple. My brother the king, and the rest of us, continue to know less of Enki than does an ordinary citizen such as Ashgab!"

The old scribe nodded thoughtfully to the words of his lord, and suppressed a smile. One never knew what turn life might take in the palace. *A devotee of Enki, at my age!* He had to laugh, inwardly, of course. Enki was a young man's god. Very popular now, but, *for an old man like me?* It made him think of his frivolous friend Dubsa who had suddenly, after his fiftieth birthday, begun to wear lapis necklaces, as did only women, or, in the last few years, some of the youngest of men.

"Yes, I understand the situation, Lord Diku. I will do as you say." He turned his head downward and to his left. "In the meantime, however, I have not finished with all I have for you, sir. There is a bit more, you see," he gestured to his side, "another set of tablets, a little more to tell. I have a poem here, from the song of a poet I heard many years ago. It was on my voyage to the Land between the Two Waters. They do not inscribe such things over there, not yet, not there; they can only think to record their business accounts. But I wrote it all down myself. I trans-lated to our own form, while I was on the road. I have it word for word. It will refresh our memories. It concerns the Sumerian version of the story I just mentioned, the 'Descent' tale we know so well.

"But first I would like, my lord, to bring to your notice the role in that story of Father Enki. Today as you listen, think not on Inanna—She to whom we have attended, always, in the past," and the old man mum-bled something then, which Diku could not hear. *Forgive me, O my Queen!* He was praying to the goddess. Then the old scribe began to read again, in his slow, deliberate manner:

"The servant hastened to Eridu to the heavenly house of Enki.

The good Ninshubur entered the heavenly house of the God of Time.

The servant pleaded:

'Oh Glorious Enki, do not let the Queen of Heaven

Be assassinated in the Netherworld!'

The servant pleaded:

'Oh Merciful Enki, do not let the Queen of Heaven be restrained by Ereshkigal!'

And Enki cried:

'Ninshubur! What has my beautiful daughter done? My Inanna! The Shining Maiden!

What thing now has my willful daughter done?

I am vexed.

I am grieved.'

And from beneath his fingernail Holy Enki took a piece of holy dirt—"

"Yes, yes, Gudea that is quite sufficient!!" Diku, who had rejected the undersize chair and was seated now, far more comfortably, upon the thickly woven carpet, a beautiful carpet of many colors, pushed himself to his feet once again. "Thank you so much, my friend!"

Diku paced a little more, cleared his throat, and put his hand upon Gudea's shoulder. He was not blind to possibilities of offending this intelligent old servant.

"Gudea, you can see, though, can you not, how all this—this poetry—concerns but one little episode in the life of Enki? And that episode lives only in the shadow of Inanna! The Descent story is Her story, not Enki's. In truth, it is this very problem which is embarrassing the king! You have perfectly illustrated to me the limitations of our knowledge!

"Tonight you must go, Most Respected Scribe Gudea, and all the nights from this time hence, to the Enki services at the home of Ashgab-Agal! And early each morning I will come here to meet you. You shall teach me all that you learn.

"But, right now, my friend, be so kind as to send a couple of your boys to my quarters; they can fetch a couch for you to keep here, a nice one of my own."

Diku put forth his huge right hand and grabbed the small frail hand of Gudea. He pulled the old man up to stand beside him. Then he kissed Gudea once on each cheek and departed, in troubled mind, from the *edubba*, the archives of the king.

10

High School Graduation

east of San Francisco
June 1963 A.D.

> "What can I say to deceive my mother Ningal?
> I will tell you, I will tell you.
> Inanna, most deceitful of women, I will tell you.
> (Say) 'My girl friend took me with her to the public square.
> There a player entertained with dances.
> His chant, the sweet, he sang for us.'
> Thus deceitfully stand up to your mother, While we by the
> moonlight take our fill of love…"
>
> —from a two-column tablet of Sumer,
> third or second millennium B.C. translation in "O Ye Daughters
> of Sumer," by Samuel Noah Kramer, in *The Light of the Past*,
> *A Treasury of Horizon, A Magazine of The Arts*

The sun was low and a breeze had come. Her arms were covered with goose bumps. She closed her book, collected her glass, her tanning lotion, her nail polish and transistor, and went into the house. At dinner she was quiet and thoughtful. She would not tell her parents and she would not tell her friends that her teacher was going to paint her. She had never consciously chosen a deceitful action in her life as far as she could recall, but this was different. Instinctively she wanted, from the beginning, to allow whatever was about to happen between the two of them to remain unsoiled by the mud of other peoples' judgments. Particularly her mother's and her dad's.

She had scheduled to meet him on the first Monday after graduation. It would be so easy to keep the appointment private; her parents knew that she wanted to go looking for summer work, and she would not have to tell a lie. She would simply meet Mr. Romier in Berkeley and then, after they parted, she truly would go hunting for a job.

*   *   *

Graduation day came, and with it several honors and two sizeable scholarships for Maria Ananin.

Sitting with her husband in the midst of the crowd on the bleachers of the football field, Ellen Ananin pulled one after another tissue from her purse. She sneaked a glance at her compact to check if her mascara was smeared. An overwhelming guilt vied with her nostalgic tears, a guilt that was sudden and unforewarned. Unwanted memories were crowding her pleasant thoughts.

...and then I forced her to play with that irritable child next door— what was that child's name? I know Maria wasn't happy with that kid, but I forced her, to help overcome her terrible shyness—not that the shyness improved much, but, still, she was much better off, with a playmate, I think...she always did need a little pushing...I pushed her into the dance lessons, too, which I'm positive was for the best—the way she moves, I know it's thanks to me...She would have kept to herself if I'd allowed it, remained solitary to this day, but she has some friends now. It's too bad, though, there wasn't someone else around back then, besides that bratty little what's her name—that child was so mean, I suspected the kid of milk money extortion...Maria had a lot of tolerance; she was always too passive; she took a good share of bullying. From myself, included, I guess...I

still can't forgive myself for that time in Olivia's hallway—Maria was four, I think . . She came running…I was waxing Olivia's floors. And I shoved her away. I was so concerned for my wax job. I'll never forget that sight— my darling little girl, losing balance, falling…Oh God, I'm lucky it was just two steps, and not more…She was such a little innocent. I remember how she came that time, to tell me some exciting thing that happened. She was always doing that. It annoyed me sometimes, invaded me. But why couldn't I listen a little more? I loved her so much, though. Yes, I have loved my daughter…Somewhere along the way, I think, she gave up on me…She doesn't tell me anything now; I haven't got a clue what she even thinks about. She doesn't tell her father either. But he's like her, in some ways, both of them with their noses in their books. Too bad it's not the same books, they might talk more. But they have a good relationship, I believe that…All that religious stuff she reads, for all I know she's going to end up turning into some kind of fanatic…When Olivia died it must have thrown Maria off course, somewhat—they say it can be impossible to tell if a child is grieving. So they tell me…But did we give her an unhappy childhood? Could that be? Is that the reason she's so shy, why she escapes into the books? She should be having more social life at her age, much more. But at least she has poise. And she's a good girl, obedient, completely trustworthy…She never was popular like I was. I doubt she'll pledge a sorority when she gets to Berkeley. That was the heart of my college life; but it goes without saying it won't be that way for Maria. It isn't my fault though, not really. I'm too hard on myself. After all, I was so preoccupied when she was small. Pete's affair, that's all I could think about in those days. I didn't ask for it to be that way. All the same, she was special, a special child, why didn't I let her know that? Why don't I let her know now? God, I hope she doesn't end up a religious fanatic…"

The ceremony was over. The woman seated to Ellen's right, a neighbor whose son was also graduating, leaned over toward Ellen's ear.

"You must be so proud, Ellen!" she marveled. "Such a pretty, gifted daughter! All those awards and scholarships! And acceptance to Berkeley! What happiness for you and Peter!"

"Yes, she's given us a lot of happiness," replied Ellen, her tissue again at her eyes, as she analyzed the complicated possibility that her neighbor's comment might actually be true.

11

Marsh Birds at Twilight

east of the Euphrates
circa 2700 B.C.

As we came to the outskirts of Orom, I began to revive from a deep
and lasting trance. In the concluding hour of a hot dry afternoon, when
the traders sat us down to rest, the aura of light upon a reed-edged river
awakened me once again into the world.

I saw a flock of little birds feeding on the shore. One at a time, as they
ate their fill, they flew across the river to take their bath on the opposite
side. I watched their little red tipped black wings splashing in the water.

One by one, as the birds finished bathing, they flew back again across
the river, above the birds yet gleaning, until they reached the bushes further on. There they rested, settling into the leafy branches, ruffling their
feathers and chatting to each other.

Soon the sun would go down. I watched the last bathing bird, who
lingered long at his splashing. Suddenly he looked about him and discovered that he alone remained at bath. Then he, too, took flight for the
bushes. He flew across the river so much faster than had the others. He
was anxious, it seemed, not to be left behind.

*   *   *

I did not see my own journey. From my village to Orom, I witnessed nothing. I returned, instead, into myself, to the dance of my life. I saw that which had been. I watched inside, as though I were a grandmother, sitting at her doorway, silently recalling, chewing her gums on memories. I knew nothing of the journey to Orom, and nothing of the two men, Ursunabi and Kerem. They were no more familiar to me than when we first set out from Fa-Orszag. Only my body had accompanied them.

I learned later that my condition had worried the traders greatly, for they feared it was possible that I had lost my mind. In truth, it was my senses I had lost. I always kept my mind.

The traders feared that the gate to abundance, which had so recently opened before them, had immediately slammed shut in their faces. But they were not to be so unfortunate.

12

The Gates of Orom

Before the first time ever I saw Orom, I had my knowledge of cities, risen from tales I heard as a child. But the day I beheld Orom, I thought not of those tales. I thought, instead, of the safafi bugs of Fa-Orszag. For the towering, terraced mud structures which rose above the level walls of Orom were formed with the geometrical intricacy of the mud-sculptured cities of the safafi creatures. I do not say that the city seemed not of humankind, however, or in any way lacking in the beauty of human design. It was, in truth, a glorious sight, set upon earth against majesty of sky.

It all became, as we moved closer, ever more glorious. I began to discover gold and jeweled images embedded in the wall, a wall which was so smooth and shining, the surface appeared to be made of rose-hued metal rather than of mud. Against the clouds, above the walls, I could recognize the fronds of tall date palms, palms which I know, now, wave from the gardens and parks of Inanna's temple courts.

In my heart, I felt a not unpleasant thrill of undeniable, and unwelcome, anticipation. And interest. Then I knew that the ferocity of life is strong, for the depths of woe through which my wonder had pushed were no less than infinite. I was somehow going to survive. But toward that survival I had neither relief nor regret, only surrender to the mystery of my fate.

*   *   *

I have a memory of a certain morning in my childhood. It was after the first partaking of food; I was washing my bowl and my cup. My mother was pounding grain nearby and she saw my clay baby cup slip from my hands and break upon the ground. I had loved and used that simple little cup all of my life, and though I was of good age, nearly leaving childhood, I wept. My mother ceased her pounding.

"Anarisha!" she called softly. "Why are you crying? You have lost your cup, and now you feel the wind of Enlil inside you, the wind called 'change.' This wind is always there. Always. Only now you are allowed, for this moment, to see it moving. As it passes, let it teach you, as it always will, the more clearly if you be still.

"You may not be shown just now what it is that you are taught, it may take the aid of Utu, passing many days before you. But remember this, Anarisha, that all the winds of Enlil come firstly from the breath that lasts forever. And this breath is made of beauty, of wisdom, of strength and of love. But the vapors of woe that pass through mortal time are like wisps of smoke, with but apparent force."

The great loss that had befallen me now—was this all a teaching also? I thought I knew that my grief, itself, would be eternal. But I knew, as well, that the insights of my mother were to be trusted. I carried both these certainties and though they were opposite, the one would not push out the other, for they were equal in my heart.

I knew not how my mother had come to learn what she did; her knowledge was from her own mother, I supposed. I knew that she meditated much, perhaps more often than anyone in our entire village, and that she spoke each evening, as she taught us to do, with the grandfather-tree of Fa-Orszag.

And I knew, too, that her words had connection with another treasure that had come into my life.

There was a scribe in a neighbor village who had taken thought to make tablets of the tales told by his people. My teacher, Old Man Ummia, kept those tablets in his home. For like myself, this unknown scribe had been a student of Ummia. To read those story-tablets was to come into enchantment. It was like sipping the juice of *soma,* in part.

I begged Ummia many times for those tablets and I read them again and again. I can not account for the number of times, but it was many! The tablets sent me to the worlds of the tales, even as hearing a tale told by voice. But I traveled in a way that was different than with hearing. Though yet in my heart, I journeyed also with my mind. Moreover, I could return whenever I wanted, simply by taking up the clay. Because I did this often, the tales became of import to me, as if they were my family. And since these tales were unlike any others, but for the ones my mother told, I came to be half stranger to the people of my town.

As I neared the gates of Orom, I wondered if it was because of the strangeness which I had brought upon myself that my village had sent me so easily and so readily from it's midst.

*   *   *

All thinking ceased. For we were making our arrival.

I beheld the Gates of Orom. And never had I seen such a wonder. The dazzling elegance of the gates, the finely cut figures, the intricate carving within the wood. (Although the walls are mud, the gates themselves are of the wood of *sitar.*) Silhouettes of beautiful men and women in beautiful interlacings of love, cut into ecstatic timelessness within the wood. The thick plating of gold, shimmering upon the top edges of the gates, appearing as golden silhouettes of tiny mountains.

Those who have not seen may perhaps in fantasy find a dreamer's portion of the awe which comes to those who truly do approach this marvel. Awe that is most powerful at the instant of first sight.

The gold is more abundant than imagination can conceive—enough gold to pass through Fa-Orszag, I believe, only after a thousand double-years of time! And therefore, the gates can shine! They glowed that day as though Utu Himself were standing there before us, reigning in His midday sky. And at the moment of our arrival, as if all that glory were not sufficient testament to the sanctity of the city, there perched upon her gates two living white birds of tremendous size and beauty.

When I beheld all this radiant wonder, the great Utu, in truth, was present. For, in truth, He spoke to me.

"Daughter, do not linger as you are—stricken and afraid, without the warmth of love within your blood," he admonished. *"There is far more yet to come of your living. More than you have ever dared to assume. This present interval is simply a time when you are being given to swallow a new and unfamiliar broth. Your customary food is finished—it now has been consumed."*

At first these words, which floated to me as castaways upon my own thoughts, seemed inane, and cold-hearted. To think thus of Utu! But such was my condition at that time. The words offended me. In the passing of the years, as I reflected upon those words, the greater portion of discernment they seemed to contain, and the more of sense. But on that day, I was not ready to accept such musing. I wanted no thought of a tomorrow. I wished only to go deep within my grief. And to find there the soothing nectar of serenity which, my mother's wisdom promised, would be hiding in the midst of sorrow's many folds.

We passed through the gates in the confusion of a crowd of other travelers. More than one road leads to the city, and all meet together at the gates. The thought came to me that not I alone was walking to slavery in Orom; that amongst this throng there must be others like me. I did not gaze upon the faces of those wayfarers, however, out of strong need to keep holding to myself.

The footfalls of Ursunabi and Kerem turned brisk and of a new rhythm as we entered their city. The traders were no longer fatigued, it seemed. Nor was I. As we entered, they pulled me to the side of the road. The road was covered with small stones, to keep dust from the city-dwellers, I concluded. And I thought how such pebbles would be useful in my own Fa-Orszag.

Once again, this time in the hot dry breezes of Orom, the traders decided to disrobe me.

"Orom must whisper in yearning for the new slave who passes this day through her streets. Tonight they shall whisper over their fires," Ursunabi said to Kerem, "and they shall talk of this woman in the morning, at the marketplace. But none shall have sight of Anarisha again, not for many days. We shall let them wonder." He folded my clothing and put it in his sack.

Thereafter, I saw nothing of Orom but the stones of her cobbled streets and the finely sewn hems and sandaled feet of her citizens. For I kept my eyes downcast and did not look upward. Not even when they stopped to greet their acquaintances, inventing tall tales about me as they talked. I did not look upward, not until we came to the gate of the house of Ursunabi.

*   *   *

As a child in Fa-Orszag, when I was told of the temples in the cities, I would see, with the vision of my heart, buildings almost like the structure now standing before us. Magnificently large and lustrous, walls caressed by the loveliness of fruit trees and flowering vines. But this was not a temple; it was the home of the trader. It had two levels, and rooms abundant as date clusters, with balconies, overhanging a yard which they called a court. This enclosure was made beautiful with potted palms and ferns, trailing jasmine, blossoming and fruited lemon, orange and loquat trees. It beckoned to the weary to recline on its cedar couches or take refreshment in its pools.

We did, indeed, seat ourselves in the courtyard, the fatigue of travel having returned to overwhelm all three of us. Kerem mumbled something about having his fill for awhile of donkeys and boats and dusty roads. And it was then that I realized that some portion of our journey had been taken in vessels upon waters. I had made my own journey so far into the secret center of my soul, I knew not that my body was moving upon anything but land!

The household had seen us coming from the balconies. They had immediately prepared a welcome. As we sat there in the courtyard we were brought jugs of cool water with slices of lemon, by two very young little girls. I knew at once that the girls were slaves, although they were the first I had encountered in my life. It was not that they, like myself, wore no clothing; for no doubt many of the smaller children went about so as they do at home. It was something else, something I cannot put to words, which spoke to me of slavery. They had only about six years, each of them; they appeared to be twins. I knew it not then, but to possess such a pair was another sign of the wealth of Ursunabi.

Two older girls brought clean sandals and a bowl of bread, crushed dates with almonds, and slices of orange dripping with honey. Ursunabi gave each of these children a smile or a pat on the head or a stroke under the chin as she waited upon him. I noted with surprise that this man could be more tender with his slaves than some fathers with their daughters. This was my first, misleading, introduction to slavery. I saw later that he treated all of his animals in a similar fashion.

They led me through an arched entranceway and I was in the house. It was another marvel. I felt a little thrill, again unwillingly.

*   *   *

The bricks of both floors and walls were shining, Anurei. Shining as nothing in our village of Fa-Orszag, my beloved, save the silver and the copper upon the table where you work. The bricks are painted in lines of deep blue possessed with the azure brightness of the day sky and a red like the shade of ripened plums. Beneath the blue and red is a hue that glows like the heaven of the setting sun.

And the walls are made with niches, as in our village storehouse! In these foreign holding places, however, are no sacks of bulghur or barley or nuts. Instead there stand huge vases, of copper and silver and clay. The vases are of a type of beauty similar to that fat little jug you made for me so quickly and so long ago. So very pretty you made it, in the season when we wed. It was young, inexperienced, charming and delightful, that jug. But Ursunabi has nothing such as you can make me now, Anurei, the beautiful jugs that come of many double hours.

His vases hold branches of blossoms and flowers with long stems. There sit jugs, also, in some niches; these wait to fetch water from the pools of the court, though from the largest recess of the wall, itself, comes a small flow of water in a steady stream.

Anurei, you see, I am writing to you. I can not comprehend this feeling that pushes me to do so. I am writing to you beloved, and somehow you become nearly real, more than just the dreaming of my mind. Though, in truth, even were you to learn tablet, I know you shall never see these words.

From the beginning, they allowed me to inscribe. Ursunabi knew that I was able. How he discovered that, I do not know. I can only suppose that the people of Fa-Orszag told him everything about me. He sent damp tablets and a stylus to the room of his wife, which was where I slept at night. The first morning I awakened early, and the woman woke to find me at work. She did not prevent me. Not for many moments. Finally she found her voice and cried out for me to cease. The next day it was the same. She stood back and gazed upon me as if I were a sacred creature or a holy figure of clay. What spirit or deity sent this blessing of her tolerance I could not tell.

Early every morning, a child came quietly to place a new tablet with the stylus in the niche of the chamber wall, and for a little while, until Kukuda wakened, I was able to write. Then my captor would rise and look upon me. And finally she would cry out. Yet she never said a word of it for the remainder of the day. I would put my things away and she would begin her daily routine of ordering me about.

But I shall speak to you further of the entranceway, as it appeared to me at first.

The most interesting sight, for you, I think, my husband, would be the household water supply. A flow of water enters from a pipe inside the wall, streaming into a large and colorful basin. The bottom of this bowl is centered with a circular hole, a hole of perfect roundness without compare. The water runs into the hole and back into the wall. Perhaps it then goes somehow flowing into one of the pools out in the courtyard. How eager you would be to learn the precise means of the water coming and going. Myself, I cannot understand the workings of the famous water systems of Orom, though as we stood there, Ursunabi told me of them, proudly attempting to inform.

I noticed, also, lamps fixed upon the walls. These are lamps, Ursunabi said, which burn goat's butter for their fire. The butter is held in vessels of copper and silver and gold. The glow from the lamps is not like that of our own common torch lamps. Not as striking, yet I believe you would approve it. The light is playful, cheerful, of good will, with no danger implied. The only danger that I can see would be if a man or woman were to take the lamp from the wall and walk through the streets in a mood of derangement made of hatred and ill intent. And, in truth, beloved, that very thing has happened in the city of Orom.

13

A Slave

Upon the floor were three woven woolen coverings, of vivid colors, all. These were my first acquaintance with Oromi carpets, of which the citizens are proud. With good reason, for the workmanship is fine and the dyes remarkable.

Upon one of these rugs, at the end of that hall, upon a silver table, was a large golden drinking goblet. From its base came a tall sturdy stem, centered midst two slender branches reaching upward to the rim of the cup. At the rim two beautifully formed doves perched, tilted as if drinking. As far as I could tell, the entire goblet—birds, branches and vessel—were formed from one great sheet of gold. You would know for certain, my Anurei, could you only see. I learned later how greatly the family values this goblet.

As I stood gazing upon this treasure, momentarily distracted from my grief, a little girl peeked through the doorway, followed by a small woman, who pulled the girl away. The woman entered the hall and approached us.

She was a thin person, bony and dry, but dressed with a splendor such as we have never seen, in linen of gold mixed with the same soft blue as that of the walls. This was Kukuda, wife of Ursunabi. I must tell you, though, my dearest, this woman could not have been less aptly named. "Kukuda" means "sweet" in faraway Erech, the city of her birth, a city so distant that people do not speak our language as they do in Orom, itself so far from home.

The woman came forth and knelt before Ursunabi and Kerem, who then knelt also, in a most bizarre fashion. All of them were on their hands and knees. And they were nodding their heads up and down. I could not help but think of donkeys. I have since learned from Kukuda that this "form of address" is very ancient, going all the way back she says, to the time when people lived as beasts. (In all I learned from Elder Ummia, I never heard of such a time.) She says proudly that only the most noble of families continue in this custom.

Seeing the three of them so, I felt a sudden nearly unpreventable urge to laugh, made the worse as there came a sudden loud rumble from the barely-filled stomach of Kerem. But I held my silence, even as the sound, ignored by all three, came forth a second time.

"My Ursunabi, you have returned to me at last," smiled Kukuda, still down and nodding. I saw, as she smiled, that several of her teeth were made of gold. The husband and the wife gazed into one another's eyes for a moment. But the gaze was quickly broken by the third and loudest growl from the innards of Kerem, to whom they both now turned their heads. At this instant, observing their serious nodding and their turning, it became hopeless, though I imagined terrible consequence, to restrain my laughter any longer. That pitiful lack of containment came of my fear I suppose; there was nothing I could do. I pretended to be coughing.

But Ursunabi was not fooled. "Anarisha," he said sternly, "Where is your reputed dignity?" He looked upward at me—I alone was standing—and I coughed again, while I wondered, *and where has gone your own?*

They all rose to their feet. "You are now in a cultured civilization, Anarisha; no more the backward village. You must behave accordingly," he admonished me again, with a forbidding regard.

"And just why is this one here in our home, o my honey-of-the-bee?" Kukuda's voice startled me with its strange lilting sound.

"I wish to prepare her here," said Ursunabi, then he quickly added, "With your assistance, my savory."

"Prepare her? In the name of Inanna, for what?!"

"I have but one intention. To sell her to the Temple. To the chief priestess of the Temple of the Lady."

"Ahh…Yes, I see. I do see. And it is quite clear to me what you further intend, my husband." She spoke knowingly, a brightness coming to her face.

"And what is that, Kukuda?"

"It is in your mind that this one shall sit as priestess. High priestess, to be more exact. Am I not correct, Ursunabi? And you foresee a worthy recompense.

"Ah, my Kukudi. And how did you guess?" He stroked the back of her neck.

"Oh, it is most clear, is it not? This is why you bring her here to your home. To your wife, Kukuda of Erech. Of all the women in Orom, it is I alone who would know the preparation. How to develop her for that unique position. Though, of course, the rites are different here, much less appropriate. And in Erech I am certain they would never think to use a slave," she added.

"Yes, that is it, it is as you say, my dear." Ursunabi's smile was wide and lasting.

Now Kerem brought his hand to his mouth, himself muffling what I thought was a chuckling sound. He turned to me, looking me over, up and down. "Yes, I am certain you can teach this woman plenty, Kukuda," he said. Kukuda continued to be pleased, but a frown replaced the smile of Ursunabi, who darted a quick glance of disapproval at his partner. Most fortunately, only Kerem and I were standing where that look could be perceived.

*   *   *

She took me straight to her bedchamber then. She gave me a cloth to wrap around myself, and a pillow, but I was given no mat. We would spend the nights together, she upon her couch, and I beneath her, except for one occasion, when she pulled me to herself.

She had no children. Nor did she seem to have true friends, though there were many acquaintances. She owned slaves. Her life was occupied almost entirely in mastery and control over those who swarmed about, serving and indulging her in every whim.

Already, that first night, she spoke as though I myself had forever been a slave. She could not imagine otherwise.

"Anarisha," she said in her strangely rising and falling voice, as we entered her bedchamber. The room was dazzling; an enchantment of white and sky blue fabrics with tiles of a golden rose like the color of apricots. "If you are to become a priestess in our temple," she enunciated slowly, to make certain I understood, "you will need to observe some habits of cleanliness. Do people not wash themselves where you are coming from?"

I understood her. The accent was difficult, much less clear than the speech of her husband, yet I knew what she had said. But I did not answer. What was there to say through my shame and my anger? She knew that I had come from that journey, captive of her husband and his friend for many days. To bathe or not to bathe had clearly not been my prerogative.

"Your odor offends me," she muttered, as though to herself. "Please take this jug, and come with me to bathe yourself."

I passed through her halls within a cloud of shame.

She led me to a room with a floor that sloped toward a hole at the center. This was the chamber where her servants took their bath, midst tiles of intricate patterns of curves and angles, in green and red and gold. I began to admire the beauty of the tiles, but she spoke before I could appreciate them further.

"I can see by the way you move, Anarisha, that you cannot be a decent woman. There is something unclean, altogether. To the essence. A nastiness, I believe. I pray my husband knows what he is doing."

How powerful are the words of another when they speak about one self. The effect upon me of those cruel phrases, spoken in that room of that brittle-as-dry-wood woman's house, in her city of unending enigma, was profound. I did not accept those words; I knew they were thoroughly untrue. And yet, somehow, in my shameful rejected state of grief, those ugly lying statements smoothly placed me beneath her. And under her authority I remained, save for my short occasions of writing tablet. From that evening I began to know what it means to be a slave.

14

To Guadalajara

east of San Francisco
1963 A.D.

In the center of a valley surrounded by green hills, in narrow corridors of learning, a privileged generation of light-skinned youth shuffled noisily and somewhat awkwardly. For it was the early sixties, in northern California suburbs, and not some other place or time. Amongst these descendants of villagers of cold climates, a boy of foreign rhythms, of heritage more varied, strode with different movement—which altered all their movements as he passed.

He was much the same in color, and in feature, as Anarisha. He resembled her enough, in fact, to be taken for her brother, had they not been separated by the generations, over three hundred of them. Even to the lustrous black hair streaked with copper that was the envy of the women of Fa-Orszag.

The teachers and the student body only began to notice Michael Dagan in his senior year. Previously he was so unobtrusive, so reserved, even aloof, possessor of an aura so subdued that it lost him in the crowd, no matter what his coloring or rhythm. But now his golden skinned, quicker-moving, suddenly six foot-two inch body was too exceptional for Anglo-American Castro Valley, or for anyone, for that matter, to ignore. And his thick-lashed, serious eyes seemed more alive, his voice unmistakably more compelling. So compelling that old Mr. Davies, the music director, gave him a lead role in the fall musical, *The King and I*, and two lengthy solos for the "Spring Sing."

Mr. Davies also persuaded Michael and three boys who played in the school band to form a rock group. The group, the Untouchables, was good enough to play for the "Sock Hop", the Jr. Prom, the "Sadie Hawkins Dance" and several private parties of that year. They specialized in slow, romantic rock. Michael thought that, hopefully, he sounded a little something like Elvis, as when Elvis did his slow songs, like "Love Me Tender" or "Just for Old Time's Sake." But the music director couldn't stop telling the boy he was "another Yul Brynner."

That year Michael also tried out for the basketball team, and the team became the first group of American friends which the much relocated teenager had thus far had. Among these new friends was a tall, fast-talking, skinny, sandy-haired, freckle-faced boy named Tom Muir. It was at Tom's house that Michael first heard the music of Miles Davis, of John Coltrane, of Woodie Guthrie, Pete Seeger and a rising star named Bob Dylan, none of whom the rest of Castro Valley had yet discovered in 1963. It was also Tom who coaxed Michael into reading Jacques Kerouac and Henry Miller, replacing the Superman comic books that Michael always carried around. From a silent, no-nonsense "jock" who saw no reason for studying, Michael suddenly returned to being, as in his childhood, an unashamed book lover—though he still couldn't find time to do any homework. "Lately," said Tom, who didn't know Michael before high school, "you're turning into a real *egghead* like me." Tom elbowed his friend in the ribs as he labeled them both with that already dated insult from the Eisenhower years.

It was Tom who introduced him to Rosie Hestia one day, at the locker the two boys shared—though Michael would have met Rosie soon enough, regardless, because she was a cheerleader, one of the new girls, for their team.

Michael immediately liked the way Rosie looked. Very neat, just slightly plump, with short blonde hair—bleached, it was, but he never found that out—fresh and clean. *Cute,* he thought. He loved the way she smelled, and the way she jumped—the way she threw her arms up in the air—when she did her cheers. He did not agree with Tom that she looked like Debby Reynold's sister, but then he usually didn't agree with Tom about most things.

On the day that basketball season began, when the principal introduced the team and the cheerleaders, one by one at an assembly, Rosie joyously ran out to the center of the auditorium for her moment of glory as the principal's booming voice yelled "Rosie Hestia!" But she slipped and fell as she ran, her skirt flying up way too high in front of the entire student body. Michael watched as the big smile disappeared from her excited little face. He felt so much embarrassment, such concern for her, and such a strong desire to do something at that moment, that he almost ran to help her to her feet—but the coach extended an arm to keep him in his place. As soon as Michael received it, in the middle of the season, Rosie was wearing his green and white school sweater, with his letter on it, and no Castro Valley girl ever mentioned Michael Dagan without bringing up Rosie's Hestia's name as well.

On the evening when she was awarded her CSF scholarship to Berkeley, a balmy spring evening with an orange moon shining full in the sky, Rosie went to an honors dinner in the school auditorium and gave a short thank you speech to the faculty. She rushed through it to the end, and then she concluded, "To all you fantastic teachers I just want to say a great, huge Thank You. Thank you so very, very much. For everything! And I want you all to know that this is truly the most exciting light of my nife!" Everyone, even Michael, who'd come with Rosie to the dinner, couldn't keep from smiling while she hurried to her seat. Later, spontaneously, he asked her to marry him as he walked her home in that full moon night.

*   *   *

It was to be a long engagement. Tom Muir made the decision to postpone college in favor of seeing the world. He was ambitious; he wanted to run for congress and change the world, but first he needed to see it. He asked Michael to come along.

Michael didn't need to think that offer over too much. For one thing his grades were too low for anything but a "junior" college. Easy enough to get into later, he told himself. And he wasn't receiving encouragement to go to college, anyway. Except from Rosie, that is, whom he placated and humored right up to the first week of September. Then Tom and he departed, beginning their long-lasting, life-changing journey to Guadalajara, Mexico. A city which neither knew a thing about.

But Guadalajara had caught Tom Muir's imagination. It probably was the exuberance of its anthem. The song played perpetually on the jukeboxes of Hayward, the town next door to their own. Hayward's *simpatico* ambiance and climate, with its seductive immigrant employment opportunities, had long enticed new hopefuls from Jalisco, where Guadalajara was the capital. Tom relished the sound of *Guadala-hharrrra* whenever, which was often, he heard or said its name. And for him that name, plus some childhood notions from *Zorro* and "The Cisco Kid" (he mistakenly assumed that both took place south of the border) was enough. He was completely enthused about going, and only secretly a bit nervous, because his knowledge of the world beyond California was hardly enough to inspire any fears.

Unlike Tom, Michael already knew life outside the United States; and he, as he said his good-byes to Rosie, to his family, and under his breath to Castro Valley in general, felt excitedly on top of things.

*   *   *

Tom had a car, an outwardly smooth and suave though inwardly troubled '55 black convertible Chevrolet, and he had two thousand dollars, a graduation present from his grandfather. Both boys had their summer savings, money they'd earned along side emigrants from Guadalajara, in canning jobs at the Hayward Hunt's tomato factory. There they had all together existed, for forty hours a week from June to August, under the unique spell of the aroma of tons of tomato sauce— an aroma so pervasively powerful that it dominated even the summer breezes in Castro Valley, causing all the children growing up in that part of the world a lifelong destiny of recalling long-gone summers whenever they ate pizza or spaghetti sauce which, for most of them, was nearly every week.

Setting forth from Castro Valley very early on an overcast September morning, Michael and Tom pulled up to the gas station by the bar near the entrance to the freeway. Michael was returning from the restroom when a pink complexioned, apparently inebriated middle-aged man strode towards him from a white Edsel now parked by Tom's Chevrolet. The man's stringy hair was disheveled and his yellow plaid suit was gashed with deep wrinkles, as if he had spent the night sleeping in his car, incapable of driving home.

"Hey, you from Cas'ro Valley?" the man yelled, directly into Michael's face.

"Yes I am," Michael replied.

"Got yourself a damn good tan this summer, di'n' you kid?"

Michael said nothing this time. He looked back at the gas tank.

"Lissen, kid, I don' wan' soun' too pushy, but lemme tell you boy— Seeing you here, hangin' 'roun' Cas'ro Valley, tha's all. My three lil' daughders, you unnerstan'?" His face was filled with disgusted bravado as he looked up at Michael. " I don' wanna soun' pushy, but lemme tell you, kid—Say, what are you, anyways? Oriental, A-rab? Mulatto? What the hell, I know you get my meaning, huh, kid?"

Michael quietly and quickly walked away and got into Tom's car.

*   *   *

"Does that happen to you a lot?" Tom asked after he'd paid the attendant and stuffed his free coffee cup (with a picture of Wild Bill Hickcock and the logo "—'s Wild West") into his glove compartment.

"In Castro Valley? Naw, nothing like that," Michael slumped down, as he liked to, in his seat.

After getting on the freeway and driving for awhile in some silence, Tom spoke again. "You know, Mike, we should have shaken that guy up, at least a little bit." He took both of his hands off the wheel as he lit a cigarette. Michael saw, with an inner *Oh no*, that his friend's eyes were narrow, the way they always got when Tom was angry.

"Aaaaa, what good would that do?" Michael looked at Tom, who was looking at him, instead of at the road.

"Given us some satisfaction, obviously." Tom finally returned his left hand to the steering wheel.

"Forget it, O.K.?" Michael said.

"Hey, did you ever read *The Wretched of the Earth?*…Well did you? Do you hear me, Mike?"

Michael stared silently ahead. Suddenly he turned.

"Is somebody wretched, Tom? Just who are you trying to say is wretched?" Michael demanded. He was growing angry, at last, himself. "You? Or that jerk? Or me?"

"According to the book—you. And you shouldn't put up with that kind of shit."

"Why don't you just forget about it?"

"Assholes like him make me sick."

"Sorry you're so sensitive," Michael paused. "Look, Tom, if you want to make it up to me for that drunk—after all he was one hundred per cent all-American white boy, just like you—all you have to do is marry some girl who's kind of my coloring, or maybe some other color, if you prefer, and you and her can go get down and make some babies and then you all can get insulted, too, or you can get fired, or maybe you can go south and get lynched, or whatever else you fucking feel like—"

"Fuck you, yourself, Michael. Don't take it out on me," Tom muttered.

"Take what out? Who's got anything to take out? You're the one who's upset. Hey, man, can you quit changing lanes?! And keep your eyes on the road!"

Doing exactly that, Tom Muir fell into a long stretch of silent attention to the road, his lips pressed tightly, his eyes still thinned.

Michael shut his own eyes and thought, *Wretched of the earth! What does he know? Did he grow up with maids and nannies like I did? Shit, his dad's an underpaid schoolteacher. I don't even see how his family could afford to buy him this Chevy.* The next thought that came was one that he told himself to disintegrate, it made him feel so guilty and rotten to consider his father's death, but the thought was indestructible—*So Tom has his Granddaddy's two thousand. I'll have more than five hundred times that one day, when my trust comes.*

And when I do, he told himself, pushing his thoughts on to a less villainous track, *I'm going to rescue that little suburb from the evil forces of stupidity.* He soon calmed down and in a few moments was half-asleep, happily transported to the scene of a newspaper office in the trouble-plagued city of Metropolis.

15

Paris

Paris, France
the nineteen-fifties

> "Just as the sun rays vivify everything living, so does reverence in
> the student vivify all feelings of the soul…feelings are for the soul
> what food is for the body…veneration, homage, devotion are
> like nutriment, making it healthy and strong…"
>
> —Rudolph Steiner

In addition to that astonishing phenomena which the twentieth century once called "relativity" (while we of this more poetic century say
"dancing with the light") there exists a second mysterious aspect to the
passage of time.

Like "relativity," this other oddity also belies common sense. But
unlike relativity, it is not a cosmic trait. For it occurs solely within the
human realm.

The uniquely human anomaly of time is this: time disintegrates fact,
but it strengthens fiction.

At first, as anyone who ever played the children's game of "gossip" is
aware, a story will tend to keep changing. But when a sufficient amount
of time has passed—anything from a few days to a few centuries—most
tales finally establish themselves, with not much significant variation

thereafter. Myth eventually assumes a more powerful firmness than does an actual event; and legend is remembered when biography is not.

Take Odysseus and Superman, for example. The stories of both those heroes have attained a longevity that prohibits tampering with the basic details of their lives. Incontrovertibly, Odysseus returned to Penelope. And Superman was raised by the Kents. But how many people are sure that their own Great-aunt Isa truly was the belle of the ball, or that Uncle Basho was really the war hero he always claimed to be?

Does inviolability occur for myth, because myth, filled as it is with primordial images from far within the geometry of our being, lies deeper than unadulterated fact, as is often pointed out? Or because fiction, universalized from a gathered mass of similar lives and incidents, plus imagination, is therefore greater than fact—"larger than life?" Or that made-up stories, like meticulous Japanese tea gardens designed to mimic wilderness, can be more refined, and hence more pleasing to many than true wild nature is?

Aren't there other more mundane, prosaic reasons, too? Various everyday reasons, not always the same, but numerous enough to add up to a story-telling—in every sense of that word—proclivity in humankind. Reasons such as, for example, the human need to be logical, since fiction can make much more sense than pure reality. Or convenience; it is easier to stretch the truth than to painstakingly piece together memories of exactly what took place. Or the reason for mixing fact with a little fiction might be, sometimes, compassion; real people could be hurt by passing down and keeping alive the sordid or otherwise unpleasant facts. Or, yet again, there is compassion's opposite—the desire to do harm, in the case of vicious gossip.

And there are other reasons, too.

Take for example, the story of the childhood of the hero of this tale. It was not actually solid truth that Michael Dagan's father moved his family from Africa to California (as the son implied in several interviews some forty years after). Michael omitted, as he had always omitted to friends and acquaintances, an entire segment and location of his youth.

Efficiently, and automatically, he deleted the time, and the place, when he most came to know love, and need, for the man who was his father. It was a portion of time that he wanted to own, and not hand out. This was one reason for persisting to tell a version of his life that hardly said anything, compared to the truth. Which, it might be argued, somewhat altered that truth.

This was one reason why Michael did not say to any interviewer, for example, "When my father returned to us and we all left Africa, we traveled for half a year. We went to Indonesia, to China, to Japan, and to the Philippines. And then to Europe, where we settled in Paris for five incredible years, a time that seemed as long as a life."

Those years included the age—ten-years-old, to be exact—which the philosopher Rudolph Steiner named "the golden age of childhood." That year in the life of a child which parallels the golden ages of civilizations, the harmonious and creative "good old days" of the cultures of the world.

*   *   *

Michael's father, David, a conventional man in many ways, was a renegade in others, including the raising of his children. David had always participated in their education (even if that meant by mail) but during their time together in Europe he suddenly developed, as was often his style, a sudden obsessive involvement. After much thought, and his wife Felipa's approval, he placed Michael and Estelle and Shoshanna in a "Rudolph Steiner School," an unusual place whose rooms held the fragrance of beeswax candles and calendula soap.

Both parents were fascinated with the exalted claims the school proclaimed. The teachers spoke of "the True, the Good, and the Beautiful," as goals for "the whole child." Hand, heart, and mind; all three must be involved. And it seemed these ideals glowed with more than just a golden rhetoric, for the children were clearly remarkable, and graciously self-assured. The teachers gave practical attention to the true, the good, and the beautiful, with an impressive understanding of the sequence of human growth. Like their founder, the teachers believed that the growth of a child parallels the growth of a civilization.

A good friend, a psychology professor at the Sorbonne, first told the Dagans about the school. "David, I swear to you it is at least a hundred years ahead of it's time!" he exclaimed, in 1954, "But it rests on arcane foundations, which are very ancient." This friend bestowed upon David and Felipa many persuasive discussions as well as books of Steiner's ideas and knowledge. As the Dagans investigated, forcing themselves through the erudite books and, with greater gusto, through the freshly fragrant classrooms, they grew intrigued. But both were fully persuaded when they learned that Steiner was an early foe of pre-Nazi fascists, fleeing for England when those hate-filled beings set fire to the buildings of his beautiful *Goetheanum*—the most tangible creation the architect-philosopher-scientist-educator had produced.

The "Waldorf" school in Paris was named after the first school Steiner had founded—"invented" might be a better word—at the beginning of the century, for the nature-deprived children at the Austrian Waldorf Cigarette factory. As in the original school, the Paris children received, interwoven with every academic lesson, abundant offerings of music and craftsmanship and art; the blackboards were covered with masterpieces in colored chalk. Pupils learned the histories and customs of civilizations, while immersed in the wisdom, devotions, and finer subtleties of other times. And like humanity throughout most of history, great portions of their days were spent in nature, under the sky, feet upon the earth.

The children sang songs that long ago were offered to Apollo and chants which praise Krishna to this day. They made nearly flawless wooden bowls and other handiwork of mindful intricacy and refinement.

Observing the mysteries of water and fire, of earth and air, animals and plants, of the sun, the moon and stars, and of themselves, they drew illuminated diagrams in the style of Leonardo. They practiced the artistic techniques of Raphael, played Chinese and Celtic scales on the recorder, and Brahms on the violin. The older children knew the details of the life of Siddhartha, of Saints Francis and Jean d'Arc, the visions of Black Elk, the ideas of Mamoinades. And they could make up mathematical conundrums as Souleman might have done. Michael, the eldest of David's children, spent an entire semester on the life, times, and meditations of Marcus Aurelius, who, the teacher said, was the only authentic philosopher to rule the western world.

Especially gratifying to the father, his youngest, Shoshanna, won two wreathes of laurel leaves for discuss throwing in the contests of the fifth grade pentathlon. The contests were held at the end of that year of her studies which centered on the Golden Age of Greece. Shoshanna won one wreath for throwing the farthest; the second was for the beauty of her throws. The fact that the Greeks had placed such a high value upon beauty as to reward it in sports events was known by David Dagan, but not entirely appreciated, not until the day his daughter came home with her wreathe. The incident was, in fact, the beginning of David's new obsession with Greece, climaxing, just a few months later, in a "business trip" to Paros, an island off that land.

Monsieur Dagan, the charming and slightly overweight American who lived, *sans* visible occupation, with his "adorable" South Pacific wife and their three children—all four possessing a classic grace and exotic good looks—in rooms of a *Tahitienne*-like decor that the wife, Felipa, it was said, had styled in so astonishing a simplicity, with such a tasteful inspiration that the apartment felt "nearly sacred"—was known for speaking endlessly with his friends, old and new, about the talents of his children.

Something in Dagan's manner, something primitive and joyful, permitted those listeners to share in his pride and delight, rather than to shun this father who bragged so frequently about his daughters and his son.

The Steiner school was, in Monsieur Dagan's view, responsible for his children's talents and accomplishments. And what he conveyed to others was far more a gratitude than a boastfulness. Oddly enough, neither nature nor blessings of wise nurture, from himself or from his wife, were linked in Dagan's mind to the brilliance of his children. But, in reality, the school was only the cornerstone around which David and Felipa were shaping the fates of their kids.

Felipa Dagan, for one thing, held certain well-cultivated beliefs. Constant and inert, filled with a richness and long-evolved simplicity, beliefs surrounded the roots of her mothering. Beliefs softly cushioned and fed and filtered, like a fertile valley of rich soil of earth.

David, on the other hand, had a *joie de vivre*. And this too, fed Estelle, Shoshanna, and Michael. The father enthusiastically took his children, during that European chapter of their lives—often one at a time—on excursions through the neighborhoods of Paris, throughout the country, the continent, and even a bit beyond, to Turkey and the Bosporous, on the weekends and *les vacances* of those years.

And everywhere he led them, along city sidewalks, through cathedrals and castles, into gardens and museums and metros, and in and out of the restrooms of the world's most elegant hotels, he would be chatting away, almost non-stop. Telling them stories and anecdotes of his life, or of the locale, or of history, or oddities of the day just past. Sometimes he liked to make up guessing games:

"Look here, Estelle, in this window! Exquisite little pastries! These cakes make me so curious…Put on your thinking cap now, sweetie! Can you tell me which cakes are made with ingredients—or maybe tools— that the bakers didn't have back in the old days? Back when Marie Antoinette tossed off her sassy cake advice, before the revolutionaries chopped off her head?"

Years later he set a similar task for his grandchild Emily, at the same Rue Fauberg *patisserie*, only adding—it was the eighties by then—"and do you know, sweetheart, which American president copied Marie, when he declared, 'Let them eat catsup,' or some such thing like that?"

The Dagan children accompanied their mother and father, separately and together, to many private parlors of that city. They visited most often the flats and apartments and rooms of artists and writers but also the homes of scientists and shop girls and milkmen, most all of whom did not normally welcome strangers into their midst.

But David Dagan tended to seduce, into intimate friendship—at the least—nearly everyone who captured his imagination. This was both in spite of and because of his tendency to talk. For his talking was partnered with a rare gift: David also listened. And even more seductively, he grew fascinated with what he heard.

*   *   *

There was one more offering which this father gave. It, too, had a lasting effect upon his son. Incrementally, gradually, David purchased for Michael, in both English and in French, the most tremendous comic book collection (the boy was convinced) in all of Europe and Africa, in all, very possibly, of the entire world. Only Michael's best friends, an inventive little dare-devil from Pondicheri, India, named Valmiki, and another rambunctious class-mate named Antoine—a boy whose spirit might have fit with society more smoothly as a hunter-gatherer than a twentieth century *Parisien*—only these two shared in the secret of that stupendous, and very well-hidden comic-book cache. But Michael did not tell any interviewer about his thousand and twenty-two comic books, nor about those years, nor even about his friends. And of course he didn't talk about their overwhelming obsession with their hero—Superman.

Running, sometimes pogoing, or skating or scooting through the alleyways and parks of Paris, the three boys played that Superman was flying, fighting, rescuing, and leaping from high buildings in a single bound. Swayed by their ancient surroundings, they took their hero back through time. Superman rescued gladiators—sometimes from lions, and sometimes from each other.

All three had learned in school that it was Marcus Aurelius, not Superman, who saved real gladiators, from death by dueling. For as Emperor, Aurelius had decreed the blunting of the swords. Like fact and fiction, the Emperor and The Man of Steel mixed together; together they vanquished evil, together they conquered time.

16

Gardenias versus Pigs

east of San Francisco
June, 1963 A.D.

> "They stood there in the forecourt of the goddess with the glorious hair and heard Circe singing in a sweet voice…She brought them inside and seated them on chairs And mixed them a potion, with barley and cheese and pale honey added to Pramneian wine, but put into the mixture Malignant drugs, to make them forgetful of their own country. When she had given them this and they had drunk it down, next thing She struck them with her wand and drove them into her pig pens, And they took on the look of pigs, with the heads and voices And bristles of pigs, but the minds within them stayed as they had been Before."
> —*The Odyssey, Book X,* Homer, reprinted from *The Norton Book of Classical Literature*

Jean-Marc had arranged for Maria to meet him at the fountain. It was best to have her come to Berkeley by bus. Easy, just a couple of transfers. But the alternative, his driving to Castro Valley for her, no, that was much more difficult. He would have to face, if he drove out there, the matter of arranging to meet her somewhere—certainly not at her house. And such arranging implied, of course, secrecy. He would meet her at the fountain. She could acquire a feel for the place. Then he would take her to his apartment and she would pose.

*   *   *

The wait between buses was long. It took Maria an hour and a half to reach Sather Gate. Only a forty-minute ride by car, she guessed, wondering why Mr. Romier never offered to come pick her up at home. Was he keeping everything secret? Like she was?

But, anyway, she liked the bus. She valued the meditative quality of simply sitting, observing the people and the passing scenes, her thoughts in motion, on the road. It always made her feel peaceful, even on this day.

As usual, she could sense that the eyes of several of the passengers were on her. She was about half way to Berkeley when she noticed a woman whose eyes had never left. The woman's stare was invasive, and unfriendly; Maria felt like moving to another seat. But her thoughts were on a different track that morning, a path that led elsewhere, not to the obvious response.

She'd been daydreaming, off and on since breakfast, about a book she was reading. She'd read it often, always completely enthralled—it was the *Odyssey*. Particularly, she was thinking that day about the woman Circe, that sorceress who transformed men from humans into pigs. She kept wondering if such a woman could have ever truly existed, if people truly once possessed such gifts. Maybe they all lived in a different awareness back then. Without the education and life that children have nowadays, she reasoned, those ancient minds might have made other patterns in other directions, perfecting strange skills, like their stories talked about.

The idea came to her that if only she knew how, she would, herself, transform this rudely ogling stranger. *But I wouldn't change her into a pig,* she thought. *No, I could make her sweet, fill her mind with beauty,*

· 159 ·

something pure and good. Like gardenias, she mused, remembering the fresh flowers in the bowls of the Tonga Room, a restaurant in the Fairmont Hotel. Her parents had taken her there that week, to celebrate her graduation. The memory of that evening filled her with joy. In a spirit at first of play, she focused her mind on gardenias. *Fragrant and lovely. Fresh. With white, shiny green leaves…*

Since long ago, since she was a little girl in Oakland, Maria had liked to practice meditation. She'd learned it from instructions in her great-grandfather's books. Her ability to think of any object, to contemplate its aspects, to imagine herself becoming that object, was perfected by years of practice, to a high degree. Now, for more than fifteen minutes, she rested in her concentration—gardenias so true that she could smell their scent. Inwardly, she saw the white gardenias floating through the woman's brain.

When at last after those minutes she sensed the task was finished, she glanced up from her lap to the face of her "subject." She found the angry woman to be glaring at her, quite vehemently. Maria watched as the woman hoisted herself up from her seat across the aisle and then, with great huffiness, move to the back of the bus. Maria gasped. Her efforts had not been in vain.

It had never crossed her mind, however, that the woman would take such offense. Apparently she'd sensed the flowers as alien and fearsome, more invasive, no doubt, than her own rude staring.

As the woman walked to the back, not waiting for the bus to stop nor even for it to slow down, Maria could not keep from smiling. But she felt a little bit odd now, herself. She seemed to be newly powerful; and she had no idea what to think of this extraordinary gift. She quickly dismissed the worry. She thought of Mr. Romier instead.

Yet even her thoughts and feelings towards her favorite topic were now strangely colored. A mysterious, unfamiliar quality radiated from the secret disarming incident on the bus. It began to fill the world.

*   *   *

She found Mr. Romier, along with many others, sitting on the short concrete wall surrounding the pool of the campus fountain. A toddler standing next to him balanced her little body by clutching the wall with one hand and Mr. Romier's pants leg with the other. In front of them both a gray, floppy-eared wiemaraner leapt to catch a Frisbee. Some of the people were reading, some chatting, some just watched as life went by. One girl with bright brown eyes and long auburn hair strummed a guitar and sang of temporality—of ephemeral blossoms and tastes of strawberries and sweet wine. Maria saw that the girl did not wear a dress or a skirt, but was actually daring to appear on campus in pants—black "capris."

She spotted Jean-Marc Romier. Quickly, before he noticed her, she took in his receding hairline, his thin, somewhat crooked nose, his wide mouth, his sloping shoulders, his pale skin, his bespectacled eyes; and she saw before her the most attractive man she had ever known.

He stood the moment he realized she was there, carefully reestablishing the little child in position at the wall. Then he grinned as he took Maria by the arm. "Come sit down here beside me, and you'll see what university life is like."

The shyness she felt at that moment was even more overwhelming than what she had known with him, before. She feared she was going to turn speechless and remain that way forever, as though bewitched by a cruel Circe, herself. Anything she could possibly say would sound foolish and awkward. And wrong.

Jean Romier watched her as she sat. He observed the fluidity of every nuance of her movement, the delicate radiance of her skin, and he knew that he might never be worthy of such a creature. Then he looked on with pride as he caught sight of two students standing near them. Those boys, too, were checking her out. *Just having her sit beside me is an honor*, he reflected. And the thought crossed his mind that at last he knew what worship was about.

Yet at that same moment, Maria was having thoughts of her own. The idea had come to her that if she didn't figure out something to say very quickly, Mr. Romier was going to go back home. He would soon abandon her, growing so bored that he couldn't possibly endure more than half an hour in her company. But she had nothing whatsoever to tell him; there was just one thing on her mind—Mr. Romier, himself.

"This is a lot like a park, isn't it?" It was Jean Romier who finally broke the silence. "But much more interesting. Sometimes people make speeches here, just as they do in London, in Hyde Park. Anyone who wishes comes here and speaks on any topic he likes—the Pope, the Freedom March, over-population, Christine Keeler and the Profumo Crisis—any issue that moves one. But I hear the Board of Regents is becoming—"

Of course! Mr. Romier was from Europe! She could ask him a million questions about that. The mention of London was a godsend, it immediately freed her. She loved to think or talk about far away places. She breathed a small sigh, with big relief. "Have you been to London?" she interrupted.

*   *   *

"Oh yes, Maria, I even lived there for awhile, as a matter of fact. My father was an entertainer. An actor and a dancer he was. We traveled a great deal, depending on what work he found—or didn't find. We lived in so very many towns, so many cities—"

"Your father was a dancer!? That's so exciting!"

"Exciting? No, Maria, I'd hardly say it was that, not much, not for me. I didn't enjoy moving all the time as we did. But I suppose one could say it was an interesting childhood. An educational childhood, I suppose," he shrugged and lit a cigarette.

Then he told her about all of the places he had lived—London, Stockholm, Copenhagen, Amsterdam, Paris, Madrid, Naples, Budapest,

Zagreb, and other towns and even countries she'd never heard of, from one end of Europe to the other. "But, just before the war broke out," he finished, "we moved to Boston. And I have not gone back to the "Old World" since, except for very short visits. I know nothing of wartime Europe. I served, though, for a short time, in Honolulu with the American Navy, just before the war ended. Until then, I was too young," he added.

"And you like it here in America the best?" she asked.

"Oh no, not exactly," he laughed. "I like my apartment, my friends, my job—you kids—it's all worked out nicely, but I'm not overly enthused about America, itself, no, not really. America has great freedom and openness, yes. It is in many ways advanced, I am grateful for all it has given the world, and all it has given me. But for my taste—America, it is much too new, still inwardly unsettled. And therefore, at least for me, unsettling. My ideal country would be my father's homeland, Switzerland. So very pretty, so well thought out. Lovely villages. Especially, I like it in the winter. The snow, the skiing, the peaceful way the rhythms of life occur."

She herself disliked cold weather and had no desire to live where it snowed. "Oh," was all that she replied.

"You are displeased because America is not my favorite land?" he smiled.

"Oh, no, Mr. Romier, it's not that. I appreciate this country, too, but, actually, when it comes to what I really want, I would love to spend the rest of my life traveling. But to hot countries, not places that are snowy and cold!"

He looked at her and laughed, with an enjoyment that was becoming more carefree. "The rest of your life, Maria? Maybe that would be a little too long a voyage, possibly?"

"Oh, no, I don't think so at all," she said. "I intend to go to so many places—Greece and India and Sikkim—you know Sikkim, where that American girl is queen?—and Spain and Italy, France, Greece—I really want to go to Greece! and Africa, Peru—so many other lands, too—almost everywhere, really."

"Sounds like a lot of adventure in store for you." he smiled.

She had forgotten to be shy. "I want to know what it feels like to live in those foreign countries, what it feels like to be me in those places. And I especially want to be where everything isn't modern. Where people live in little villages, for instance. I don't care much for the newness here, myself. I wish I could become one of the people in each country. I would love to put on cultures the way we put on clothes."

"Spoken like a true Californian," he laughed. "We all have so much variety, here, don't we? So of course we want to sample more!"

"It's the ancient cultures I want to know, that's what I mean," she said, annoyed, but just a little, that he hadn't understood.

"Well, Maria, life can be interesting right in your own backyard, don't you think?" He considered her beautiful, young, hope-filled face, her lips—such pretty, exquisite lips.

"Let's do something interesting right now," he said. "I'm going to take you to my apartment and we'll begin the first sketches for this painting of ours." He took her by the arm again and they walked the few blocks to his car.

He had *KJAZ* on his radio and as they rode to Oakland they listened to Nancy Wilson, then Bill Evans, neither of whom she knew, but whose albums she bought the next week. There was no conversation, but his right hand rested lightly on her thigh.

His apartment seemed nicely familiar, due to the visit she'd made that evening with the class. She was pleased to find that she felt very relaxed, not at all her usual experience with visiting other people's homes; they often seemed too cold, less cozy than her own.

Immediately, she noticed a painting on an easel near the window. It was a partly finished portrait of an elderly woman. The eyes of the woman were black, and they seemed both kind and sad. The eyes had been strongly outlined, as was the bright magenta lipstick, and the dangling earrings. The woman's gray hair and her dark brown face were softly painted so that the bright eyes, lips and golden earrings stood out against everything else. The vivid portions created a separate abstract image; while the face as a whole was realistic and old-fashioned, in many shades of brown it evoked the renaissance.

The painting was not finished, but the portrait kept drawing her attention. It already had a finesse and a power, with that fascinating duality. She saw that Mr. Romier had painted the physical woman in one style, and her spirit in another.

Jean-Marc was moving about the room, looking for something.

"Who is this, Mr.Romier, in the portrait?" she asked him.

"Oh, that's Marta," he glanced up from the box of drawing pencils he had just located. "That's my…my mother-in-law. Rather, my ex-mother-in-law," he smiled as he watched Maria's expressions change.

"You weren't aware, I suppose, that I'm divorced. Well, yes, I was married for six whole years. No children, though. It's been a while now. I have, no longer, any relationship with my former wife. But as for Madame Marta, and myself, as for us, we're family, and always will be. Someday I'll show you the other paintings I've done of her."

"I like this one…It's a very good picture, a very good painting, I think."

"Thank you, Maria. But you don't need to say 'I think,' honey. Just giving your opinion is sufficient—I value it highly, you know." he said.

She felt a warmth flow through her as she heard the word "honey." She had never heard him use the word before. Certainly not with her. It was actually a word she disliked, if it came from anyone except her family. But she was not surprised, only pleased, with the feeling it gave her as it came, so easily now, from him.

"Well, I believe we're ready to begin. You sit down over there—" he motioned to the sofa, "and I'm going to do a little sketch, just a figure drawing, to start off with. You can be looking at this while I draw." He handed her a coffee-table size book, *Treasures of The French*

Impressionists, and went to open the drapes to let in the afternoon light. Then he took a record album from a table—Handel's *Water Music* the cover said—and placed it on the hi-fi. Finally he positioned himself carefully, in good relation to both Maria and the sunlight, and began to sketch.

For awhile she leafed through the pages of the book, but after a short time she closed it, glancing instead at the Turkish rug beneath her feet. The tones of the swirling reds and blues and purples in the labyrinth design were so vividly alive, the rug seemed nearly to vibrate with its own energy. It called up old feelings, feelings from when she was small, when she played on the Persian rug in her grandmother's house. She felt wonderfully serene.

"Oh, that's good, that's good. Beautiful! Mmmm, yes!" He seemed excited. "I've always wondered—do you actually suspect how lovely you are?"

He was silent for a moment and he paused in his sketching. "Maria, do you realize you are one of the most seductively beautiful girls I have ever known?" He felt a wonderful exultation come over him as he confided to her his secret, frequent thought, and an exultation in just saying her name; it felt intensely erotic to pronounce it. He thought of *West Side Story,* which he had just seen, and he sang a bit of "Maria"—under his breath—but she heard him.

"I see that my book is not so interesting to you, is it?"

"Oh, but it is, I love the impressionists, it's—"

"Here, let me get you something more interesting, I have something very fascinating—"He was quite excited now, and as he rose he knocked the easel behind him so that it almost fell. *It will be perfect to give her my new book,* he thought, but somewhere out of nowhere a doubt came: *She's only seventeen. She's my student. The book is not appropriate. But of course it's appropriate! What am I, a church youth leader? This is valuable and enlightening for her.* He handed her another large coffee-table book,

The History of the Nude in Art. It was a beautiful, expensive work of art itself, which his girlfriend had given him for his birthday.

"This will be good for you to see, Maria—to study the poses of the models, the girls and ladies who inspired the great masterpieces throughout history. The way they position their bodies, how they hold their hands, their facial expressions. This is good for you to absorb, so you can be a good model for me."

He was silent for a while, sketching her with complete focus, delineating his lines in time with the *Water Music.* Then, still sketching, he said, "I would like you to pose for me, Maria, not just this one thing, but many more paintings. Does that sound O.K.? You are very good, already, you know—your posture, the way you place yourself, your exquisite bone structure—exceptional! Nice high cheekbones, deep, pretty eyes, delicate nose…and such lips…you really are an inspiration to me, do you know?"

She could hardly believe the afternoon was happening. Beginning with the woman on the bus, and going on from there, the world had taken on new aspects. An unusual mood pervaded everything, a mood that was both strange and familiar. Either unreal or supernatural, she couldn't decide which.

He drew several sketches. He didn't want to stop. He didn't know what he was going to do when he stopped. He knew what it was he wanted to do, and he knew that he would do it, eventually. But this day was not the proper time. The girl was an innocent, defenseless. A virgin, no doubt about it.

He was aware that her classmates, many of her classmates, did not fit into that category. The high school had acquired, in fact, a rather far-reaching reputation. Local newspapers dubbed it the "Peyton Place of the West." So far had the stories spread, in fact, that the governor of California had signed a letter to the principal reprimanding the school and the community for the outrageous number of teen-age pregnancies in 1960-1962 in that small unincorporated town. The high school seemed to be having a not too subtle competition in female sexuality, stimulated, Jean decided, by the omnipresent influence of an onslaught of public goddesses. *Marilyn Monroe, Bridget Bardot, Elizabeth Taylor, Sophia Loren, Diana Ross, Ursula Andress, Carol Baker*—his current favorite, *Zsa Zsa Gabor, Britt Eklund, Nancy Kwan, Ann-Margaret, Raquel Welch...and all those Playboy centerfolds—Do the high school girls look at Playboys?* he wondered—and he let a few lesser corollary goddesses pass through his mind. Sexy women were visibly abundant. And of course there was no place in Castro Valley for the girls to go for fun, except to the one movie theater, or maybe to get their hair done, or to park with their boyfriends. Whatever accounted for it—the role models, the boredom plus hormones, maybe mixed with a suburban commitment to the self?—whatever the causes, the time and the town were fertile and ripe for provocative attitudes. Attitudes that grew, he believed, more calculated and overt with each new semester.

Maria, however, occupied this highly charged environment like an encapsulated astronaut. Securely and unaffectedly, she breathed in from her own private atmosphere. Naive, and unknowingly sensual. Provocative, yes, but without intention. He would do nothing today but sketch her face. And make just a hint of a suggestion.

"Do you like my new book, Maria?"

"Oh, yes, I do, it's very well done. It's fascinating, like you said."

"I believe the human body is the most aesthetically pleasing aspect in all of nature." he declared with earnest enthusiasm.

Surprisingly, she laughed. "Of course," she answered. "You're supposed to feel that way." She smiled and he thought he saw in her face a sudden hint of mockery.

"I mean," she explained, as she saw that he was stunned, that she'd taken him aback, "I'm sure that a fish knows that fish are the best looking things on earth, and the same goes for birds, or monkeys. Or even the way pigs look at each other, especially at the opposite sex..."

"Pigs? I thought, somehow, you were a more romantic girl, Maria!" He smiled also, but it was obvious he was annoyed.

"Romantic? I don't know if I'm that or not," she laughed. "No one has ever told me, or in any way made it clear, what I am."

"Don't you know for yourself?"

"Oh, I don't know. I guess—no, I don't. When you talk about 'romantic,' for example. In a way, I don't know what that word actually implies. I mean, I can define it. Or use it in a sentence, or even maybe apply it to someone else, someone I see from the outside. But me—I only see myself on the inside—so how do I know anything of what I really am?"

"Well, you've made at least one debatable assumption there, young lady, what you just said. But we won't go into it now. You mean, perhaps," he suggested, "you don't know what are romantic feelings?"

She felt herself losing her shyness with him. She was becoming aware that she could tell him what she was thinking. It didn't matter if he was going to agree or disagree. She might even have fun arguing, like she sometimes did with her father. She didn't articulate it to herself, she wasn't capable of it at that moment, but somewhere in her that afternoon she already began to see that as much as she wanted this man, he was wanting her even more, with a greater intensity.

He remained quiet and thoughtful for awhile. Then he spoke again, a little less intimate, suddenly, than he had been all day. Now his tone was one she'd heard very often, a tone he used in class. "Do you know, Maria," he asked, "that when Leonardo painted his *Last Supper*, he had all of his models pose in the nude, including, of course, the model for the Christ? And then afterward he added all the clothing. He was able to achieve much more authenticity in the flow of his lines that way, you see."

"Oh, is that so? I never heard that before."

"Yes, it is the old traditional method, you know," he laughed, "No, you didn't know, but you do now." He felt suddenly confused, though happy again. But, why, he asked himself, was he taking this whole thing in the direction he was taking it? Why didn't he just grab her hand, pull her close, and kiss her good-bye in the way that he wanted to? Just as he had done when he first met Mei, and others? She would realize then, as the others had, just how he felt.

But he did not do so. "It would be very good for this fountain painting we are making, my friend," he said, "if you would be so kind as to allow me to follow the example of Leonardo, if I may—to do a little initial sketch of you in the nude, I mean. But please don't answer me now. You go home and think about it for a while. You can come back and let me know next week." She heard a tone of voice that was as though he'd said, "and your essays will be due on Monday."

*   *   *

On the bus-ride home, perhaps from emotional exhaustion, she fell asleep. The bus driver, aware of where she usually got off, kindly woke her before she missed her stop.

When her mother greeted her at the door with "So how did the job-hunting go, honey?" she realized she had completely forgotten her intended agenda.

"No luck," she replied.

Feeling somewhat deceitful, yet also composed, she put her purse down and went to the refrigerator. She poured herself a glass of iced tea, washed a bowl of cherries, and took from her purse a semi-sweet chocolate bar. She didn't bother yet to change her clothing, a raw silk, cream-colored Chinese sheath, or her shoes—her black French-heeled sling-backs—but immediately carried her treats, on a tray with her book, out to the patio. Then she curled up on the chaise lounge and began to settle her mind into the story in the book. Her little white cat, who had followed her out, snuggled up at her feet, his paw soft and cozy against her bare ankle.

17

The Slave Holders

Orom,
circa 2700 B.C.

Kukuda of Erech, as the gaunt and brittle wife of Ursunabi the trader
was known, could not vividly recall her native city—though she made
much of second-hand knowledge of the place. This was no doubt
because she had never taken any interest in remembering it.

Kukuda had departed from Erech when she was only six years old, a
gift for Ursunabi. That sophisticated but very young man was the only
child of Kukuda's father's closest friend, Daddasig of Orom. Daddasig
was a world-trader, of Sumerian descent, as was Kukuda's father.

When little Kukuda—"Kukudi" she was called at the time—arrived
at the home of her future husband, she discovered that the fearfully
imagined foreign estate was not really so very different from her own
home, now so far away. The house was only slightly smaller than her
father's, and like her father's it included many pretty secret hideaways
for a little girl to claim—balconies and stairway nooks, secluded corner
niches and mossy, fern shaded grottoes by fountain pools. Kukuda was
then at the easily fascinated, easily inspired, pretending age. When she
wandered from one corner to another in the house, playing at being the
grown-up wife of Ursunabi, which she played quite often, she would
travel whole-heartedly into her role. So completely did she immerse

herself in it that even fifteen year old Ursunabi would forget that his betrothed was still but a little girl. Whenever this would happen, Ursunabi's mother, Miri, would instinctively bring herself to the doorway, and finding Ursunabi and Kukudi together, talking softly or looking into one another's eyes, she would take the child by the hand and lead her, most often, to the kitchen courtyard. Then Miri would show Kukudi how to prepare some delicious savory or beverage—a palm-nut candy, a milk and honey with rose petal tea, a spicy butter-cake—a special delicacy intended for making only by the woman of the house. Miri, an Elamite, come from afar herself, was a kind and thoughtful woman and she did not want little Kukudi to miss the wholesome sort of childhood which she herself had known.

Miri was a motherly companion to Kukudi, cheery and cozy with her small daughter-in-law-to-be. Had Miri lived longer than she did, who could say how nicely Kukuda would have turned out? But the girl was only nine years old when Ursunabi's mother died of a sickness in her lungs. Young Kukuda was at the stage of life, then, of newly discovering herself, of knowing herself to be herself, poised on the brink of unveiling the world that waited behind her childish visions.

But with Miri's death Kukuda no longer glimpsed or sampled that unknown adult world in tiny, safely portioned pieces. Rather, she abandoned her need for Miri and her need to be a child, all together and at once, suddenly and quick. Childhood had, after all, already given her the loss of her own birth mother. Without slowly ripening, Kukuda became like a small hard fig, picked too soon. Or like the bud of an unopened rose, cut at the stem, then entirely forgotten, all young loveliness left to wither and dry alone.

*   *   *

After Miri's death there remained in the house Daddasig and Ursunabi, when the father and son weren't traveling, and the family's fifteen servants. Ursunabi did not at that time take Kukuda to his bed. For Miri, who lay ill for many weeks, had had sufficient time to make clear all her wishes. Ursunabi promised his dying mother to wait for Kukuda, until his betrothed was old enough to bear a child. This restriction was the single exception to the girl's sudden maturity. In all other ways, she assumed the position of the woman of the house, so fully and capably that it astonished them all.

Kukuda possessed a natural disposition to manage, and she soon found that taking complete charge of so many underlings greatly helped to fill the terrible emptiness of life. She began immediately to perfect her skills in establishing her will upon the servants, backed by her neighbors and by the entire society of Orom, as well as by the servants, themselves, who felt strong need to continue in the security of an orderly household, devoid of conflicts with each other.

Ursunabi, who had been charmed by Kukudi the little girl, and who had actually loved her, was slow to see the new development in her character. He was more and more away from home, making trade with his father; once they did not return for more than a year. And Kukuda did not mind their absence. When Ursunabi and Daddasig were out of the house, she possessed complete control. But whenever they returned, she adroitly disguised the unattractive habits of bossiness, ill-temper and even cruelty, which had gradually become her style while the men were far away. She created, when they were home, as endearing a manner as she could conceive.

Kukuda balanced between her two personalities for many years; it became second nature to move from the one to the other. The servants said nothing to Daddasig or to his son, for fear of Kukuda, and from a sense that the men, though genial enough, did not actually care what happened while they were away, as long as the house ran smoothly. The servants, like Kukuda, herself, became accustomed to her duplicity, eventually almost ceasing to discuss it among themselves. After all, their young mistress was rarely physical in her abuse and there were much worse situations for slaves to come upon in the houses of Orom.

Therefore, only the servants were aware that two Kukudas existed. Ursunabi merely had a sense that he barely knew his young wife, whom, without thinking about the matter, he no longer loved nor even liked.

Once in awhile Kukuda remembered Miri and Miri's ways, the gracious ease which Ursunabi's mother had always shown with everyone—with herself and with the slaves. Kukuda did question, then, how she herself had become so "firm," as she came to think of it. But she had no wish to change. She was quite in love with her power, quite satisfied with her life, or very nearly so.

18

Anarisha's Dance

I was with Kukuda for fourteen days and fourteen nights. She struck me only once in that time. But she hurt me often with her words. These she thrust at me like stones, throughout that slowly passing time. Her constant avowals of my ugliness, my unclean spirit, my stupidity and my certain lack of worth, all mingled with my grief, spreading a shame throughout me which kept my gaze down in her presence, and my head bent down as well. Her apparent confidence in whatever she spoke was overwhelming, for I was as weak then as I have been in all the days of my life, before or since. When I called upon Heaven, or upon the memories of the teachings of my youth, all seemed to flee from me, like wisdom from a fool, and I cried inside myself to the Anunnaki, asking why I was forsaken.

On the fourteenth night, Ursunabi came to the door of the chamber of his wife. I had seen him only from a distance in all those fourteen days.

"I have come for her," was all he said to Kukuda, who laughed without mirth.

He accompanied me then to his own bedchamber. And in my weakened and humiliated state he took me to his bed. He spoke words to me then that opposed everything I had been hearing from his wife. He repeated again and again, in pleasing and simple statements, with a quiet masculine tenderness of voice, feeling words of my beauty, my radiance, my quality, and my worth.

He was pleasant looking enough, and he handled me with respectful refinement. And with desire that was undiluted—powerful and full. In spite of my undying love for my husband, in spite of all I held dear in my life, I was overcome. In the end, I joined him willingly.

To this hour, so many long years later, I yet wonder, can you ever forgive me, my beloved?

*   *   *

I said nothing to Ursunabi that night. But when he lay quietly breathing in sleep beside me, I recalled how once he fretted that I would take cold, when first we set out from Fa-Orszag.

I knew his concern that day was for the high price at which he hoped to sell me. I knew that such thinking was in his mind yet. Even, and especially, it was there when he entered me and when his sacred water flowed.

In the early morning I awoke in Ursunabi's bed, to the chatter and the song of birds. The trader had awakened first, and I opened my eyes to find him standing, combed and dressed, looking down upon me.

"Tonight is the night, Anarisha! Tonight! Tonight we present you to the priests," he smiled, "and perhaps a few householders who think they can compete!" He laughed. "And I do believe we are well-prepared! Your destiny is splendid: to bring joy and prosperity to the city of Orom!"

The sun was not long shining when Kerem arrived at the door of the house. I heard the sounding of the gong, and a scampering of the slave-children. Kerem was shown into Ursunabi's chamber, while I yet lay upon the bed. There is to be no end to my shaming, I realized, but no feeling came with the thought. For, oddly enough, and I knew not the reason, I was no longer, in truth, ashamed. Now I believe that this change occurred because I never ceased in my praying throughout those evil double-hours of my life, and the gods at last rewarded my persistence. Finally they returned to my life to give help. I found that on that morning, the powerful force of life was with me once again, stronger, perhaps, than it had ever been before. I no longer allowed myself to feel any shame; it was a simple matter of decision. Whatever was to befall me, undeserved shame was of no use. If I allowed it to come, I was very weak and very much a fool.

This change in me was, of course, just what Ursunabi and Kerem were wanting. A shameful woman would never inspire the desires of the priests. Ursunabi had successfully balanced the accomplishments of his wife. I was no longer degraded, only humble and obedient, and passive as a cow.

As I rose from my bed, Ursunabi took me by the hand.

"Come, my dear one, we are going to the bath," he smiled. "Kerem and I shall bathe you for this day."

"Yes," Kerem nodded agreeably to Ursunabi, "Our final parting gesture."

The bath chamber of Ursunabi was much larger than the chambers for Kukuda and her slaves; it was larger than three of our houses in Fa-Orszag. The bricks were highly polished and they shone with recent application of coloring, for the servants maintained constant fresh tint on all the walls and the floors of the house. The patterns on the bricks were of circles, spirals, and small flame-like shapes, in rose, deep blue, and bright jade-green, the same hues as most of the other rooms.

The chamber had six shining lapis-blue pots of great ferns, all perfectly kept, and fourteen—I counted them—pots of flowering plants, all in healthy bloom. The room was fragrant as a garden; the fragrance of the gardenia reigned. There were no furnishings except for three rose soapstone sitting stools clustered near the drain hole in the center of the floor.

Two youths with beards barely showing, stood in the room, holding several white cloths and two large jugs of water. Two more jugs and several smaller vessels sat on the floor at their feet.

Ursunabi and Kerem removed and folded their clothing. Each man took a jug from the boys, who took the clothing. Then the men themselves poured warm water upon me. Afterward they took the white cloths to dry me off. Next they took the aromatic oils from the small jars, carefully choosing, with some discussion, which scent they would apply to which part of my body. The fragrances were lush, beautiful. It was my first encounter with the ritual that would become my morning routine in the years to come, but performed by priestesses. They dried my hair with the white cloths and ran their fingers through to comb it, as though they were my sisters. And then they began to kiss me, Kerem with such enthusiasm and in so many places that finally Ursunabi intervened. He pulled me away by the hand. "You are very alluring, Anarisha," he said, with an appraising look devoid of all emotion save the crystalline sparkle of the hopeful eyes of a trader.

It was at this moment that I became suddenly dizzy. I sat down upon one of the stools, and immediately a strange thing happened. As though I were asleep, I dreamt.

A woman, in a cave, her hair wild, her face terrible, giving orders, "Take Her!" she is screaming to someone, "Take Her jewels, take Her lapis, take Her clothing—take everything, all of Her disguise. Each in proper order, you know what to do…"

I cry out. "No, Sister! This cannot be…"

"Silence Inanna! Thus it is ordained! Thus speaks Ereshkigal!"

I remembered her name clearly afterward. I had never heard the name until that hour, but I would hear it many times again.

*　　　　*　　　　*

Throughout that day the entire household was busy with preparation. The rooms became even more resplendent than before, with new additions of fine cedar furniture—exquisitely carved stools, small chairs, and serving tables; and many potted palms. These arrived from morning until late that afternoon. The servants hastened about, under perpetual direction from their mistress. All were in a quickened commotion, making ready for the banquet of the night.

The chief priestess of the Temple of Inanna and the other guests were to be served the finest, most delectable dinner ever to be offered by a householder of Orom. Or so Kukuda said. Some of the preparation was begun earlier, but most was accomplished that same day, beginning in the dawn.

I was occupied all that day in rehearsing the service of the meal and in rehearsing my dance. Kukuda and another woman, a famous dancer and a family acquaintance, had been training me in this dance since the morning after my arrival. Now a slave woman, loaned from the estate of another acquaintance, refined and perfected my movements. This woman was much kinder than either Kukuda or the famous dancer, but by this time it almost did not matter.

The guests began arriving at sunset. They were seated on mats at low cedar tables, all loaned by friends of Ursunabi. On fresh fig leaves, placed within large and small alabaster bowls decorated with images of lions serving fruit, we served the feast. The people were given four kinds of breads, warm from the oven; slices of roasted chicken, roasted lamb and roasted fish; three grains with herbs and leeks; delicacies of citrus fruit—lemon, loquat and orange; tender green lettuce leaves with spicy nasturtium petals; the honeyed cheese, the sweet goat's milk with butter-cakes; the nut-filled dates, the rose water and barley ale. I carried bowls and goblets to the men and women who were gathered in the house. Slave girls and boys assisted me. The guests, many of the men, and three of the women, reached out to touch or caress us as we served. I was unprotected, as in all those days, by any clothing, or by custom. I thought of you, my Anurei, my true protector, whom the gods struck to the ground.

Late that night, when dinner was finally finished, they left the servants and Kukuda in the house, to do the cleaning up. But as for me,

Ursunabi led me, at the head of his guests, to the principal courtyard. There came, just behind us, a boy who held a drum and a young man with a lute. This man looked upward at the stars then immediately began to make music, as soon as he was out the door. The breezes were warm and the melody was soft and sweet, much filled with melancholy.

Ursunabi took me by the hand to the brightest center of the moonlight, and told me to begin my dance.

✳   ✳   ✳

Anarisha danced. All were silent, but for the trader.

Standing against the wall, Ursunabi clasped the bony hand of the Chief Priestess, while he spoke to her in whispers. "You can see before you what you see, great Mother—but please allow me to point out a few subtleties. If you will. To bring all the nuances to your notice, Your Reverence. You see how the movement is so innocent, so childlike? Do you not agree? Graceful, soft, seductive. But without sophisticated artifice—a village girl, you see. From the northeast! Delicate bones—another sort of allure than our beauties possess, Your Reverence; she would be set apart for that alone. You see how the structure defines—" Ursunabi was going on, but the Chief Priestess put her finger to his lips. He ceased his talking and, like all the others, simply watched Anarisha dance. He watched her somberly, trying to rein his nervous passion.

When the dance was over he looked intently at the priestess.

"She has a touching sadness in her eyes. And purity," was all the old one had to say.

✳   ✳   ✳

The night when I stood before the "Important Ones" of Orom—Kerem had named them thusly—serving them their splendid feast in that great House of Ursunabi, watching them, in their garments of shimmering, beautifully crafted linen, as they gazed back upon me in my nakedness, during this night something altered deep inside my soul. Then I remembered Ma Agghia, and the sparkling river of which she once spoke.

In a few days the Chief Priestess of the Temple of Inanna would strip me even of my name—no more my "Anarisha." She would designate me "*Inannanindigur*" instead, Priestess to the Heavenly Queen. But before that ever was to happen, there was first this night. It was from those hours that I knew myself to be a *Woman Who Looks and Sees,* as we say in Fa-Orszag. The night of my dance; when I, Anarisha, gazed outward.

The stars were bright as tiny suns that night. But it was I who was the center of awareness, the center for all the eyes of the Important Ones. Eyes which gleamed with intelligence and power and "civilization," as Ursunabi named the thing which makes the people of Orom the way that they are; it is a thing for which I myself have no single word, but it contains a certain lack of clarity and has instead an arrogance, even in some of the most gentle of them. I gazed out at these "civilized" ones and they gazed back.

As I danced the dance called "*Mystery*" which the three women had taught me, I kept in mind the teaching of the slave woman who had come to me that day. It was the slave, not the famous dancer, and certainly not Kukuda, who most clearly showed me the meaning and the purpose of this dance, as she moved before me on that afternoon. My friend Kukuda never danced, she merely told me what to do.

I entered the spirit of the drum, and the spirit entered me. With only the mantle of the music of the lute, I moved before those people. I showed them all I have been given, all that is my own. And that which is more than my own, which can only be danced—the *Mystery*.

When all was finished, they were silent. I saw they had become at one, in peace with me. They were seeing as I see. No longer "civilized;" they had become, in some way, like villagers of Fa-Orszag. In truth, they were with me more than that; they were like you, my Anurei, or your father, ones who know the forest. Fully grown, they were, and some quite old, but on that night, in the silence after my dance, they seemed like village children. My children.

I could hear the crickets, and a soft breeze blew, caressing our faces. The starlight shone clear, piercing the soft sky of a full-moon night.

On the courtyard bricks, the Oromi people, more than twenty-five of them, sat gathered beneath me on their mats, careful of their fine clothing. They looked upward to me. As once I looked to my mother when she and the others danced. While I stood there, covered with moisture, breathing heavily, exhausted, but in peace, I could see in their faces, in their eyes, that they awaited something. They were hoping for loving comfort, and praying that I would speak.

But I do not speak as they speak. I was able, from the first, to make sense of the words of these people of Orom. Most words are the same as our own in Fa-Orszag. Yet it has never been possible for most of the Oromi to make sense of the statements I give to them. It is so to this very day, even now as I write, so many years later. (For I have waited long to tell of that night!) In truth, even now I do not form my words as the Oromi, and most of the people can understand nearly nothing of what I say. But I understand the Oromi, all the words they speak, no matter how odd the voice. Many know not that I understand. (And so, Anurei, you can see, my love, how in this fine city of Orom sometimes there does come a time for laughter.)

*   *   *

I saw before me that night many kinds of souls. Some were happy souls, bright and fun loving. There were those who were despairing, dissatisfied, confused. Some were intense, ever-seeking, ambitious and complex.

There was one soul among them who was blissfully serene. It was this one who compelled me, at last, to gaze upon only her, she who was Chief Priestess of the Temple of the Queen.

And it was this one who, on the following day, for twenty-one pieces of gold, each much larger than the two that Ursunabi and Kerem had given to Fa-Orszag, was to purchase me from the traders. That I should fulfill the sacred office of High Priestess to the Lady Inanna: Inanna, Goddess of the Morning and the Evening Star, the Guardian of Serenity for the Eternal Protected Kingdom of the City of Orom.

Part III

Mystery

1

The White Robe and the Tree

east of San Francisco
June, 1963 A.D.

"By the river, by the marshlands,
She found a struggling tree.
And the maid Inanna knew:
The huluppu needed care.

So she took the little tree
To the orchards of her home.
One day the tree would thank her
And provide her throne and bed."
—from *The Twenty-One Hymns of Orom*

She rose from her bed almost as soon as she awoke. Dreamily she undressed, folding her blue Rayon baby-doll pajamas and placing them neatly under her pillow. Then she went to the closet and took her white Velveteen robe, cherishing its softness, the snowy perfection. It was brand new, her father's graduation gift. Without glancing in the mirror, she savored herself in the robe, half-consciously sensing her own beauty, as if it were a mood. She thought of her unpretentious, sometimes exasperating father.

In the bathroom before showering she washed her face with orange blossom lotion. Its fresh scent flowed through her morning happiness. Then after she had showered she smoothed upon her shoulders another fragrant potion, a gift from her mother, solid gardenia perfume in a pretty rose-hued jar. The gift was inexpensive. But her mother had driven all the way to San Francisco, a cause for nervous anxiety, in order to purchase it. Maria loved such jars of jelled perfume. She had always begged for them, always gardenia, since she was a child, whenever the family went to Chinatown, the only place that they were sold. An overwhelming glow of love for both her mother and her father overcame her as she again put on her robe.

She went down the stairs to breakfast, dreamy with that glow. But she didn't speak to her mother as Ellen passed hot chocolate. Her thoughts were moving on.

What does he want of me, anyway? Does he actually want me for his girlfriend? Or has he something else in mind? He wants to make love a few times, then he's tried me? And then he's tired of me. Is that what a man like him does? She pondered this question, aware of *Emma Bovary*, another second hand sophisticate. Like Emma she possessed an abundant experience of novels. Also, movies, popular songs, plays and musicals, a couple of operas, and television (with lots of *Ovid*, besides). But none of that was for real, nothing of her own. She knew the truth was that she knew nothing, or next to nothing. *I have to just think that the best is about to come, for both of us…Now that I see I have him. Now that I see how he wants me. All that urgency I've been feeling, I almost think it's beginning to disappear. There's none of the usual intensity, not this morning. I wonder if I even still love him? It's almost like I just feel sympathy— maybe compassion?* and for awhile, as she often did, she absorbed herself in analyzing which word most aptly fit.

"Maria, you look lost in space." Her mother's voice was hoarse, and filled with waking grumpiness. "How 'bout starting your vacation right for a change by helping me with chores? Since you haven't found a job. You could begin with these dishes and then mow the lawn and do some vacuuming."

Maria's glow disappeared, but she was relieved to find, by the time she began the vacuuming, that her familiar longing for Jean Romier had returned, strong and perfectly intact.

*   *   *

When she arrived at the campus fountain the following Monday, she was late, and he wasn't there. She asked someone where the restroom was; the girl pointed back to the student union.

As she walked toward the building, a middle-aged man, possibly a professor, passed by and exclaimed, "Good Morning!" She found herself blushing, because of the look in his eyes as he saw her, and the tone of his voice. She was still recovering as she passed a large group of boys. One of them called out, "Hey! Where are you going?" She glanced his way and saw that the entire group was staring. She felt caught and helpless, though she liked their attention. Another of them yelled, "Want me to come along?—Aww, don't turn red on me!"

There was raucous laughter and she wished she could evaporate into the morning fog. She hurried to the steps of the student union. "Hey, you looked cute that way!" trailed after, as she left the group behind. At the door she nearly bumped into someone going the other way. This boy smiled, a nice big brotherly kind of smile, and she smiled too, grateful he was giving back the poise which had been taken.

Before she entered the building she looked behind, to the fountain, to check again if Mr. Romier might be arriving. There was, in fact, someone who looked like him. She rushed into the building to find the restroom. But when she hurried back out again to the fountain, the man was gone. Maybe he thought she'd already left; it was getting so late.

The fog had lifted, the Campanile bells were chiming noon, and the day was becoming hot. She waited twenty minutes more, a sick feeling in her stomach, but still he never showed.

Finally she walked through Sather Gate and up to College Avenue to catch the bus, the two long bus rides home. All the way to Castro Valley she wondered if it had been wise to leave the campus. She pondered the possibility that she would never hear from him again. If he, who had never called her, would even be able to call her—how would he know the number? It wasn't listed; her wary parents kept it to themselves.

She felt terrible. And she marveled how, just a few days before, she had imagined that all she felt for him was sympathy.

*   *   *

That night around eight o'clock the phone rang. Pete Ananin answered, then he yelled, "Hey Maria, baby, it's for you! It's a man!" He returned to his recliner chair and the "Perry Como" rerun he was watching. It did not occur to Pete that he might have embarrassed his daughter. He only thought, *What's that jerk calling her now for? This is no hour to be calling a girl about a job!*

Maria, humiliated, heaved a sigh, and came out of her room. *Oh, please God, don't let it be him.* How could her father yell that way?

She went downstairs to the only phone in the house. It sat on a small table just outside the living room, where her father was sitting.

"Hello? Oh, hi!" She sat down on the little chair. "Oh, no, it's O.K., really. I—Oh, no. I had to leave for a few minutes. I guess so. Right, yes. I thought that might have happened. Day after tomorrow? But I have a job interview. In San Francisco. A receptionist. In a disc jockey school!" she laughed, suddenly amused at the thought of being surrounded all day by people who were trying to sound like disc jockeys, "Oh, you do? Nine-thirty? Yes, that would be nice. Yes, me, too! Good-bye!"

She hung up the phone and rested her chin on her hands, her elbows on the table, rerunning the conversation through her mind. It was good, it had felt right. Then she remembered her father, sitting so close by. But she had spoken very softly, and the TV was going loud and strong; she was certain her father hadn't heard her. Everything was fine. She went back to the words of the conversation. Who had sounded more intense and excited—*Mr. Romier? Or me?*

"Who was that Maria?" Her father's voice came booming, like a radio announcer, into her thoughts.

"Oh, just a guy I was supposed to meet this morning about a job." That was pretty much the truth.

"Well, what the hell did he call you now for? It's past eight o'clock! He should have phoned hours ago. Not a good sign, honey. That's not someone you should hook yourself up with…" And her father's voice drifted away as the television again seized his mind.

In bed she thought happily of Wednesday. For Mr. Romier was going to meet her at the fountain and drive her to "The City," to her interview. In his chocolate colored car, maybe with the top down. His jazz on the radio. Her hair, and his hair, blowing in the wind. And his hand…*maybe like last time?*

It's strange, she thought sleepily, *this summer it feels as though the hours are moving more slowly the longer the daylight lasts…*" She gazed out her bedroom window.

Suddenly she thought of something that sent her scurrying out of bed. She grabbed her white robe and wrapped herself in it, running quietly, barefoot, down the stairs, out the back door, over the soft wet lawn to the garden corner beneath her room. There, in the filigreed moonlight, she could discern the silhouette of her own much treasured lemon tree. The little tree was a gift from her parents, the year before, for her sixteenth birthday; her mother and father had known very well exactly what would please her. They had taken her to choose the tree, to a nursery in Hayward. Then all three had planted it together. Now she cared for it, watered it, fed it, mulched it, watched it thrive and grow. It was in bloom this summer for the first time.

Those Beautiful Eyes

She ran to the lemon tree and gently pulled a branch of blossoms to her face. As in the morning, delicious fragrance flowed into her being, blending with her bliss.

2

Fascination

Oakland
the next evening

"It's Almost Like Being in Love"
—a popular mid-20th Century song

"Sometimes, once in awhile, unrecognized, unacknowledged, teachers come into your life, and they show you something, not necessarily intentionally. Something important. Then they pass on, finished. They come and they go." Mei Wong looked down at her half-finished martini.

Jean-Marc stared at Mei's shiny dark hair, slightly disheveled it was now, for Mei, that was. Her hair fell a little over her shoulders as she leaned forward. It fell in glowing waves, a magic to it. Just like everything about her, he thought. Such a special quality she possesses, of something,—of what? He'd never been sure.

I'm sorry, what was that you just said, Mei?" he asked, "I didn't hear you, I guess my mind was wandering."

"I was telling you good-bye."

"Oh, you're leaving?" his voice was caring. "But what was that you said about teachers?"

"Nothing Jean. Nothing. You know, I think we always did have trouble listening to each other."

He stood up from the sofa. As he helped her with her jacket he leaned down to her. "You're right, I suppose. You and I are in two different worlds. It's just how it is. But the way you are, Mei—you have a lot of magic. Promise me you'll never change too much. Okay?"

"The song says it shouldn't matter," she said, no feeling in her words. "You know, 'two worlds' and all that."

"No, actually I don't think I do know. What song are you referring to?"

"Oh, never mind, Jean," now her voice was quicker, sharper. "It's not important. I'm leaving now. Thanks again. For everything." She adjusted her purse strap on her shoulder. "I learned a great deal, I think. Everything will be fine in the end, I'm sure. Good-bye Jean-Marc. Have a good life. Enjoy."

She went down the apartment stairs, looking a little business-like, as she often did, in her light-blue linen dress and jacket. Then she walked down the block to her car, in a daze. A part of her noted that the feeling was not much different from the way she had felt just after her sister's funeral, three years before. It wasn't grief she'd experienced, not then, and not now—that would come later. For now there was just that deep calmness, with the pain still somewhere distant, only hinted at in the thought that what was happening just could not be. And that there was nothing, absolutely nothing, she could, or would, be able to do about it.

*   *   *

He was having second thoughts. About the drive to San Francisco. Wouldn't it lead, he asked himself, down a much too predictable direction? Not the route he was presently taking with Maria Ananin, with the painting situation.

He was beginning to realize that his fantasy of becoming intimate with this girl while painting her portrait had subversively transformed itself. It was now quite different from what he had intended at the start.

It had to some extent moved out of his control. Gradually he had become more and more involved, not with his end, but with his means.

The act of painting her was, to be certain, what now preoccupied him, a goal in and of itself. For days he had been filled with fantasies of how it would be to have her sitting there, slight and tender, a little afraid, yet with a young and healthy power, in the nude before him. His thoughts had gone down various paths, creating visions of various subsequent scenarios.

He sat down at his kitchen table, got up again, paced a little and then began to do his dishes. It seemed to him that if he drove Maria to San Francisco as planned, and home again, with some hours in between, they would end up feeling, inevitably, cozy and much more acquainted with each other. Sentiment would overcome; it would be easy to suppose they were in love. As opposed to happily lusting after each other, which was what it had been, he thought, until now.

On the other hand, if he did not take her to San Francisco, never took her anywhere, in fact, but simply painted her, one painting after another, never meeting for any other reason, wouldn't something quite different occur? Something less prosaic, and more undilutedly erotic?

For a moment, as he searched for the dishtowel, his preference for fascination seemed to him debased, more cat-like than human, and he felt a twinge of self-doubt. But then he thought, *So what?* So he preferred intrigue to the commonplace. That was simply a tendency he had developed.

No doubt half the world feels as I do, he assured himself, *if they're honest, they even admit it. And the other half needs the security of love. It's all understandable."* Unfortunately, it was not in his nature for the more balanced, expanded notion to occur that someone might want, and have, a life that included both satisfactions. Then, again, maybe he was afraid.

*   *   *

He wasn't driving her to San Francisco.

Maria put down the receiver and went to her room. She put her new recording of Albeniz and Lizt concertos on the phonograph and lay down on her bed, burying her face in her pillow, feeling empty and forlorn, though the beauty of the music poured through her.

The next morning she canceled the San Francisco interview. She had not slept all night and was in no shape to have a stranger, let alone a self-confident disc jockey instructor, pass his judgment on her. Besides, she told herself, if she did get hired, the commute by bus would be much too long.

She had done a lot of thinking in the night.

She picked up the phone again and called Mr. Romier. Then she canceled their meeting, too, claiming her interview was rescheduled for that day. Hanging up, she couldn't tell if she felt better or worse.

*   *   *

But eventually they did meet again, and again, always now at his apartment. It was on the third visit that he once again stated his well-remembered request.

She complied. In his tiny, immaculate bathroom, she removed all of her clothing, hanging her things on the same hook as his navy blue terry-cloth bathrobe. She stared at the clothing for several seconds, talking herself into composure, which came with unexpected ease, smoothly, without wavering. Then she walked into the living room, where he was waiting with his drawing pad and charcoal. He was looking down at the pad as she entered.

When he looked up, he said nothing. His eyes were wide, like an excited child, and she thought, *I'm making him happy.*

She watched as his moment of dream-becoming-reality suspended itself. Then he made a gesture. "Here, Maria," he said seriously, motioning down toward his carpet, "Please sit here. Make yourself comfortable." And he too sat down upon the rug.

He did not speak a word as he sketched her that day. When he was finished he murmured a quiet thank you. As she was walking out the door, he said only, "Again, thank you, Maria. I'll call you soon."

When she was gone, he sat down at his piano. After several minutes had passed he began to play the somewhat aggressive and agitated composition which he himself had lately been composing. But he stopped after only three or four chords. He got up and went to the drawings, carefully gathered them, and brought them to his kitchen table. Then he sat there, looking at those sketches of Maria Ananin for a time which was so long and so lost that when he finally became distracted with hunger pangs, and glanced out his window at the darkened sky, he wondered where the day had gone.

*   *   *

Maria, using her fork to pattern the peas upon her dinner plate, supposed that she was happy. But the never-ending questions inside her kept asking, in several ways, *What is this, I've begun?*

*   *   *

She ran in the shadows of the afternoon streets and sidewalks, up the hill, past the grade school, past the neighborhoods where suburban developments ended and country farms began. She sped by spacious, puddled grasslands, past long, old, ranch houses with winding driveways and white-fenced horse corrals. A cool wind in her face and a hearty barking of dogs gave a glorious awareness that she was escaping from the confusion of her own thoughts.

Then she walked, until she passed beyond the last paved road. She found herself in tall-grassed meadows of a still older incarnation of the town, midst birds calling to each other from gnarled, ancient oaks and thick blackberry brambles. She thought of Artemis passing through glades and woods and glades again.

In the distance, in the dusk, she could see the silhouettes of a gathering of cows upon a hill. This world is the truer world, she thought, but what about the other? As she pushed her way through the sharp grasses, not caring that they sometimes cut her skin, she felt safe in this wilder place. Here nothing was at fault, unlike the world she lived in, of phones that rang, or didn't—either causing confusion—and people who, out of some incomprehensible ignorance, had to make up complicated games, forcing you to play. And you played, trapped, because you couldn't help yourself.

No, she didn't seem to care much for romance, nor other "once-removed dramas," as she named what she thought was going on. People who wanted each other had no good reason not to get on with pure ecstasy, to let it happen, she was sure.

I do like having desire, and I like to feel it grow, at least for awhile. But then, isn't it best, eventually, to fulfill it?

It was almost dusk when she returned. She did not call Jean-Marc to cancel their next appointment, as she had planned. It seemed best not to do anything at all. She lay awake for most of the night, gazing toward the slow, imperceptible setting of a solitary star; she watched it through her bedroom window, at one with the cold bright sparkling in the night.

3

Invasion

Oakland
October, 1963

> "Inanna cared for her tree,
> Yearning for her throne,
> Yearning for her bed.
>
> But there came a certain serpent.
> Deep within the roots,
> That power-creature nested.
> Next flew there the Imdugud.
> High in the huluppu the bird settled all its young.
> Now came the shadow woman Lilith—
> To lie within the tree!
>
> And so Inanna wept.
> The young Inanna wept!
> Long did Inanna weep!
> But none of those invaders
> Made move to leave from there."
>
> —from *The Twenty-One Hymns of Orom*

She sat at the kitchen table as he made charcoal sketches of her feet. Just her feet for now, though he had asked her to remove all of her clothing. Soon he would be moving on, sketching more.

This was the first chance in three weeks that she had found the time to come to him. She was always busy. When she compared herself with her happy-go-lucky, "soshey" roommate, she wondered if she was too much of a perfectionist, studying too much, and too much alone. At least she had a roommate now. For two weeks there was none—for unknown reasons the dormitory never assigned her anybody. But Rosie Hestia, a girl down the hall, soon requested a change. Rosie was from Castro Valley, too, and she pleaded for Maria to come to room with her, to replace the "disastrously mismatched" girl they "stuck me with."

On the rare occasions when Maria did join her new roommate in fooling around—in the roughhousing, pillow-fighting and teasing that went on perpetually between Rosie and the other girls of Eighth Floor—she didn't get so tired. But she would feel guilty. Then, too, her hours of homework were increased by the difficulty of keeping her mind on her books. Her thoughts ran constantly to Jean-Marc. The effort to focus, she supposed, added to the fatigue she felt so often. Many evenings she would struggle, and fail, to stay awake. Sometimes, she'd fall asleep before eight, dozing until the pile of heavy texts came crashing from the bed down to the floor to waken her again.

*   *   *

Jean-Marc's window was open. The warm early autumn breezes drifted through the lacy curtain and played with Maria's hair, which Jean had loosened from its band. The moment was still as he looked back and forth between his sketching and her feet.

Rodrigo's Concerto de Aranjuez, playing on the hi-fi in the bedroom, united with the cozy intensity in the kitchen. The music filled the balmy October evening, an "Indian summer" evening, bringing suggestions of exotic landscapes, palm-filled oases, or shadowy courtyard gardens of a moonlit Spanish night. She loved this music; he seemed to always to play it. She was so near to him, so relaxed, enough to reach out and run her fingers through his soft, fine hair, to touch him on the back of his neck. She could have done that, she imagined, and he would have made no move, just continued with his sketching. Except for adjustments of her posing, he never touched her, never tried.

Suddenly the doorbell buzzed loudly. Both of them froze. Whoever it was aggressively pushed the buzzer several times more. Then there was shouting.

"Hey you up there! Romier! Let us in! It's me—Steven! I know you're home!" the visitor's voice came through the open window, invading like a criminal intent on doing evil, "I can see your f—ing Alfa right in front of me." The loud volume of the rough voice crashed into the Concerto, interrupting its climactic crescendo, and expected ecstasy.

Jean moved quickly to peer down. "Be quiet, Steven, for heaven's sake! I have neighbors!" He hissed loudly out his window. Maria saw that the back of his neck was crimson with emotion. She had never before seen him so angry, not even in the French class, when every so often somebody forgot he was in charge.

The visitor was yelling more. "What the hell is with you, Jean? You were supposed to be at Blake's two hours ago!"

"Oh Good Lord, I forgot!" Jean-Marc looked back at Maria.

The yelling from below continued. "You're the one who set it up! In the first place! Now press your f—ing buzzer and let us in!"

There were four of them in the station wagon. Jean watched as Steven motioned for everybody to get out. Then he turned around to Maria. "They're coming up," he said helplessly, "Quick, go get your clothes on!"

"Why doesn't he think of something?" she wondered as she rushed to the bathroom. It wasn't necessary to invite these rude men to come up. What was the matter with him? She tried to imagine what he could say to send them away, as she rapidly buttoned her blouse. But before she returned to the kitchen they had already entered and were filling the apartment with themselves and their odors of sweat and cigarettes and beer.

"Well, well, well, and what have we here?" the man named Steven beamed in surprise as she entered. She felt a little sick to her stomach.

"Let me introduce you," said Jean irritably. "Maria these gentlemen are basketball acquaintances of mine. *Mes amis,* this is Maria Ananin." She caught a look of pride pass over his scowl for an instant.

The men stared intently in silence at the exquisitely pretty—and sullen—seventeen-year-old now standing beside Jean Romier. Her golden brown hair was long and wavy and shining. It was not "ratted" and not lacquered—unlike the hair of the wives of the men. Her skin looked flawless and seemed to be without make-up. She was not—extraordinarily, in 1963—even wearing lipstick. A thin white shirt and khaki skirt allowed them to envision a body that was both lush and delicate. *Incredible...*thought Steven grumpily, *Leave it to Romier.* They all remained silent.

Three of them were smiling and two scowled, like Jean.

Finally someone muttered a "Nice to meet you, Maria." This man, a man with decent-looking eyes, introduced himself as Ben and apologized for the yelling.

"Your friend here arranged a basketball practice for seven, young lady. But he never showed."

"We've been sitting at Blake's all night," mumbled one of the less friendly, turning to Jean. "Why didn't you answer your phone?" he demanded, then made a slight smirk, as if the reason now was obvious.

"You should have gone on without me," said Jean coldly.

"We were being considerate."

"So what do you want now?" Jean made no attempt to hide his impatience.

"Why don't we just stay right here and party?" suggested Steven looking again at Maria.

She thought she saw an odd expression suddenly, a satisfaction, pass over Jean's face for a fraction of a second, then the frown was back.

"I'm taking Maria home," he suddenly said, and immediately ushered them out. He motioned to Maria to get her purse from the table, then he led her, trailing the group, down the stairs. He drove her home, speeding, without conversation, but apologized for his "ill-mannered friends" as he dropped her at the dormitory grounds. Then he waved a good-bye from his window and sped away, his eyes on the road ahead, new thoughts suddenly filling his head.

She walked into her room in a daze. But nevertheless she noticed that her roommate Rosie, stretched out on the bed, was reading a letter. Another letter from her fiancé, no doubt. Maria heaved a deep sigh, without considering the cause.

4

A Fertility Rite

Orom
circa 2700 B.C.

Once each new moon, on the *Day of Inanna*, they walked her to the public plaza of the temple, where three great pools of water caught the light of early dawn.

In strict procession the lesser priestesses came following, hand in hand. Formally the priestesses came, in a line, wearing only honeysuckle blossoms in their hair, with simple strands of carnelian encircling their wastes. But on the head of the high priestess was an elaborate gold and lapis lazuli headdress—an intricate wreathe of golden leaves and bright blue inlaid berries. Decorating her ears were large and heavy rings of finely polished copper.

She alone entered the largest pool, while the lesser priestesses quietly remained, standing in their traditional choreographed formation of "*anna*," the "cluster of dates," before the wall. In slow formality she entered the clear blue water and then walked, immersed to the calves, to the center of the pool. There the cascade of a magnificent fountain embraced the golden light of the sun in a sparkling celebration that reached upward to the sky and back to earth again.

In the years that passed, the ritual never changed and always, over the years, when she gazed upon the cascading water, she marveled.

Momentarily she would forget the crowds of devotees who stood watching her, in dawn adoration, as the morning of the new moon began.

The Oromi people, who worked throughout the daylight hours of all their days, gave devotion in the midst of life. The first day of the moon, as well as the myriads of other holy days, was honored during the spaces just before duties and just after—those beautiful double-hours of time when nothing must get done, and a man or a woman can be as free as any child. Except of course, for slaves.

*   *   *

"She removes and passes her headdress to a priestess, then enters the pool and walks calf-deep toward the fountain. Beneath the fountain she descends to a simple kneeling position, as though coming to sit at the feet of her father. Quickly she reaches for the clay disk at the center of the fountain pipe, while the water falls upon her, as if she were a cow maid of the hills, watching, unprotected, while the rains come pouring down.

The cascade ceases. Now the chanting of the devotees breaks the silence of the early dawn…

The merchants, the housewives, the lawyers, even the servants, already on their way from one errand to another, blend their personal mantras with the mantras of young virgins of both sexes, and with the chanting voices of elder supplicants who recite more ancient verses certain to please their Queen.

All watch as Inanna-nin places her vulva before the phallus of the fountain.

Further down she eases herself, down upon the tiles of the pool. She reclines now in the water. Resting on her forearms, her feet firmly planted and knees raised upward, she tilts back her head. Long streaming locks of copper-black hair, abundant and glowing, spread upon the surface of the water as the sun lights both her belly and her throat. And the fountain flow—now coming forth in a single unity, a torrent of power that comes from the clay, rushing forth to meet her thighs—now it caresses and shapes her flesh. With living force, the water pushes upon her waiting loins.

Such is the New Moon *ceremony of Orom.*

She reclines there in the water, dutiful priestess, in the position which the temple teachers have shown her, while Enki, God of Water, of Wisdom, of Semen, and of Time, bestows His ecstasy.

Inannanindigur, she who is the living embodiment of Love, of Beauty, of Prosperity, of War and of Peace, receives. And we who adore her receive, as well, together.

(The great ones of Orom, and those who make journeys, are convinced that no foreign city possesses a High Priestess who can compare. The ordinary citizens know no other; her predecessors have been forgotten.)

The gushing water, hard and strong and very warm, comes upon her, enters the waiting vulva of the Queen. As the water of Enki caresses, rushes upon her, excites her with its gentle and powerful force, the people watch, each in trance of ecstasy themselves. Those men or women who beg and pray to the Queen of Heaven to give them babies or to find them love, those who are diseased or lacking in prosperity, those whose small city vegetable gardens or orchards do not thrive, now step forward, over the wall, to join her in the water. Staying close to the pool's edge, they raise their voices in joy-filled chants of gratitude and adoration. They direct their song toward Inanna-nin, but they pray, as well, in their hearts, to he who embodies the Husband. Dumuzi the Shepherd, Beloved of the Goddess.

Dumuzi, too, has his human incarnation. It is the King of Orom, Asimbabar Himself. But the King is not with us this morning. Only on one singular day of the year, on the First Day, *can we know that greater rite. Then the water of Enki will enter the vulva of Inanna through the true phallus—the organ of Orom's own King.*

As for now, the day of the New Moon, we have the holy foaming water, and the clay facsimile. Many are the duties of Asimbabar; we must be practical. Until that holiest of days, the citizens must take their Spirit of Love and Prosperity only from the Lady and the Water. Thus we receive our Power which is the Gods' to give. Thus is Orom made joyful and fer-tile, in our loins, in our hearts, and in our homes!—from the tablets of Gudea of Orom.

*　　　　　　*　　　　　　*

When her time of fulfillment came, and she herself gave not a thought to Dumuzi, not to the king, but rather to the village man whom she had left behind her in that home so far away, the crowd of devotees took up a single chant. Always this chant was the same, a praise created long ago, time out of mind, the chant of the first *Great Mother*. The merchants, the housewives, the lawyers and the scribes all joined their voices with those of the slaves, the virgins, the supplicants, the priests of Enki and the priestesses of Inanna. And in the end, Inanna-nin herself raised her own voice, joining with the throng.

Then she rose, departing from the "pool of holy waters." Her priest-esses followed, hand in hand. Young voices chatting softly now, they strolled down the narrow palm-lined walkway, returning through their temple's jeweled and shining gate.

5

Mystery

east of San Francisco
late October, 1963

> "Mankind when created did not know of bread for eating or garments for wearing. The people walked with limbs on the ground, they ate herbs with their mouths like sheep, they drank ditch-water"
>
> —from a Sumerian hymn, as quoted in *The Sumerians*
> by C. Leonard Wooley

The most ancient spiritual teachings have in them, if nothing else, if no literal, fundamental knowledge of cosmic divinity, as some still say they do, at least another revelation. They infer, inevitably, the knowledge which humanity once sensed directly, purely from instinct. For the world's ancient scriptures were born in days that were nearer to the days when our ancestor, a being something like a monkey, was so much more instinctual, up there swinging in the trees. Swinging in the trees, while fully sensing the love and beauty and wisdom in the universe, as well as the terror and the pain, whenever those aspects showed forth.

But in a latter day, in a time when millions no longer owned old teachings to hold onto, and instincts lay buried beneath millennia of biased training and acculturation, minds and lives began to slip off course. It was with confused desperation that humanity reached then for wisdom—much like slippery-handed monkeys grasping at elusive, muddy branches while floating down a raging river in a terrible time of flood.

*　　　　*　　　　*

Maria's art history class was an introduction to the great art of all times. It began with prehistory. The animals of the *Caves at Lascaux*. The *Venus at Willendorf*. The *Ritual Dance of the Caves of Addaura*. Maria doodled the Venus' pregnant-looking body in the margins of her notebooks. All her notebooks, not just art history. She added cartoon-like eyes, nose and smile to her Venus's face, hoping that the face she discerned in the book was not just an illusion of random indentations.

The *Ritual Dance of Addaura* intrigued her. For the twelve thousand-year-old figures seemed to be doing a dance which she knew. The positions were remarkably similar to the *kahiko*, a dance she had just recently observed. She had even attempted to dance it herself. One cave figure was doing the step called the "*hela*"—Hawaiian for "arm stretch." The cave figure bent at the waist and placed his arms exactly in the hela position.

Her new friend, Marta, had placed her arms that way, the night she performed the sacred Hawaiian dance. An expert in classic ethnic dances, Jean-Marc's ex-mother-in-law had danced for Jean and Maria late one Friday night. She'd appeared unexpectedly at Jean's apartment, on her way home from teaching a class. She stayed a while, demonstrating some simple steps and postures. Studying the photograph of the dancing figures of Addaura, Maria could almost hear Jean-Marc beating on Marta's gourd drum—the "*epu*," Marta called it.

Maria read and reread the questions which scholars asked about the figures in the caves. And she added questions of her own. Were the figures depicting the use of dance for attaining a union with all Nature? As the Hawaiians had danced? Did the Addauran dances move in harmony with the Gods? With the *Tao*? Or The Father, or Mother—or whatever the ancient Addauran artists had called the central power of Reality? (Jean-Marc, who had no religion, optimistically called it *"joie de vivre."*) She wondered, as she often did, if all those different words, which since childhood had confused her, didn't simply point to different aspects of the same thing, the ineffable something which she herself thought of, more and more, as the *"Mystery."*

*   *   *

Oakland
Late October, 1963

She is mystified. She cannot understand what he is trying to tell her. Something is up. She asks herself if other girls ever have this confusion reading a man's mood, the trouble she is having tonight. She thought she knew him better. But this evening she barely recognizes his voice on the phone. And interpreting his meaning is impossible. It could be, she supposes, that he intends to be unclear. For some peculiar reason…

She presses the buzzer—#116. He takes longer than usual to respond, but in a few seconds there is a short buzz. As she opens the door to the building, she glances up at his second story window. Sometimes he's right there, smiling down. But not tonight.

She goes up the old, dirty stairwell. The carpeting is patchy, stained, in horrible condition. Jean's apartment is definitely tasteful, but the building is unpleasant, rather decrepit. *It's depressing*, she thinks. An old, musty smell, mixed with something like overboiled broccoli, permeates the hall.

He's not waiting in the hallway to greet her, as he often is. She knocks at his door and waits.

But then he's with her, giving a kiss on each cheek, as always, smiling, taking her by the arm, leading her to the kitchen. He seats her at his table.

"I have something I want to talk over with you, Maria. Would you care for something to drink? A little wine, perhaps? Red? White? Something else?" She chooses red and he rises to get some burgundy, the glasses, a corkscrew. He doesn't speak while he bustles about, and she begins to feel a little nervous, not the way she usually feels in his kitchen. Usually it's so relaxing, coming to him. She notices and regards a tiny orange stain on his white tablecloth.

Finally, as he pours the wine for each of them, he comes to the point. "I've invited some other people." Now she becomes aware of the soft slow jazz coming from another room. Not his usual classical music, but the music he likes when he drives—pleasant music, also.

"Invited some other people?" she echoes his words.

"A few, yes. My photography group. Kind of a club. You met one of them the other night—Ben, remember? A few weeks ago. Nice fellow, don't you think?"

She stares at him for a moment. "Yes, I suppose so. I only saw him for a minute. But yes, he did seem nicer than some of your other friends." She doesn't want to sound rude or edgy, but her feelings about that Friday cannot be disguised. And why should she bother to try, anyway? His friends, for the most part, were crude, obnoxious.

"Well, it's not the same people, tonight, except for Ben. Yes, I agree, they were terrible. I'm sorry Maria. It was bad for you, was it? No, these people are quite another sort. Much more cerebral. You'll like them, I know. Quiet, well-behaved people."

Her wineglass is still nearly full to the top, but he pours some more burgundy, and more for himself. The buzzer sounds.

And now the guests are filing in, first two, introductions, the buzzer again, one more, the buzzer, another man, introductions. "Everybody's here." No one is late. They're all men. *He invited no women?* Maria notes their expressions, their movements, their clothing. Their jackets; the fabric, the cut, all the jackets are casual, yet costly, definitely more expensive than what her father, or Jean, would buy. And the men's voices…they're so obviously comfortable with each other; they must know each other well. Jean was correct. These people are more subdued, more reserved. More subtle.

She does not feel wary, not the way she did that night, with the basketball players, but, rather, she feels curious.

He offers them drinks. Rum? Scotch? Vodka? He mixes something for someone, then brings the wine, pours a little more for her. She takes a sip and goes to the couch to sit down. She glances out the window. The moon is orange and full, moonlight is on the lake.

The men are talking politics. Someone speaks of something called the "Trilateral Commission." Then it's the resignations of MacMillan and Adenauer. Kennedy's visit with MacMillan. It seems that one man, a boyish looking guy with red hair and beard, actually attended grammar school with Bobby Kennedy. This fellow goes on and on, too much. He says "I" and "me" constantly. They talk of the Freedom March. "It will only have a marginal effect," the redhead says firmly. Silently, over in her corner, she disagrees. Now two of the men are arguing. About the record album Jean is playing. One claims John Coltrane is with Miles Davis on "Someday My Prince Will Come," the other insists he isn't. Someone else analyzes the "quality of Jean's sound," and they discuss "stereophonic equipment." The redhead owns this latest improvement. He talks about his "*woofer*," and Maria suppresses a giggle. Then he guides the talk back to himself, his recent move from Washington. "The culture is superior in D.C. So much history. Absolutely great for the kids!" He laughs at the effect the *Mona Lisa* had on his nine-year-old; "—on loan to the Smithsonian—the sixth time I've seen her," he informs them. "'*Daddy, the lady stared at me from another time,*' that's what my Sherry—" Someone interrupts to defend the "cultural richness" of San Francisco.

She tires now of the conversation and concentrates instead on the music, which is mesmerizing. When she notices the men again, it is Ben, the man she recognized, who is the center of attention. He draws graceful lines with his hands and arms, pulling the others into talk of time and space, galaxies and light years, and *quasars*. She likes the sound of the words, and she likes Ben's voice. She listens curiously to those phrases she can catch from her distance on the couch.

Gradually, the entire group becomes louder, dissecting the politics of San Francisco, where, it turns out, most of them are from. One lives in Tiburon, the Marin County suburb, but he knows as much as the rest about the "byzantine intricacies" of The City. Even Jean seems to know, or at least he does an adequate job of faking it. The conversation is moving too fast for her now—subjects and people she herself knows nothing or virtually nothing about, with little interest in finding out. She'd be more at home if they were talking about the Roman Empire, in the reign of Marcus Aurelius. She stops listening and begins to focus on their gestures, the body language, the faces.

Jean has the heat turned up high. Everyone is growing warm. Almost all of them have removed their jackets. Maria feels relaxed with her perpetually filled wineglass in her hand. No one seems to pay her much attention, except for Jean, coming over now and then to fill her glass, and to give her a pat or an uncustomary stroke on the cheek. Nor does anyone expect anything out of her. She sits curled up in a corner on the couch, passively, as if she were a cat. The jazz, something Brazilian now, soothes and nourishes. At least two of these men are, her inner voice affirms, definitely attractive, and one especially so.

All of them appear to be nice enough, even the self-promoting redhead ("just insecure," she tells herself). Now that the discussion is settling on books and theater, it's more intelligible. Absorbed completely with their talk, she finally finishes her wine. She rises from the couch and goes to the kitchen. For the first time in her life, she mixes a drink, rum and coke, as she has seen Jean do it. Jean suddenly, instinctively, turns his head toward the kitchen. Out of the corner of his eye, he watches her. He turns a little more, smiles to himself, then returns his attention to the talk.

She goes back to the couch, nestles in and sips tentatively. She's made the drink too strong. She can taste strong rum. But she keeps on sipping regardless; actually she likes the taste. The jazz is delicious, too. She feels delicious. It feels good to be here tonight, so relaxing…

Now one man leaves the standing cluster. He comes to sit beside Maria. He has barely given his name when a second man arrives and stands beside them. The second tries to make conversation. It goes awkwardly; she has no response to his comment about the "travesty" of "leaving you alone over here." The two men don't know what to say next, either. But now the others are coming to join them. Jean-Marc is coming, too.

Jean tells them then that Maria is his model. "She's been posing for me since the beginning of the summer."

Someone asks if they can see the paintings. "There's only one," he says "but I've made a lot of drawings." He looks at Maria, "Oh, maybe some day I'll show them to you, I guess. They're all put away now, though, troublesome to get. Maybe some time." *He's just making excuses*, she thinks, *I know he'll never show them. Do they guess he does me nude?*

"Oh, so, you're a model, Maria," someone says, "I might have guessed."

Somebody asks how she'd feel about allowing them to photograph her. After all, that's what they are, a photography club. *What does that mean, anyway?* she wonders. *Do they make field trips together to take pictures, or what, exactly?* "It would be all right," she replies, not expecting that they want to take the pictures right then, this evening, this minute.

It seems they have cameras in their cars. And Jean has all of his, all his cameras, lots of film, and his lighting equipment. No problem. Great idea.

"We'll set things up right now, if that's okay with you, Maria." "You look just great." "Don't worry, sweetheart, we won't bite. It will be fun.

And we'd certainly appreciate it..." They leave for their cars to get what they need. She listens to the music. Now it's a song she knows, sometimes she even sings it, with the radio. "A Certain Smile" passes through her, like a secret soft caress.

*   *   *

When she was seven years old she would make a wish, only one. A prayer that she always repeated, always the same. She would wish that one day she would grow up to be the queen of an island of her own. She blew a dandelion in the wind—"I wish I could be queen of my island," she whispered. She broke a wishbone with her father—"I wish I could be queen of my island," she thought. She gazed at the first star of the evening, "I wish I could be queen..."

On her island, none of her subjects would be without food or without a home. "No meanness allowed" would be the law of the land. Mothers and fathers would be brought before the queen if ever they were unkind to their children. There would be no punishment for the bad mothers and fathers; the queen would simply explain to them how to be better the next time. No one would eat the animals, and music and dancing would happen every day. If you worked hard you might become a little rich. But not too rich, just enough for the houses and gardens and farms to be pretty. And people who couldn't work would be given help by everyone else, so they wouldn't get sick and die or be miserable—the queen would see to it. Gardens and forests of animals and plants would be everywhere. There would be no pavements, or billboards, or other ugly things. People would not drive big, noisy cars. They could have very little ones, just for fun, but mostly, they would walk or bicycle wherever they went. Or they could row in boats or swim and, of course, they could fly in airplanes to exciting far-away places. There wouldn't be any money either, everyone would trade and share.

Maybe, when it was warm enough, they wouldn't even need their clothes. And the whole island would be, always and forever, happy…

Now in Jean's apartment as she sits in the center of this small circle of various-aged, tanned, balding and graying men, all intently and even excitedly eyeing her as they set up tripods and cameras and lights; as she finishes off one of the oddly salty chocolate brownies that Jean has been passing around, she recalls her former fantasies. She imagines herself transformed. She is a benevolent queen, a radiant servant of mankind, bringing joy and excitement and contentment with her love, her beauty, and with her magically powerful wishes that all shall, indeed, know bliss…

Life is mystery, she sees, immersed in the strangeness of the moment. *I feel like my life is becoming a movie. There's a story in it; maybe everything's going to turn out to have a plot. That's possible I suppose. And every new second is in suspense, a mystery. Such a "Twilight Zone" feeling I have sometimes. Do any of these men ever feel like this? About their own realities?…I think they've finished setting up. The photography equipment…could it be that the equipment is a symbol…*The man named Ben is coming toward her now.

Ben speaks in a low voice and reaches out his hand. He takes her own hand, and holds it for a few seconds, as he makes a request. His eyes are respectful, serious. She rises from the couch and he escorts her from the room. They go to Jean's bedroom, which she has never seen.

The room is beautiful. The three Asian pots, all of graceful shapes, the low bed covered in white fabric, perhaps damask, or something like damask, a small cedar chest, polished to a warmly golden glow. And on the chest, a blue china vase with a bouquet of tiny-blossomed flowers of purple and orange and white, with fragile forest-green stems and tiny leaves. *Wild flowers*, she thinks. *Where did Jean get them?* Her mood goes deeper upon entering the simple purity of Jean's bedroom, deeper into her own spirit world of being-in-love with Jean-Marc Romier. Ben observes her and goes to the vase of flowers. "I'm certain Jean-Marc would want you to have these, Maria," he says as he arranges three stems of tiny orange flowers behind her ear.

"Would you sit here, please, beside me on the bed?" he requests. He asks seriously, and almost *as if he were going to conspire with me about something?* She wonders. She sits on the edge of Jean's bed, close beside this stranger, feeling that something disturbingly unlike her life, thus far, is taking place. The fingers of her right hand pass slowly back and forth over her left. She looks at Ben, a slim, darkly tanned, green-eyed man, a man graying at the temples, a dignified man; perhaps he is ten years older than Jean-Marc. She looks him in the eyes and she waits.

He begins to speak. His voice is somewhat slow, thoughtful, assured. He talks on and on, hypnotically relaxing. When she speaks to him, in response, or with questions of her own, he listens intently. Finally, such a long time has passed, there is a knock on the bedroom door; someone has been sent to fetch them. This other accompanies them to the living room. The men in the living room cease their conversations now and watch as Maria and Ben walk by.

All of them are watching us, she thinks, *but I don't mind…Ben wants to take me to that corner…He has a kind touch, good, loving…Alyosha, he makes me think of Alyosha Karamazov…*thoughts come of her beloved Dostoyevsky hero. *Alyosha, would Alyosha touch me like this?* Thoughts of this Ben, thoughts of Jean-Marc…She focuses on helping Ben to remove her pullover sweater, in a way that won't make tangles of her hair. Three crumpled little wildflowers fall to the floor.

*   *   *

Together Maria and Ben are bringing the white cashmere sweater up and over and off. Together they are moving with such grace and such a minimum of gesture that the men who watch are breathing as one. All feel the dance that reveals itself in the movements of their self-possessed companion and this shyly assenting college girl.

Ben places her sweater on a chair. Now he lifts a delicate, rose-peach piece of silk, the unexpected undergarment of a child, or of women of days gone by—it once belonged, in fact, to her grandmother. It is a thing the men's mothers might have worn, when the men themselves were children (a popular "Victoria's Secret" camisole it could be, in a future era; but so oddly old-fashioned in 1963). Up and over her breasts. His fingers barely touch her as they pass.

When he lifts this final covering away, she raises one arm in a slow, tentative gesture, and the observers notice that their throats are dry. She puts her fingers to her tousled hair, pushing strands from her eyes, while the men drink from the glasses they're holding or retrieving from the coasters on the tables of the room.

The quiet jazz from Jean's hi-fi passes through them all—soft, tropical, seductive, of the night. The photographers nervously make adjustments to lighting equipment as Jean turns off his lamps.

Ben places one warm hand on her waist. Her skin is also warm, in spite of no protection. He walks her to her place upon Jean's couch. Before he goes away, to align his own equipment, he bends down to kiss her, one kiss on the left breast. *I'll help her take her pants off later*, he decides, as his lips pass slowly across a soft warm nipple...

6

The Curse of Guilt

"Then the Queen of the Netherworld spoke:
Silence Inanna; make no stain upon my home.
With the Glance of Death,
Ereshkigal screamed her hatred. With the Curse of Guilt,
She struck Inanna to the ground."
                    —from *The Twenty-One Hymns of Orom*

Several hours later, Jean Romier locks the front door of his apartment. He takes Maria by the hand and they proceed slowly down the stairway and out into the cool evening breezes surrounding the inner city lake.

It has been a night far distant from the realms of other nights. She wonders if anyone has ever known such a night. So beautiful and free. She will review it inside herself forever, she thinks, and probably she will never fully understand. Already, she retraces the amazing enfolding of the final hour.

She has never felt so heavenly. There is euphoria in every cell, and in all the world around. Sleepily, she savors the joy which they all together made.

As she walks arm in arm with Jean-Marc, arriving at his Alfa, she sees that it is nearly dawn. The morning star, the planet Venus, she believes, glows in the brightening sky. She can see why the ancients thought that it was Venus who brought the dawn. The sun will now be rising. And there is much dew, almost a light rain, coming in the air.

Suddenly, before he opens the door to the car, Jean takes her chin in his hand. He tilts her face upward to his own. With his usual tender look he smiles. Then he speaks, affectionately, cheerfully, the last words that she will hear from this man, once her teacher, for many years to come.

"I always suspected you had it in you, Maria," he smiles, "You know, many women these days aren't strong and healthy enough to have even one…But you, Maria!…You exquisite little slut, you!…I wonder, though, did it never occur to you, honey, that sometimes nature and human decency can be at…at cross-purposes? I know you are aware—"

His words are echoing in her brain. Sharp, acidic, they repeat themselves. In the tissues of her stomach there forms a hard, tight knot. For a moment she stares at him blankly. But then the blankness clears, her eyes pierce his, and she turns away.

Then she is running. Speeding through the streets.

He calls out, yelling while he chases. "Maria!" he shouts, "You don't understand! It was only love! I only speak with love! Like a father, Maria! Don't take it this way! Just my stupid words! Please, Maria! I didn't mean to hurt you! Come back! I worship you!"

But no one hears him, no one except a few annoyed insomniacs tossing in their beds as he runs below their rooms. She is already far ahead; she couldn't hear him if she wanted.

She's been running through the streets for years. She runs like Artemis—like Diana. He'll never catch up, no matter how he tries. She runs like Hermes, like Mercury, like a being of the light.

*　　　　　　*　　　　　　*

Some women, some men, are born to inspire the fertility of the race. They are nothing less than a sacred instrument of Nature, a channel for Her purposes. Their genes are such that just to see such women, or men, and just to be near them, is a catalyst, pushing anyone and everyone, to be fruitful and to multiply. Or at least, to want to make the first moves in that direction…"

It is the knowing words of the man named Ben, spoken in Jean's bedroom, and not the words of Jean Romier, which echo in her mind as she finally drifts to sleep, beneath the oak tree in the courtyard of her dormitory's grounds.

7

A Letter from Venice Beach

October 29, 1963

Dear Rosie,

I miss you, too, Rosie. And I'm sorry to hear about your grades. You just better quit messing around so much.

We're in L.A. now. Venice Beach. I've been thinking maybe you and I will move down here some day. I know you'd like it. Everybody's pretty much for real, even the old people. And I hear you can rent a little cottage near the beach for next to nothing.

There's plenty to do, too. Tom and I are learning to surf. And we drive around, explore the town, go out on the pier. Mainly we've been hanging out with some people we met the first day on the beach. At night we all go down to the pier, or over to their place to listen to music. Sometimes they let us crash—their apartment is nothing to write home about, but it's a step up from trying to sleep in Tom's Chevy. Mattresses and sleeping bags on the floor is about the extent of their furniture. But to tell the truth, Rosie, I wouldn't mind if you and I ended up living like that. It's better to live simply, don't you think? Not get too tied down with property and stuff. Then you're free to spend your time off where you really want to be—outdoors, like on the beach, or climbing a mountain or something—not home taking care of your boring old possessions. That's the way to a satisfied mind. Which is what I think is the most important thing you can have. Like that folk song says. Which reminds me, I met this guy. He hitchhiked here from Greenwich Village. He plays guitar and writes folk songs, at least that's what he calls them—anyway, last night I actually sang with him in some little hole in the wall club. He's not too bad, and he says he's even getting to be semi-famous. Also I met a girl who's a fashion model. But she's going to be an actress.

They have a great jazz station down here, Rosie, that's another thing. And there's a good club we can get into easy with no I.D. We heard Howard Rumsey last week. Remind me to send you the names of some albums you need to get.

I've been taking lots of photographs. Another guy we met has a darkroom, so I'm printing my own stuff. I'm not sending you anything now, though. You'll see what I've been doing when I get back. I want to be there to see how you react. All I need now is a Nikon. There's so much around here, so many cool subjects, especially near the beach. The ocean, the people. The old buildings and piers, the way the light and shadows fall on them, you know, and the shapes and designs, especially on edges and corners. I can't explain it; the light on the forms just gives me a satisfied feeling sometimes. The darkroom guy's mother is an artist and she was looking at the prints I was developing yesterday and she sort of started going crazy over them, like I was a genius or something, that's what she said, because she'd never seen images of buildings that made her feel so "emotional." And she said my stuff makes her think of Rembrandt. Because I'm "so in love with light." It was funny. Anyway, I think I'd like to get me a book on Rembrandt. Also, I'm becoming sort of interested in anthropology. Tom's influence again, one of his paperbacks. (I still know how to read, Rosie, even without college!) I'm into this book about pygmies in the forest. Yeah, Tom and I are still friends—amazing isn't it? You guessed right, it's not the easiest thing in the world to travel with him, but I'm managing. At least his driving's improved, somewhat. He still spaces out when he's talking, and he tailgates like crazy, but he doesn't get a speeding ticket every five blocks these days. By the way he says to say hello.

It was great to hear your voice on the phone. Do you know it's already two weeks since that call? Anyway, I was glad to get your letter. And I'm glad you switched to be roommates with that girl from Castro Valley. Maybe now you'll be happy. But I hope Maria Ananin isn't too quiet for you. Yeah, I do remember her. She was in my world lit class. She was really quiet, though. I hardly got to know her.

I hope you write soon. Remember to write to the address in San Diego I sent you—Coronado, I mean. That's where we'll be by the time I get your next letter. Then we head south of the border. Tijuana and beyond!

In spite of what you seem to think, I really do miss you, Rosie. In fact, you're what I mean when I think of the word "home." I don't know why exactly—maybe it's because I grew up in so many places—but I don't particularly think much about any of them. Only you. But anyway, Tom's hungry now. Gotta go. Like I said, write soon.

Love, Mike

8

A Camera

from Los Angeles
Nov. 1, 1963

Dear Rosie,

Maybe you really are a wise woman, the way you say you are. Anyway, I like the way you figured it, this time. If you'd mailed me a package, who knows when it would get here, and you're right—just sending money for my birthday would be cold. But your "contract" with the check—that was cool. And the artwork—I didn't know you had it in you! Too bad you want it back. But here it is, all signed and sealed, my promise to buy myself a camera. As a matter of fact, I went out and bought it yesterday.

I couldn't find a good deal on a Nikon. One of these days I'll get me one. What I did buy for now was an 8MM movie camera. It has three lenses, a wide angle, normal and telephoto. You rotate the turret so you can take pictures through any of the three. And it has reflex viewing, which means, Rosie, that when you look into the viewfinder, the scene you see is coming through the same lens used for taking pictures. Very boss.

Also, there's a spring-wound motor. You wind it with your hand like you're winding a kid's toy or a music box. It's a used camera. I discovered it in a pawnshop. A bit old, but it's in great shape. And the light metering is done with a built-in light meter. It's selenium, which doesn't require any batteries!

I don't know if you're understanding any of this, Rosie. But I want you to know a little about what you gave me. The fact is, I'm kind of excited about it. Maybe this is the beginning of my "chosen career," the way I'll earn our daily bread. Who knows? But, anyway, thanks!

Love you,
Mike

9

A Rainy Night in November

Berkeley
November, 1963

In early November, on a cold gray day, in a week so gloomy and lonely as to forebode a winter devoid of cheer, Jean-Marc Romier took the day off from teaching and stayed in bed. Around 5:00 P.M. he rose and dressed, fixed himself a can of chicken soup, and drove alone to Berkeley to the university, to see yet another French-made film.

Last Year at Marienbad was showing in Wheeler Auditorium. It was a strange and compelling film, a film about time and memory and *nothingness*, he told himself; *it's about me.*

The night was dark, except directly beneath the campus lamps, when he walked through the doors of the auditorium to return home. The rain was coming heavily now, and the wind was strong, the beginning of an icy storm blown in from the north. He walked across the puddled pavement rapidly, with the other straggling loners and a few couples who, for one reason or another, had come out to see that film on such a night. A few feet ahead of him, even more quickly than he, walked a girl, probably an undergraduate. She was thin, too thin, with long hair—it was mousy looking and damp. She had no umbrella. He thought of catching up, which he did, nearly, and offering to share his own umbrella, but he decided against it. That would be too forward; besides, as he came closer he noticed her stooped shoulders, a dull expression, the hair was unkempt.

Yet—and it was crazy—in some indefinable way, now, as the girl walked beneath the light of a street lamp, she somehow reminded him of…but possibly every second or third young woman he ever saw was going to conjure up that image in his mind…for the rest of his life, perhaps? He crossed the street to his car, never knowing that the girl was, in fact, Maria Ananin.

As for Maria, herself, she did not see Jean Romier, so near, but walking behind her in the dark.

10

Coronado

November, 1963

Dear Rosie,

It's so strange to be here in Coronado. After all these years. I was eleven when we lived here. In 1956, it was just for a couple of months. I told you about it once (when we were at the Cliff House, having breakfast after the Senior Ball, do you remember?) Remember about the three Filipino kids I played with, how we made a swing with some rope, on a grapefruit tree? We had these great wars with rotten grapefruits. (I don't know why that seems like such an important memory to me.) Huge grapefruits, in Coronado. And they still are. But everything else has changed.

I get the impression everything is going to change, from now on. Everything in the world. Since last week. For everyone on the entire planet, except maybe China. The U.S. has tremendous influence nearly everywhere else. Most Americans just aren't aware of it, but we rule an empire. Maybe one day people will realize that, maybe not. But it's true, even in the towns of Liberia, back in West Africa—America rules. Even in the little villages, somewhat, sometimes.

Where were you when he was shot? I heard it on the radio, myself, in the car, back in L.A. on the way to the beach. We ended up not going to the beach. It can get cold in L.A. in November.

We went to Van de Kamps instead, for coffee and danishes. Tom sat there in the booth and cried. To tell the truth, Rosie, I felt like it, too. That girl I was telling you about, Kari—the model—she got a little hysterical. At one point she told Tom she never wanted to see him again, because he went and announced that maybe the assassination was a good thing for some people, like for the Vietnamese and the average Cuban, for example. Tom tends to say what might possibly be the true thing, but at the wrong time. Like I said, though, Tom was crying, himself, at first.

When did you hear about it? Right then or later? I think myself that the shooting had to do with civil rights and the war on poverty. Kennedy tried to go too far, with the help of his brother. Too far for the men with the real power, the business hoods and the traders who actually own the world. Those guys need to feel, at a gut level, that they have complete control. Too many of the little nobodies, people who might almost as well be slaves, have been getting uncomfortably big for their britches while Kennedy's been in office. And the world's been cheering him and Bobby right on.

But the "Unknown Variables," as Tom always calls the guys who handle the big money—what they feed on is mastery and control and expensive living. Their egos are weak, insecure. I don't hate them, like Tom does—what good does hating do? But I know they cause most of the horrors in the world. I've known that since I was a little kid in Africa and Paris. I feel pity for them, when people get so confused about how to be human. The craving for money is an addiction. And lately they've been feeling the threat of withdrawal.

You should see all the poor families—really poor people, I'm talking about—friends we've made down here, people who own less than nothing, they have these huge portraits of JFK hanging on their walls. Along side Martin Luther King. But what's going to happen now? Who's going to get killed next? And whose portraits could go on those walls, in their places?

Anyway, to move on, speaking of Kari, I don't know why you get so upset about her, Rosie. Isn't it best to be honest and tell each other everything? I'd like to know what's happening with you, in the same way. You and I are eighteen years old, now, Rosie! We both need to meet people, all kinds. Have lots of experiences, learn about life. If not now when? Kari's a nice person. Besides, she helps me out by posing for some shots. Like I told you before, she's a professional. And she does it for nothing because she's my friend.

I don't own you Rosie, and you don't own me. Not even after we're married. I see it like that. I mean, she's only hanging out with me and Tom. She has a boyfriend. I'm not going to cheat on you. That's a promise I'm making. And keeping.

Maybe my big mistake is writing to you about everyone I'm getting to know or whatever, if it hurts you. Maybe I wouldn't be bothering to tell you that stuff if I was right there with you, in the same town. Oh, well, live and learn, I guess. But anyway, nothing comes close to the way I feel about you, and I mean it. I just wish there were some way to prove it and make you see.

I'm not too surprised about your major. Home Ec is just the kind of thing I'd expect you to end up with. I guess that means great food for me some day?

And I'm glad to hear you liked the Joan Baez album I sent you. I knew you would. You know, Kari actually helped me pick it out.

Have fun on your break. And don't forget you're the one I want to be with for the rest of my life. I hope that's the way you're seeing it, too. Remember, you and me are going to make babies together. And soon.

All my love, Mike

*   *   *

November, 1963

Dear Rosie,

What kind of a letter was that supposed to be? I just don't get it, Rosie. I never thought you were the type to make mountains out of molehills. I thought you'd be happy to know I'm thinking about you, even when I'm with somebody else. I only asked her opinion about your birthday present because she's a girl, and because she has good taste. I mean it seems like yours. Which I thought was good. I mean, I still think so.

Anyway, Rosie, I don't want to waste time writing back and forth about this. Do what you want with the album. But I'm glad you had the sense to stop yourself and didn't break it. Give it to your roommate or someone. Hope to hear from you soon.

Yours, Michael

11

Near Descent

Berkeley
January, 1964 A.D.

"Hello? Yes, yes she is, yes, just a moment, please—Maria!"

Rosie Hestia leaned against the wall and looked on while her studious, 'grinde' of a roommate slowly placed a pen in a pen-holding coffee cup than slowly rose from her desk.

Maria never received any phone calls, or almost never. For months now. Rosie wondered who the woman could be. Maybe a professor or a TA. Or Maria's mother? She listened intently for Maria's response.

"Oh, oh, hi! Oh, it's so nice to hear your voice."

Rosie, now half-reclining on her bed, watched Maria, who nervously balanced from one foot to the other by the wallphone.

"Oh, he told you to? Oh, he did?" Maria's voice was colder now than at first, only politely interested. "Oh, yes, I see. Well, I'd really love to Marta, I would, but I have so much studying to do. Yes, it's hard to keep up. And finals are coming soon. It's very thoughtful of you, though. I'm sorry. One day, maybe. I really have thought about taking lessons with you. But not at this time. Please, let me write down your phone number."

She went to her desk for her pen and her address book. As she returned to the phone, she glanced back at Rosie who continued to watch every move she made.

"Yes, I have it. 626-2–323. Yes, when I'm less pressured. Thank you, Marta, I will. For sure. Yes. Good-bye." As she hung up the phone, her thoughts were blasted by a loud shriek from across the room.

"Ma-ri-a!" Rosie was jumping up from her bed and running across the room to practically leap upon her roommate. Rosie grabbed the startled girl by the shoulders and gave her a small firm shake.

"What's wrong with you? You should have done it! Whatever she was talking about! Don't you remember how excited you were last fall, when you met that woman? Marta! I even remember that name! You were so excited! And you haven't gone anywhere or done anything in ages. Not anything that remotely resembles fun! What's with you, girl? Anyway?"

Maria stood frozen, Rosie's hands still on her shoulders.

"When I first met you," the agitated Rosie continued, "you were an entirely different person. I was so glad, I was so relieved to have you for my roomy. Instead of that first fiasco I was assigned to. You were nice, you were happy—you were alive! And you always looked so bitchin'— sometimes I even used to think you could be a movie star! I'll admit, in a few ways you seemed a little socially backward. But now! Ever since you came in late that night… it's so easy to pinpoint it—and by the way, you never even had the decency to tell me what happened that night! And I worried plenty! You know, that time last fall when they put you on restriction. I mean, experiences change people, maybe, sometimes, I guess, depending on the person. But not so completely, not the way you've changed. Didn't you ever, ever get into trouble before that, Maria? Actually, I'll bet you didn't!

"You have nothing to do with anyone any more, including me! The way you kind of slink around the dorm, nobody wants to have anything to do with you, either! And frankly, you've become such a physical disaster—I think you're way too skinny now for your own good. And your complexion—Why don't you eat with us? I'm not sure you even do eat!—"

Maria turned, pulling herself from Rosie's hands, which had remained gripping her shoulders, not tightly, but softly, in a gentle contrast to her words. She gave Rosie a short, cold glance and returned to her desk and her physics book.

"Listen, I'm sorry," Rosie, who remained at the wall, was almost crying. She felt so terrible for her. "I'm really sorry, what I just said. But you make me so frustrated. You could be really happy. Didn't you have any friends in high school?

" Why don't you ever call anybody? Why do you always need to study so much? Nobody else does. You just told that woman that finals are coming up. I heard you. This is January, Maria! Finals are a month away! I haven't even opened—"

"You know, Rosie," Maria interrupted without looking up from her book, "I'd really appreciate it if, in the future, you'd try not to eavesdrop so completely on my phone conversations. That is, if a 'disaster' like me ever has another one."

"Crimeny, Maria! I give up!" Now Rosie was almost screaming. "I need some fresh, healthy air. Excuse me, I'm going down the hall!" She grabbed her pillow, her smallest teddy bear, and a box of tissues and hurried out into the hallway.

"I feel so awful for my roommate," she announced as she entered the room next door.

*　　　　　　*　　　　　　*

Two weeks later, returning from another visit next door, Rosie looked immediately, instinctively, to the two large windows on the far side of the room. Immediately, she dashed across and grabbed Maria's hand. Carefully she helped the dazed-looking girl down from the chair on which she was standing.

Then she led her to bed and tucked her in. She carried the chair back to the desk and made sure it was properly aligned in its place. She returned to the windows to shut them. As she did this, she looked downward, disregarding the vertigo which always came whenever she gazed from her eighth floor room to the street below. Her heart pounded so loudly that she couldn't hear the sound of traffic coming from busy College Ave. Nor did she hear Maria's soft "Thank you, Rosie," as it drifted from the bed.

*   *   *

In February that year, as in many East Bay years, the winter temporarily masqueraded as spring. It disguised itself with pink fragrant blossoms on magnolia trees and cherry plums, with a glory of early daffodils, and a delicious mediterranean temperature that urged co-eds to put on bikinis and study on the balconies; while the boys grabbed binoculars from fore-thinking friends.

The warm breezes of healing change were already trying to blow through the colder winds, which, in that winter of American trauma and grief, had been powerful enough to wreak havoc for decades.

In this limbo-like interlude of very early 1964, Rosie Hestia occupied herself with memorizing the nutritional values of artichokes and avocados, and the differences between iceburg lettuce and romaine. She short-sheeted her friends and was short-sheeted; she learned to play bridge; to dance the jerk and the twist and even, sometimes, she attempted the limbo. She stumbled through a beer-bust in Tilden Park, and two winery tours in Napa. She attended a Harry Belafonte/ Nana Maskouri concert, ate lots of sourdough french bread and lasagne and had her palm read by a gypsy at the Spaghetti Factory in North Beach. In between all that, she found time to exchange long letters with her fiancé. And to study for finals. On Sundays she often went to church.

She gave up, that month, the task of trying to pull her silent, uncooperative roommate into her own fun-filled life. She became satisfied instead with simply being orderly, considerate and undemanding herself; though every once in awhile she did ask Maria not to smoke another cigarette.

But she never could bring herself to say something about the record album, the one and only album that Maria insisted on playing nearly every single night. It was the very Joan Baez album which Michael had sent to Rosie, herself. Rosie had passed it on to Maria—as Michael suggested—for the reason that she just could not accept the outrageous circumstance under which the album had been purchased.

Maria listened to that record over and over, particularly one song, the one about fair maidens courting their men. Rosie would get up, rush out, go down the hall to her friend Alice's, escaping the frightening metaphor about men and summer stars—how they appear and then are gone—before the line lodged in her brain. The pretty melody and Baez's poignantly beautiful voice only made the words more difficult to take, since every time Rosie heard the song she always thought of the one who had given her the album, and of the unknown rival named Kari who had selected it. Then her worst fear, that any day now Michael was going to write to say he was leaving her for someone else, would surface, harmonizing with the sadness in the song. It irritated her that her roommate, who obviously loved no one and knew nothing of romance, could so ignorantly torture her this way.

But there was almost nothing besides listening to the album, other than studying, that Maria ever did. Rosie didn't really have the heart to take away the poor thing's one diversion. And she certainly didn't want to do anything that would lead to a rerun of that incredible chair scene back in January…

12

Desperate Move

Berkeley
March, 1964

The false spring ended; the cold returned. It was March, a storm-filled, frosty month. Finals were over and Rosie Hestia could not stop fretting about her roommate and the hermit-like existence which Maria continually endured. It was time for something to be done.

On an overcast Sunday morning, Rosie sat beside her friend Christine in a neighborhood church and listened to the minister begin his sermon, a sermon entitled "Am I my brother's keeper?" She listened for about one minute. Then her mind began to wander to the familiar corner of concern.

"Yes, I am her keeper!" she exclaimed suddenly, an hour later, to Christine, as the two hurried through the sanctuary doors into an icy-winded downpour.

The girls decided to run. Church bulletins clutched atop their heads, they dashed up the stormy maple-lined blocks from Grove Street to Dwight and College, heading for the shelter of the dormitory cafeteria.

"And I don't care if it isn't any of my business!" Rosie turned and shouted to Christine, a few paces behind her. A crash of thunder seemed to punctuate her words.

Later, after leaving her friends in the middle of lunch, she rode the crowded elevator up to the eighth floor, teeth chattering, throat already getting scratchy. She made efforts not to sneeze on her fellow passengers, while her thoughts grew more and more certain and determined about what it was that she must do.

Summer is coming, and after that I'll be in the sorority, she told herself. *If I don't act now, I never will. Besides if I wait any longer, it might be too late!*

The elevator approached her floor; the door opened and closed again before her, but she didn't notice. She rode back down to the lobby and up again to the eighth. When she finally reached that floor for the second time, she had no idea she'd been there once already. But her plan of action was complete.

The room was empty. Just as she'd hoped. "Of course she's in the library," she muttered to herself. Immediately she headed for Maria's side of their room. Efficiently and carefully she combed through the top of Maria's desk and through its drawers.

All was orderly, meticulous, very easy to search. After not much time or effort she found what she was looking for in the middle desk drawer. Maria's address book.

Hastily she riffled through the pages, located the entry that she needed, and copied it onto a slip of paper from the desk. She sneezed, replaced the book exactly where she had found it and shut the drawer. Then she breathed a sigh of relief, which turned into another sneeze; she grabbed a tissue from the box on the desk and went across the room to the phone on the wall. Midway she hesitated when she thought she heard footsteps near the door, but it was only her imagination. She dialed the number on the paper. When an elderly female voice answered, she crumpled the paper in her hand and tossed it into the wastebasket.

"Marta Diaz?" she inquired in a very hushed voice. "My name is Rosie Hestia. I'm a friend of Maria Ananin. Do you have a couple of minutes? I need to ask you—Marta do you think you could do me a little favor…"

After she hung up the phone, she peeled off her soaking wet clothes, put on her long flannel nightgown, and scurried into bed. Soon she was fast asleep, dreaming feverishly.

It seemed she was in a hospital room. A colorless room, with the dark mood of an old British mystery movie. She was visiting her sick grandmother, who was sound asleep and snoring. And immediately Rosie saw an opportunity—she found herself, half against her own will, desperately attempting, for some strange and important reason, to rob her sick sleeping grandma of her wallet! But as she pulled her grandmother's purse from out of a cabinet, all the contents spilled out, tumbling down upon the floor. At that very same moment there came a rustling at the window. Rosie looked up in terror, certain she was going to see The Wolf. But, instead of a horrible creature who would eat her, into the room flew Superman. Shining in red, yellow and blue Day-Glo, he looked fantastically strong and handsome. His piercing glance caught Rosie in the middle of her act. He had just begun the process of gently closing handcuffs on her wrist when she suddenly awakened with a start.

She looked at the clock. It was six p.m., time for dinner in the dorms. Rosie felt exhausted, but her stomach was rumbling with a loud demand for food.

13

A Healing

San Francisco, the Mission District
March, 1964 A.D.

"My religion is kindness."
—The fourteenth Dalai Lama of Tibet

The apartment was old for the West Coast. Like much of San Francisco, it dated from the turn of the century, the Victorian reconstruction that followed the fires of the earthquake of 1906.

The kitchen was narrow, neat, and shining clean. A huge wood-fired, cast iron stove overpowered everything. From one of the stove's burners a low fire glowed beneath a full teakettle, while another fire burned beneath the oven, though baking was done. The oven gave some warmth for a chilly afternoon.

Above the kitchen sink a large window provided sunlight—a surprising amount of sunlight, considering that the window faced the neighbors' brick wall. But enough light somehow entered the kitchen, in fact, to sustain a large potted geranium and three smaller pots of herbs—lavender, basil, and sage—upon the windowsill, as well as several ferns and a bonsai thriving in various niches of the room.

Next to the sink counter stood an ancient wooden grammar-school desk, covered with two neat stacks of cookbooks. It was this desk, and the books, which most often caught the wandering eye of an afternoon visitor—a tired looking young woman who sometimes glanced about from her seat at the kitchen table, where she partly faced the kitchen and partly faced the hall. At the table, a little round card table covered with white linen, there sat the two women: the hostess, a pleasant aquiline-featured, thoughtfully focused, seventyish lady who listened with unrelenting attention; and the guest, an intensely serious and much younger person who spoke in tones so low that she was difficult to hear.

When the clearly distraught visitor at last, after nearly an hour, finished with her sad and much convoluted tale, there followed a long silence. The ticking of the old brass clock on the kitchen wall was suddenly loud and paramount.

Finally the kind-eyed hostess began to speak.

*   *   *

"Your life is not finished, yet, Maria," the older woman said softly. Her small brown face peered just perceptibly above the tiny, elegant bonsai tree in the center of the table. "Imagine a maze, a labyrinth. You clearly picked one of those dead-end pathways, your first try." She paused, smiling, watching the younger woman's eyes. "Now you must just go back. You observe where it was you started from, and you make another try.

"You're lucky, dear—you're still so young—many of us follow confused paths for entire lifetimes before we see that we've chosen blind-alley alternatives. Though our choices may have appeared very compelling back at the entrance, when we first began. And, then, Maria, when we finally see what's happened, we're so very worn-out to go back and start over again!

"But, as for you, my dear, you're still at the beginning! It's easier. Eventually you'll find the way that isn't a cul-de-sac; the way that takes you home."

Maria studied the new growth of leaves on the bonsai, a miniature Japanese maple, and she thought of winter and spring. Then she looked up. "Marta, I'm not so certain everything was a 'blind-alley,' the way you say," she spoke rapidly, before the old lady could go on, "Not altogether. I think that what happened to me, that kind of thing must have a purpose, even if it feels so terrible at the end."

Did people suffer for nothing, as Marta was implying? Was there nothing to be learned from life, nothing but the knowledge that life could have been happier some other way? Nothing to be gained from a bad experience except regret and wasted time, and the immediate need to start over again? Marta meant to reassure; Maria did not feel reassured. She made scratches with her fork across the top of the coconut pudding that her hostess had placed before her.

Then once again she let her mind go back and examine that last evening at Jean-Marc Romier's. She tried her best to recapture the feeling of those minutes just before he had suddenly, lastingly, poisoned both her thoughts and her heart with the venom of his ugly words.

"'Exquisite slut,'" she silently repeated it to herself, once again, as she had so many times since that night. But as usual she could not bring up the emotions which were there just before that entrapping pronouncement. She fell, instead, automatically, into the only emotions that still remained—the shame, and the pain of Jean's betrayal.

Marta watched Maria's face, as the girl changed from contemplation to a struggle to hold herself together. Then the older woman softly closed her eyes.

"But it's all right, *hija*," said Marta, finally, in a completely new tone. There was a sudden, unexpectedly joyous triumph in her voice.

"It is all right. Everything is going to be O.K. " She smiled and reached across the table to pat Maria's hand. "Please, won't you try some of my coconut pudding? You need more meat on your bones."

Strangely, this grandmotherly person's last, simple, everyday suggestion caused a greater effect than any wisdom she had yet attempted to convey. The words struck the girl like a sudden powerful splash of water, a healing ocean spray that misted across her face.

In fact, Maria's face did suddenly seem fresher, more pure and clean. Something fresh and pure was flowing into and coming out of her very cells. It was traveling inside her, into her blackened mind, into her heart.

Through the center of her being, so refreshing. And outward with her breath, back into the atmosphere of the kitchen. Marta's voice was…But Maria was not able to recall the sound, though only a moment had passed. It was frustrating; the voice was leaving no imprint in her mind. *There must be a reason I can't recall it, this isn't natural*, she told herself. *There's something magical—the law of some magical process she just used. For some reason I'm forbidden to recall her magical tone of voice…*She knew these thoughts were foolish, but they came to her with force.

Marta, just then, spoke again; she was asking a question, "—like drinking from a mountain stream?" This time the words came as a clicking in her face; Maria was instantly snapped from her bewildered enchantment.

"What? Pardon? I'm sorry, Marta, what did you just say?"

Marta, herself, did not reply, now, at first. Instead she looked at the girl for awhile, seeming to assure herself of something, before she could answer, "Oh, I was just wondering, Maria, what is it you're thinking, this minute? You do look deep, you know. You don't mind telling me, do you?"

Marta's melodious voice was different yet again, though still intriguing. Now aloof and reserved, it conveyed, at the same time, an intimate quality. Maria wondered where Marta was born, where she grew up. The woman had never even mentioned what country she was from. She spoke with an accent; Maria couldn't place it. Was Marta from the Caribbean, or from South America? Somewhere in Africa? But her surname was Spanish. Maria knew only that Marta had once attended a university in England…

The girl hesitated; she didn't want to sound as outlandish as her thoughts were. How could she say out loud that she suspected magic was in the room? Her fingers reached out and traced the top edge of the porcelain container of the little bonsai tree. She felt moist soil on her fingertips and wondered if Marta minded that she was touching. She put her hands back to her lap, and glanced at her food. She was actually beginning to feel a little hungry.

"I was effected by what you just told me, I guess, Marta—that everything is O.K. By the words, coming from you, yourself. Especially since I've just told you everything—all the secrets about me." She hoped her own voice was as calm and down-to-earth as Marta's had become. "The fact that those words were coming from you, not just anyone, that was important—and the way you seemed so certain. Your tone, the rhythm; it had a strong effect on me, that's all." She began to eat. The pudding was smooth and soothingly delicious. She was overcome with an uncustomary and immense gratitude for the pleasure of food.

Marta ate too. For a long while, both women were silent. For several minutes, they both thought only of the pudding, it's texture and it's taste, and the coconut from which it came. The only sounds to be heard were the clinking of spoons against bowls and the ticking of the clock. When they finished, both were subtly altered. "Well, now" Marta smiled, "It is true what I said, everything is O.K? Am I right?"

Maria hoped Marta would say more, go into some of her beliefs, her philosophy, maybe even at length. It would be strengthening. It would give something to hold onto, more than just a confident declaration that everything was fine. It would be, above all, fascinating, to learn more of this woman's perspective, more of what she'd spoken of the first time they'd met. In that other lifetime, when they were both together with Jean-Marc Romier.

Marta had performed her hypnotizing dances then. Of Africa, of the Americas, of Polynesia...

But the old woman just hoisted herself up, with a slight difficulty, it seemed. She rubbed her knees, and went to the stove. She lit something—a wooden shish-kebob skewer it was—on the flame under the kettle, and carried the burning stick to a brass incense dish on the windowsill. She lit the incense in the dish, and returned to the stove to turn down the flame. A fragrance of myrrh, unfamiliar to Maria, yet almost like a memory, filled the afternoon kitchen. The younger woman watched each of the elder's movements, mesmerized by the grace of one who had given her life to the art of dance. Then, once again, Maria passed into the world of her thoughts.

*   *   *

"You are some-kind-of-girl, Maria!" Marta, who had been quietly studying her, exclaimed suddenly.

"Some kind of? What do you mean, Marta some kind of?" Maria was startled. She nervously pushed her empty bowl forward.

The slender, cocoa skinned seventy-seven year old stared silently at the skinny, pale adolescent. She continued this staring with the same piercing attention as she spoke. "I don't know, love, I don't have the words." She made a mock frown and shrugged her slight shoulders.

"But, please, Marta, tell me. How do you see me? Nobody ever tells anyone that. Not the people I know," *except for Rosie*, she thought, and she had no desire to learn any more of the terrible things Rosie Hestia saw in her. "But I really need to know. How do you see me? Especially from you, please, I need to know."

She spoke like a sincere child; Marta saw the extent of the earnestness in her eyes. There was a sad longing in this girl's eyes that appeared to be nearly unbearable in its magnitude.

"Now why do you need to know that so badly?" Marta laughed, a sparkling in the center of her own black pupils.

Maria saw that Jean's ex-mother-in-law was intensely interested in her. She liked this woman. Here was a person who possessed the same acute curiosity, the same tendency to become fascinated, which she herself had. Or rather, once had had.

She began to explain herself. But it was difficult.

And then, out of nowhere, without warning, there came a sense of manipulation, of being tricked. A feeling that the old woman's questions were actually part of some slick examination.

Marta already knows the correct answers to her own questions, she decided. *As well as the wrong answers, the foolish ones. Marta is interested in me, all right*, she thought. But the obviously alert woman came with a hidden agenda, possibly not a benevolent one.

Marta watched with concern as a coldness stiffened the girl's countenance.

Fortunately, however, the unfounded suspicions subsided as quickly as they arose. Maria was too rejuvenated, too newly energetic and alive, to make false blunders. She was able, like an accomplished skater, to spin on the ice and stop herself in her tracks. Almost immediately, she turned from her rigid—and of late, habitual—mood of paranoia.

She grabbed for her purse beneath her chair and took out her cigarettes and lighter. *No*, she assured herself, firmly, *Marta is not playing games with me, and her question is not a test; her question was completely innocuous. The problem is with me. That I don't have any answer.* "I don't really understand," she said carefully, "why I need to know what you think of me, Marta: I simply know it feels urgent right now to know what you think."

Marta did not laugh, as Maria thought she might.

"Well," said the woman, chewing at the shish-kebob stick which remained in her hand. Even that action was done with such a refined awareness, once again Maria was reminded that Marta was a dancer.

"The way I see you, dear, is this," the old woman said slowly, "You are strange, quite extraordinary. That's for starters, I'm just telling it like it is, O.K., sweetie? You are not what I would call 'usual.' To put it another way, I never met anyone with precisely your aura, those shadings of colors. The way you are at this moment, your aura is, well, it's definitely different from the way it was an hour ago when you first walked in. You know something about auras, and etheric bodies, Maria?" she asked—for it was nineteen sixty-three, not ninety-three, and not every Bay Area girl did know such things. But Maria nodded. "And then, too, you seem completely unlike the young woman I met on that first occasion, when Jean-Marc (Maria did not blink) introduced us. You're apparently very mutable. Maybe it's your age. It's interesting. But, now, Maria, can I fix you a cup of tea? Lemon-ginger perhaps? I make it, all fresh, myself."

Maria was disappointed. Marta, she decided, could be as full of b.s. as Rosie. Nevertheless, she couldn't deny that the woman made her feel more at peace than she'd felt in ages.

*   *   *

"Now, before you go, dear, I have one little good-bye present. The fact is, I normally hate to give advice. It's way too risky, for one thing; it's dangerous, as well as annoying. But, today I'm taking my chances. This is advice I'm going to give you. Do the best you can with it, and I promise to never give you any more," the old woman smiled warmly as she helped the girl with her coat. Maria noticed how small and shining and straight Marta's teeth were.

"Maria, I said before that you are a strange girl. I did not say a beautiful girl. I think you already know that. But then, maybe you don't." She paused, smiled again, and looked at her intently, "Well, you would be, if you'd eat a little more. I know, I've been a beautiful woman, myself," she laughed, a deep and musical sound.

And you still are, Marta, Maria told her silently, awed at how truly pretty the old woman was, in her simple blue gingham dress, with her radiant eyes and complexion; her soft grey curls framing her delicate face. But the girl said nothing and Marta went on.

"I will tell you how you can use your power. Because there is much you can do. Go ahead, be what you are, your spirit has come to have this body, this pleasant form. But that does not necessarily lead to a good life for you, does it?

"Beauty can lead to good or to bad, like any other power. But if it's beauty your spirit chooses to create, then go for it, go for all of it. Go the whole way, don't just make a flimsy outer shell. And don't confuse sensual with spiritual. It's incredibly easy to confuse those two, you know. The ambiguity, the trickery in that netherworld between *eros* and *agape*, that is really not much fun to live with. I think you know that now?

"As for your thoughts—strive to direct them to the most beautiful. Keep thoughts matching face, or even the physical thing will go away."

She laughed again. "I know you been keepin' some ugly thoughts in there lately," she deepened her voice as she said "ugly," and altered her accent—which persisted in hinting at one ancestry after another—as she gestured to Maria's forehead.

"It's easy to create something that is ugly, true? How much easier to do angry, hateful scribbling than to make a lovely work of art. The same goes for life. Stop being easy on yourself, Maria. Straighten up and fly right! Remember to forgive. Don't hate nobody, never! Just get out of their way, and be sorry they're so messed up! And wish them well, too. At least for your own sake! What use, if someone hurts you, to fill your mind with blame and other ugly poisons? It only hurts you more. Even the physical will lose its grace if you carry on like that. You'd be surprised, if you could see, how many of us old folks, those of us with bitter uptight faces, began as pretty, glowing children!

"Work on yourself, Maria, train yourself to be strong, not lazy. You can figure it out; you don't need me to tell you how. Wisdom and good character will grow like muscles if you just exercise them. Let your mind create kindness, nothing else. Look for kindness everywhere, in everything, in everyone. Let the actions you do and the choices you make be loving and full of peace. Actions are much more real and lasting than anything we see or touch, infinitely more real; one day you will know that.

"Practice with perseverance. Until acting in beauty becomes second nature, like the practice and perfecting of an intricate dance. Then everything that is you will be made of beauty, not only your body and your face. And if your essence goes on forever, beyond this dream, and beyond the final tired old dried up shriveled shell, as I believe our essence will, then it will carry on, a gift back to the universe, in harmony with all.

"But, you know, Maria, even supposing that no spirit does, after all, keep going, you will still live one satisfying life, that way, won't you? Do you hear me? Do you understand?"

Maria nodded. Then Marta patted the girl's cheek with a small warm hand, nudged her outside, and shut the door behind her. But immediately she opened it again, slightly. She peeked out the crack and called down the stairway, "One last suggestion, *hija*—if you want your teeth to sparkle like mine, be strong—you quit that smoking, now!" Then she shut the door again. She returned to her kitchen, went to the stove and poured herself a second cup of lemon-ginger tea.

*   *   *

Maybe I am strange, like she says, Maria thought, looking down from the bus window at a lone mud hen floating on the waters of the bay. *And so is she.* She pictured the old woman, tried to remember her elusive voice, the gestures, the expressions that had crossed Marta's face. She had seldom, if ever, been in the presence of someone with such an exquisitely heightened sense of grace. Not then, not ever, did Maria suspect that what she had seen in Marta was not the gracefulness of woman, but was, rather, that of man. For Marta was not, and never had been, Jean-Marc Romier's mother-in-law. The transvestite dancer was, in reality, the eldest brother of Jean's second wife. Another secret that Jean Romier had chosen not to tell.

...I do feel good that Marta phoned me again. And made me come to see her. Maria lit a cigarette. *My last,* she told herself. Nevertheless, as the bus left the Bay Bridge, and her view of the water ended, she lit a second one, obdurate for the moment, as she had a different thought. *So she thinks I'm weak and lazy, does she?!*

Part IV

Travels through Time and Space

1

The Morning Flute
and the Morning Fire

circa 2700 B.C.

Each dawn, from high above the waking city, from the rooftop of the temple, there came the slow and honeyed largos of a mellow low-toned flute. Laden with melancholy, the song seduced the young morning into timelessness and mystery, revealed within the sad sweet brevity of life.

The date palms swayed before the clouds, fronds waving serenely through golden rosy mists. Birds departed their quarters in the branches, calling good morning and *ciao*! in the languages of birds as they winged above the world.

Another new day in Orom, thirty-second year of the third Inannic dynasty, twenty-seven hundred years before the birth of Christ, was about to begin.

*   *   *

In the shadow of the temple wall a lone figure stood, watching the seventh sacred rite of the new moon. Thoughtful he stood, not chanting, in solitary stillness. He observed each movement of the high priestess, and observed above her the streaming clouds as they passed over heaven to welcome the sun. He saw the play of gentle breezes that moved through the palm fronds, the patterns of rainbow colors in the coming and going of the people in the throng. And he observed, also, within his own soul, the ecstasy which made reply to the beauty of all that came before him.

All is harmonious, he thought; *it goes well in our city. The priestess of Inanna and, therefore, all the people of Orom are dancing with Divinity. We live in harmony with the Lady, with Her Heaven and with Her Earth. Our own natures move with all Nature. The hour is beautiful; it is right and good.*

Thoughtful, yet, he walked to his home, a modest house, on the street of the bakers; his father and the fathers of his father had been bakers. The street was not far west of the center of the city. He would change into his finest holiday attire and quickly walk back, to the Palace of Asimbabar.

In one double-hour he was to meet with the king, with many nobles of Orom, and with ambassadors of three cities of the west, from the Land between Two Waters.

The meeting concerned a tremendous matter. The king of Orom was, after several years of hesitation and deliberation, at last prepared to begin the construction of a second city temple. No longer a subject for planning or political debate, a second temple was an imminent necessity, if the king was to acknowledge the impassioned popularity— among the city's prosperous—of Enki, the mighty and active God. The temple was to be erected in the center of Orom, directly facing, and exactly equal in size, to the Temple of Heaven's Queen. And he, Gudea, son of Nergal and scribe of the king's eldest brother, was to receive the king's appointment. Through no desire of his own, Gudea would soon be Enki's priest.

*　　　　　*　　　　　*

As he walked from his home to the palace, Gudea told himself to pray to Inanna for counsel. The goddess, he believed, could only give approval to an increased beauty, an increased harmony in Orom. Kind and just, she would be pleased to share her great domain. Ecstasy would only expand under male and female, two instead of one. Good fortune would be doubled, Gudea assured himself, or perhaps it was Inanna who assured him. If only he acted correctly. He must never fail to consult both deities, the goddess as well as the god, to learn the will of each. He saw that truth with clarity.

It would, the old man realized with a trembling, be necessary to work closely not only with the chief priestess, the elderly administrator, but also with Inanna's vessel, the high priestess—the young Inannanindigur, herself—in devotion to this task…

*　　　　　*　　　　　*

At that same hour, in Fa-Orszag

Simbaya sat huddled with her husband and children by the warmth of the early morning fire. Absent-mindedly, she stirred the soil at her feet with a little huluppu twig while she gazed up at the crescent moon and the morning star, fading now, together, between the fronds of a tall date palm. She began to squeeze her lips together as the urge to cry became more and more powerful within her throat.

Two years had passed since they had taken Anarisha.

Simbaya had wept too often. Her husband had shown her little, if any, sympathy. She was certain he had had enough of her tears. She kept her face looking upward toward heaven and silently pleaded with the Anunnaki to help Anarisha, wherever she was, whatever had become of her.

She was my comforter and my companion, a part of me, the kindest person I have ever known.

Simbaya silently repeated '*the kindest person I have ever known*' over and over, like a mantra, pleading with Heaven and giving steadiness to her heart.

2

In a Bookshop of Nayarit

Nayarit, Mexico
1964 A.D.

> "In the warm afterglow of the lover's night, the land fills with contentment, security, and the continuation of life through sexuality and food."
>
> —*The Time Falling Bodies Take to Light,*
> William Irwin Thompson

"Hey Dagan! Dagan! Come look over here!" Tom Muir's loud baritone boomed across the aisles of the tiny Mexican bookstore. "I found just what we need! Just what the doctor ordered!"

The middle-aged shopkeeper glanced up from the thick reference book he was perusing at his counter. He removed his reading spectacles to better observe the two young gringo customers.

Tom waved a thin paperback in Michael's face. "It's for somebody who speaks Spanish. But we can learn it all backwards," Tom hardly decreased his volume, though his friend was now at his side. "Then I'll tackle the novels, they look easy. Cut the look, man. What's so funny? This thing is chock full of handy phrases. And see how it's in categories:eating, shopping—"

"Big deal. Language books always do that. Did you ever do your French homework?" Michael glanced at the book and at the other five Tom was holding. "Let me see that." He pulled *Ingles Fantastico Sin Maestro* from Tom's grip and flipped through a few pages, then he started to laugh. "Oh, yeah, just what you need, man, phrases for your present way of life. '*Pude usted decirme donde puedo comprar unos hele-chos?*' That's how you say 'Can you tell me where I can buy some ferns?'" He turned to another section. "'*No puedo decir, a usted lo que se de sus negocios, porque no tengo tiempo que perder.*'"

"Which means?"

"Which means: 'I cannot tell you what I know about your business, because I have no time to lose.' Oh, that one's real useful, Tom. Fundamental. There must be thousands of people who need to say that. Everyday."

"Well, you never know what life might bring, I always say. Give me back my book, Dagan."

"Oh come on, is this really what you want to spend your hard-earned money on?"

"Yeah, Dagan, actually it is. And the price is right—twenty-five pesos. Look—here's the medical section: '*Tome chocolate caliente para esa ron-quera.*' You could save someone with—wait, give it back, Dagan! Let me see, that means—'Take hot chocolate for that hoarseness.' No—wait, listen, can't you see it…There you are, Mike—you wake up in bed one morning and you're lying beside this gorgeous senorita…and she opens her big, thick-lashed eyes. Sleepily, contentedly, she murmurs to you: '*Buenos Dias, Michael, mi amor.*' And lo and behold—the poor little chiquita's voice is hoarse! So you reply softly, in your irresistibly deep, well-practiced Spanish, '*Tome chocolate caliente para esa ronquera, mi corizon.*' Now she gazes at you gratefully. Seductively, she slithers from your bed to go make scrumptious Mexican hot chocolate…"

Michael raised his eyebrows, then grinned benignly. "It's your money, Tom."

The shopkeeper smiled, also, as Tom paid for the book and the five others. Then, after making change, the slight, middle-aged man stared intently. But not at Tom. "Your name is 'Dagan,' senor?" His accent barely differed from their own.

"You speak excellent English!" Tom exclaimed.

The shopkeeper laughed and Michael sighed. Just like Tom to say something so absurd; the man had uttered three English words. But how did the guy know his name?

"Thank you," said the shopkeeper to Tom. Then his gaze returned to Michael. "Your name is Dagan?" He asked again, very seriously.

"Yes, senor, that's right. But how do you know that?"

"Well, I couldn't help but overhear your friend here," the shopkeeper replied, smiling again. "And I have some interest in that particular name, you see. Though, never before, have I had the honor of meeting an actual authentic Dagan!" At that instant both Michael and Tom observed the acute awareness in the man's eyes.

"This interest was passed to me by my father, my late father. My father was a history buff, you see, among other things. Researching ancient history was a favorite avocation. And he was a collector of antiquities." He paused for a moment to reach for something beneath his counter, then looked up again.

"Particularly, he was interested in the middle east, in the original civilizations. Yes, Babylon, Elam, Egypt, Canaan; the civilizations referred to in the scriptures. He had a consuming interest in the gods of those lands. Most specifically, he was fascinated with fertility. He spent half a lifetime learning what he could about the fertility gods—the original gods and goddesses of love," he hesitated, "And that is where you come in, Senor Dagan."

Michael looked at Tom. It was Tom who raised his eyebrows this time, and smirked.

"The name 'Dagan,' you see—excuse me, but," he interrupted himself, "are you yourself cognizant of the derivation of your name?"

Michael stared at the man blankly. "Well, I don't know, I mean, my name, my father told me it's from Palestine. His side of the family is Jewish. I know Dagan is not a European name, even though my father's father was from Eastern Europe, from Russia, a place called Pinsk. I do know the name comes from Palestine, but exactly when it was that my family emigrated from there, that I don't really know for—"

"But do you know what the word 'Dagan' means, young man?"

"No. No, I'm afraid I don't My family always intended to find out, but uh, no, no one in the family actually—" Michael's voice began to trail off and Tom recognized his friend's embarrassed look and tone of voice.

The shopkeeper noticed, too. "It is not necessarily likely that you would be privy to that information, senor," he said, sympathetically. "To most of us in the west, that name relates only to obscure history. Your name is an ancient name, you see. Very ancient, even before Babylon. We can trace it all the way back to Sumer. Very far back, *verdad*?"

"Sumer?" Both Michael and Tom repeated the word at once.

"Yes, indeed, to Sumer, the 'Land between the Two Waters;' the Land of Ur, where Abraham was born, where he came to know his God. Wait now, let me show you something." He bent down and brought up a small, well-worn book from beneath the counter. Placing it upon the huge encyclopedia he'd just been reading, he quickly flipped through its pages. "Here we are. the Sumerian 'King Lists.' They kept lists, you see, of their kings, their dynasties. Very methodical people, those Sumerians. List-makers, bookkeepers, wonderful accountants. Accounting—that's how writing began, you know. They thanked Nisaba, their Goddess of the Storehouse for bringing it to them. Accounting first, literature second. Business is business, true? Or maybe you boys aren't so aware of that, as yet. But you will be, not to worry. An old American expression: 'not to worry,'" he laughed, "Maybe Jewish, I think. I learned it years ago, a little stint I had at Cal Tech. 'Not to worry.' Unusual grammar. I've always remembered it. Here, read this please. It's in English, my friend," This time he turned to Tom. "You see, here are the names of the Sumerian kings (and a few queens). Centuries of them. Here, look on this side." He pointed with a pencil. "Here we have the Dynasty of Isin. And there they are—you see! Two kings with the Dagan title! 'Iddin-Dagan': reigned two years, hardly at all. 'Ishme-Dagan,' twenty years. Now, do you have some time boys, would you like to hear more about all this?" he asked, hopefully.

Michael and Tom looked at each other. Tom nodded with enthusiasm; he was easily interested in knowing anything obscure, besides the shopkeeper possessed a compelling voice, with a tranquil sense of timing that encouraged listening. And the man was speaking clear English! Michael nodded also, a bit somberly, concealing his emotion. The truth was he felt, just then, unexpectedly elated to learn about his name.

"Good. Good I'll go on, then. Now, to comprehend the special significance of why the 'Dagan' comes hyphenated at the end—at least this was my father's theory—it is because Dagan is the name of an incarnated god. A god of fertility. Look here. What other name do you see that is used in this way? I'll show you. There: 'Ishtar.' 'Libit-Ishtar.' You see how the title of the goddess appears at the end? Just like the 'Dagan.' Because Ishtar, just like Dagan, is a sacred reference. Ishtar is a sacred name; Dagan is a sacred name," he paused, for effect, and also to see Michael's reaction. But if there was any reaction, the young man was not revealing it. The shopkeeper continued.

"Ishtar was originally named 'Inanna,' you understand, in Sumer. 'Ishtar' is the later Babylonian name. And the persona of Ishtar turned, in fact, a little more foreboding than Inanna ever was, just like Babylonian law was more foreboding, compared to Sumerian. The goddess is 'Oshun' in Africa. In the Greek world, she is 'Aphrodite'—perhaps that name is more familiar? For the Essence of Feminine Love and Desire? Here in Central America she is 'Ixchel,' among other designations. In India, 'Rati.' And she has more names. She has so many, many designations.

"So. 'Inanna' was the Sumerian title. Inanna, the Goddess of the Morning and the Evening Star. That 'star,' of course, is really a planet. Venus. The Roman appellation. I find it fascinating, by the way, that all over the world the fertility goddess was one with that particular heavenly body, whatever her local name was.

"But, to get back to your own name—Inanna's consort was the shepherd king, 'Dumuzi.' The man once actually lived. Very probably. And just like the Hebrew's David—who was another intimate of the Divine, I might add—Dumuzi was a shepherd. Perhaps it is the shepherd's nightly interlude with the stars that explains the divine connection, do you suppose? Like David, King Dumuzi's first occupation was shepherd. Then he became king.

"In the Inanna-worshipping cities of Sumer, the kings who succeeded Dumuzi were thought to be Dumuzi's incarnations. Apparently something like the lineage of lamas in Tibet. Ah, never mind, boys, not many in the west know about that interesting topic, either. Maybe one day, maybe by the end of the century?" he laughed, and Tom looked at Michael and shrugged.

"But I digress. 'Dagan' seems to refer to the deification of this continually reincarnated mortal, Dumuzi. That was my father's idea about the title. Inanna and Dumuzi were the sacred husband and wife of Sumerian religion. Those two lovers were, in other words, the accepted rulers of the universe: The Lady of the Heavens and the Shepherd-King of Earth. In those early days, of course, shepherding was quite an up-and-coming profession. People were impressed with the newest technology—the domestication of animals. And they were impressed with the shepherds, the men who had the know-how. By the time of Christ it was just the opposite; shepherding had become an ordinary, humble job. This can all take on a certain significance for us today, we who know of David, the shepherd king, and of Jesus, who was both the 'Good Shepherd' and the 'King of Kings.' It is interesting to see that there were holy shepherd-kings way back in those early days—centuries before David and more than two thousand years before Christ. I believe it can be quite thought provoking to realize what is innovative and what is tradition, don't you agree?

"But, anyway, to get back to Dumuzi and Inanna: Inanna breathed her spirit into the body of her high priestess, a woman who served in the temple of the goddess. Usually this woman was from a family of the upper class. When Dumuzi and Inanna came together in the annual sacred rite—the sacred fucking, so-to-speak—the king of the city made love with the high priestess. By means of that New Year ritual, the Sumerians called forth their highest, most holy power: fertility. New Years was extremely important to the Sumerians, just like to the Chinese. In fact, for many reasons, my father believed the two cultures evolved from the same Central Asian people.

"Humanity's fertility, and Earth's fertility—these were united for the Sumerians. The two were entwined, wrapped up together, inseparable in the Sumerian psyche. The people needed and revered both. The Sumerian hymns move back and forth between images of human love-making and images of thriving fruits and vegetables, of meat and milk and honey, cheese and butter and barley ale.

"One of the great erotic poems in all of human history is the Sumerian hymn to the intercourse of Inanna and Dumuzi. It was sung by the Inanna-Dumuzi worshipers, which is to say nearly all of the citizens. You must see the words of the song one day, my friends. It's much like the beautiful 'Song of Songs' in the *Torah* or the *Old Testament*— filled with luscious images of fruit, you understand. In fact it's probably the parent of Solomon's song. But it is much older and far more explicit. Anyone who possesses the name of Dagan owes it to himself to look it up. You see, what I'm trying to tell you boys is this: 'Dagan' is a title for the kings who were Consort to the Goddess!

"Subsequently, in later mid-eastern writings, we find references to 'Dagon' with an 'O'; the name is that of a fertility god, pure and simple.

The poet Milton even mentions him. You might want to look that up, too, Michael.

"Now, the most famous of the two Sumerian Dagan kings was Ishme-Dagan, 1884 to 1856 B.C.; you see the dates, there, boys? Ishme was a writer, or at least he made dictation to his scribes. In his tablets, Ishme-declared that he was divinely appointed to 'guard the life breath of all lands.' Quite an unfamiliar image isn't it, to 'guard the breath?' But breath was numinous to the ancients.

"Do I make sense to you? 'Numinous' is a fantastic word, don't you agree? The sister of 'luminous.' Not only do they rhyme, but their meanings have such kinship. Numinous means 'evincing the presence of a deity.' *Verdad*? Just like 'luminous,' the word refers to Light! If we're talking about a benevolent deity, of course." He laughed and, seeing the bewildered eyes of both Americans, decided, matter-of-factly, that these two, like most of their compatriots, cared less about the nuances of the English language than he did. Then he continued, his voice suddenly hushed, and a bit dramatic, "In his tablets, Ishme-Dagan spoke directly of the sacred marriage. He declared, 'I am he whom Inanna, Queen of Heaven and Earth, has chosen for her beloved husband!'

"So, there you have it! Whether you are a true descendant of Ishme-Dagan, or simply a descendant of some ordinary citizen who took the name—that, Michael Dagan, is the question! In my opinion, it would have been unlikely that anyone, other than the true descendants, would have been allowed, in such a religious and legal-minded society, to use that particular name. It was not the custom in their world, as it is in Mexico. I don't think ordinary Sumerians would have found it feasible to simply snatch up the most loaded title in their world, and—"

"And claim it for their own, just because they wanted to?" inserted Tom. Tom was now painfully tired of keeping quiet, not only for the last few minutes, but for the last few months, during which time the limitations of his Spanish had kept him from nearly all his usual habits of conversational domination. With the one exception that he could still be loud.

"Si, senor, that is correct," said the shopkeeper. "Yes, indeed, your friend Dagan, here, has quite a name for himself!" he smiled, "And I must say, I am experiencing, in meeting you, today, Michael, a great excitement. The excitement that my father would know, could he be here in my place!" Tom gave Michael another raised eyebrow of mock admiration, but Michael was oblivious to everything except the expression on the shopkeeper's face, which conveyed a respect that was nothing less than awe.

"I was not aware—it was rather foolish of me," the man continued, "I was not even aware that your name was still in use. It is quite satisfying to learn that your family history does, in fact, go back to the Middle East. Just imagine what treasure is there in your genes, my friend! And what memories! They claim these days that ancestral memories are not passed on, but I don't believe that. We know virtually nothing, as yet, about DNA, or about the relationship of thought to chemistry. Who knows what somebody will prove some day in the future! Now, please, if you will, if you are not in any hurry, gentlemen, have a seat. You see, I have some stools back here, let me bring them out for you. Perhaps you would care for a glass of beer? Some *tapas*? Let me go for you. I'll be back in just a minute—make yourselves completely at home," he looked at them imploringly; it was obvious he was anxious for them to stay. Before they could even think to refuse, he had rushed out of the store and down the street.

"Well, well, well, now," said Tom.

Michael said nothing.

"I guess it does explain your father, doesn't it?" said Tom. Michael had, on a couple of occasions, divulged a few details of his father's personal history.

When the shopkeeper returned to the store, he was flushed from haste. He set his purchases on the counter, three bottles of Corona, and a plate of various tortilla-rolled dishes, chips and cucumbers with lime, guacamole, and salsa. "I am so sorry, I have forgotten to introduce myself. My own name—I have completely forgotten to tell you!" he laughed. "I am Enki Rodriguez."

"An unusual first name," said Tom.

"It's Sumerian," smiled Enki. "A god. My father, you see, was truly obsessed with that subject. If you knew anything of Sumer, you would immediately recognize the name 'Enki.' But, of course, you are not alone in this ignorance." He handed Michael a glass and poured him some beer, then some for Tom and himself. "Not many are knowledgeable on that subject, as yet. I grew up in an unusual family, in many ways," he laughed. "The information from Sumeria is relatively recent, you know: the excavations, the comprehension of the cuneiform, all comparatively new. But the tablets are numerous; we have so much. Even the school children's homework. One day the world shall know Sumeria as it knows Egypt or Greece. More and more material comes forth. My father himself wrote a book, and several monographs. Here, allow me to show you his photo." Again, he reached under his counter. This time he brought forth a faded and wrinkled photograph. A hefty young man, whose face and whose entire bearing conveyed strength and virility. The man wore what appeared to be a Hemingway style safari suit; he seemed, altogether, a sort of Mexican version of that American novelist-adventurer. Perched on his shoulder was a large parrot, and, incongruously, a bouquet of flowers was in his hand. "They're a kind of *frangipani*," said Rodriguez, pointing to the flowers. "This was taken in 1932, in Guatemala. My father, like the century, was thirty-two. I have to confess," he said, as he passed the photo to Michael and squeezed a slice of lime over his cucumbers, "I am showing you this so that my father can, in some way, meet with you this morning." and he smiled sheepishly.

As Rodriguez continued to quiz Michael about his family history, interspersing his questions with stories of his own family, Michael found himself developing a comfortable feeling about the man. The guy was so interested. And interesting. Tom liked him, too, though he gave Tom but minimal attention. It was purely circumstantial that the two travelers did not, after that one meeting, ever see Enki Rodriguez again. They did search him out, on the day they departed San Blas, but unfortunately, Sr. Rodriguez was not, on that day, at his bookstore.

The visit ended at noon when the shopkeeper declared he needed to close for siesta. He sincerely expressed his regret, but it was necessary, he said, for him to honor an afternoon social engagement. He wrote down his phone number as he avowed that Michael and Tom must visit his home, to meet his wife and children. The boys had no telephone where they were staying, but they promised to stop by the shop again.

"Yes, definitely, you must! My family will be thrilled to meet you. My eldest son, he knows all that I know, about the fertility gods—I have seen to it!…Well, my friends, it has truly been a pleasure! But today I have asked Michael here so many questions. I have yet to talk with you, my patient young friend," and he turned at last to Tom. "But, then," his bright eyes grew even brighter, "*No puedo decir, a usted lo que se de sus nogocias, porque no tengo tiempo que perder!*"

"Come again?" said Tom.

"Oh, you do not understand me, *amigo*?" smiled Enki. "You must look it up. It's one of those 'handy phrases' in your book. But I will translate for you: 'I cannot tell you what I know about YOUR business, Tom, because I have no time to lose!'" Sr. Rodriguez shook their hands and accompanied them to the door, he and Tom both laughing, while Michael remained completely lost in thought.

3

Far from the USA

from San Blas, Nayarit, Mexico
April, 1964

Dear Rosie,

Aquei que juzga menos es el que juzga mejor. That means, "He who judges least is he who judges best." And it's all I have to say to you about your last letter. Except for one more thing—you are way off base. Also, I miss you. All your funny ways. I miss everything about you.

If only your mom had let you come here last December. Lately you're beginning to seem like a character in some book, you seem so far from reality, at least this Mexican reality.

I wish you could see the place we're in now. It's an old-fashioned, coastal town. San Blas, in the state of Nayarit. We're by the jungle, by a river, and by the sea. When you're out on the river you can see alligators and birds, fantastic tropical varieties of birds. This area is known for its birds. There's this nice elderly British couple we're friends with—they've come to this town every year for the last ten years just for bird watching!

We live in the poorest section of town. Which is also, in my opinion, the most interesting. Funky and beautiful, both. Kind of like a bouquet of gardenias in a Corona bottle. Which happens to be what is sitting here in front of me on the table—it's Ana's arrangement. Ana is Louis' wife. We're staying with these two guys (they're brothers) and their wives, and a baby. Nice people, just a couple years older than we are. I'm learning a lot from them. Especially Rico, he knows so much about Mexican politics, all the nuances of how the Indians are so screwed. He belongs to a local literacy organization, and he brought us with him to a couple of meetings. The people have a goddess here. "Amara"—that's her Spanish name. The Goddess of the Sea. I learned the *wixarika* name, but it seems so private and sacred, I just don't want to pass it on. They thank her for the rain for their harvests, and for the fertility of the women. Some of them are worried that tourism's going to claim their sacred place. I'd like to get a little involved, in fact, while I'm here. People seem to trust me. And nobody speaks much English so my Spanish is improving, though Tom's, I have to say, can only be described as a bad joke. And he's embarrassingly loud. I guess he thinks more volume makes him lucid. Whether it's Spanish he's speaking or English.

The baby is Rico's and Marcela's. She's incredibly cute. You'd really like her. I watch her for Marcela a lot. I take her out on walks and stuff, and it makes me think about you and me. I've made loads of movies of this kid. You'll see.

Rico and Louis are letting us stay here while they help us on the Chevy. It broke down again. This time near Manzanilla. Rico was driving by and he pulled over and offered to help. Then they invited us to stay with them.

I think I could live here for a long time, at least until Louis' wife decides to kick us out. But it's not like we're parasites. We help with the chores, and the baby. Even the girls, the wives I mean, seem to like having us around, at least most of the time.

Being away from America is starting to feel normal. I miss home of course—I mean I miss you. But at the same time, like every once in a while when we get hold of a *Newsweek*, or a *Time* or something, it kind of brings me down, to tell the truth. The more I learn about what's happening over in Vietnam, the more I wonder what the hell is America doing, killing everybody over there? And the more I just want to disassociate myself.

It seems to me that right from the beginning, taking the land and killing the "Indians"—an ignoramus expression; it's about time somebody came up with a new name for indigenous people—and slavery, expansionism, the Monroe Doctrine (have you studied that yet at Berkeley? I hope they explain it better than they did in high school) all of it, the policies toward the rest of the hemisphere, and beyond—all of it sucks.

Look at how the U.S. just plain stole California from Mexico (who, of course, also stole it, to begin with). Because of gold, the Americans grabbed it. Greed. And look at the disgusting military take-over of the Hawaiian Islands. They just imprisoned the queen in her palace with no provocation whatsoever. Total disgusting greediness. I could go on and on, right up to this war right now. For all its history, in fact, our great democracy, which really is great, for certain people, has been practicing might is right. While preaching freedom and equality for all. "All" meaning, of course, that certain qualified part of humanity called "ourselves." Just like Rome did, as Tom says.

By the way, I'm reading an anthology of classical literature that my Dad gave me, I guess he thinks I'm not learning anything here. But he couldn't be more wrong...

4

A Generation Gap

San Francisco
1965 A.D.

> "Barney, hoose yr herows?"
> "well, lemme see—Cleaver, Dillinger, Che, Malcolm X., Gandhi,
> Jersey Joe Walcott, Grandma Barker, Castro, Van Gogh, Villon,
> Hemingway."
> "ya see, he i-dentifies with all LOSERS. that makes him feel good.
> he's getting ready to lose. we're going to help him…there ain't no
> heroes. it's all con. there ain't no winners—it's all con and horse-
> shit. there ain't no saints, there ain't no genius—that's all con and
> fairytale, it makes the game go…"
> —*The Gut Wringing Machine*, Charles Bukowski

David Dagan creased his completed stack of escrow papers slowly
and firmly. Absent-mindedly he stuffed the documents into a manila
envelope, placed the envelope in the "out" basket and arranged the
cover neatly over his new IBM Selectrix. Then he rose from his desk and
went to check the floor by his door for mail, returned to the desk and sat
down again. All his motions were in automatic; his mind was a thousand miles away, on his son.

The boy was becoming one magnificent headache. So much potential, and now, in the dawn of manhood, the kid was turning into nothing but a drifter. Nearly two years with nothing to show, only drifter's jobs, just enough to get by. And no mention in his letters of even a plan about college. David had never, at least not for several years, urged anything whatsoever on Michael. David Dagan was not a nag. But he had silently supposed, simply had expected, more from his son. A good deal more.

Felipa, too, was becoming concerned; their son was, in fact, the only thing his ex ever wanted to talk about whenever she visited or phoned. Michael's sisters were fine, settled, secure. David and Felipa hardly gave a worried thought to the girls.

Michael, the bum, was on a perpetual vacation. Since high school. One extended carefree vacation. Like a lot of kids these days. All those excursions through Europe—the music, the museums, the talks and the meaningful anecdotes...all the books he'd given that boy! The expensive private school education—all come to nothing, just going to waste. The parochial school, the Steiner school...He sighed, remembering the beautiful classrooms in Paris.

You could say—as Michael's younger, but wiser, sister did say—the kid was passively-aggressively throwing it all back in his father's face. He always did have his mother's *chutzpah;* he was born with it. Now he was insolently heading nowhere. Nowhere except, David guessed, in and out of the *palapa* bars of Mexico. Refining his knowledge of *tequila* and *cerveza* and how much he could hold. If he didn't enroll in some university soon, it wouldn't surprise any of them to see him ending up in Vietnam.

By his age I was...Oh, hell, what's the point in even thinking about it!

David had an afternoon coffee date. The girl was due any minute now, any second, right there, in his office; a vivacious, wonderfully joyous girl named Essie, a girl about the age of his son. A waitress in one of those new topless joints in North Beach. But he'd met Essie downtown, at Blum's, the candy store, of all places. Buying chocolate covered cherries, just like he was. A girl who liked to satisfy herself.

Maybe they should just remain right here in the office. But he would have to straighten the place up a bit.

He rose from his desk again and went across the room to arrange the pillows on his sleeper-sofa. *Michael needs to be shown, somehow…No, no sense in butting in. It's his life now…his bed he's making…*David punched a firm tapestried pillow in its center, a gesture only psychologically necessary. Maybe it would be a better idea to talk to the girlfriend. Rosie. That one seemed to have a good head on her shoulders. David didn't want to interfere in the relationship, but it seemed to him that the girl might be a bit more capable of seducing Michael into coming home, more capable than she had thus far bothered to be. Young and inexperienced she was, he supposed.

All she needs is a little fatherly advice he told himself. So many girls these days seemed totally ignorant of how to use their more subtle feminine wiles. Not the way it used to be, back in his day—in Felipa's day—back in the forties and fifties. Yes, he'd have to call Rosie Hestia and take her to lunch, as soon as possible.

He bent down to search through the record cabinet for his newest album. "*Boss Tres Bien.*" He wanted it on the turntable before Essie Esurient arrived.

"Essie's gonna love the Conga drums," he declared out loud.

5

A Singular Circumstance in the City of Orom

east of the Euphrates
circa 2700 B.C.

The people were astounded. Never had the high priestess spoken in public. Never, in time out of mind, had any high priestess spoken in public.

Some, those standing near to the wall of the sacred pool, perceived the first words, no more than a murmuring to herself. A few amongst those closer listeners, some of the lesser priestesses and a few devotees, even caught the meaning, difficult though that was with her accent, so foreign and so strange.

"Come to me Kukuda," were the words they thought they heard.

Then she rose from the water. She looked about, gazing forthrightly at certain of the people standing in the crowd, a moderate crowd that day.

Many of them gasped. Those who were sleepy, waiting half-consciously in the dawn, instantly awoke. A great hush fell upon them all. The lesser priestesses, the devotees, the supplicants, the passing traders and the housewives, the servants, the others, all turned still and silent. The priestess was speaking, and this time she was loud and almost clear.

"Kukuda!" she called, her voice resonating with the strength of two years of daily chanting, "Kukuda, if you are there among the people, I beg you, now, come forth! Come now, please Kukuda, come to me."

The people looked about them. Some were acquainted with a woman named 'Kukuda.' "She calls for the wife of the trader," they murmured. The name was unique. The woman was not of Orom. She was a foreigner, like Inannanindigur herself.

Some began then to catch sight of the woman. Yes, she was there, amongst them, rushing, coming from somewhere in the center of the crowd. A small, bony matron. Quickly they made way for her. All eyes watched as the wife of Ursunabi moved towards the Pool of Sacred Waters.

Transfixed herself, Kukuda stared straight ahead, seeming not to heed the crowd. Yet she moved through the people with quick efficiency. She was determined to learn what the priestess could possibly want with her.

When Kukuda arrived at the wall of the pool, Inannanindigur walked toward her from her place at the center. Kukuda, confused, looked down at the water. The priestess spoke, "No, my lady, you need not descend. I am coming."

Kukuda waited. Every new moon she came to this ritual, compelled, though not really knowing why. She supposed the priestess had observed her constant attendance. But what could the village woman want of her? Kukuda's bowels churned roughly, enlivened with guilt and fear.

There was a muttering in the crowd as those near the front informed those behind just what it was they believed the priestess might have said.

When the Holy One reached the quaking matron, she took both her hands and assisted her into the water. All was silence again while the people strained their utmost to listen. But once again, only those who stood most near could discern the words. For now the priestess spoke in the softness of private conversation.

"Kukuda," she said, gazing into the eyes of Ursunabi's wife, and continuing to clasp the sweating palms in her own. The matron heard a voice that was richly loving, young, and sincere.

"In truth, your name is good. Do you remember when you were a child? Sweet Kukuda?" Inannanin spoke tenderly, repeating "sweet" in the tongue of Orom and of Fa-Orszag, which were essentially the same. "Forget, now, what you have become. Return; go back to your child-time perceptions. Remember the little girl you used to be. Kukudi. You are that one. I have seen you. I see you now. I see you in my temple, I see you in my sleep. I see you with your Miri. Do you understand? I am your friend." She smiled, and, the people gasped once more, for her smile was so beautiful, and they had never seen it, not until that time. Then, to the astonishment of all, Inannanindigur pulled the woman to her breast. She held her, hugging her gently, but not for long. Without a parting word, she spun around, quickly returning to the fountain at the center of the pool, where she resumed the New Moon rite. Raising her thighs for the strong, hard push of water, she let it press her holy loins. Slowly moving, at one with heavenly bliss, she shared her sacred passion with the city of Orom.

Kukuda, still standing in the water near the edge of the pool, waited for the ceremony to finish. As it came to closure, the crowd's chanting softening into silence, she lowered herself to her knees. Then she prostrated three times, right there in the water, before that holy woman, that one of whom she had made a slave.

Then she turned. Soaked clothing clinging to her body, she stepped from the pool to hurry through the crowd. Through the street of the potters, the street of the granaries, the street of the stone workers, and onward to the more affluent neighborhood of her own home.

*   *   *

For the remainder of her life, whenever she felt overcome with sadness or great confusion, and on other occasions as well, Kukuda would think of Anarisha (whom she never learned to call by any other name). She would be reminded of beauty. Then the sadness or the anger or the other pains would be transformed, mixed with the compassion that now defined her world—a netherworld no more.

6

The Winter of Love

San Francisco
Winter, 1967 A.D.

"I am that I am"

—the *Torah*, the *Bible*, the *Koran*

"I'm mixed race, mixed nationality, mixed religion. And I don't comprehend this narrow, insular way you have of looking at things." Michael tore open a bag of potato chips as he spoke.

Rosie glared at him. He was speaking matter-of-factly; it was clear he was frustrated, not intentionally obnoxious, simply stating his confusion. *But that's just as annoying as if he were acting stuck-up about it all,* she decided.

"I don't get it," he continued, "the interpretation that you give to those words. '*I am the Way, the Truth and the Life.*' Sure, the man said, 'I,' Rosie, but I really don't think he meant 'I' in the same way you do. Not 'I, Jesus of Nazareth,' not the egocentric 'I.' He meant it like 'I am that I am,' that kind of I. The God within. The 'Kingdom of Heaven' that is within. The 'I' that is Krishna. Or the Sufi's 'Beloved,' Ahknaten's Aten, the Jew's Nameless One. The Buddhist 'Nature Mind.' I could give you—"

"Where in the world do you get all this, Michael?" Rosie was irritated, but she attempted patience. "How do you know what Jesus meant? You're not even a Christian!"

They were sitting on the edges of a spacious lawn of Golden Gate Park. A band played upon the outdoor stage. The stage was quite distant, so that Michael and Rosie were not, as the majority of the crowd, silently and hypnotically immersed in the inner world of the music, the psychedelic, spell-casting songs.

The band playing now was Country Joe and The Fish. They were doing their extremely slow and dreamy "Porpoise Mouth." For the entire week this band had been playing "Porpoise Mouth," in one manifestation after another, always enigmatic, always mesmerizing, to the people in the houses and apartments of the Berkeley neighborhood where Country Joe shared a home. Mesmerizing to those, that is, who were attuned to such things—such things as an ecstasy that drifted on waves of sound into your window, floating through your rooms like an almost visible ghost stream of light or steam or smoke, and then whirling into your ears to take you slowly dancing into the spaces of your deeper mind.

Maria Ananin was one of those attuned to such things. All week long she had lived with "Porpoise Mouth," as that short hallucinogenic symphony wafted not only into her apartment but also through her street. And up into the trees of Berkeley, where the sparrows, the robins, the starlings, and a few lost or set-free parakeets, along with the students walking down below, all came together with that sound. This weekend, though, The Fish played in "The City," for the people in the Park.

The noon sun was shining and the euphoric fragrance of sensimilla was everywhere. Michael and Rosie sat with Maria and her new boyfriend, a Beatle-haired anthropology teaching assistant named Rick, on a multi-colored woolen Mexican blanket. The blanket was one of Michael's presents for Rosie, brought back from Guadalajara a couple of months before. Michael lived in San Francisco now, in a small studio apartment not far from the park, just across from the 'Panhandle.' He attended the Academy of the Arts, enrolled in cinematography. He lived alone; Tom Muir had been drafted and sent to Vietnam.

The girls had not seen much of each other in the last year or so. But about ten minutes before, Rosie had spotted Maria—barefoot and tan, with golden waist-length hair encircled in a wreath of eucalyptus leaves (*more gorgeous than ever, in that long gauze dress*, thought Rosie). Rosie invited Maria and her boyfriend to share the blanket, and to share the picnic food, of which she had prepared a great abundance.

Maria and Rick listened without comment to Rosie and Michael's arguing. They quietly helped themselves to fried chicken, to Caesar salad, baked potatoes with chives and sour cream, then apple pie and sodas, as the soon-to-be-married couple became less and less involved in anything but their own heated discussion. All but one of the group ignored the occasional joint which passed their way, and three of them even forgot about the band, a new favorite of Michael's—in fact, his main reason for being there. It was only Maria who really heard the music, thinking, *This feels like a déja vu—have I heard this song before?*

Rosie's voice was growing louder. "It's all your interpretation, Michael—just what you're not supposed to do—interpret, I mean. The Bible says not to interpret. We have to be very careful not to—"

"Oh, wait now, Rosie," Michael interrupted. "I know you were taught that, but everything you were taught, it was all only interpretation, itself. To me it's as clear as, for example, '*Thou shalt not kill*,' which sounds simple, but even that, because there is no…" he paused for a second.

"No direct object!" said Maria unexpectedly.

They all turned to stare at her, and then Michael smiled, "Yeah, right, Maria, no word to say what it is you can't kill. Anything? People? The people in your own tribe? Who? What can't you kill? You're forced to make an interpretation. From my point of view it's you, you and your fellow fundamentalists, Rosie, who are—"

"We are meant to follow Jesus," said Rosie firmly. "That's the way it is, sweetheart, pure and simple."

"But what if you follow, instead, the Christ? Using the more esoteric definition—"

"What do you mean 'instead,' Michael? It's all the same thing. You're going in circles. This whole darn conversation is going in circles!"

He looked at her, exasperated. She, strong and sure, looked at him, loving him so very much and praying that he would one day come around (where did he get those words, like "esoteric," anyway; he hadn't even been to college?) He smiled now, loving her, too, and feeling tolerant, even of her rigid religion. It was, after all, San Francisco, 1967. And though it was winter, two seasons early for the "Summer of Love," it was a day that most truly deserved that name.

Rick and Maria watched Rosie and Michael for a few more seconds. "You know, I think I'd like to move a little closer to the stage," Rick said. "That isn't Leary up there now, is it, Maria? Hey, Mike, Rosie, nice meeting both of you, and thanks for the great fried chicken."

"And the delicious apple pie," Maria added. "Let's keep in touch more, Rosie. Nice to see you, Michael." It seemed, she thought, like centuries had passed since high school.

*   *   *

"You know what I read, the other day Rick?" Maria asked, trying to keep pace with her long-legged boyfriend as the two of them wound their way through the clusters of chemically and musically altered bodies sitting and lying upon the grass, " I read that '*You can't establish the identity of the Lord by mental speculation.*' That's what it says in the *Sri Isopanisad*. That seems obvious, doesn't it? But people always try." He looked back at her blankly. "Wha'd you say?" was all he muttered, not really interested in finding out, as he noticed a dark-haired woman who gave every indication that she might possibly be Grace Slick.

"Oh, nothing, Rick, nothing. Go ask Alice," was her soft, and unperceived, reply.

7

On an African Riverboat

Uganda
two years later

> "I am the fresh taste of the Water: I the silver of the moon, the
> gold o' the sun,
> The word of worship in the Veds, the thrill
> That passeth in the ether, and the strength Of man's shed seed.
> I am the good sweet smell
> Of the moistened earth. I am the fire's red light,
> The vital air moving in all which moves, the holiness of hallowed
> souls, the root
> Undying, whence hath sprung whatever is..."
> —*The Bhagavad-Gita*

"C'mon Maria, let's walk around a bit, have a look at things," the young ponytailed American sounded confident and authoritative, as he motioned to his wife.

Rick Ford craned his neck to better observe an imposing, turbaned East Indian man, tallest among the crowd of arriving passengers who were swarming up onto the deck of the "Orishi," the ancient steamer ferry on which they all would soon be crossing Lake Victoria. The

Orishi noisily, but patiently, awaited her much delayed departure from the Ugandan shore.

The atmosphere on the steamer was remarkably different from anything in equatorial West Africa, where Rick and Maria Ford now made their home. Rick was anxious to see everything that he possibly could while aboard this exotic antique. It was, he thought, straight out of a thirties adventure movie, or an old Lowell Thomas newsreel.

The boat was noisily filling with a teeming humanity, piling together down below, sending up their shouts, their ceaseless children's cries, even their drumbeats and snatches of music—African xylophones, and singing—up to the more quiet, more privileged ones preparing to enjoy the formalities on deck.

Rick made quick, excited progress through the crowd, but his wife began to lag behind. "I think I'd rather just sit right down here for awhile, Rick, if you don't mind, I'm becoming a little hot and tired after—"

"Becoming a little tired?!" Rick was incredulous. "I'd say you're becoming a little insane! How could anyone want to miss this? But, O.K., Maria, go sit somewhere in a corner, if that's what you want. I'll see you in the dining room for dinner."

"Fine, Rick. The dining room for dinner. See you later."

Maria seated herself down against a wall, on a narrow wooden bench.

The bench was almost fully occupied already. But she squeezed in at the end, next to a youngish, pink-cheeked Caucasian man. She saw he was wearing the collar of a priest.

He smiled and said hello. And then, with startling instant familiarity, brushing a mosquito from Maria's cheek, the man proceeded to draw her into a quite intimate discussion of his life. He was much older, it turned out, than he first appeared to be.

He was on his way, he said, in a slightly unusual French accent, to return home. To Quebec City, which he had not seen in fifteen years. He had been living all that time at a mission, near a small town somewhere along a river. He was teaching grammar school.

He wanted to confide in her, especially to talk about celibacy, he said, how he had endured it for so long. Through faith. But how difficult that had been. She seemed to be a nice girl, he saw she was a sympathetic soul; he had not found anyone he could speak with like this in years. She made him think about celibacy, which was often, he sighed, on his mind, as it was. He wondered whether he really, truly believed that it was really necessary, for having an authentic religious life, that is. And how or if he could endure it much longer.

After awhile the discussion turned to abortion and birth control.

"But we're on a sinking ship, Father," she interrupted the priest's musings. "And on a sinking ship, the rules are changed. I read in *Life Magazine*, or was it *Look?*—anyway, they say that by the year 1980, the earth might reach a population of four billion! Four billion! I'm not sure I can believe that. But, anyway, the article said that beyond four billion we'll pass the threshold of what the planet can comfortably maintain. After that, if we do allow it to reach four billion, the whole earth will be spoiled. The seas, the atmosphere, the air itself will change. Over-crowding will bring terrible social problems, as well. Growing crime rates, mental illness, depression, heavy drugs, wars,—gangs—just like with over-populated rats! New diseases will come like plagues; droughts and famines will be common, maybe even before the end of the century—"

"My goodness, Maria! Cheery little person aren't you? Don't you have any faith, yourself, dear?" he sighed, and moved on to talk of Africa, as he had come to know it. He spoke of East Africa, and the ways of African villagers, which, he said, were more and more becoming his own ways. Then he went on to the strangeness of the decade, what he'd heard was happening at home in Canada, and in the States. "Tell me about the hippies," he begged, excited that she came from California.

Rick passed by with a rum and coke. He didn't stay, and the priest's talk continued, while the sun set majestically, East African-style, before them, covering the lake with brilliant pink and golden orange. Sometimes she became entranced with the sunset, or with the bobbing of something she couldn't quite make out, or with the water itself, and she entirely missed what the priest was saying.

"From what remains of Christ's words, minus all the political tampering," she caught, after one long contemplation of the colors of the clouds, "what we can tell from His words, it can be seen that Jesus of Nazareth was a Man who was loving. *'Love your neighbor as yourself.'—'Judge not that ye be not judged.' 'Father, forgive them for they know not what they do.'* Love—that is my God. If Love can create the universe and then defy, with miracles, the very nature of what was created, I am not at all surprised. It was to this Love, which Jesus knew to dwell within Himself, and in us all, in all creation, that He referred, I believe, when He said, *'I am the Way—*"

"Oh," she said. "I've thought about such things. And you know what else I believe? I think it was Christ's forty days and nights in the wilderness, in nature, alone in the desert, that brought him to his love. And understanding. Like an Indian yogi. And it gave him the strength to suffer so much for the sake of love, to be an example of love. For our continuing evolution, I think. And I guess it also brought him to the extreme forgiveness he attained…But, it's just very sad, and puzzling, to me, Father, that after all he did for love, so many people, throughout history, have used his name against his purposes. Like, for example, the way some of his 'followers' have always judged others, or righteously ended other people's lives, or even destroyed whole cultures…"

The missionary turned more closely toward her. "Hmmm. Yes, Maria…But what you said before, I guess you meant to say that Christ was able to discover who He was because He went inward, in the desert? To the Kingdom of Heaven that 'lies within,' as He put it. As when He said "*I am the Way.*' It is my own belief that He was not referring to the sort of "I" that was a personal…"

But now she wasn't listening; her mind, once again, was floating on the lake. As she gazed out at the undulating reflections of tangerine sky streaming across the deep blue water, suddenly, seemingly out of the blue, but also out of the half-heard, half-remembered phrases of her present companion, there drifted fragments of a similar conversation, and she thought of Michael Dagan. And with those thoughts, simultaneously, came the first evening breeze—a light warm African breeze, like a caress, so soothing it was, and so blissfully soft.

8

Morocco

Rabat, Morocco
1970 A.D.

> 'With patience, fortitude, and purity...An unrevengeful spirit never given
> To rate itself too high—such be the signs...'
>
> —the *Bhagavad-Gita*

The air was cold and damp in Morocco in February. Even in a not so elevated city like Rabat. It would be necessary to buy her a sweater. His *Gbandi* country-cloth jacket would be good enough for keeping warm, himself.

She looked so cold and insubstantial here, like a plant transplanted to the wrong climate zone. Rick noticed how it was when she spoke to people; she still used the soft, slow, gentle rhythms of the tropical equator. Of course she did. Mannerisms didn't fade away in two days, whatever age you were when you acquired them. The Moroccan men seemed to find the way she spoke interesting, perhaps more than interesting. Enticing, tempting, and no-good? He wondered.

The way she moves, never thinking about it. She doesn't even know how she moves, he decided. *She's a bit like Kima, I guess, yeah, a certain delicate, sensual motion they both have.* And then, too, she always looked up to Ma Mehma, the older woman next door—she might even have picked up a bit of that practical, peaceful thing that Mehma had. Yes, serene like Mehma, wise, a little grave. Sensual like Kima. A few of the village women had been her role models. He understood it now.

She'd been just a girl when they came to the village. *She doesn't know any other way to be a woman*; he had a sudden realization how it happened, the coming of age of his wife. He understood with all the acumen of an intelligent, well-educated, twenty-seven-year-old Berkeley anthropologist.

And he—how had the people initiated him? Influenced him? For the first time in the two days since he said his farewells to the village friends and neighbors who stood waiting in the mist of early dawn, standing somberly in two sad parallel lines at his door, with the characteristic West African formality of such an occasion, for the first time since then, he felt his eyes cloud over. Not quite full enough to make tears, only just enough to let the world go blurry in front of him. It was to become a habit.

He fingered the rough cloth that the shopkeeper had handed him. Maria stood examining something in a corner on the other side of the shop. He looked around. He saw a boy in the light of the entranceway. The boy was staring at Maria as she bent over to pick up another article, a small engraved metal plate. She bent from the lower part of her body, below the waist, at the joints of her legs, just like a West African woman. *So easily influenced*, thought Rick.

He tried to see her through the boy's eyes, but it was impossible. Was the boy noticing her grace, was he seeing her beauty? Or was he categorizing her: a "money-woman"—unveiled, thin, light-haired, maybe-European, maybe American "money woman," as they said in West Africa. Maybe the boy simply thought she was bending kind of strangely. Rick didn't know Morocco, at all. And if he did know it, if he and Maria had lived in Morocco for three and a half years as they had in West Africa, or even longer—if he had lived here all his life, been born

Moroccan, of Moroccan parentage that stretched back to the dawn of oral history—*would I then*, he asked himself, *need any more confirmation that this insolent kid is standing there right in my face imagining that he's fucking with my wife?*

Many years later, he remembered that shop as the defining symbol of the unhappiness that she had always caused him. And he understood, when he thought about it, why it was that he sometimes had to strike her.

*   *   *

One morning she awakened, in the lovely, mysterious rose-hued city of Marrakech, to a serene and settled recognition that marriage was not for her. This conclusion had been refining and polishing itself for months, even years, but only on that cool, full-moon night, in deep sleep, had the insight attained sufficient clarity to call complete attention to itself. Within a week she said good-bye to Morocco, and to Rick Ford, whom she never had really known, anyway.

She decided without deliberation that she would not return immediately to the United States. She would take her portion of their savings, which amounted to a long-enough lasting sum for her purposes. She and Rick had been generously funded for the research project on the religious beliefs of the *Vai* people of Liberia—how the Vai incorporated Muslim belief into pantheistic traditions—a project which proceeded smoothly and successfully because both Rick and Maria were conscientious workaholics, whatever they decided to put their minds to. It was the one thing they had in common.

Rick would finish up the rest of the paper by himself. The research was, after all, his project; he was the anthropologist, she was the wife (an ancient history graduate). But even if her name was never to appear anywhere, never to be connected with all those satisfying, exciting hypotheses she'd given him, Rick was nevertheless generous and at ease about dividing up their small "estate."

Since she knew no passionate relationship with money, but cared only about being where she wanted to be, in minimum comfort and hopefully maximum beauty, she was thoroughly satisfied with what he gave her. She took it all in traveler's checks and kept them in her gold and plum silk purse in the rucksack on her back.

She would go on to the land that had always called to her most clearly, since childhood. She reasoned that if she stayed for a time in Greece, somehow, by some inexplicable but intuited dynamic of the universe, she would find out "who I am," a perplexing question not only for her, but for millions in that era. Which nevertheless didn't make it any less troublesome. Already that decisive week she'd begun to make progress towards answering the question. She now possessed a string of 'nots': she was not meant to live forever with just one man, she was not monogamous, not naturally, and she was not a victim. On the other hand she was not cut out to be so independent that she could live perpetually alone and lonely. She required a community of intimates. She could see a satisfaction in becoming someone like a village widow-woman, perhaps. *Or maybe a courtesan,* she thought light-heartedly, *like an ancient Greek hetaera.*

But a painful memory pushed away that playfulness. Her mind filled instantly with thoughts of Jean Romier. As usual something blocked most of the memory. But she still retained one piece—some phrases that were spoken in Jean's bedroom on that night. They were the words of Ben, Jean's trance-inducing friend…

"The reason men want you, Maria, and the reason that you want them, is the desire to blend your life forces together. Don't be afraid, it's very simple. This is what sexuality is about. This is what life is about. And, the way you are, Maria, I doubt even Aphrodite herself would inspire more of that desire. You could take any man on earth straight up to heaven with you."

Those Beautiful Eyes

She knew that Ben believed, at least for the moment, in what he was saying; it was his sure and powerful conviction that had betrayed her.

9

Memories of a Marriage

inscribed on clay tablets in Inanna's Temple of Orom
circa 2700 B.C.

He was a shining star, brighter than the stars, in my nights. And a sun that moved before me, lighting all my days.

Anurei of Fa-Orszag was the firstborn child of Erishoul the woodsman. Erishoul was a unique man of our people, a village man who lived like the solitary ones of the grasslands, making his home just beyond the edge of our village, beside the grasses where the fruit groves finish and the forest begins. Anurei grew to be a man there, often entering the forest, going deeply within its realm, in company with Erishoul. From the time when he was a small one in his father's arms, they would go. Then, when he had completed the time of drinking from his mother, he would walk hand in hand with his father into the deepest center of all the trees, the holy place. And there they would know Abu and be known of Him, or sometimes Her, as Anurei has told me, for the God of Nature could be both man and woman.

The father and son had no fear of Abu, no fear to walk among the mighty pines and the green growth of the forest, with its beasts and its mists and its ghosts. That is why we of Fa-Orszag knew that Erishoul and his eldest son were Good and Brave Ones of our world.

Anurei came to my family's door when we were both small children. I can still recall those early mornings, the glowing morning light and the glowing little Anurei standing within it.

He was sweet to me, and funny as well, making faces and gestures that caused me to laugh. He learned that it was not always easy for me to cease my laughing, and he delighted to see me so.

He loved to make me smile, as well, then and ever after. He spoke kind and funny words about me, and my family and his own, and all the people of our village, telling tales of what one or another had done, making me smile as I saw the world through those eyes of his which were fatherly even as a little child.

He taught me to walk gently into the forest and to be not only fearless, but happy and loving there, as the still-standing deer mothers or their playful fawns.

I was in the company of Anurei for a part of every day, all the days of our childhood. When we grew to a good age we married, as all Fa-Orszag had known we would. I remember the moment, however, when first he came to speak of it.

We were on the river-path, fetching water for our families, walking the path in silence.

"Anarisha," he said, suddenly, "I desire to sleep upon the mat with you and to enter and keep you in the night."

And so we were married, in the sight of the entire village. Around our shoulders we placed wreaths of the fragrant leaves of the *lauroa*; and the wreathes neither loosened nor broke throughout that night. We led the people around and through our homeland, through the trees of the orchards, almost to the forest, the drumming of Erishoul and of my father, Oresh, and the chanting and the singing of us all, guiding our bodies and spirits in our dance.

In the early dawn, when at last we departed from the people, and at last lay down upon the new mat, in our new home that was crafted so carefully by our loved ones, a great feeling of contentment, woven with curiosity, came upon me. I had always felt so very much wonder for the thing which was about to happen. Delicious mystery hovered in the flickering torchlight of the room.

Then Anurei came into me. With great, smooth power he filled me with the wondrous organ of himself. And at last I knew full loveliness and what it is to be as one with the most god-like man in all the valleys and the kingdoms of the world.

One day, if not in this dream, then in some other, I shall be returned to you, Anurei. And you shall forgive me, my husband, you shall understand with your great kind heart, all that Anarisha has become. I, your Anarisha, who enfolds and caresses you forever, in the private softness of her longing soul.

10

The Greek Island:
a Second Encounter

Paros, Greece
1971 A.D.

"Either the world is a mere hodge-podge of random cohesions
and dispersions, or else it is a unity of order and providence. If
the former, why wish to survive in such a purposeless and chaotic
confusion; why care about anything, save the manner of the ulti-
mate return to dust; why trouble my head at all; since do what I
will, dispersion must overtake me sooner or later? But if the contrary be true, then I do reverence, I stand firmly, and I put my
trust in the directing Power."
—Marcus Aurelius, Emperor of the Western World
(addressing himself) 161–180 A.D.

A retired sea-captain, a fatherly pharmacist, two middle-aged fishermen, a young modernist artist with a witty Scottish wife—good
friends, all of them, speakers of English, all but two of them—had
taken a liking to Rosie Dagan. They were showing Rosie their island.
She spent more and more of her time with this amusing, cafe-loving
group, while her husband wandered about by himself. "He's just doing

his own thing," Rosie explained to her Parosian friends, introducing, with due respect for Michael's inborn inclinations, that new Haight-Ashbury phrase (which later turned so sarcastically pejorative as it spread beyond sixties San Francisco to a more philistine America and to far more cynical times).

One night Rosie went out, minus her husband, to a party at the home of the captain, a handsome, graying man named Apostoli. Apostoli entertained with sophisticated style, in a great white room—with a baby grand—that viewed the sea. The house was in a section of Paros that Michael did not even know existed.

They returned her very late that night to her hotel, straddling the back of a pregnant donkey. She was high with *ouzo*, laughing, and completely ready for making love.

Michael was relieved to see that Rosie, too, was enjoying a resurrection on the island.

As for himself, he wanted only to be alone with nature. He would leave early in the morning, not long after sunrise (Rosie never could make it up in time). He strapped his Nikon over his shoulder, but he seldom used it. The world appeared to be perfect; he temporarily rebelled against separating fragments from the whole of it, even into the frame of his film. Often he would simply sit on a hillside, lean against a rock, and look about, absorbing.

He did not, like Rosie, frequent the cafes, only when it was necessary to eat. He did not get high drinking ouzo. He was high without it, from the light and the sea, the hills and the rocks, the braying donkeys and the vivid wild flowers, the blue sky and the shining white houses.

In the weeks since they arrived on Paros he had not again seen Maria Ananin, not since that first morning, when the two of them had so strangely stood, spellbound and silent, on the road by the sea. He wondered if he never saw her because he was afraid to see her. If it was possible that he could instinctively, unconsciously, be avoiding whatever place on Paros that Maria happened to be. Or if, by the laws of chance, it was simply unlikely that he would run into anyone twice, given the size of the island.

Neither he nor she had asked the other, that morning, where they were staying. They had barely asked each other anything.

But late one afternoon at the end of the fourth week, his final week, after another tranquilizing day of exploring the terrain, a day which had not included lunch and had left him feeling tired and hungry, but content, he did run into her. It was in one of the small, family-run restaurants on the wharf near his hotel.

He had returned from that day's excursion around five o'clock. He went to his room to check if Rosie was there, maybe napping. But of course, she wasn't. So he went down the hall to shower, he dressed, and went out to have his dinner, early and alone—he was starving. He walked quickly down the street to the restaurant, musing about that strange concierge, the man who had spoken English and had somehow known his name. He had never seen the guy since that first morning.

As he approached the restaurant, he glanced at the tables near the entrance. And there, at a sunlit table half indoors, half out, facing toward the sea, sat Maria Ananin.

She was dressed in white, a simple sleeveless dress, with sandals on her feet. Her long hair was loose, blowing in the breezes from the sea. And she sat alone. He did not know if she had come to the island by herself, or if she was with others. Or with one other. He knew so little of her, actually. But the little that he knew had been on his mind for the last four weeks.

When he saw her, it was one of those odd moments—like on that first morning—a feeling not of surprise, but of affirmation, as if he'd known all his life that this was where, and when, he would see this woman.

He went straight to her table. There was no alternative. Turn around and walk out? Pretend he didn't recognize her?

*　　　　　　*　　　　　　*

So they sat together. At that homey, fruit-decaled-oil-cloth-covered table by the sea.

And, as they waited to place their orders, waited for her moussaka and his grilled bass, for their calamari and their salads, their chianti, and later for the coffee and the flan, and then the check; while they gazed upon the lengthening shadows on the wharf, at the glistening, not quite yet chemically ravaged Aegean, as they watched the coming and going of a glorious sunset above and upon that water, relishing their slowly disappearing dinners and glasses of sparkling ruby wine; while they caught the facets of the other's laughter, half-sensing the bustling family at the stove in the back and the three tired fishermen who came in at nine, who gazed toward them as well, and then later, as they both stared fixedly at the flickering flame of the candle in the wax-covered wine carafe, and came to the dawning comprehension of the other's mesmerizing eyes, with discoveries of the nuances of every subtle change; and finally, as they glanced at the now blackened sea, at the now victorious shadows, at the crescent moon, and the piercing, distinct constellations of singly appearing stars in the unspoiled clarity of a primeval, non-electric-light-reflective sky of night; while all of this went on, they talked.

They spoke as neither one had ever spoken, nor was to speak again. He confided his carefully guarded years in Paris; she confessed her private dreams.

"Wisdom, strength, a good and loving character. That's all I wish for. A kind, good character—I guess I've come to want that more than I want anything." She said it seriously, earnestly, not even caring if she sounded corny, not feeling embarrassed to tell him. He smiled and told her that, basically, he felt the same.

"Plus one more thing," he laughed, "I'd like to save the world."

They marveled at the coincidences, that both had lived in West Africa, both in Castro Valley; and "Now we both are here!" They relived together the potent sultry magic of the tropical forests of Africa, and he told her of some small, but "far-out" revelations he'd had in the jungles of Mexico and the Philippines. She told him legends of the island of Cypress, where she'd been the month before. They discovered that they both had, every day, been sitting alone on the hillsides of Paros, filling themselves with the beauty of the island and the sea. She said that she began the day at dawn by running along the shore, and then she climbed the hills.

Sometimes, she said, she read a little—"Have you heard of the Dhammapada?" They spoke of who they were, of the universes from which they'd come. He told her of his comic book collection. Of his heroes, his best friends, and much about his Dad. He divulged his private causes and silently rejoiced as she agreed. Then, softly, slowly, he spoke of the loss of Ishme, his son.

She told him about her secret fern-garden. Her childhood vision of a woman in the mist. "I think that wishes do come true. But only if you forget, like a little kid does sometimes, that they probably won't."

She didn't speak of her French teacher, nor of her evening with Jean's friends. She'd thought for a moment that she actually might, because it was her life, but then the cook came to their table and said it was time to close.

It was very late. Maria knew Michael should be going home, back to Rosie. She told him she would walk to her hotel by herself; they both agreed the island was safe.

It was only as he came to the door of his room and reached out to turn the key that he realized he still had no idea where on Paros Maria Ananin was staying.

Rosie wasn't in the room when he arrived. When at last she entered, tiptoeing, two hours had passed. By then he was asleep, his spirit in the room, yet far away.

*   *   *

Rosie stared at her husband, sound asleep, before her. Then she put on her poncho, which she had just taken off, the yellow and red poncho which he had long ago given her, a souvenir from Mexico (she hadn't actually cared much for it, at the time, but now it was in style). She slipped her loafers back onto her bare feet, grabbed her purse, and went back out the door, down the stairwell, passing the old man's desk. She returned to the cool, starlit night.

Then she walked until she reached the wharf, where she sat down, her back against a wall. For a long, long time she sat there, gazing into the starry sky, which seemed filled with a thousand sparkles of light. She wondered why the stars were so much brighter here than at home. And she thought about how Michael used to tell her what he knew about the constellations and astronomy while she sat upon his lap, on the cozy old swing on her front porch, long ago in the days of high school. She remembered something about "nebulae," and the speed of light, and the birth of black holes.

After a time, she opened her purse and took out a notepad. She searched for her pen. Then she began to record the thoughts which were coming so very quickly now, and which she did not want to forget.

This black hole inside me is longer, much wider, than what's been in there before.

And, it's deeper, much deeper. Deep enough to suck the whole world in and make it explode.

The black hole is in me. It has that in common with the other things that have been there before.

For example: when you were a new life in there, Ishme, a new tiny little someone, just beginning to be—then you were what was inside me, at the time. I felt you in there, Ishme, even before they said I was pregnant. That's why I made the appointment, because I felt you, small and new. Something I loved. And cute, I could tell you were very cute. But a black hole isn't cute—anyone knows that—and that's what's inside me, this time. Now that we've come full circle; now that you've gone back, way beyond me, somewhere, beyond inside me.

Back to where you came from, I suppose, to begin with. A place of light, they tell me, much longer, much wider, much deeper than any black hole.

But that's where you are now.

Not in me. Not with me.

It's the black hole that's in me. I feel it there.

Much longer, much wider, much deeper

Than anything

That was ever

In there,

Before.

11

Back to Berkeley

Berkeley, California
the nineteen seventies

> "For the time being philosophers had better be patient and willing to live with an 'unfinished' view of the world…there can never be conclusive reasons for saying we have a complete theory. The last word, then, is that there is no last word in the endless quest of science."
>
> —"The Philosophy of Science," an essay by Herbert Feigl,
> from *The Great Ideas of 1969*

After Paros the days went by faster and faster, as though the hours of the central portion of life were the vortex of some swirling storm in the universe; a place where time increased its speed in ratio to the hours of days gone by.

Michael and Rosie left the island, each provided with their own elixir for the soothing of their grief. Returning to more everyday moods, they became closer than they'd been before. Once they shared a memory of their child, fragments of a happy night when they'd bathed the baby in the kitchen sink—how he splashed them sopping wet and laughed and laughed at what he'd done. Both could hear, inside them, the unbearable echo of their tiny child's delighted sounds. At long last they held each other and cried.

Behaving as if they'd been given a new lease on life, they moved from cool, collected San Francisco to warmer, multi-dimensional Berkeley, choosing to completely begin anew. Traveling approximately fifteen miles, they re-entered the alternate Bay Area culture.

Then Michael took the advice of his mother, to continue juggling part-time jobs in photography stores, but to also learn to sell life insurance. "Your good looks, honey, and that nice smooth style you have—you know, sometimes you remind me of Gregory Peck, the way he was in *David and Bathsheba*, or *Roman Holiday*—you'll do so well in sales, I'm positive," Felipa declared, with softly passionate certainty. "And you can help a lot of people," she added, knowing her son's motivations like the back of her own hand. "People need an intelligent, honest insurance agent. But just to make double sure it's for you, I've consulted my cards. And they say you should definitely go into insurance! That's the interpretation I get."

Michael's friend Tom, home from service in Vietnam, to which he had been unhappily but, in the end, willingly drafted, tried to dissuade him from deserting the old dreams of film-making. "This is really unbelievable," Tom exclaimed, "this unadventuresome direction you're taking!" But Michael was ready to find meaning in devotion to Rosie and to a second child. He made decisions within the walls of his own reality, not Tom's. For the first time in their long friendship, Tom was ineffectual in his influence.

So Tom Muir decided to settle down, himself. He moved close by, into a student apartment, taking a job in a bookstore called "Moe's," on Telegraph Avenue, a street which was, at that time, only slightly past the prime of its famous rebelliousness; and to which Tom, therefore, was drawn, like a run-away kid to a circus.

In the evenings he hung out with Michael and Rosie, watching "Star Trek"—the reruns were on every night at dinnertime. And Rosie's dinners—in the seventies she made tacos, beef stroganoff, chicken teriyaki, lasagne, or barbecued spareribs—were irresistible. Before dessert, of cheesecake or homemade chocolate chip cookies, Tom and Michael would share a joint or two, supplied by Tom as a gift to his hosts. But Rosie was never tempted to even try "the stuff," as she called it, and finally Michael also declined, tired of making her feel left out.

In the summer they sat on the swing in the overgrown weeds and grass of the backyard, under the loquat tree. They gazed at the few muted stars of the Bay Area heavens, if the Berkeley evening stayed warm, which it seldom did. Mostly it was in the tiny kitchen, eyes on the Rorsach patterns of the faded chartreuse linoleum, moods adjusted to the sounds of Chicago Transit Authority or Taj Mahal or Cat Stevens or Santana, that they would discuss, or argue, politics and anything else that Tom was upset about. Usually this was some issue he'd heard of on the radio—always *KPFA*—earlier in the day. For Tom Muir had come back from the war an extremely moody young man, somewhat paranoid and acutely capable of discerning hypocrisy and lies. At times Michael felt he was learning a lot from his friend, at other times he felt like he was Tom's therapist. But he didn't mind. It so easily could have been he himself who was sent to "'Nam," with Tom at home protesting. Their roles would have been reversed, if only were their lottery numbers. Or so he told himself. But deep in his gut he knew he would not have given in, would have even abandoned America, or gone to jail as a political prisoner, rather than become a part of the evil nightmare from which Tom returned—Michael had, in fact, endured two brief sentences for demonstrating. But Tom, professing equally strong objections, had nevertheless, like a romantic young man of 1918 or '42, gone off to battle with visions of camaraderie and heroism in a far-off land, and a boy's fascination with courage and death and war.

After several months of troubled talk, the conversation faded, along with their need to expand their taste in rock. More and more, they played Segovia or Williams. *Spanish Etudes* became their background for "*Go*," the Asian game of logic that they learned when they were teenagers, escaping off to North Beach on bleak suburban nights.

Each evening, after Tom went home, Rosie and Michael would make love, and/or do their homework. And then, if there was any time left, or even if there wasn't, Michael would stay up reading: science fiction (*The Dune Trilogy*), political theory, some anthropology, some ancient history, the Dhammapada, and the Tao Te Ching. There was one book that he studied as much as his insurance manuals, a book about the filming of *Beauty and The Beast*, the journal of Jean Cocteau.

Rosie was always the first to fall asleep. She had quickly succeeded in becoming pregnant again and, for other reasons, as well, was nearly always exhausted. She worked very hard at a nursery school, supervising over twenty three-year-olds, and she also was back in college, this time to study child development. That subject, she often reiterated, was the most important subject on earth. "If everyone got 'enlightened,' like you say, Michael—only not about the cosmos or whatever—but about how to bring up their own children, then there wouldn't be any more troublemakers. And there wouldn't be any more troubles, either. For you and Tom to drive yourselves crazy over." She sometimes mocked her husband's opinions, and she became increasingly annoyed as he began to leave the house at night, to tutor "at risk" teen-agers or to coach a sixth-grade basketball team, kids who were "economically disadvantaged." She scorned these new terms he used, without really knowing why. She was bothered, too, by the growing number of organizations he sent their meager savings to. She fretted over bills and watched the junk mail piles grow larger and larger, their names traveling from one do-gooder mailing list to another. She complained frequently, though a small, nonverbal part of her was actually a little pleased that he gave.

*   *   *

Rosie had heard that drinking raspberry leaf tea would create an easier labor. And, oddly enough, she was terrified of labor; it was odd because her experience the first time around had been so nearly painless, nearly perfect. But back then, she'd been a naive optimist.

She planned to take the raspberry leaf tea. As it turned out, she was so busy, decorating the baby's room, making sure everything was perfectly ready, finishing off her job at the preschool, and a million other things. Somehow she just couldn't manage to get over to the natural food store in the Haight, where her friend Julie said they sold the best leaves. She considered planting her own raspberry vine, for the freshness. But finally at the end of nine months, a week after the due date, she bought some prepackaged tea at the Berkeley Co-Op, hoping that it wasn't too late to ease her labor, at least a bit.

She never learned whether the remedy was effective or not, though, because the pain she experienced was not from any cause which the plant could have helped, not from her female organs, but rather from the jangling of a nerve. It was a nerve located at the end of her spine, the obstetrician explained. This terrible piece of her body tortured her with fourteen hours of sharp unanesthetized excruciation. After fourteen hours had passed, and the monitor screen by her hospital bed showed that the baby was nowhere near ready for pushing out, she finally relinquished her wish to give her child a healthy, natural entry into life, relinquished her desire to prove herself as strong as any "natural woman," and buzzed for the nurse, to whimper for a caudal. She tried to console herself by remembering the flawless birth of her first child, but that barely helped.

Michael stood by her side, telling her to scream or yell if it made her feel any better, or to get off the bed and walk. But it was 1972, and her birth instructor had told her not to do any of those things. Just to keep her body still and concentrate on her breathing, with her eyes focused on a single point somewhere in the labor room. Rosie had faith in medical authorities, including the birth instructor, and she wasn't about to listen to the inexperienced advice of her husband; the pain would no doubt get even worse if she did as he said. If that was possible.

Michael smoothed her wet forehead and tried to soothe his own worries. They were as powerful, in their way, as Rosie's pains. The length of her labor tortured him, not only to watch her agony, but also to wait so long to know that she, and the baby, were going to be all right.

It was a time to meet his fears. And a time to confront the unknown depths of his feeling for this willful, stubborn woman. With panic for her fragile mortality playing at the margins of his mind, he faced the truth of what she meant to him.

In newly acute focus, he saw that not only was she a part of him, of every breath he took, and that he could not be himself without her, but also that whatever he would do in life would be done because she was there, somehow in it, with him. Life's purposes came from their unity, not from just himself.

He saw that the conflicts they had, constantly, were as valuable as their empathies, that their differences were as compelling as their mutual hopes.

But, he suddenly realized, what really brought them together was deeper than either the differences or the affinities; it was something beyond words. For completely unknown reasons, one filled the other; for mysterious causes, the two of them fit. They came together at such a depth, so completely unconsciously, it seemed, that most of the time he took no thought that this was how it was. No more than he took thought that his heart was busy beating or his lungs were filled with air.

He pondered these things as he watched the graph on the screen. Her labor was going nowhere. The fear for her safety grew greater; though it seemed irrational, wildly increasing beyond his control. He considered praying, but he didn't know how. Never, though he'd studied much about religion, had he been able to decide whether there really was a God. But he very much wanted there to be One, at that moment. Rosie once believed in God. Years ago, until they lost Ishme. He guessed she didn't really believe anymore, at least she never went to church. But he wondered if it was possible she still had a Bible—he knew she used to keep a small paperback version in her purse. Now he grabbed the purse from her bedside and searched. He was surprised; the book was there. He flipped through it, searching for the Psalms. He was familiar with the Psalms. In Mexico, an American preacher had loaned him a Bible, and a little later, curious about some details which that shopkeeper, Enki Rodriguez, had brought up, he had read the whole book through. Then, too, there had been a year back in his childhood when his father used to read to him from the Torah, every Sabbath in fact (in a fleeting passion to make Michael more Jewish). Always, his father read about his own first namesake, David. Michael liked those stories, David fascinated him, with all his strengths and weaknesses.

Now, in Rosie's book, he turned to the Psalms, because he thought that, mostly, they were David's. He read where his eyes fell, in Rosie's unfamiliar, modern Protestant translation:

"*Our inner selves wait for the Lord,*" he read "*He is our help and our shield. For in Him does our heart rejoice, because we have trusted in His holy name. Let Your mercy and lovingkindness, O Lord, be upon us in proportion to our waiting and hoping for you.*"

He put the book back in Rosie's purse. *And that can be difficult, can't it, David?* he silently spoke to the legendary psalmist—the shepherd and the king, the fighter, the lover, the betrayer, the husband and the father. "*You know about the torture of that, don't you, David? The torture of waiting and hoping...?*

*   *   *

Ishme Frederick Dagan, Mar., 1968–Feb., 1969, was killed in the arms of his baby-sitter, a girl of sixteen. The girl was jay-walking, in the early evening, across a wide, insufficiently lit highway, on her way to buy an ice cream cone to share with her little charge. The person who hit the baby and the teenager was a middle-aged woman who was not wearing her distance glasses; and who, therefore, did not clearly see the darkly clad pedestrian in time. Nor could she bring her station wagon to a sufficiently quick stop, when she finally did notice the girl with the baby, for she was traveling so very fast, faster than was legal on that road. The reason she was speeding was that her adrenaline was pumping; the woman was very angry with her husband. He had cruelly criticized her in front of many friends, at a dinner party on the previous night. The husband had humiliated the woman, claiming she was talking too much. This put-down came, unbeknownst to the woman, because the man was feeling irritable with his boss. The boss, just a few hours before the dinner, had given the man yet another undeserved reprimand—not comprehending the man's unusual work style, a style which was actually quite efficient, but which included several disconcerting habits, the habits of a man of very different culture than the boss.

Little Ishme Dagan was in this wrong place at this wrong time due to the circumstance that Ishme's mother and father, Michael and Rosie Dagan, were beginning to greatly miss the romantic underpinnings of their marriage. They had decided the time was way overdue for them to go out together for a few hours, just the two of them, to an early movie, then to dinner at a favorite restaurant. Ishme's parents were in a theater a few miles away, viewing the concluding scene in *2001, A Space Odyssey*, when the baby's accident took place. Like all events, the accident had many interconnected causes, and many interconnected effects, some obvious and some not even known.

Anger with the participants, with the driver and with the baby-sitter—who was not killed—was, for Rosie, one of the main effects. But not for Michael. He knew his wife was extremely angry; they once discussed her feelings. It was painful to force his mind in that direction, but one day Rosie said she absolutely needed to talk about Ishme's accident. Hearing her out, he became mystified at himself, at his own absence of any anger, whatsoever. He didn't believe he was suppressing anger, as Rosie claimed he was, and he knew he wasn't purposefully attempting to conquer it. He simply didn't possess the emotion; the accident had brought him only a strong sense, all through his body and his mind, of sad inevitability. Everything had fallen together to create a destiny that left him entirely empty and sad. That had been enough to do him in, without the anger.

Fortunately, two years later, on Paros—"Paradise"—the radiant light had pierced and diffused his grief. No longer was it the entire substance of each and every circumstance of life, though the sadness would continue to remain, giving a toning and shading to all his remaining moments.

Sadness was still with him, giving its shading, at the moment of his second child's birth. But at that moment, when the tiny head of the new infant appeared from between the quivering—though benumbed—legs of the wide-eyed mother, the father's sadness transformed immediately, into an ingredient of bliss, one of a plenitude of ingredients, all blended fully, triumphantly. Michael seemed, in fact, to leave his own body and to float above the scene, right up to the ceiling. From there he looked down on the obstetrician and the nurses, on the table, and on his wife, and on the miraculous face of his wailing new child, in whose features he could detect every persona of every known member of his and Rosie's families, including their greatly longed for and permanently vanished first son. The last thing he saw in the face of his newborn was the radiant promise and hopefulness of all the beings yet to come. Then the father returned to normalcy, as he heard the doctor say, "Don't you want to come and have a look at your baby?"

Later in life, on two occasions, the topic of 'out of body experiences' came up in conversation. On both those occasions no one in the group had actually lived through that legendary event. But, even though the talk was all skeptical speculation or approving fantasy, Michael didn't insert his own first-hand knowledge. The experience had been too intensely personal and full of awe. Besides, he hardly believed by then, that it had actually occurred.

12

Maria and San Francisco

San Francisco
1972 A.D.

Sometimes on Sunday mornings she would waken to the sounds of the *taiko* drummers as they marched up Buchanan Street. She would rise from her bed and, from one of the many windows on the Buchanan side of her second story flat, she would watch the black-haired young men as they marched around the corner and down Bush. Then, as the rhythms softened into the distance, she would gaze down the foggy early-morning hill, toward the Japan Center Plaza and the Kabuki Hotsprings (which she could visit in three minutes if she wished). She did not feel aggravated that the enthusiastic drummers had awakened her; she was only thankful to be living in such an enthralling part of the city, in a pale blue-Victorian with a fireplace in the bedroom and a beautiful old cherry tree growing in the small front yard. In spring, when the large tree was spectacular, a prima donna among blossoming cherry trees, groups of Japanese businessmen—guests of the Miyako Hotel—would visit her corner to contemplate the plaza and to take photographs of the tree and of the house. Sometimes, if she was out on her front steps, reading a book, or writing, or just observing the neighborhood, the dark-suited men from Japan would smile and laugh and ask, usually by pantomime, if they could take her photograph as well. Then they would take turns posing with her.

This pleased her, as did the sounds of Japanese conversation and Japanese love songs coming from the shops as she passed on errands in the early evening. She would walk down her hill after work, almost daily, like the *Nisei* women, to buy fresh fruits and vegetables and tofu or to do the laundry. Or sometimes she just meandered about the neighborhood for the sheer delight of it: the aromas of tempura and miso, the peaceful presence of the cherry trees and maples, the stones and pools and cooing doves of the plaza, the quiet meticulous mothers with their adorable well-behaved children, and the fine-complexioned grandparents.

Everything in the neighborhood was of a piece, a refined and quietly bustling little world of its own, serene as a fantasy of pre-war Japan. Even at the bank. She went about her own business quietly, herself, observant, so obviously different from her neighbors, but wondering if perhaps she and they might be inwardly alike. Why else would she feel so inexplicably and happily anonymous, so pleasantly unbothered here?

She did not drive a car in San Francisco, though she easily could have; her boyfriend, with whom she shared the flat, kept his Volkswagon parked in the garage. The garage was a lucky bonus—finding parking was becoming nearly impossible in 1972. Her boyfriend, a man named Matthew Johnson who, like Maria, was a "personnel analyst" at City Hall, usually preferred to walk or take a bus, using the car only to leave the city. Maria preferred not to drive at all.

Except for herself and for Matthew, who was black and from North Carolina, everyone in their Western Addition neighborhood, it seemed, was either Japanese-American or Japanese. Many had grown up in that very district (so the landlady said). Many had been sent to the concentration camps and then had returned to this city where they'd left their hearts, and whose guardian, Francis, would hopefully, from now on, remain unthwarted in his loving protection.

Except for the kind and nearly deaf landlady, Mrs. Oda, who lived downstairs, Maria had had only two or three conversations with any of her neighbors. They seemed to be as introverted as she (actually, her own shyness was beginning to thaw in the heat of her new profession). She only occasionally sensed the neighbors' sad history, during certain lonely, windy moments while walking through their streets. One day, perhaps, she and Matthew would marry, she would become pregnant, quit work, and while strolling the baby about she would get to know these people whose lives defined the small unique community that she now called home.

Then again, she still didn't believe that she would ever marry again. Though she did care a lot for Matthew. He was generous, considerate, and not bad looking. Especially with his Afro and the beard he had just grown. But what attracted her to him most was his mind—he was so impressively logical and curious, interested in everything that she was, and he always made sense. On top of that, he was verbal in his satisfaction that she was a fantastic woman, telling her, for example, how extraordinarily seductive or sultry she was, and then, in his characteristically inquisitive fashion, asking her for her own definition of his words. Both of them had a fascination with the meanings of words.

She knew he was intelligent, and that his Ph.D. was in computer science; but she didn't know that he had it in him to create, two years after they parted, a computer company that would gross in the tens of millions, with headquarters in both the United States and Europe, before it was put out of business by IBM. Nor that he was capable of becoming a father who possessed exceptional wisdom and love, nor that he would not live to see old age, dying of cancer before he reached the age of fifty, before his youngest daughter had turned fifteen.

Nor did she ever realize how completely she came to hurt him. When he learned that she didn't love him, not in the way that he loved her. It wasn't that she told him so, not directly. It was something that he found himself, in the diary on her bedside table.

She occasionally read her entries to him. That was why, the first few times he picked up the journal and browsed through it, he told himself that what he was doing was all right. Later, when it happened on a regular basis, he began to loathe himself for invading her privacy, for stealing her thoughts. But by that time he was uncontrollably addicted. When he found the poem, he was already feeling so bad about himself that his first reaction, combined with the overwhelming grief and shock, was that he felt justly punished. Years later those feelings had muted, but they still were there, the same disturbing mix. The poem, unfortunately, was titled "Matthew" or he might have convinced himself it was just a poem, a fictional situation, and not the reality of her lessened love.

He never allowed himself to believe that the poem might have come only from a moment of a mood. Instead he copied it over, and many years later his wife Diane found the copy in the pocket of his plaid bathrobe, soon after he died. By then, it was virtually unreadable, wrinkled and faded from folding and the fingering of too much study of the meaning of the words. For Matthew, the deterioration of the paper hadn't mattered; he had long known the lines by heart.

Matthew stayed with Maria for awhile after he discovered the poem, not quite certain what to do next, not divulging anything, trying to figure out further how it really was with her. When he finally moved out, it was the end of the year, Christmas—almost Kwanzaa time for him, the first Kwanzaa he acknowledged. When he left, she assumed it was he who had ceased to love.

She quit her job at City Hall. Then she moved to a small studio apartment in the Mission District and went to work for a community center, performing jazz dances and teaching children. When she looked up her wise old friend Marta, she was told that Marta had "passed."

She tried to figure it out, herself; why love couldn't last. She decided to abandon all hope for romance. She would devote her life to dance, would give her being, all her force and love, to the "disadvantaged" little girls in her classes. She would help them find their beauty and their courage, as Marta Diaz once helped her.

It was 1972. The moon had relinquished its mystery; Americans had camped there. And as for Venus, that heavenly body was under-going a "probe"—a Soviet spacecraft, Venus 8, had soft-landed on her surface; instruments, like the searching fingers of a gynecologist, examined the Queen of Heaven, the Morning and the Evening Star.

13

Meanwhile in the Suburbs

Castro Valley
1979 A.D.

By the year 1979, Castro Valley, California, yet unincorporated, but with a population of close to forty-five thousand, had lost nearly all traces of Mexican-horse-ranch-chicken-farm ambiance which it once had called its own, even as late as the middle of the century.

Like its neighbor Oakland (once upon a time the quiet homeland of beautifully evolved *Ohlone* families who liked to purify themselves in their sacred heated *temescal*, a people who, perpetually at peace, dwelt in three villages surrounded by acres of well-tended, almost-gardened meadows midst extensive oak groves and forests of redwoods so numerous and tall that the stately arboreal silhouettes came to serve as landmark for Spanish seamen coming up the coast; a land Mediterranean in latitude and climate, with soil so rich and fertile that it was the "fruit vale" of California when the Mexican and then the gringo ranchers arrived and, even to this day, as a city, remains nurtured by an invincible protection of thriving woods and glens), like this Oakland, Castro Valley became a land of "progress."

As in Oakland, the meadows and hills of Castro Valley were suddenly forced, by a growing human population, and by a handful of hungry-spirited moneymen, into the presumably irrevocable invasion of concrete, stucco, and asphalt which delighted the greedy financiers.

But unlike Oakland, where non-agrarian civilization conquered in the first quarter of the century, Castro Valley did not urbanize until the third. No custom-designed craftsman houses, Julia Morgan churches, brown shingles, Spanish adobes, nineteen-ten bungalows, nor Victorian manses for the former estates of Don Castro. Unlike Oakland, Castro Valley was fated to be mantled with blocks of tracts: postwar fifties, sixties, and seventies suburban real estate developments.

These were not "little boxes," to be fair. They were not identical and were often more elegant, complex, and thought-out than the stereotype which that song of the California suburbs—specifically hillsides south of San Francisco—soon memorialized. But like those hillside tracts, the houses of Castro Valley were, at mid-century, filled almost entirely by young Euro-American couples, with two baby-boomer children, two automobiles, and at least one pet. There were almost no servants or grandparents, and precious few cousins or uncles or aunts. Having very busy mothers and scant kin, with no grandmas' or grandpas' laps to nestle upon, the children grew into elder-starved cliques of rootless, restless second-generation suburbanites.

And though suburban gardens were sometimes very pretty, the landscape at first remained too young and immature, especially the trees, to offer much nurturing power. For the most part, those early tract children did not spend time with the trees anyway, preferring to stay inside, in their *rumpus* or *family* rooms with their telephones and television sets. Or they would go to the *shopping center*—as mall-like collections of stores were then called—to make recreational purchases. On the whole, those early tract children led lives of conscious boredom and unconscious aesthetic deprivation, either of natural countryside beauty or of the artistic refinements of the more cultured and urbane city-life. But, never let it be forgotten, as for survival and comfort, these suburban children were far more fortunate than most other children of that time!

The youthful malaise and ennui that were born in these circumstances had their effects. For one thing, the local high school was a hotbed of teen-age gossip. Unlike the wildlife of that area, the gossip was on-going, thriving and evolving—abundantly fertile and alive.

*   *   *

And so it was for nearly three decades when, in the spring of 1979, a particularly choice and unusual conversational tidbit began to make the rounds through the classrooms and the cafeteria, the lavatories, and the high school's halls.

The gossip had it that the popular French teacher, Mr. Jean-Marc Romier, was leaving the school. And not because he had been given a short sabbatical, as was first reported. Nor had he suddenly quit his job. Rather—and this was fairly certain—he was leaving because he was fired by the principal. Mr. Romier was dismissed, it was told and retold, because he was caught abusing himself with drugs. Whether this meant marijuana or barbiturates, cocaine, LSD, speed, or something else again, was never officially divulged. Somebody joked that maybe it was the teacher's espresso habit. Because the details were not known, the topic persisted over the summer and through the entire next school year, kept alive by the virile powers of unimpeded imagination. There never was a firm consensus concerning that matter; but most parents were disgruntled and some were horrified, and some of their sons and daughters felt pretty much the same. Others, those students who said the man was "hella bad," and another fringe group who said he was "brilliant," were authentically saddened, or, in the case that they themselves were users, were inclined to empathize, regarding Romier as a fellow "freak." Some thought he was a veritable martyr, and they eulogized over what a fascinating teacher he had always been. What did it matter, they reasoned, about his private life? Maybe his habits made him more inspired and creative, whatever drugs he was into.

But the students who had actually been in Romier's classes that last semester had another view. They said the guy was lately "pretty out there." He was strange and unnatural, they concurred, even a little scary. In fact, they claimed, he'd been getting "really sort of weird."

Part V
Inanna and Dumuzi

1

Let It Flow

Orom
circa 2700 B.C.

"He caressed my breasts,
Like ripe fruits of his orchard.
...my thighs,
Soft grains of his field.
His love, sweet wine, sweet honey,
Flowed freely
In my garden.

His hands found my 'sheepfold,'
And he took me with sweet appeal.
My king, my lion, my beloved.
He let flow the cream.
Dumuzi, I will take your fresh cream.

Now I, the Queen of Heaven,
Will keep safe your house,
The great storehouse,
Where the breath of all life is contained.

O my shepherd,
The fate of your people,
The fate of your land
Is secured.

—"Composition for a *tigi* (harp)"
from *The Twenty-One Hymns of Orom*

Early on the morning of the New Year, the twelve temple priestesses filed in procession to the palace to fetch their king. The graceful, chatting young priestesses of Inanna led the dignified king of Orom, in lengthy promenade, to the temple of the queen. They brought their fine and solemn king to the sunlit chamber of the waiting priestess, to the waiting bed of Inannanindigur.

On the following day, when the sun blazed high in the heavens, the king returned to his palace. The people loudly rejoiced. Lining the borders of their streets, all of them, the older ones and the younger ones and the children; all sang songs to Inanna and Dumuzi. The lutes and the *vinas* celebrated with heartfelt melody, the drums and the tambourines grew ecstatic, the dancers danced into dream-like trance. The people tossed their blossoms of jasmine, their roses, their gardenias and lilies. They chanted the praises; they gave thanks, as the king and his retinue returned.

The fate of Orom was sealed for the year. The life-breath of the people was guarded. All was secure in the land.

*   *   *

Standing beside my golden table, he took my hands in his hands. And I made farewell to Asimbabar. For another year again I would not see him. Then I lay, alone now, face down upon the bed where the king had caressed me, where I had caressed the king, where we had taken our bliss for all those just past double-hours. I wept then, tears for

Asimbabar, who confessed "I long for you all year," but more for my Anurei, and myself—and our unchosen destiny.

2

The Rain Forest

Berkeley
the eighties

Long ago, when he was a small boy, playing in a warm world where the lush green forest was a loving second mother, a mother who held and comforted, who taught and caressed, he had no idea in his head what it was like to be lonely. Though both his human and his forest mother sometimes grew ferocious, with thunder, lightening and rain raging and pouring from their souls—making him a little bit afraid—he was not ever, not in any moment, anything that might be called alone.

And all around him there thrived the moist warm essence of a people who took the brevity of this life as a thing that is granted. A collective gratitude for earthly existence therefore prevailed; this also kept the little boy, and all of those people, from ever feeling too empty or alone.

He did sense, however, deep down inside himself, somewhere from his chest to his heart, as well as in his tummy, and even in his throat, the knowledge that something very crucial had been taken from him. But he tried not to remember what. This something very important was actually his father, who once had been right there beside him, in that very same land, but who, for unknown causes, had gone away—far, far away. Yet was maybe coming back. In some distant unknown time. Or, maybe, wasn't coming back at all.

For this reason, the two mothers, both his human mother, and the forest one, seemed even more necessary to the little boy than they might have seemed otherwise.

Sometimes when he was with his human mother he would sneak up behind her. And he would throw his arms around her neck, because he was so very happy that she was his. And sometimes, playing on the soft living floor of his emerald green jungle, beneath the roof of its rustling leaves, deep inside the powerful embrace of its fragrant frangipani and wild gardenia and ginger, he would know a blissful contentment, know that everything was as it should be—a feeling so profound that for all his life he never would forget it. When he had grown to be a man he could recognize that satisfaction in the moment of climax when he was making love.

This was why, on a strange day when the world seemed to come to a stop, and his long-gone foreign father stood in the center of the funky little airport of that land, smiling and calling the boy to run into his arms—when that day came finally to its confusing twilight, and the boy sat thinking there, behind his house, beneath his trees, embraced by the warm soul of the rain forest for the very last time, he cried and cried, as though his heart would break, as though leaving that jungle meant leaving the dearest person that he had ever known.

Now many years later, contemplating his own son, who sat alone and quiet before a loud and ubiquitous television set, Michael felt, for unknown causes, as distant from that boy as his own father once had been from him. And he remembered his jungle. But now, unlike the days when he was a boy, a panic of emptiness, or aloneness, grew inside him. Powerful and terrible, it overcame his mind.

3

Childhood Friends

Berkeley
January, 1983 A.D.

> "...There is one common substance, though it is distributed among countless bodies which have their several qualities. There is one soul, though it is distributed among several natures and individual limitations. There is one intelligent soul, though it seems to be divided."
>
> —Marcus Aurelius

— So, now, Dagan? What do you think?

— Oh, I think it's good.

— Just like my mother used to make.

— Yes, it's actually quite good. Delicious. I think it would catch on. You can move here Valmiki, and make a fortune. People go crazy in this town over anything that's exotic and tasty.

— So I've noticed. My guess is that what that's all about is your post-sixties disillusion; that's why this place is so insatiable. Berkeley used to be overflowing with political ascetics, now you're all gourmets! Next time I'll show you how to make this, yourself, Michael. It's called "*chai.*"

— You know, Valmiki, I was thinking, in some ways, you're the one person who comes close to being anything like a peer that I—

— Oh, I know, I've thought that, myself. You realize it's because of Paris. We were strangers in a strange land, kids without a country. Both in the same unusual circumstances. Both of us thinking too much. In trouble too much! Running wild through those streets. Upsetting those quiet, suave, soulful streets! "Leaping tall buildings in a single bound"— even on the Rue Fauberg—remember? You remember Antoine? So hyperactive. They medicate kids like him these days. If my own kids were like we were, it would drive me crazy. As a matter of fact, I don't allow it.

— You don't allow fun, Valmiki? But, what was that you said—'unusual circumstances?' I think everyone grows up in unusual circumstances. Of some sort or another.

— Everyone? Who knows? The question's so absurd, no way to test that one, Michael. I guess I'm just inclined to assume that other people's lives are ordinary. But, tell me, do you ever think about those days? Remember Marcus Aurelius?

— Oh, sure, sometimes. Sixth grade. The play we wrote. I'm amazed at how contemporary the guy was. He was overly busy—trying not to make excuses to his children, concerned about not spending enough time with his kids—

— Yeah, I like that. And he had a lot of causes for stress, more than most, in that millennium. His emperor job; not always nine to five, eh? Imagine—the whole western world hassling you! Do you still read the *Meditations*?

— Once in awhile…his attitude was…

— Stoic. Almost Buddhist-like: "*If you work at that which is before you, following right reason seriously, vigorously, calmly without allowing anything else to distract you, but keeping your divine part pure, as if you might be bound to give it back immediately, if you hold to this, expecting nothing, fearing nothing, but satisfied with your present activity according to nature…you will be happy—*"

— "*You have existed as a part, you shall disappear in that which pro-duced you; or rather, you shall be received back into its seminal principle by transmutation*"—yeah, it's true, Valmiki; he sounds like Siddhartha.

— It was probably more of a global village back in those days than we realize, for a Roman emperor, at least. But, to be honest, the thing I like about reading Aurelius is that he makes me think of Roman villas. Roman gardens, a little like the old gardens in Pondicheri. But not exactly. More rosemary and lavender in the courtyards, alexandrine mosaics and statues, heads of lions spewing water into fountains. I read him and I'm there, strolling in the gardens of the emperor. Though I doubt that he, himself, actually did anything like that—strolled in his gardens, I mean. It's too self-indulgent for a man who chose to sleep on a plank. Most of his writing was done in battle camps, not in his gar-dens...You know, you and I are old-fashioned, Dagan...

— What do you mean?

— Well, let me put it this way: How many people do you know, of our generation, I mean, who are still in love with their first wives? Who are still even married to their first wives?

— That's surprising; I'm surprised to hear you say that. Aren't mar-riages for most people in India long-last—

— I'm not "most people in India," now am I?

— Could you pass me more of that chai of yours?

— Certainly. Glad you like it—don't let me forget to show you how it's made...Anyway, for one thing, for a good part of the year I'm not even in India. I'm somewhere else in Asia; in Japan, Hong Kong, Singapore. Or I'm in England or France, or the States. And when I am home, most of my friends are really so cosmopolitan, not in the least traditional. It's they I compare myself to. Madhouri and I, in spite of the others, our sophisticated friends, I mean, in spite of everything, I would have to say we're quite traditional. And I would give you that same label, Dagan, in your own way, as well. In the middle of your self-indulgent society here, you—

— When you say "traditional," in what sense, exactly—what do you mean by that?

— In my own provincial particularity. In the sense of a devoted follower of traditional Hindu beliefs. In the sense of someone who loves Rama, someone who does his best to follow the *Dharma*...Do I surprise you?

— No. No, not at all. Except that—you put me in that category with yourself?

— In a way. Abstractly. I can see you going down a similar path as myself, but without your necessarily being aware that you are even on a path; you do not define anything. You have no names for anything. But you still have reference points which are similar to my own, to which I give my traditional names, you understand. Like "the Dharma." When we're out in nature, like at Point Reyes or the Sierras, you always go silent. And sometimes you just sit, even here at home; it looks to me like meditation.

— Maybe what you're talking about is simply the effects of our education. Paris—the Steiner school, some of the things they taught us, like Aurelius—

— Oh, yes, I agree, that definitely had a lot to do with it. We had an incredibly old-fashioned education, you know. Old-fashioned isn't even the word for it—"ancient" would be more on the mark. Rudolph Steiner was an initiated mystic; did you know that, Dagan?

— Actually no; I don't know what Steiner was, nothing about him. They taught us virtually nothing about his life, did they? Nothing of his beliefs, or his ideas, not that I can recall. All I have is some vague image of his face, from that photograph in the school office. Remember? He looked so damn serious, I used to think. How do you know anything about him? You've read something since?

— Oh, yes; a good deal, in fact. For one thing, I learned the man was a child genius in the field of philosophy. By adolescence he'd already digested just about everything western philosophy had to offer. He was especially influenced by Goethe—remember all the colors, that atmosphere in the classrooms? My kids go to a Steiner school, in Cambridge. I'm surprised you never considered it for your Aaron. I'm sure I wrote you. I know quite a bit now about the context in which you and I were raised. You'd be surprised. That is why I used the phrase, "under unusual circumstances."

— Valmiki—When you say you "love Rama," what exactly do you mean by that? And why do you relate that to me?

— Are you at all familiar with the Ramayana?

— Just what we learned in school.

— Fifth grade, yes. It was my father who came and gave a talk to the class.

— Yeah, I remember. You were embarrassed. Your father was at school, lecturing like a teacher, in front of everybody.

— I was proud, also. But yes, it was strange to bring my private life— my father, the Ramayana—into school.

— I remember some things, in the story. A monkey…and the ending, the part about the woman going into the ground with her mother…

— Sita's mother, Mother Earth, yes…The Ramayana is, of course, a story with many, many implications. To me, to make a long story short, it's my life inspiration. To be a good man, a strong man. And for my wife, it's the inspiration to be a good woman. Madhouri and I, sometimes at night, you know, we read the story to each other; throughout the years we have done this, as my father and mother once did; it's our family tradition. And to the children—we tell the tale to them, we don't read it. It is better to tell them. So the nobility, the strength, the faithfulness, the heroism of Rama and Sita, so these examples are kept fresh in their minds, and in our minds. Otherwise, it is very easy, I believe, to forget about these things. Especially in today's hodge-podge world. The Ramayana is sometimes a basis, as well, for my psychology lectures, and inevitably—

— Well just how do you relate this to me?

— I am under the impression that you, like me, are constantly reminding yourself, as best you can, of certain priorities. I think they are crucial to you, Michael. I've seen it in your correspondence, in those quotations of yours, which you love to site. From your usual sources—Emerson, de Chardin, Buber, Merton, the Dhammapada, Lao Tse, eh? I know how you still play with those notions we used to get so excited about as kids. Your ideas are old, Dagan; I say that with approval, you realize.

—

— But to make you more up-to-date—I also think you still want to be a "Superman." Strong and heroic, of service to humanity. And in disguise—an ordinary man, unacknowledged, a middle-class, mid-life Clark Kent. I see this in your home here, this simple, rudimentary lifestyle you have. I know how you've been doing; I know your business is quite successful. Rosie and I had a talk, last year, on that hike in the Sierras. And I have to say, before I really stopped to think about it, I was amazed, the first time I visited here. Your home, to put it tactfully—it does not give evidence of much prosperity, does it?

— I hope I've outgrown super-heroes, Valmiki.

— Too bad. But, actually, I don't believe you.

— As for my house—you sound just like Rosie. Of course with Rosie, it's a complaint.

— Your wife isn't in agreement with your lifestyle?

— Well, this house isn't exactly everything she would have it be. If it were up to her. But to be fair, she's the one who accommodates, she compromises. She does her best. She spends freely enough on herself, though. That's not my business. She has her nails done every week, for example…Yes, she'd definitely like to spend more on the house, to have a bigger house, in fact, a finer house, a new car. But she accepts my idiosyncrasies. She's the one who usually accommodates. She seldom complains, to be honest. I wasn't being fair to Rosie, to say what I just did.

— It came out wrong.

— Yes…"You think too much," that's her real complaint. "Why don't you just enjoy life?" I guess she simply wants to make me happy.

— But you ask yourself, "How can I fiddle while Rome burns?" Or some such thing?

—

— I imagine you're giving a lot to charity these days, aren't you, Dagan?

— Not so much.

— Do you mind my asking what charities you support?

— Do I mind? What do you want to know that for?

— Oh, well, forget it. I suppose it's none of my business. I just wondered if it would be, oh, somewhat similar to what I might choose. Probably. But never mind. I see you think I'm getting nosy.

— No, it's all right…You were always nosy, Valmiki. "Curious," you used to call it.

— Well—

— I still remember your schemes, you know. That summer when you were trying to get yourself into all the neighbors' apartments…remember, Valmiki? How you just had to see what the interiors looked like, in our building? You talked me into going through the halls and ringing doorbells with you. Remember that?

— Oh, I—

— You told the people we'd lost our pet turtle. That we absolutely needed to search inside their rooms for our turtle, if they didn't mind. Because we'd found turtle droppings on their doorstep! Do you remember? "La merde de la tortue"—after awhile you could barely get it out with a straight face—

— Oh, yeah! I do remember! We said we were certain the turtle must be hiding inside! Yes. I'd forgotten all about that. The neighbors were so damned aloof and private, where we lived, that's why I—

— Do you remember the astrology experiment you made with the teachers at school?

— Yes, I do. I haven't forgotten that one. It was rather clever of me, for my age; I still think of it sometimes. It showed signs of the budding psychologist, the research scientist. Can you remember the details?

— Some of—

— I asked the teachers to give me their birthdays, and to fill out a personality questionnaire. I found it in a library book. I kept everything anonymous.

— Oh yes. Your questions were kind of personal, as I recall.

— Then, without knowing which birthdays, or which questionnaires were from which teachers, I matched the personality profiles with the birthdays, according to what I knew about astrology. I had you and Antoine match them, too. Then we went back to the teachers to see how accurate we were. Most of the teachers were very cooperative.

— Yeah…I figured you did it to find out which teachers were virgins.

— I was a little kid, Michael! You misjudge me.

— Sure. But, as you say, you were clever.

— Do you remember that we were correct to an accuracy of…of something like—oh, something like 30%?

— And what did that tell you?

— Absolutely nothing. It was a lousy experiment. No control group, not enough subjects, not enough questions, not enough data on the astrology—I only asked for their sun signs, remember? And our deductions were worse than chance. I was smart enough, though, to admit the failure, that I learned nothing. I learned something about how not to do an experiment. And I learned that Mlle. Bressier was a latent nymphomaniac!

— Ah, there we go.

— I'm still mystified by astrology; I still haven't seen sufficient data anywhere, to either reject it or accept it, though I'm inclined not to accept it. But many highly educated people in India completely accept it, you understand. They wouldn't marry without the horoscope charts. That's because people assume the inevitable interconnectedness of everything. But over here, it's a different story, people regard the world as a closed system, they leave out infinity. And then, even within that closed system, the perimeters for cause and effect are limited more by the current temporary status quo of science; whatever is still mysterious isn't allowed to be included in the sequence of events. Not a truly scientific attitude, if you ask me. On the other hand, the daily forecasts in the newspapers here are enough to make a non-believer out of anyone. But what interests me more these days, concerning personality formation, isn't astrology. It's genetics.

—

— I'm involved now, in fact, in a study on identity. It's fascinating, my theory. It concerns the inheritance of identity awareness, the idea that the awareness of self-existence is in the DNA, that it is passed on, probably to even more than one individual. But skipping generations, so that—

— Wait, before you go on, Valmiki, back when you were talking about Rama and Sita—I had a question. Do you see yourself as the hero of your life? Do you see your existence as a sort of mythological epic? Each difficulty an occasion to fight for good against evil?

— That's how you see yourself?

— I'm asking you.

— I'll tell you, Michael, if you really want to know. I live my life inspired by Rama, as I said, and also I live by a vow I made, some twenty years ago, it was. I took the vow with a teacher I was with for awhile, in Nepal, a Buddhist. You would have liked him. I wrote you about it at the time, in fact. You recall the episode?

— Vaguely. I'm sure I was intrigued. But frankly, it's hard enough remembering the events of my own life, let alone yours.

— You may have heard of this vow yourself. There's so much interest in Buddhism these days, no? Since the Chinese take-over and the exile of the Dalai Lama and his people, of the masters, the lamas. A horrible thing for Tibet, but an incredible good fortune for the rest of us. Have you heard of the vow of the *Bodhisatvva*?

— No, I don't think so. I don't know much about the Tibetan take on Buddhism, to tell the truth.

— It isn't Tibetan in origin, as a matter of fact. The version I know is Shantideva, an Indian, but he's a favorite of the Tibetans: "*Thus for every single thing that lives, In number like the boundless reaches of the sky, May I be their sustenance and nourishment. Until they pass beyond the bounds of suffering.*"

— It sounds like a hard promise to keep. Christ-like.

— That's absolutely right. Or you might think of a saint, like your local patron, there, across the bay. Francisco.

— And you, you really take it seriously?

— Well, I try. Of course I have very far to go, I'm only at the beginning. But I'm not one of you Americans; I'm not in a hurry, not anxious. I have enough lifetimes; there's plenty of time.

— I read somewhere that Tibetans don't really call themselves Buddhists. Is that true?

— Well, it depends. I guess what you're referring to is that the Tibetan word for those who practice isn't a direct translation of the word "Buddhist;" their word means something else. The word is "*Nangpa.*"

— And what does "*Nangpa*" mean?

— One who goes within, who seeks within the inner mind, not outside.

— I see. Like Aurelius. Or David…So tell me, Valmiki, what do you think of Aaron?

— Your son? Oh, he's a great kid, Aaron. I've observed his strong integrity. He has a solidity. I like your son.

— You like the blue hair?

— A significant color! Auspicious, isn't it? But, seriously, why do you even ask me that? What difference does it make to me what color your son's hair is? Does it matter to you?

— Well, it has certain connotations…and no one else his age…he probably got the idea from the students…He did a summer camp at the art college, I think, maybe—

— Self-expression? Identity exploration? Probably he's just ahead of his time. From what I've seen, if an eleven-year-old in your Bay Area here dyes his hair blue in the eighties, than half the world will have blue hair in the nineties…But, your son strikes me as a kid who owns himself. I trust Aaron. I've not seen a lot of him, as you know. But, on those occasions when I've been here, over the years, I've seen his evolution, and his consistencies, too. He's a fairly quiet kid, but it's easy to pick up that he has a good heart. I've witnessed several incidents. The way he is with animals, insects, even. And with my Maya, for example—remember how he just picked her up all of a sudden and carried her on his back, on that trek last year, when she was so tired? And she was a big girl—six years old—he wasn't much bigger, right? I remember his smile. Great smile, Aaron has.

— He's failing at school now. And he barely speaks to me these days.

— Well, Michael…But, maybe…

— But maybe? Maybe what?

— Maybe, do you think it is possible Aaron senses that you are not whole-heartedly there for him? And not there for his mother?

— "There" for them? Don't tell me you've started using that kind of—but what are you talking about?

— You know, Michael, sometimes…it isn't what we do or say that makes the biggest difference to the people we care about. It's what is on our minds; that's the crucial thing. It shows in our presence. If there's one thing a loved one can sense, it's how often you think about them. I know you, my friend. As well as I know anyone. And I sense that you are, in your heart, pursuing, or being pursued by, I don't know which, by something, how can I say, something other than the needs of your family. There is this aspect about you, it's in your look, your gestures, your posture. Especially I've seen it in your correspondence over the years. Those ideals we were just talking about, those are there, yes, but...have you ever wondered if you are fully committed to your own priorities, Michael?

— And what the hell do you mean by that?

— How can I say this? Have you ever heard of *Kama*? There is a Hindu god called "Kama"...

4

Kama, the God of Love

Berkeley
February, 1983 A.D.

> "The representation of the instincts in consciousness, that is to say their manifestation in images, is one of the essential conditions of consciousness in general..."
> —*The Origins and History of Consciousness* by Erich Neumann

> "Question Reality"
> —A popular bumper sticker of the late twentieth century

When he located Funk and Wagnalls' *Standard Dictionary of Folklore and Mythology and Legend*, he didn't bother to take the book to a table. He just stood there by the library shelf, searching through the entries. When he found what he was looking for, he read rapidly through the phrases, intensely curious.

"Kama (Desire): the god of love of Hindu mythology; in the Rig-Veda called the first-born of the Mind. He was a beautiful young god, carrying a flower bow with flower-string and five flower shafts (Exciter of Desire, Inflamer, Infatuator, Parcher, Carrier of Death;) or sometimes he is depicted with a bow of sugarcane, the bowstring of bees, the arrows tipped with flowers, riding on a parrot. Kama holds the mastery over every

human being and even the gods are "disordered" when the spell of love touches them. Thus is insured the perpetual creation of the world, which is never finished."

He put the reference book back on the shelf. His body responded ahead of his mind. A chill startled his skin and his heart beat faster. He suddenly felt so unexpectedly and profoundly sad that he turned and glanced about the room of the library. But everyone and everything appeared to be normal. He picked up the dictionary again, and read the last lines over:

"...holds the mastery over every human being...even the gods are disordered...Thus is insured the perpetual creation of the world, which is never finished..."

"Thus is insured the perpetual creation of the world, which is never finished..."

Then a deep calm pervaded him, and the thoughts came. The realization that all his life he'd been waiting for some message, some voice from elsewhere saying "yes." Yes, there is another world you once called home; yes you are able to see through walls.

Almost immediately after this first reaction, he considered what had caused it. A subterranean stream of flooding memories. The English-speaking concierge in Greece—that mysterious man on the island of Paros. He recalled a caged parrot, the wildflowers in the man's hand. The fantastic light. And his first, overpowering desire for Maria Ananin. Then he remembered the bookseller, Enki Rodriguez, back in Mexico, and his talk of the shepherd-king Dumuzi. And the meaning of "Dagan." He remembered Enki's father, in the photograph—there were wildflowers, in Enki's father's hand. And a parrot on his shoulder.

Is everyone a spirit in a human disguise? It all came together now, one flash following another. For an instant (but then it was gone) there came a clear awareness of a secret, hidden story in his life.

Ah, yes, so it does all make sense. But this knowing, which came and went almost immediately, departed when he realized that the "sense" was not an answer at all, but rather a million new absurd and unanswerable questions. Then came the final settling thought, the one that brought some balance, that kept his sanity, the thought that he held on to: *It's all too crazy. Too extreme and supernatural. I guess it's just coincidence.*

It was from that day, however, that the ideas began to come to him—the new ideas, the revelations. He began to write them down at stop signals, on a tablet he kept in his glove compartment. In the middle of watching the new "Star Treks" with his son—he was always, these days, with his son—he would jump up and write down his notes; or while he was mowing the lawn or helping with the homework. It got to be annoying to his family. When he finally closed his business and announced to Rosie, "The time has come; I'm ready to make my film," no one was taken by surprise, neither Rosie nor Aaron, nor himself.

*   *   *

Pehutbit enters the woods astride an animal. Together they fly through the forest with grace and with fire.

There can be no doubt; it is his lion that the young noble commands! Leaning against a cottonwood, Isis-Taia watches from the distant meadow. She stretches. Admiration and pride are like flames in the girl's eyes as she beholds her lover returning, at one with his beautiful beast.

The young man jumps from the back of the lion. Then he guides the animal by the collar, leading him to a second tree, another great cottonwood. He ties him there. With strong affection he slaps the lion's sweating haunch.

Pehutbit goes to Isis.

"I've made another song for you," he says casually, as he carefully lifts his famous lyre from off his lover's lap...

So it was, that the ancestors presented themselves. From genetic memories. From cellular geometry to thinking consciousness. From unforgetting DNA to timeless daydream, in that singular season of

Michael's life. The ancestors appeared on the screen of the newly opened mind of their distant descendant—a contemplative twentieth century descendant, a descendant whose observer, film-maker perceptions tended to interpret life as if life were one long Indian serial, made in collaboration with a French surrealist, most likely taking place in a rain forest of West Africa or Mexico or the Philippines.

The film he made, the *Dance of Life*, which was conceived that season, was never discovered by any fan or critic to be what it actually was in the mind of its creator—a visit with his own ancestors. But that didn't matter; it was aesthetically nearly perfect, as more than one critic avowed. And it had a quietly reverberating influence, though it never made "Michael Dagan" into a household word. Which didn't matter to Michael, or to anyone, not in the long run. The *Dance of Life* gave birth to his other films. One of which, ultimately, accomplished much more than anything Michael ever could have dreamed of. It helped to insure, in effect, the perpetual creation of the world. Not, however, that Michael Dagan was still around when that finally came to its fulfillment. He never got to know that stupendous consummation. For such is the timing of the universe.

*   *   *

He did not begin his project with the writing of a script. He diagrammed instead, for two hours on his father's computer, his own unusually encompassing, hallucinatory, self-generated family tree. And it was this diagram which then became the basis of the script for *Dance of Life*, starring Maria Ananin, who played all the female leads—young women, mostly, though the dancer was nearing forty; for, like Michael, Maria appeared to be no older than twenty-five; and also starring six brilliantly conscious actors and dancers from Oakland, Berkeley, San Francisco, and Marin, plus himself—seven men of varied race.

He found Maria easily, the first place he searched, in fact. Right in his phone book. He'd never known where she'd gone to, after Paros. He hardly could believe it, but there it was—her name; she'd actually come home to the Bay Area. He laughed to himself. *Maybe she's been here all the time.*

Ann Cowart Lutzky

The Hallucinated Paternal Genealogy of Michael Dagan

a temple priestess of an Inannan city-state & a king of the same city-state

Ishme Dagan, King of Isin

/

Sukkal Dagan, Babylonian emigrant   Irefaa-en-Neith of Egypt. & Astakhbit of Egypt

to Egypt & Mara of Egypt

(poet)   (baker's daughter)   (chief-singer to Pharoah)   (noblewoman)

Isis-Taia Dagan   &   Pehutbit

(poet's daughter)   /   (chief singer to Pharoah)

/

/   /

/   /

Aaron Dagan, Palestinian emigrant to Russia   /

& Esther Solomon, Jewish Russian

(farmer)   (farmer's daughter)   /

Saul Dagan, Jewish Russian & Sophia Lutzky, Jewish Russian descendant of David, shepherd-king of Israel

(farmer)   (farmer's daughter)

Michael Dagan, Jewish Russian emigrant to U.S.A. & Hester Kaplan, Jewish Russian emigrant to U.S.A.

(coat factory-worker)   (seamstress)   /

David Dagan, Jewish American & Felipa Patriarcha –and that's

(entrepreneur)   another story

Michael Dagan, multicultural American

husband of Rosie Hestia, father of Ishme and Aaron

5

She Opened the Door

Oakland
May, 1983 A.D.

"Dumuzi stood waiting.
In the doorway of her house
Inanna appeared before him, shining.
She opened the door.
The Daughter of the Moon was shining.

His eye beheld her.
His heart rejoiced.
He brought her to him,
Like a medal of precious lapis or gold,
Placed close against his heart.
He kissed her..."

—from *The Twenty-One Hymns of Orom*

Her porch was strangely similar to his father's veranda. The flowery pastel fabric of the sofa, the potted orchids, even the gardenias—all were elements of his father's haven, though his father had a Spanish colonial in the hills. And this was an inner-city bungalow.

There was a beautiful potted orange tree on her porch. His father had no orange tree. *But I know he'd like one,* thought Michael. Actually, he remembered, it wasn't his father who had decorated the porch, it was his mother—no longer the wife, but ever his father's "help-mate," as the Torah put it...

As he stood there waiting, the fragrance of her gardenias overpowered his thoughts. The scent unveiled a potent, fleeting instant of well-being, a lost souvenir from his tropical past. It was a fitting prelude to the following moment, the moment when he saw her, appearing at the door.

When she arrived, showing herself behind the screen of the doorway just before she opened it, the sight of her standing there took him beyond any observance of her beauty, so full he was with excited anticipation, overshadowed by a sense that his coming to her home could hardly be for real. And soon would not be; would be, instead, for the rest of his life, only a memory. But as for now...

*   *   *

He immediately recognized the man standing in the shadows just behind her.

The guy was much heavier, his hair thinner, his posture less self-consciously assured than the previous time they had met. But the narrow, intense blue eyes, the large grinning mouth, the shiny, unusually high forehead with the greasy bangs straight across—all of that was the same. And Michael seldom forgot a face. He stared for a moment without speaking, strongly certain that this was the pompous graduate student she'd been with long ago, in the sixties, in Golden Gate Park. Her ex-husband. He remembered a few things she'd said back on Paros. The thought occurred that maybe she never actually divorced the guy. He noted the sinking sensation in his stomach which this thought seemed to cause.

It was this man who asked Michael to come in. But after Maria introduced them (she didn't say "my husband," just simply "Rick") the intruder immediately left them in the entryway, disappearing into a room at the end of the hall. She led Michael to a small indigo-blue futon in her living room. It faced the windows and her sunlit porch.

Curled up at her end of the futon, her long white spring dress pulled over her knees, she listened attentively to his ideas, ideas which were not yet very definitive. She quickly became enthusiastic. He'd hoped she might get excited, and she did. His speech quickly took on more gusto. He'd also, equally, been expecting that she wouldn't be interested. But, undeniably, she was. And she became more and more so, the longer he talked.

They made an appointment for lunch at the Bay Wolf, a nice, many-starred restaurant a few blocks from her house. He needed to talk more specifically, about how each of them envisioned her roles, about the financial details, about a contract.

He told her, just before leaving, how it was that his ideas had come to him—he felt crazy telling her all that, but he remembered the way it had been back in Greece. This was someone he tended to open up to. In fact he felt compelled.

When they said good-bye, he gave her a light kiss on the cheek, as he often did with women, as everyone did in the Bay Area in those days. It was ridiculous, but while he drove back to Berkeley from Oakland along Tunnel Road, comfortably pushing his old '71 Volvo to unusual speed and performance, with the *KRE* volume uncustomarily high, that kiss began to make him feel guilty. Guilt invaded, unfairly, he thought, into the exhilaration of the afternoon. And there were a couple of other things, too, besides the kiss, that began to bother him—the presence of Rick (he knew Rick shouldn't bother him) and one more thing wrong with the picture. He had noticed a faint blue circle under her right eye;

it was covered with noticeable make-up. But there was no such circle under her left.

*   *   *

In nine months the film was finished, funded partly with Michael's entire savings, except for Aaron's college fund—Aaron was twelve by then. But mostly it was funded, with much eager encouragement, by Michael's father, who readily turned over what would have been Michael's now sizeable trust.

Michael was meticulous, demanding, and courteous with his crew, all twenty-two of them. Each was treated with the same reserved respect, no matter what the position or part, no matter what charm or damagedness he or she brought, no matter how much immature naïveté and youth. He conveyed, also, just beneath the surface of his politeness, a contagious excitement, as if something crucial were happening.

Many of them fell into infatuations, or a little hero worship, for the boss. Before the film was half finished, at least that one particular aspect of his reputation began to spread. Some of the younger ones secretly, privately, began coming to Michael for personal advice. He had no shyness, now, inspired with his work.

Though he'd known her before filming started, and though she was there, after all, in several leading roles, he did not single out Maria Ananin in any obvious way. The crew noted, immediately, a subtle "chemistry" between the two of them, but then there seemed, also, to be a degree of chemistry between the actress-dancer and every single member of the crew. The women, even, had a sense that interaction with Maria Ananin could get a bit discomfiting, a little too overtly sensual, and she seemed to be one of those people who acted as if you, whoever you were, were the only one in the entire world who presently really mattered.

None of the others were around the night he kept her late. He wanted to go over the Egyptian scene. She played the girl named Isis. And he played her friend, Pehutbit, chief singer of Pharoah's court. He wanted to run through the scene alone with her, to achieve a degree of intimacy they couldn't otherwise attain. Later, before the camera, they would repeat whatever they developed. It seemed to him a straightforward matter; the scene was short, it wasn't even very intense. It only involved his singing a song to her, and playing a lyre, which he would, that night, simply mime. He was focusing on the technicalities, though he imagined that people might think otherwise if they guessed the two of them were in his studio that night. But he knew he was in a professional creative mode; nothing would happen.

And nothing did happen, except a little thing at the end, when she kissed him goodbye, just on the cheek, as he himself had already done with her. But she looked embarrassed, and shocked at herself. Then she muttered an aloof good-bye.

That was it. Nothing more. Yet somehow he saw the truth. She wanted him.

As she walked out the door, he spoke to her back: "You should stop seeing your crazy ex-husband," he said, wishing that the loathsome character hadn't forced him to feel so protective. She instantly spun around.

"It's inappropriate, in your situation, to be so nice," he added, "Forgive, forget, but don't see him any more. Rick's no good for you."

*   *   *

Later that night, after dinner at home—for he'd worked with Maria less than two hours—he and his son competed to see who could put the most dishes into the dishwasher.

"You think you're hecka fresh Dad, but you're losing. I go way faster than you," declared the boy.

"Your Dad has a lot on his mind," commented Rosie, who was plastic-wrapping left-over spanikopita.

"He does? I don't see anything on his mind," answered Aaron, and he roughly patted his bending father on the top of the head.

"Oh, you don't see anything?" replied Rosie. "That's because you're a boy, and not a Mom. I see plenty on it," and she gave her husband a look, a penetrating look that coincided with a glass suddenly slipping through Michael's fingers and crashing to the ground.

As he swept up the pieces, Rosie noticed the wrinkles of tension in Michael's forehead. But she couldn't read his thoughts.

I am never, he was thinking to himself, *even if it's indelibly programmed into my DNA, I am never going to repeat the mistakes of my father. I will never cause Aaron and Rosie the pain and suffering which that man has given my mother. And my sisters. Given to my mother and to my sisters, and to me.*

6

The Journal of David Dagan

On a humid August evening of 1991 in a spacious overhead fan-blown bedroom of the Oakland Montclair Hills (known during the days of the '91 fire as the "East Bay" Hills, by media who, for some reason—ignorance? prejudice?—could not fit the word "Oakland" into the same sentence as "beautiful wooded estates") the following words appeared on the screen of the laptop—one of the first—of a pre-diabetic, white-haired insomniac named David Dagan:

My Somewhat Scattered Ruminations which have come to me upon the anniversary of the death of my beloved ex-wife, Felipa Patriarcha Dagan:

For all my life, since the first day I met her, I never did fall out of love with Felipa Patriarcha. You could say she was the "love of my life." Felipa's small, exquisite golden-hued hand was not the only hand I ever took into my own to place a wedding band upon; nevertheless, we are talking about the mother of my children, Michael, Estelle and Shoshanna—the only children, I am fairly certain, that I have ever had.

Felipa and I were good friends after the divorce, "best friends" you could call it. In the last years, the years when she took my advice and went on estrogen (she was one of the early pioneers to do so, I might add) and she mellowed out, we'd even come to the point of having dinner together some-times, on Sunday nights.

We never made love again, however. That was not possible for her to agree upon. Which I understood.

I would have been entirely content if the marriage had continued eter-nally. That was always my expectation, in fact. But I thoroughly under-stood her point of view. Any idiot could see where she was coming from. She had too much pride and self-respect to be married to a "philandering man" (her words).

She thought (mistakenly, in my opinion) that she emotionally required her man to be there with her, at all times. She probably told herself that after the divorce she'd find a man who would be. But she did not.

She knew, I am almost certain, that, in spite of my faults, I whole-heart-edly worshipped her. I don't believe she ever really doubted me on that. Because she understood me. I'm speaking with complete accuracy there. In fact that was one of the many reasons that I loved her. She understood me better than anyone I ever knew. And believe me I've been grossly misun-derstood by a lot of individuals.

And I understood her. We never fell out of love, neither one of us. But she simply couldn't put up with me. For that I've never blamed her.

We didn't argue much over how to raise the children; that was never an issue. How our kids were brought up was important to both of us, extremely important. Our top priority. I once heard a TV psychologist claim that this very factor is the single most essential requirement for rais-ing children—that you make them top priority.

Now somebody might ask me, how can you sit there with a straight face and consciously hunt-and-peck out this incredible statement—that your kids were your first priority? When you didn't even give enough of a damn to be there on the same continent with them? For a good portion of their childhoods, you weren't there, you hypocritical old so-and-so. Well, that is true enough. But I was somewhat out of my head in those days. I didn't act wisely. Basically, I was immature, a kid myself. In my heart, my kids were always my first priority—and there were a good many times when I did act accordingly. I can tell you, truthfully, whenever I was in the physical presence of any of our three children, I always listened to them, always was intrigued with them, as a matter of fact. And the time I did spend with them was no insignificant ratio to the total hours of their overall child-hoods, I might add.

But I was sometimes an idiot. Over women, over girls, instead of their mother, the one I truly loved.

Today I see what was what. I can call a spade a spade. Much better than I could back in the forties or the fifties or the sixties, or the seventies even. Back in those days it was all craziness. The other marriages, my "affairs." Obsessive-compulsiveness, that's how I diagnose the cause. I say "affairs" in quotes, you see, because sometimes I didn't even have sex with some of those ladies. And, as aforesaid, I wasn't in love with a single one of them. Including the three other wives. I liked them, they "turned me on," as the kids say, and fascinated me, yes, but so what should you expect?

That I should be home enjoying forever the company of my beloved sec-ond wife Felipa, and our three children—that's what you're thinking, am I not correct?

Well, it sounds swell. But I don't suppose you'd believe me if I told you that this second wife of mine happened to arouse in me so much passionate feeling, with such a constant intensity, in both body and mind and whatso-ever else there is of me, to such an extent, that I just had to get away. Just had to force myself to get up and escape—to go beyond an extremely wide circumference of wherever Felipa Patriarcha Dagan remained at the axis of. In order to recognize myself again, to recogitate my own identity. "Rebirth" myself, my daughter Shoshanna would say.

What's with this machine, anyway, speaking of Shoshanna?

She's very impressive with computers, Shoshanna. In fact it was she who gave me this very laptop which I am at this moment in immediate rela-tionship with. This lovely machine which from the start brought me so much joy and excitement, from the moment I first took off her wrappings.

She was Shoshanna's birthday present, you see, this year. My 78th. My daughter tied a magnificent ribbon—gold and burgundy velvet—and this goddamn little computer looked to me to be almost sacred. Especially so when I put her onto my lap, and I first gazed upon her deep blue screen. It meant so much to me to possess her.

I'm not a young man, you realize. If I'm to devote my precious remaining hours to clearing out the old attic that I call my brain, to recycle all the clutter for you future third millennium generations of Dagans, you understand (I assume some of you future Dagans, or maybe just one inquisitive one of you, will be interested in knowing, firsthand, the often confused, sometimes eventful life and times of David Dagan, your ancestor, who lived from 1913 to somewhere into the 21st century—knock on wood): if I'm to devote my precious hours to this, then I am naturally grateful that I have been enabled to do so on a portable. As opposed to my lumbering, unadventuresome clone in the kitchen. No, I'll be living these days with my delicate little laptop.

Sitting myself on the hammock, in the shade of the loquat tree. Or on my nice warm front porch, among the potted orchids and gardenias. Or down by the Bay, in a waterside cafe at Jack London. Maybe up on top of Mount Tamalpais. In fact, wherever I damn well please. You understand. I am not an "indoor" cat.

So I am reverent of my machine. But I don't understand her, you see, not much. Though, believe me, I have had many good, understanding relationships with mechanical instruments. Beginning with my mother's pedal-pushing sewing machine and my Uncle George's shoe-shine machine (which he invented, himself) and going on to the Naval communications equipment I was in charge of during the War, and the Piper Cub I owned, 'til two years ago. But I guess computers are meant for the young to understand, and maybe a few individuals of my own generation. Not, however, individuals of my own sort.

My laptop acts, sometimes, like a touchy woman, you see—logically incomprehensible, more so than the clone does. And I simply don't have around me the expert, Shoshanna (she's in Panama), who could explain to me what I need to know. Like why the machine just clams up, goes cold on me, as she did just a minute ago.

She's doing fine again, for now, though (the computer, I mean). So. Back to my "missive," as they used to say in mid-twentieth century Liberia, a nation of importance in my life which I hope to get into later. Back to my "memoirs"—

Obsessive compulsiveness you can call it—my condition of life (or a part of my condition, to be more precise, which I'm compelled to be). Obsessive Compulsive Addiction.

They've learned how to drug that out of you these days, don't you know? Simply a matter of a prescription from a psychiatrist. But how can people place their souls in the invisible clutches of some stranger-healer they don't even know one damn thing about? Less than they know about the friendly cashier at the local supermarket. Not I, my dear descendant.

You need a good recommendation for a good psychiatrist, and that I do not have. Not that I haven't known admirable psychiatrists and, psychotherapists, too, in my day. The salt of the earth, wise men, wise women. They've passed on, however, or I have.

Maybe I don't want to change, anyway, when push comes to shove. Incredible—drugs for obsession. I don't suppose that awes you future Dagans, but it awes me. Like drugs for depression, or for schizophrenia. Drugs to balance you. I wouldn't need to be a Buddhist like my son, or whatever he is—I could get the "middle way" right along with my other pills at breakfast.

Though, like I said, I don't know that I'd want a transformation like that. I've had a satisfying life, in spite of everything, all said and done, thus far, knock on wood.

I got obsessive, I got compulsive, I got obsessive—who could ask for anything more?

At my age it doesn't matter, anyway, everything's all just a little game—like bridge—that's what it's come to, between myself and the universe. And so far the score breaks even. You know what Estelle (my youngest) would say: maybe it's not a game, Dad, maybe it's a dance. And my son would agree.

When I was a kid, it was amazing (I never told anyone this about myself, you know, never; but you, dear reader, are family)—when I was young, nobody had a clue that I could get myself inwardly so worked up about certain topics. I did an adequate job, you see, acting out the role of "sanguine-tempered child," as the Steiner people would say. I played the role so well, matter of fact, that I've continued to act it out all the rest of my life. It suits me fine. I knew instinctively from an early age, who I wanted to be—an easy-going "sanguine" soul. Of course I didn't have a name for it then. But deep inside I was actually a closet "melancholic."

Nobody knew, for instance, that every time my father—alav ha-shalom—my father, who was still religious in those days, back before the second war, whenever he said, for example, the word "shabbot," I would make myself blink my eyes seven times, as soon as no one was looking, out of respect. I had to do it—I was absolutely firm with me. And that childhood saying—"Step on a crack -break your mother's back"—? Well, you can guess the story. A little voice, like a nagging Jiminy Cricket, would prod me: "Those words, all that break your mother's back stuff, they just might, for some scientific, but as yet undiscovered, mysterious-workings-of-the-universe sort of reason; those words just might be true. You never do know about such things, do you now?" The truth is, I was in my early teens before I finally allowed myself to ignore the necessity of keeping my eyes down to guard the way I passed myself over the sidewalks! Then it struck me that no one I knew had ever had a broken back, and not just a few of those folks were mothers! Of my friends, who carelessly stepped on cracks! At least I assumed my friends stepped on the cracks. I'm not going to say that the thought occurred to me then that all my friends might be slyly, surreptitiously avoiding the cracks, just like I was; and I won't say that I began to slyly check them out.

I won't say that because, after all, I'm talking now about my thought-life during my youth. And I don't want you to get the idea that I was, at that age, a ridiculous meshugener.

After all, a lot happened in my youth, to tell the truth, a lot that I'm still, frankly, quite proud of, even if it was eighty-two percent good luck.

Everyone—or most folks—have, throughout my life, liked me, sought my advice, and given me their advice. There's always been a lot of intelligent, you might say, give-and-take between me and the rest of the universe. When I was a kid no one guessed at my compulsive side except for my mother, and, I think, my Uncle George. If Felipa had been around then, been kids with me, she would have guessed, too, would have gotten me into some sort of strange conversational labyrinth where I would have been forced to talk about my little personal eccentricities. She always had the ability to do that—to act, in a subtle way, the part of a therapist. Somehow I'm sure she had that trait even as a child. But she was half way round the world, then, a little baby-girl in Kavite, in the Philippines, when I was a boy. As it was, no other kids guessed my stuff, nobody found me out.

But enough about my compulsions. As for the obsessive side, my interests, you may well guess, were intense and long lasting. For awhile it was erectors. Whereas another kid might have owned an erector set that he took out of the closet once a year, or maybe once or twice a week if he really was into it, between marbles and catch and stoop-ball, I, being me, played with my erector set solidly. For three or four years straight. I don't think I did anything else but eat, sleep, and make little bridges and small gratuitous pulley machines with motors. Then there was my chemistry phase, two years. Then magic—that lasted five, one of the more powerful, all encompassing obsessions. I performed magic, watched magic, read magic, dreamed magic. Even earned my first wages, at birthday parties, doing magic. That interest never went away completely, in fact. Of course magic was more like love, or baseball, a springtime thing, don't you know. Like the way I felt about Felipa. Around the age of twelve, I got into mysteries.

Radio, books, movies. Read every mystery in existence in that one year. Even girls' mysteries, quite a few.

And so, speaking of girls, you can imagine how it was when I became devoted to a subject that already is a universal obsession for less neurotic mankind. The whole pattern was already set, before girls barely entered my picture. Girls just fell right into place. In more ways than one, in fact.

Girls, by the way—this is my own theory—girls and women tend to be attracted to a man who's obsessed with them. On condition that you maintain your dignity and charm during your insanity, and don't come out with your secret too overtly. They have to guess at it, suspect it. That turns most of them on, I believe. But don't take me too seriously, I only speak from personal experience. That is, what I mean is, it's not a good topic for generalization. What's true for one man doesn't necessarily work for another. What counts is the way the whole gestalt, the whole personality, fits together.

So it was. One obsession after another. Until I was thirty-two—the year I met Felipa, my Queen, the one I loved the best. I'd already been married once...

7

More from the Journal of David Dagan

Oakland
September, 1991 A.D.

Felipa had brilliance running through her every cell. Not just in her head; intelligence coursed throughout her body. She could dance like crazy. Jitterbug, lindy, foxtrot, tango, Charleston, rhumba. And when she was older she kept up with the kids, every dance they could do, she could do better—she even knew the names. She was supernaturally coordinated. And she could learn a new step almost faster than you could show it to her. She'd never forget it, either.

Nor did I ever know another woman who was so fine-tuned, so responsive. Making love with that woman was like playing a Stradivarius (I imagine, never having played one). She was, to be honest, a little lacking in aggression, not very extroverted in the bedroom, which I would have liked in her, I have to admit. Our whole focus was on her. Never on me. But I enjoyed her. Oh, I know what you're thinking: ahh, so that's why he ran around, "never on me." Right? But you're wrong. Yes, I myself used to rationalize it something like that, but lately, in retrospect, I'm more honest with myself. I ran around because, what I've said before—it was my nature. Not any failure on Felipa's part. My "karma," my daughter Estelle would say. My genes, would claim Shoshanna. And my son says it's my genes plus my character.

Felipa was good with math. Quick to catch on, in that area, too. Economics, accounting, legal matters. God, I admired that woman's intelligence. I honestly don't think any of our children, bright as they are, even come close. Not to their mother's innate balabosta-variety intelligence. Lucky for me she never went to college. Or maybe not so lucky. We might have been a real partnership, in business. We were that, somewhat, anyway. Except when she was "dysfunctioning."

Oh yes, Felipa had her down side. And I am fully aware that Michael and Estelle believe that their mother's depression was due to my "abandoning" them. Shoshanna is more understanding.

In the first place, I never abandoned them. I wrote them, at the very least, twice a week, during all three of the years when they were without me in Africa. I know the mail there wasn't the best in those days, but she got most of my letters. She just never shared those letters with the kids. I don't hold that against her; she had her reasons. It must have been tough, and complicated, how she felt. But things weren't working out for us. Actually it was partly her depression that drove me away. Which came first, chicken or what?

She always had that depressive tendency, as far as I know. I had a talk with her mother once. So Michael just doesn't realize, nor Estelle.

The way I figured it, as long as Felipa and I were apart, they'd all be happier remaining in Liberia than going anywhere else. I did not "abandon" them!

And I think they truly were happier. People in Africa loved her, and she loved being loved. She was kind of like a fascinating pet to them. She had lots of good friends in that village she always went off to. She fit in there, better than anywhere, I suspect. Even more than in her hometown, Honolulu. She thrived on village life. Sat around playing "Ludo" (which is West African Parchesi) with her friends. Trading gossip and "medicines," dancing, telling each other's fortunes. I've always wondered why she didn't just move over there, to Gbongayja, I believe they called it, the village where she and the kids spent so much time...

The depression. Why couldn't I stay with her and help?

The fact is I made it worse. She saw so much significance, so much malfeasance, in any little twitch of my eyebrows. Literally. I didn't believe that all the shouting and the crying, the not-speaking, the door-slamming, the pillow-throwing, book-throwing, etc., etc., was good for the kids, or for her, or me.

Shoshanna tells me that everything calmed down after I left, just like I knew it would. In fact, Shoshanna even says I did the right thing. Of course, now, myself, I'm not so sure.

Michael thinks I didn't give a thought to them, after I left. But what does Michael know? Doesn't he see that it actually did work out for the best? Particularly, as far as he's concerned...

8

Dear Maria

"If you look to others for fulfillment, you will never truly be fulfilled."
—*The Tao Te Ching*, Lau Tzu, Stephen Mitchell translation

December, 1991

Dear Maria,

I prefer to write to you, rather than speak. I think it will all be more clear that way. I've been thinking about this for a long time. Going around in endless circles. In spirals. It begins to seem impossible to return to the center, the point that contains the truth. I always come to some point where I tell myself for a while, "Yes, this is the way to go," but then, eventually, my thoughts move on, ending up on the other side of some circumference of emotion and reason, and again I think I know— "this must be the answer."

The reason this happens is the overwhelming pull of the opposing directions. On the one side is the influence of what I feel for you. I remember that morning on Paros, Just before I saw you, just before you were even there, the feeling came. An awareness, as if I were a newborn child, entering earth through some dark and apparently infinite *yin*-filled passageway that never forewarned the coming balance of a place that also included *yang*. And then you came down the road, appearing before me, like a goddess. On the one side is this.

On the other, is the pull of love, my love for the friend and axis of my life, my wife Rosie. And my son. And my own need to not betray them.

Either direction I let my mind go, I am for awhile content and then ultimately disturbed.

So, I have thought and thought, how is a lasting decision ever to be found? Not, it seems clear, not by simply looking for happiness. The only thing I can find as the truest definition of the center of my circles, is the need for something of goodness, of integrity…"

✻   ✻   ✻

As she set the letter down on the top of her bureau, she looked up at the reflection in her mirror. *Am I so transparent?* she wondered. The letter startled her. She had no idea what had prompted it. Never had she done or said a thing to cause such a letter. He wrote as if he were responding to her. To a proposal, an invitation, a seduction, a what? An "advance," her grandmother Olivia would have put it. "A girl should never be the forward one," her mother used to say, with Olivia nodding in agreement. And Maria, all her life had complied, or she thought she had.

But obviously, he had known what she was feeling, regardless. Just as though he'd read all the years of her thoughts. All the fantasies, the imagined nights. The wish to be with him forever, the wish to be his wife. And so he'd made this response. How definite he was, no question in his mind as to how she felt. She kept staring at her reflection.

She didn't know how to respond herself at first, or even if she would. In some ways the letter infuriated her. Then again, it made her happy. It also saddened, and it puzzled. In the end, when she at last replied, she was not intending to be cryptic, it was just that she felt confused. And she also worried that someone other than he might see what she wrote.

She said only, "You saw everything in such a strange mirror-image metaphor. From yin to yang? I do not understand."

But he did not write again to answer her, and neither one of them mentioned their brief correspondence. He was making his second film, *Aurelius*, then. She had only a small part in the project; they barely even spoke.

9

The Ohana Palace

east of San Francisco
June, 1992 A.D.

Over her left ear, bobby-pinned securely to her hair, was a fresh white gardenia with a single, shiny green leaf. He had carefully arranged it there for her, while she stood in the hallway, about to turn off the lights. It took him more than a minute to attach the flower properly. At last he stood back to see the result. The white gardenia was like magic for Rosie's face; Michael thought he'd never seen her looking so good. He took her face in his hands, tilted it upward, and kissed her lips. "You look very pretty," he said matter-of-factly, completely ignorant, unlike his wife, that in all their years together, he had never before bestowed that particular, highly coveted acknowledgment. When her eyes moistened, adding to her radiance, and to his own warm feeling, he didn't see that, coming so greatly overdue, the compliment had actually upset her.

It was eight p.m., exactly, when he led her through the torch-lit entrance of The Ohana Palace, a Hawaiian restaurant-club in Emeryville. Rosie halted at the doorway in astonishment, suddenly clutching Michael's hand much tighter. The beautiful Polynesian room was entirely filled with their friends. She had suspected nothing; his surprise was a success.

Rosie's first observation was that a large number of people were there from her hula class. It was only one year ago that she and Michael started those lessons, every Tuesday night, but the dancers in the class were so relaxed, so easy to get to know. She already considered them family.

Other faces dated from farther back, from her teaching jobs in various day-cares and preschools of Berkeley and Oakland, or families they knew from Aaron's grammar-school years. She spotted Aaron, too, astonishingly spiffy in a brand-new suit—he'd never seen her son in a suit—with his girlfriend, Chloe, also newly incarnated, wearing make-up and a dress. There were some neighbors, and Michael's family, his sisters, grown nieces and nephews, both his parents, her own widowed mother and her brother, and several of the actors and crew from Michael's two films, with husbands, wives and "significant others," people who Rosie had come to know even better than Michael did. She was amazed that not a single one of any of this crowd had spilt the beans. She was also amazed, and inexplicably dismayed, that the suspicion had never occurred to her on its own that her husband might surprise her like this for their twenty-fifth. But she appeared to everyone to be excited and joyous as she stood by the reservation desk, gazing around the room at all the friends and family who sat at the candlelit tables and the palm thatched bar.

Rosie's dark brown hair was currently graced with streaks of silver. She had, over the last year, dyed it to less and less degrees of blondeness, bored with the color and tired of the expense of keeping her own true brown disguised. At first she'd felt a satisfaction in the gradual lifting of her little life-long deception. But, lately the fact that Michael never seemed to even notice the change was becoming obsessively bothersome.

Her hair was tonight done in a chignon at the nape of her neck. The onlookers thought this new hairstyle was very becoming, especially with the gardenia. Rosie's mother and three other women were relieved that Rosie had finally abandoned her habitual style, with her long hair falling loosely down her back; Rosie was really, those four were certain, becoming a little too old for that look.

Around her neck she wore a thin strand of tiny white shells. Her dress, a pale peach, was made of lace, over a sheath of cream silk. It was her favorite dress; Michael had helped to pick it out. She loved the way it felt, so light against her skin.

Rosie and Michael headed for the long table in the front, by the stage, where they could see a pile of presents, gorgeously wrapped. At the table was a seated Polynesian man who was playing slack-key guitar. As they headed for the table, all eyes upon them, she felt a sudden twinge of regret. She was slightly provoked that Michael had gone and surprised her like this. She knew she should be feeling loving and grateful, and she was grateful, but at the same time, it honestly annoyed her, that he'd done it this way, as a surprise. Didn't he know her well enough by now to realize she would have had as much fun looking forward to this party as in actually being here? She could have better prepared herself. Practiced her hula more, for one thing. And she would have made alterations in how she'd dressed—worn her hair down, maybe, and chosen her green flower-print sarong. He'd eliminated half her fun. *Oh well, c'est la vie,* she told herself, *it's still sweet of him.*

As they passed by the tables, Michael greeted the guests with a smile and a small nod. It was interesting, he noted, how at unexpected moments the shyness of his youth would suddenly rear its unwelcome head, no matter how old and experienced he got. *Oh well, it's Rosie's party,* he thought, oblivious that he was taking a rather odd stance towards their anniversary. He saw that Rosie was glowing, as she stopped to talk to everyone and, for that, he felt affectionately satisfied. He went on by himself; he figured the evening would be half over before his wife made it to the other side of the room, at the rate she was going.

*　　　　　*　　　　　*

Edward Anders put down his fork as he saw that Michael Dagan was coming toward his table. Edward was an old friend of the Dagans. From way back. San Francisco, the late sixties. Edward and his wife, Julie, had lived in the same Noe Valley neighborhood as Michael and Rosie, two houses down the block. For a time, in the days when Rosie was pregnant with her first child, the Anders and Dagans had taken turns making Sunday brunch for each other, followed by a trip to the park and a game of Frisbee with Ed's golden retriever. Edward hadn't seen Michael in years, though he sometimes had lunch with Rosie. About ten years older than the Dagans, he was recently retired from his accounting firm, and recently divorced from Julie. He had informed Michael on the phone that he was selling condos these days, and traveling a lot.

Now the white-jacketed, straight-postured Edward extended his arm to give a light touch to Michael's passing elbow. Michael looked down and immediately recognized his former neighbor, though the dark wavy hair had turned entirely gray. Michael noticed, also, the pretty brunette who sat at Edward's side.

This woman, who appeared to be no more than thirty, gazed up with huge, unabashedly awe-struck eyes, stunned by the moment of actually meeting Michael Dagan. Edward introduced her as "Olive" and said that she was a cinema student at San Francisco State. Olive, it seemed, was a fan of Michael's *Aurelius.* "I've seen it three times, now," she gushed. Edward smiled; this was one reason he had brought her here tonight, instead of his girlfriend.

The next moment, however, the expression on the woman's face caused Edward Anders to question his invitation. But, *Ah, well,* he reflected, *Dagan's still too much in love with Rosie to bother with this one. And who could blame him?*

Michael smiled and nodded at the two of them. Then he moved on, rushing to the next table, as he caught sight of who was sitting there, motioning with an arm and grinning ridiculously upward at him.

"Well, so you made it! Good for you, I thought for sure you'd miss your flight!" the host exclaimed.

"Hell, no, man, after you paid for it? What kind of ingrate do you take me for?" beamed the guest.

The voices were loud, trying to rise above the music of the now amplified guitar. Edward and Olive could make out the words clearly from their table. They listened and watched as Michael's entire being grew more relaxed, greeting this guest, who, thought Edward, looked like some character he might see on Market, selling *Street Sheets*.

Edward Anders stared intently, then turned his head, wanting to observe his companion's reaction. He saw that the young woman had grown solemn and focused; she was obviously mesmerized by Michael Dagan.

"But who put you way over here?" Michael could be heard. "Get up, Muir, I want you next to me—where I can keep my eye on you," and the elegant host nudged the ragged guest's back, prodding him to stand.

Edward turned his attention back to his plate, poking his fork into a piece of pork teriyaki. He glanced sideways again at Olive, finally addressing her, somewhat softly. "Pardon me, madame, but your salivation is showing," said Edward, who was a man of little patience.

"What?!" responded Olive, who had not before realized that her husband's father could be such a jerk.

*   *   *

"Then I decided to convert to Hawaiian," Michael's eyes were wide and he wore a large grin. He was only slightly inebriated, but it was beginning, at least to Rosie, to show. She glided toward him, quite high herself. Her husband wasn't much of a drinker, normally, just occasionally he could get a bit carried away at a gathering like this one, especially if there was champagne. She knew it was his shyness, he thought the alcohol freed him; unfortunately he was correct. Soon he would be talking too much—lecturing, to be exact. Talking too much for his own good, and possibly even for hers. "Maybe you've had enough, Michael," she whispered in his ear, and she moved on.

"No, I'm serious," he was speaking with Rosie's best friend, Angela Gentry, the director of a daycare where Rosie used to work. "I've got Hawaiian in my blood, a little. And lots of Filipino. Did you know the Polynesians passed through the Philippines on their migrations? And that means, Angela, that even pure-blooded Hawaiians might be part Filipino. Sooo, my Filipino side of the family, who mostly live in Hawaii, anyway, they're not so alien to the Hawaiian way of being—the chanting and the dancing, the way the people connect to nature. Did Rosie tell you we're taking the hula these days? The *kahiko*. That's the old, classical dance, not the hotel mutation. A friend of mine got us into it; Maria Ananin, the dancer, you know, the girl I work with—she's been doing *kahiko* for years—"

"Oh, she has?—You know, I thought maybe Maria would be here, tonight, but I don't see her," said Angela, looking around while she analyzed his choice of the word *girl*. "I've never met her, though, just seen her in your movies. Maybe I wouldn't even recognize her in person."

"Unfortunately," he said, "Maria couldn't make it tonight. Anyway, she's the one who convinced me of the beauty of that dance. Rosie and I took it up, oh, about a year ago. The gestures are a lot like tai chi, which we've also been learning. It's interesting, you know, Angela, the way the two are similar, as if they came from the same roots. Then, again, some kahiko gestures look like Indian dance. The ancestors of the Polynesians came from there, Southeast Asia, I mean, according to some anthropologists and according to King Kalakaua. Kalakaua was a great Hawaiian king of the nineteenth century. He was also a scholar, both Westernstyle, and Hawaiian—"

"Yes, I believe I've heard—"

"There's a legend that long ago a mortal woman—not a goddess, as you might suppose—but a living Hawaiian woman, created the hula," he continued, enthusiasm for his topic joining his champagne. "By imitating the wind blowing through the leaves, and the motion of the sea. And yet, the hula was at one time performed exclusively by men. The dance is inspired by Laka, the deity of forests, of sea, of flora and fauna—of all nature, really. Laka's a god and goddess, both. You're not supposed to dance unless you're in the immediate presence of, at the very least, one plant. In other words, of Laka. Laka transmits the 'knowledge,' the meaning of your dance. And at the same time Laka receives your dancing as a gift. The dance is sacred..."

He paused to sip more champagne, but not long enough for Angela to think what to say; he went on again too quickly. "The Hawaiians were incredibly connected, invisibly grafted, you could say, to their vegetation. Much of the language is plant metaphor, or direct reference to flowers and plants. A Hawaiian term for people, for example, is "the flowers." Have you ever noticed how Hawaiian songs are often love songs to nature, to a mountain or an island or a flower? And the songs addressed to humans, to kings or queens or lovers, those are filled with metaphors of beauties in nature. A *lehua* blossom, a certain style of rain. As a matter-of-fact, when we were living in West Africa, on the edge of the rain forest, my mother, who grew up in Hawaii, used to always tell us—"

"Michael," Angela interrupted, in a conspiratorial whisper, "Would you dance the hula for us, here, tonight?"

"Oh, no, not tonight."

"Aw, come on, please, Michael." It wasn't that she didn't want to listen to his conversation. True, he was monopolizing, but she liked his voice. He had never before talked so much with her. She was aware that this man was either very silent or very talkative, nothing in between; it was a pattern she'd noticed in the years she'd known the Dagans. Tonight he seemed excited, in a youthful, forthright way that she was finding especially attractive. But even more, she decided, she would like to see him dance. He would be so cute; he could take off his shirt. His eyes were shining, intensely alive. "Yeah, how about a performance, Mike?"

"Maybe I've been talking too much," he smiled, and picked up his glass of champagne. "That's my personal life, Angela, I don't want—"

"Oh, come on now, Michael, you're among friends!" she exclaimed. Rosie's husband was gorgeous, otherwise she might take offense— "Personal life?!" He meant that, too, she decided. How distancing this guy could get. "Come on, now—"

"Enough, Angela."

"O.K. O.K. I'm sorry, Michael. Don't worry, I'll be quiet. I'll leave you alone. Relax. Don't look so concerned!"

"Ever been to Hawaii, yourself, Angela?"

"Of course. Have you?" She did feel annoyed; if his friends weren't part of his "personal life," then who was? Maybe he didn't even consider her to be a friend. After all these years!

"Which islands?" he asked.

The guitarist was singing, an old song of departure, of sailing away beyond the coral reef, of reluctant good-byes. Michael recognized a melody his mother used to sing.

His eyes began now to wander. He tried to locate Rosie. He couldn't make her out. Maybe she'd gone to the restroom. He reached for his distance glasses, in his pocket.

There she was, he saw her. She was standing near the stage, near the guitarist. Rosie was teaching Edward Anders how to hula.

Her hands were on Edward's hips and her gardenia was clenched between his teeth. Rosie's hair was down, she'd undone her chignon. Facing each other, Rosie and Edward presented what Michael thought was a totally westernized and absurdly inappropriate posture. Nothing like his own conception of the dance.

He didn't catch Angela's reply as he continued glancing around the room, searching, this time, for Tom Muir. He never did learn which islands his wife's best friend preferred.

*   *   *

— Aaron looked absolutely fantastic tonight!

— Yeah, he did, didn't he?

— That suit!

— Do you know, Rosie, our son actually asked me to help him shop for his suit. I took him to Nordstrom's last Saturday.

— Nordstrom's? You and Aaron? I can't believe it!

— Is that surprising? Isn't that where you always shop?

— Sure, but it isn't like you to go there, Michael. And certainly not like Aaron. Interesting…You know, I loved the way Chloe looked, too! She's quite a good-looking girl.

— Of course she is, honey. She's very pretty. I've always thought so.

— You're kidding. With that purple hair, and the ring in her nose? I'm so glad she did her hair black for tonight, and not some weird fluorescent combination. She almost looked normal. She might have really been an embarrassment, you know? That we allow our son to go out with—

— I like the way Chloe looks, always. What's to be embarrassed about? A lot of intelligent, creative people of their generation are into that kind of style.

— Oh, sure, Michael. What do you know about their generation? *Nada.* That's what.

— Our son's generation? I know a little, honey, maybe more than you think, maybe more than you do.

— What was your reaction to Tom, Michael?

— It was good to see him. It's been a long time.

— Of course…No, I mean what did you think of the way he looked?

— The way he looked? He looked like Tom.

— Tom Muir was the embarrassment. He was the one who was the real embarrassment, you know?

— What are you talking about, Rosie?

— What am I talking about? Don't you think Tom could have at least shown us enough courtesy to press his shirt? Or wear jeans that weren't in shreds? I mean, most of the men had on suits. Did you see how Edward Anders was dressed? That nice white—

— I thought that white jacket was a little over-doing it myself, to be honest. But that's Anders' business. It basically isn't my concern how somebody else dresses. Tom or Anders. I don't really give a shit, how Edward Anders dresses. Or Tom…Is that all you got out of the evening, Rosie? Pleasure or embarrassment over how your friends were dressed?

—

— Well?

— Why do you always say "your" friends, Michael? Aren't they your friends, too?

— Of course. Many of them. But a lot of them—you have to admit you know a lot of them better than I do.

— And is that my fault? Is it my fault you've never made any effort to keep up with anybody? You give more attention to some homeless stranger on the street than you do to our friends. And you spend way more time on your outdated political causes than you do on our social life. If it wasn't for me, the only people there tonight would have been the people from the hula class. Who we just met. Everybody else, from the eighties or seventies or the sixties, from our whole life—all of them could have disappeared off the face of the earth as far as you're concerned. Except for Tom. Or your family—but even my family, even your own family, I'm the one who does all the keeping up.

— What do you mean, Rosie; what do you think I had to do for tonight? To make this all happen tonight? You think it just took a couple minutes, a snap of my fingers—

— Oh, sweetheart. Look, I'm sorry. Michael, I really do appreciate what you did tonight. It was a wonderful surprise. Really it was. A very sweet thing you did. I'm really sorry. I don't want to fight, honey. Not tonight…I love you, Michael.

—

— But, actually, sweetheart, it is kind of a good thing to be talking about these matters. Don't you think? Our friends, our social life—it's about time we discussed it. We'll be better prepared for the next twenty-five years. You know, all the social stuff becomes even more important when you get to be seniors.

— We're not seniors, Rosie.

— No, but we soon will be.

— Hardly.

— You really could put a little more energy into our friendships, though, Michael. It's like you don't really care about most of those people. You and Tom, that's it! Except when Valmiki's here, which is almost never. And even Tom's always in Central America or somewhere, these days, he's hardly here in California…You know, when you two used to get together, the way you would go on and on about how people should be more kind and compassionate and all, always philosophizing about this or that—I bet you anything that's just what you two were doing in that corner the whole last half of the evening, in fact, isn't that so?!

— That's hardly what we were discussing, Rosie. As a matter of fact Tom was catching me up on Chiapas, which, of course, you don't know a—

— But really, sweetie, I think if you both did less thinking about it and more real, hands-on interaction with people, that would be so much more—more real than all the philosophical—

— Hands on? You mean like Edward Anders and you? Is that what you mean by hands on, Rosie?

— What are you talking about?

— Oh, nothing.

— Oh nothing? Now don't go saying "oh nothing," Michael; please don't say your famous oh nothing! I hate it when you say oh nothing, you know that? Why don't you say what you mean? You just made this very loaded statement, and then you say "Oh nothing." Now where is that supposed to leave me?

— Getting out of the car, and walking into the house, maybe?

— Yeah, you know, you're right, this is stupid, we've been sitting in the dark for twenty minutes. The neighbors will think—

— Rosie, can you ever, even for one second, stop thinking about what other people will think? Besides, they're all asleep.

— And I suppose you never think about that?

— Not like you.

— Look, I thought you don't believe in being judgmental Michael, that's what you always tell me. But it's exactly what you're doing this minute. To me. It's what you're always doing, in reality. You're always judging me. But it's all right, honey. Really it is. It's O.K. with me if you have some negative ideas about me. Because it frees me to have them about you. Which is ONLY HUMAN, MICHAEL, YOU KNOW THAT? And yes, so I care about what other people think. That's human, too. Humans are a gregarious species. Right? Isn't that what you were just saying the other night? But you've totally side-tracked me. What were you saying about Ed?

— Noth- I mean, forget it. It's no big deal.

— I like Edward Anders. He's fun. I like him a lot. But that's all. He isn't my type. His best friend, now that's another story…But seriously, Michael, are you jealous because I have lunch with Ed sometimes?

— Rosie, you know I've never interfered with you having men friends. Why are you saying this now? You know I trust you.

— Well, maybe. But is that totally honest of you? I don't actually, if I'm really honest I have to admit, I don't altogether, really completely trust you.

— What do you mean by that?

— Oh, I don't know, Michael. I guess I basically trust you. But deep down, part of me, I mean how can anyone ever—

— I know I trust you, Rosie. I always have, I always will.

— But maybe you shouldn't.

— Maybe I shouldn't trust you? Do you know what you're saying?

— I mean, I mean maybe you just shouldn't be so unsophisticated. About life.

. — You think I'm unsophisticated? And you *are* sophisticated? Just how sophisticated are you, Rosie?

— I didn't say—

— You said maybe I shouldn't trust you.

— No, I—

— Is there some reason I shouldn't trust you?

—

— Is there a reason, Rosie?

— Michael, sweetheart, listen to me…

— Yeah? I'm listening.

— Look, I can see, this conversation is getting…

— Yes?

— Michael. Do you already know? All about everything—you know, don't you, Michael? I can hear it in your voice! You do know, don't you, honey? And I thought all this time—My god, what a fool I've been!

— What in the hell are you talking about, Rosie?

— Michael, please don't pretend you don't know!

*   *   *

It took only three weeks to find himself a flat in San Francisco; because he was lucky and because he had almost no considerations. It was a small, comfortable Victorian, second floor, above the landlord's family, on Oak off of Fillmore. Chloe, his son's girl friend, who had always liked him and who was very saddened to hear about the separation, immediately bought him a Burmese cat as a housewarming gift. Chloe was certain, from her own devastating childhood experiences of loss and loneliness, that the pet would help. Michael accepted the animal, partly because he didn't want to hurt his son's girlfriend's feelings, and partly because he had none of the energy required to refuse.

10

The Ritual of Inanna's Descent

east of the Euphrates, west of Mohenjo-Daro
circa 2700 B.C.

They came to me in my courtyard garden. I sat awaiting them on a small linen covered pillow beneath my orange tree, a tree that was filled at that time both with fragrant blossoms and with ripe fruit amongst green and shining leaves.

The priestess Bhakta came forward. She carried, on a tray upon her head, a golden goblet and a small, gracefully formed lapis vial, half-filled with juice of *soma*. The golden goblet was from the home of Ursunabi; it was the goblet with the birds upon the rim, the vessel I had discovered in Ursunabi's home, long ago on my first day in Orom. The trader and his wife had only lately offered up this gift to our temple, with the request that it be used on this momentous day. Gudea told me that the vessel possessed such a history and was of such a value that he knew not how anyone could possibly even determine to price it.

Bhakta poured the soma into this cup. Wordlessly, she handed the vessel to me, and I drank of it. My women, who were gathered in a cluster behind the chief priestess, watched silently. I closed my eyes, then, though not tightly, and swallowed the liquid. It was pure undiluted soma. Not unlike the fine quality which was swallowed by the people of the village of Fa-Orszag.

But Fa-Orszag was so very long ago. I no longer remembered the taste. And also, perhaps, I was no longer that Anarisha of Fa-Orszag, but had become, completely, the Priestess of Orom.

Then, too, never had I received so abundantly of this medicine. The amount of soma which was given to a high priestess in the ritual of *Inanna's Descent* was lavish. The priestess preceding the woman before myself had perished during the sacred rite. And such tragedy was not uncommon, so Gudea advised me.

Yet, as of old, just as in my far-off land and time, I savored the precious moment of passage. Swallowing the drink, I savored the moments that followed, the moments of transformation from ingestion to effect.

But unlike in my village home, where the drinking of soma and the ordinary condition of living were nearly seamless, my present being was this time dissolved into a clearly distinct state of trance. Almost immediately, due to years of careful training, my body knew where my heart and mind must travel for this singular ceremony of the city of Orom.

As I prolonged my breathing and slipped more and more rapidly into the center of myself, the High Priest Gudea presented himself at the courtyard entrance gate. One of my women, waiting at the gate for his arrival, accompanied the elderly priest of Enki to my orange tree. Gudea came to me immediately and, without greeting, stepped forward to grasp the top of my forehead with one hand and the back of my neck with the other, shifting the position of my head. It was all as I expected, just as we had trained.

Something shifted inside of me, then, as well. This also was as it should be. From the length of my spine, and through the expanse of the mood inside the realm of my thoughts, I became altered.

Then I heard Gudea speak. "Inanna offers Love from the Above. The Queen of Heaven descends to offer Love to the Below. All Creation, even the greatly ignorant, desire—deep in their souls—to know Her. The rock, the sand, the lion, the human, all desire to know Her. To know the Queen of Heaven, just once, if no more, to see Her unclothed, in undisguised Divinity."

Gudea smiled shyly, and knowingly, at me, "And how She does love disguises!" he said. I knew, at that moment as he spoke those words that I, Inannanindigur, was also, and had never ceased to be, Anarisha. How often had I worried over this matter, as the years grew plentiful. But now, once again, the awareness of myself as Anarisha, beloved of Anurei, came fully upon me. And I knew that my soul had never left. I might have known this, seen it easily, had I not been fooled by my own disguise.

If ever I leave this city I shall remember Orom as the *Great Village of Disguises*. A magic place, truly! And how frightened I'd been of it when first I'd come. But I learned what Orom was, the temple teachers had told me: "Orom is not simply a big village, with village structures and family ways of being-in-the-world," they had said. The districts of Orom were not villages at all, they told me (how long had it taken me to under-stand that! Or did I ever understand?) Orom was—Gudea, himself, had taught this—a "civilization," as Ursunabi once had put it, too. Gudea pronounced that strange word slowly and beautifully, in order for me to hear its power. Yet even now, do I know what "civilization" means?

So, Anarisha's soul had never truly departed my person, and it was yet Anarisha's eyes through which I gazed. Therefore, knowing this, tears of joy and gratitude came to my eyes as the ritual continued, and something, yet again, shifted inside me.

And then it was that I witnessed, as in a dream, but moving before my open eyes, there in the garden, in front of the southern wall, a whirling apparition. It had the appearance of a great, round tablet. A perfect sphere. It hovered in its place above the earth, like a bird sus-pended on the wind.

The object was magnificent in size, taller than even the garden wall. Its surface appeared smooth, like the Great Wall of Orom. The shine on its surface was as the radiance of gold, but the coloring was as lapis, a blue that was rich and strong. That azure hue, however, did not remain.

There came other colors, even as I watched, colors of all the rainbow, and these swirled upon the surface of the circle, like oil upon water. Soon this changed, also—the swirling took forms. And I saw before me, on that strange tremendous tablet, the emergence of another world.

Then I heard Gudea speak again: "Inanna offers Herself in Loving Ecstatic Submission. Inanna is descended unto the Darkness of the Netherworld, that She may bring Light. Inanna descends, into Longing and Desire, that She may fulfill. Inanna descends, into Death itself, that she may Enliven. Disrobed now by Her Sister, The Lady comes to Her Union with the Netherworld. Thus, will She nurture new Seed within Her womb. Thus will She birth the Harmony of the Whole of Opposites. All Beauty, all that is Righteous and Complete, all that is Bliss. That which makes Union yet again with yet an other Netherworld, to make new Seed again. Eternity eternally perfecting Eternity. Thus, by will of Enki, God of Water—the Semen of the Seed. Thus, does it come of Inanna, radiant Goddess of the Morning Star."

Gudea ceased speaking. And I heard other voices come into his silence. And I knew that these were the voices of the beings I expected. Now they showed themselves before me, upon the surface of that unique and tremulous circle which suspended itself before the garden wall.

These foreign ones appeared to be beckoning to me. They motioned with their fingers and with their arms, while they called Inanna's name. They were dressed in vivid clothing of a type which is unknown, except perhaps in visions of priests. The clothing on the uppermost portion of their bodies was separate from the clothing on their bottoms, and the cloth fit closely upon their skin, moving with limited grace against the motion of their limbs. The men had little hair upon their heads, in the manner of the men of Uruk. The women had, some of them, much hair, while others had but little.

As I gazed upon them all, one of the women stepped suddenly from that spherical tablet, coming forward and down in an astonishing swirling movement.

She walked directly toward me. But even in my deeply enchanted state, I had the need to look away, to observe Gudea and Bhakta and my lesser priestesses, to know how they were receiving that which was happening before our eyes. But when I turned to my people, I saw that all of them were deep in prayer or meditation.

So I arose from my pillow then and moved, myself, down the garden walkway toward the woman's outstretched hands. I stood before her and placed my hands into the hands of this stranger.

"Anarisha," she said clearly. And I heard and understood the voice and accent of my own village of Fa-Orszag. I looked deep into her eyes. The woman was my elder, Ma Agghia.

Her hair was a shade of sand, hair of a hue that I had never seen, except in my visions. It was like sunlight, in shine and fineness. The thought came to me that Agghia was sent by Utu. Her skin was as it had always been, back in Fa-Orszag, the color of my own, and with the quality of the light of the new moon. Her eyes were as always, black as obsidian.

She kept my hands in her own and she smiled at me. It was a good smile, a smile to be trusted. So I went with this woman, without fear, as first I went with Anurei into the forest when we were little children. Hand in hand we entered another world.

*   *   *

When I entered there most of those strangers immediately departed, going through the back doorways which were in that place. Agghia, and another woman who remained, seated me down then, politely, in an odd metal chair made perhaps of silver. They gave me a silver goblet decorated with much inscription, and asked me to drink. The taste of the liquid was good, like newly fallen rain. Agghia began then to chant. In matching rhythm, slowly and carefully, the other woman removed my clothing, and as she did so her face became transformed; it turned from pleasant aspect to cruel and deadly form. When at last I stood naked before them, she gave me a look of cold finality. *She is Ereshkigal,* I thought, *She is my sister, the Goddess of Kur.*

Agghia bid me to drink once again from the silver goblet, and this I did.

Then it was that everything inside me made to shift once more, the greatest of all changes. *Oh, what is happening?* was all that I could think, in spite of years of preparation. But I recognized that which came next: a moment like the shiver of death. It was the moment of *Descent.*

*   *   *

Immediately, I found myself yet somewhere else again.

I seemed to be inside a dwelling place. And the air of contentment and safety in that place was as the feeling in my own dear home in Fa-Orszag, which I had known not for all those many years. I seated myself upon a small couch in the entrance room of the house. A pretty little cat was curled up near the doorway, asleep, but barely so.

On the wall, just above the cat, there hung three masks of fine dark wood. I saw that one of these masks appeared to be a horned cow—one of the many disguises of the Goddess. Another was a death mask; for the eyes were closed and the features truly-portioned—it was an unflawed human face. *But how can this be a death mask, when the substance is not clay? The mask is carved of wood!* I pondered the problem, and gazing at the mask more intently, I suddenly perceived that the face bore startling likeness to my own!

Except for the masks, the walls, unlike those of Orom—but much like the walls of my village—were void of decoration. There were, however, windows in that place. I turned my gaze to a wall of numerous windows. Through these large rectangles, whose vacancies were filled with something clear and shining, like ladies' mirrors of Orom, I could see the sky of night.

Stars shone in the heavens. Yet the starlight was strangely dimmed. And the blackness of the sky was filtered through a mist of amber yellow. Bewildered, I turned my gaze to my closer surroundings.

I noticed then, down a long and much-lit hallway, a second door. I immediately arose. Walking quietly on soft unending carpet, I moved toward the unknown doorway, compelled to enter there...

---

* soma: a potent drink used in very ancient times, from Iran ("hoama") to India ("soma"). Over a hundred hymns of the *Rigveda* honor this libation and its goddess. Drinking caused exhilaration beyond one's natural powers, and the juice itself, presently believed to be from a mushroom (*Amarita muscarita*, the "fly agaric"), was described as "primeval, powerful, healing all diseases, loved by the gods, even the Supreme." It is given credit for actually inspiring the *Vedas*, themselves, which are humanity's earliest still in use metaphysical scriptures. Soma is said to be a gift of the goddess Saraswati.

11

Brando

San Francisco
August, 1992 A.D.

The cat was full-grown. Not a kitten, not an old-timer, he was at the peak of the cat-prime of his cat-life. However, like his fellows in that land and that era, he had known the surgeon's knife. And therefore he did not inhabit a grown male cat's condition, but retained instead the receptive traits of kittenhood, both in innocent-eyed kitty appearance and in feelings of curiosity and playful fascination. With the passage of time, nevertheless, had come experiences of many sorts, and so this kitten-like cat possessed a portion of the wisdom and perspective of uncastrated maturity.

It happened that this cat was by nature a scaredy-cat type of animal. He could be charming and extroverted, but was prone to ferocity when frightened. Often, in the realm of humans it did happen that, because of the humans' disturbing unexpectedness, he would become alarmed. Then, because of the resulting aggression on his part, the humans would retreat.

Yet because he was small and pretty, a few retained a slight fondness for "Brando," as they called him. And, because he was one who thrived on interaction with fellow sentient beings, Brando yearned to expand that fondness, yearned for a greater closeness with the humans of his world. He was deeply lonely and unhappy when humans were near because of the neglect that they perpetually blanketed upon him.

His malaise was founded on the circumstance that the sovereign human character in his world, the man who came with the territory, was a very strange-but-uninteresting-to-a-cat sort of individual. This man went about the rooms of the flat thinking and acting in a manner that the cat could not fathom, could not interpret nor absorb. It seemed almost as if something of the man had been carried off, leaving only a moving body to go on, with not much left behind in its movement which was either stimulating or comprehensible. At least not to a cat.

Fortunately, Brando was mostly an "outside" cat. He spent much of his life outdoors in the domesticated wildness of the gardens, fences, trees and tar-paved areas of his block. It was out there that he engaged himself in myriad connections with friends and enemies, all of whom were cats, as well as smaller creatures, none of them human. For this reason he was able to enjoy a partially fulfilling existence.

The few visitors to Brando's home included human beings of varied descriptions, humans who came into the flat and went out again, some like the man in their level of interest in the cat, some slightly different. Some bent down to give a stroke or two. At first charmed by his guileless expression, these visitors were later annoyed—he scratched when they lingered too long in running their fingers through his fur. Those who knew him from previous visits came to acknowledge him with a "hello, kitty," and not much more, if they acknowledged him at all.

But at last, after a young cat's lifetime of this sad state of affairs, there appeared at the door of the flat a human being greatly different from the man and his previous friends and acquaintances. Brando saw immediately that this new female moved with the quiet expectedness of a fellow cat. None of the sudden inexplicable movements of humans as Brando had known them; in this one, all was fluidity and flow.

*   *   *

She settled herself down upon the man's sitting place, making no aggressive attempts to come for the cat as did some of her kind. The cat looked up at the woman. The look in her eyes, and all the whole of her, was very soft, as was her scent; she made him feel the way a pretty little female kitten would. Not passionate—for he knew not much of that—but a nice warm wishful feeling. Yet this was a human, and of only slightly less size than the man; Brando's feelings astonished him. He had to go right to the woman and rub against her.

The next thing he knew, the even further astonished animal found himself receiving an understandable human voice that was speaking of neither food nor water nor of coming in nor going out, but of matters far less mundane. The cat very distinctly understood that this human was perceiving him to be a beautiful, charming, and wonderful sort of animal.

He had just taken in this message when the man returned from the kitchen, where he had gone to fetch something steaming in a cup. Although the cat had never seen her before, he could sense that this woman knew the man very well. When the man walked across the room, something else was clear. The woman sensed the man to be even more beautiful, more charming and more wonderful than she did the cat. And not only that; the man was someone she wanted to share life forces with. Immediately.

When the woman and the man had spoken some words and the woman had finished her tea, the two humans stood. They went to the room where the man made his sleeping place. Brando followed. But the man gently pushed the cat away with a foot and shut the door before his face.

Brando walked, grace and dignity totally intact, through the hall to the front door. He circled to lay down to await the man's return. He would sleep, and dream a pleasant dream about the more comprehensible world of cats. When he awoke the man would let him out.

And he would go down to the street, back to the true dimensions of his own reality.

*   *   *

The cat scratched his ear and began to settle himself. But there came no opportunity for dreaming, or perhaps what happened next did take place in the sleep of a cat, unique abode of consciousness such as that is.

Brando had just turned about and made himself cozy when he sensed that someone was returning from the bedroom. But the bedroom door had not been opened, had not made its customary sound. He widened his half-closed eyes. There was someone coming from the room, a woman who resembled the woman who had gone there…

She had the same cat-like flow as that first woman, and the softness, but she was smaller and more undulating. And her fur was much darker, more like the man's. More significantly, she was not a living human being, but something else, something like those cat friends and enemies who would sometimes appear, cats who had lived and died and gone, and then come back, in new and scentless form.

Slowly this woman moved toward Brando. As she drifted by and out through the closed front door, she spoke. *What a pretty kitten you are, my little one*, she told him. Her voice, like the sudden warmth of the spring sun that follows the rain, renewed his spirit, and from that moment Brando seldom felt frightened or lonely amongst women or men again. And, therefore, from that time, the humans began to like that cat.

*   *   *

The man and the first woman returned from the bedroom.

Brando stretched and raised himself. But the man, who had removed all of his usual coverings, and all of the woman's as well, stood still, with his hands slowly moving over the woman's thighs. He did not even look downwards at the cat. The woman also appeared to sense only the man. Once again the cat wanted to go rub against the legs of her. And this he did.

The woman looked away, then, from the eyes of the man; she looked down to the animal. "Such *a nice little cat* you have, Michael," she said with attention.

"Yeah, you're right, Maria, *he is, isn't he?*" the man replied softly, and sincerely, including Brando in his love.

And Brando sensed all over his whisper-like self that the man knew at last. Knew that this small cat-self was a being-in-the-world of that flat, a being with whom to share spirit, as well as food and water and time and space.

12

Ananin and Dagan

San Francisco
September, 1992 A.D.

> "My beloved met me,
> Took his pleasure of me, rejoiced together with me...
> After he on the bed, in the holy loins
> has made the holy Inanna rejoice,
> she in return soothes the heart for him
> there on the bed..."
> —translation in *The Treasures of Darkness: A History of*
> *Mesopotamian Religion* by Thorkild Jacobsen

Under a white crescent moon, for the seventh time in seven nights, she passed over the water, crossing the Bay Bridge, from Oakland to San Francisco, driving to the home of Michael Dagan. After long and careful searching, she found a space to park, just three blocks from his flat. Walking, nearly running, she turned from Fillmore onto Oak Street. Growing more and more excited, she hurried along Oak Street, the street where he lived.

She rushed up his stairway, and he met her at the door. Then he took her, as he liked to, by the hand. They passed quickly up a second stairway, through his long and narrow hallway, through the bedroom doorway, coming down upon his bed.

Slowly now, so much more slowly, he undressed them both in sequence. Then he pulled her to him, closer than before.

Like a new devotee, all-absorbed in rapture, he caressed her slowly, cupped her breasts and brought them closer, to his mouth, then kissed and sucked each breast in turn. Slowly, with the fingers of his right hand, he began to stroke them, came to know their fullness, while his left hand found the softness of her thighs. Later, almost without shyness, her hand came to his own legs, touching gently, moving lightly; then her tongue, between his thighs. He began, and she continued, on the bed.

13

Inspiration

San Francisco
September, 1992 A.D.

"Inanna, the Priestess of Heaven, rejoiced with Dumuzi:

May the fragrant cedars stand high by your side.
May the plentiful grain grow high by your side.
May the sparkling water flow fast by your side.
May the gardens flourish with spices and fruit, with roses and
honey and birdsong.
May the fields bring forth barley, and beer,
And the milk of the goat,
With the cream, and the cheese and sweet butter.

I will keep your house of life, my shepherd.
I will flourish all your people and your lands.'"

—from *The Twenty-One Hymns of Orom*

After seven time-altering nights, a complete week, he found it suddenly and inexplicably necessary to have some time to think. Rising before the dawn, he left Maria in his bed. He quickly made some toast and coffee, finishing them off in his car just as the sun came up. Then he drove north to Marin, to the Green Gulch Meditation Center.

It was in the quietness of that retreat, walking beside the far-reaching rows of the early autumn vegetable garden, under the golden canopy of the apple orchard, and then on down the wilder path to the seashore, while the birds chattered and the September breezes carried the ephemeral fragrance of the marshlands, that he had a flashing remembrance of things past—long past, for there came a sudden thought of ancient lands. Then the *Gilgamesh* rose up inside him, filling his mind with radiance, breathing new life throughout his very soul.

He wrote the entire script during the following seven days, on his father's borrowed laptop. Down on the floor, leaning against his sofa. Slouching on a kitchen chair on his tiny back porch, under the sky, in the afternoon shade. At night, hunching over the laptop, he worked in moonlight, most often on his bed.

The filming began just a few weeks later, mostly with his regulars, his reliable former crew. The first scenes he filmed were the three in which Gilgamesh, played by himself, rejects and opposes Inanna, played by Maria Ananin. These were not the first scenes in order of his script, but he felt a compulsion to complete them before he could work on any other.

Maria took to her role, he thought, like a fish to water. It seemed she had been intrigued with stories of Inanna-Ishtar almost since she was a child. She told him that once she had read—in the summer before she started college, she thought it was—a novel about a courtesan priestess who served the "Goddess of the Morning Star." The book had left, she said, a lasting and strong impression.

He was more than satisfied with her interpretation of her role, especially her portrayal of Inanna's seething anger at Gilgamesh, when the man refuses the goddess and cruelly scorns her. He had felt somewhat wary about this scene; he had never seen Maria show any anger, whatsoever. But when the day came, he was amazed as he stood facing her, himself the target of her rage.

Her face was transformed. She was ugly, truly ugly, possessed of a hatred that gave good cause for fear. At the end of the day it was necessary to soothe and calm her. She had become disturbingly, he thought, involved with the flaming emotions of her role. But he merely said, "I didn't know you had it in you, Maria!"

Her anger fascinated and repelled him, striking various keys, accessing information that he didn't want to know, secrets about her feelings, secrets about his own.

Surprisingly there came up in the pit of his stomach a chaotic rage against his wife's betrayal, as he stood there in the spell of his lover's wounded eyes.

But, of course, everyone was delighted when they saw what was captured on film. "You can just see it! The goddess of love and beauty really is the goddess of war! It's right there, right there in her face, isn't it?!" enthused the actress who was playing the "Holy Harlot"—the bar-maid who tamed the wild man, Enkidu.

It was a great piece of fortune that the scenes with Maria were the first to be filmed. Had he waited for the proper sequence, it would have been necessary to find another actress to play her role. Or, more likely, he would not have completed that film at all.

And, if either of those alternatives had been the case, then every film, every idea, which that unknown, seemingly insignificant but aesthetically almost perfect, twentieth century masterpiece would eventually come to inspire with a fertile ever-streaming breath of life, then none of those future progeny would ever have come to be. Nor would they have borne fruit of their own. And if such had been the case, then where, if one really stops to think about it, where in the world would we humans of these subsequent, sweeter-fated centuries, we present multitudes of earth *dudes*, as some back in that century—Dagan's century—liked to call themselves, where would we all be now? The question is impossible to answer. Hopefully the world would have come to wisdom, regardless. But who of us can say?

14

Anarisha's Information

Orom
circa 2700 B.C.

in the courtyard of the Temple of Inanna, late in the afternoon

— But why was that man chosen, Anarisha? He was not a king.

— I believe he was chosen, Father Gudea, simply because he was a man of good intent, and a man of many races. The man was finely balanced. Then, too, from childhood, he always loved Abu; he loved the forest. You are correct, he was not a king; but he knew the Shepherd-King, in his heart…Gudea, in that world, in that city, there is no king!

— And the woman, why was she chosen?

— She, like the man, was of kind intent. And also…when this woman was but a child, she called for the Lady, in joy and innocent belief. And Inanna came to greet her.

— Did they understand anything, were these two ever accepted into initiation, were they trained?

— No, Father, of course not. Theirs is a netherworld. But when they joined together in love, they received me. And I imparted the knowledge—Oh, please excuse me! Father Gudea, it seems so funny, I am so sorry for laughing, forgive me, my brother, I mean no disrespect. But I am mystified, still. It is I who understand nothing!

— What do you mean, Inannanin?

— In their netherworld, things are upside down, you know?

— ?

— An example—from the strange windows of the man's entrance chamber, I beheld this sight: at night, all of the stars, all of them together, giving no more brightness than does one butter lamp!

— Hmmm…And what else?

— The people have no need to birth more children! Indeed, it is most beneficial in their world not to have any children at all!

— What nonsense are you talking?

— I am saying that the earth there is too crowded. Just as in the old story. You know the one I mean—the tale of the flood—too many humans for the gods to endure the noise…

— and therefore—

— Yes, Gudea, therefore they have no need for the Gift of our Goddess!

— !!!

—

— Please stop your laughing, Priestess, can you never be serious anymore?!

— It was…it was very sad there, Gudea, in the Netherworld. That is the only reason I am laughing now. Please forgive me; I am like that.

*　　　　　　*　　　　　　*

— Was your visit without benefit, then, my sister? Is that what you are telling me, Anarisha? The Descent was for nothing in our generation?

— Oh, no, Father. Allow me to finish.

— Please go on.

— That netherworld in which I found myself—that netherworld had great need for the Goddess. And She had compassion on them. Oh no, the Descent was of great import.

— But if our reborn ARE SO OVERLY PLENTEOUS THERE, AS YOU TELL ME—

— Oh, Father Gudea, don't get angry! Or worried. I have never seen you angry before. Please, I can not bear it. In truth, everything has gone beautifully. I am not explaining it well. Please allow me to continue. When I have finished, perhaps you will have no more perplexity...

—

— Yes, those people were plenteous; but the earth itself did not thrive. The earth was perishing, my brother—Oh, now I am crying— please bear patience dear Father, I will go on. The animals did not thrive, nor the plants, nor the lands. The very air itself was ill. Poisoned. As were the waters. But She came to help. Our Lady arrived. I invoked Her for them, in myself, the same as I do for Orom. Then Inanna and Dumuzi were united, with benefit. The lands were secured. OF THAT I AM CERTAIN. I saw the forthcoming. I traveled on, you see, Gudea, beyond that world, to yet more distant times. And those further incarnations, the grandchildren and the great-grandchildren, inspired by the ideals and efforts of a few heroic ancestors, they received the benefit from our Lady and Dumuzi. Eventually they redeemed all Nature. Earth was made fertile again. Oh, great events took place in those later times!

— I see, Inannanin...I believe I see...They tell us the netherworlds are strange, now I begin to know it. But I am an old man. It is hard for me to hear new ideas. Even this present position in which I find myself, here before you; so late in life, I have to laugh, myself, Daughter, when I think of it. Priest of Enki! It is still impossible to believe this is so! But tell me, Priestess, you did not forget to invoke Father Enki, did you?

— No, I did not forget, Gudea.

— Then all is as it should be.

— I invoked the Anunnaki, as well, every One of them.

— What?!

— All of Heaven, my brother. The great Joy in Heaven helps us, Gudea. Long before I came to Orom, I knew this. I invoked the

Anunnaki and I asked them for four gifts, for Wisdom, Beauty, Strength, and Love. That these be given to all who have died and risen again as new seed in the netherworlds. I could not prevent myself, Brother, I know it is not in our training, but I had to save those worlds, as much as possible, while I was visiting them.

— Your ways astound me, Anarisha. Your ways astound me! I believe you are not, in truth, Inannanindigur—the vessel of Inanna. Where are the ways of our Passionate Goddess? I know not what you are up to, Anarisha, but I see *Geshtinanna* hiding behind your disguise. Yes, Geshtinanna—Dumuzi's sister, *The Compassionate One*. You are a lioness, come *ansarasiggigi*, roaring over the horizon without warning. In truth, my daughter, you make me tremble now.

15

On the Mountain and Beyond

"Someday, after we have mastered the winds,
The waves, the tides and gravity,
We shall harness for God the energies of love.
Then for the second time in the history of the world
Man will have discovered fire."

—Teilhard De Chardin

Marin County
April, 1992 A.D.

Always, since she was just a little girl, when her family spent two fun-filled weeks in summer and two in winter at their cabin on the north shore of Lake Tahoe, Rosie Dagan had loved to go to the mountains. It was Rosie who telephoned Maria, and not the other way around, to suggest that they meet, not for coffee or for lunch, but to go hiking on "Mt. Tam."

The Steep Ravine Trail would be a perfect way to get together, private and cheerful. They hadn't seen each other for so long; a six hour hike would allow plenty of time for "catching up on life after college." Rosie was fairly certain that her recollection of Maria liking to be outdoors in nature was correct.

The Steep Ravine was familiar, "almost like my own backyard," Rosie said on the phone. She and Michael had often done those eight miles to the beach and back, in the days when they lived in San Francisco, the year she was pregnant with Ishme—nineteen sixty-eight, a crazy but fun year, when they were, sort of, hippies. Michael was, anyway. A few years afterward, they hiked on Mt. Tamalpais again, in the late seventies, when Aaron was little—and always running ahead. These days the trail made her think of Maui, the ferns and the waterfalls and the flowers around Hana, where she and Ellis had just rented a little cottage, only a few weeks before.

Rosie felt certain that Maria would enjoy the beauty of Steep Ravine. She would love the way the trail concluded, down by the sea. Rosie knew the encounter might get a little stiff and awkward; she and Maria always had that effect on each other in the past. But outdoors, hiking on the mountain, they would both be more at ease. It was April; wildflowers would be in bloom.

*　　　*　　　*

Maria was late. She was supposed to be at Rosie's place in Pacific Heights at 8:00 A.M., but there was "some kind of tie-up on the bridge." When Maria showed at 8:45, flushed and tense, Rosie was in the atrium, finishing a cheese puff and a third cup of cappuccino with her new significant-other, Ellis Kant. Ellis, a jocular, sixtyish developer-attorney, owned the palatial stucco Italianate which Rosie now called home.

Coffee didn't "agree" with Rosie, as her mother always put it; it made her "hyper," gave her an unrealistic sense of urgency, and opened up floodgates of later-regretted confessions and indiscreet confidentiality. Rosie knew her cappuccino was altering the mood she'd intended, but "Oh, well, that's life," she told herself, as she often did.

Strolling—it could hardly be called "hiking"—along the pleasant spring-filled trail, Rosie Dagan bared her new L.L.Bean red plaid flannel shirt. And then she bared her soul. Possibly it was the Peet's cappuccino. Maybe it was Maria's wide-eyed compassionately receptive expression.

Or, most likely, it was the powerful, incomprehensible closeness that a person—some people—can feel for the one who, deep within, beyond articulation, is perceived to be *the enemy*.

From yet another perspective, there was another reason—the truth-telling encouragement that Tamalpais itself gave. Since ancient times, when Miwok villagers lived in that territory, the mountain was known to be sacred, an inspiration for clarity and truth.

Preliminary chit-chat dispensed with—that happened on the drive from San Francisco—Rosie began to pour out almost everything that mattered, with her first few inhalations of fresh, clear mountain air. By the time they passed through the grasses beyond the wooded mountainside and she had removed her REI Vasques and her new hemp socks, to set foot upon the first sands of the shore, the sunlit Pacific sparkling before them, she had offered to Maria the secrets of a life.

She confided all her run-of-the-mill insecurities: her everyday inadequacies—too much gabbing on the phone, too much chocolate and too much cheese, addiction to soap operas and talk shows, failure to limit video games (PacMan, to be exact) when her child was young, the perpetual failure to floss; as well as more personal humiliations—how she slipped and fell and displayed her underwear to the entire student body when she was a cheer-leader in high school. She gave disclosures of best-left-unsaid truths: that she had had her tummy tucked and her nose reshaped, that she cheated on her college chemistry mid-term. And also, she confided, she had always felt—even before she'd married him—that she'd never really be quite good enough for Michael Dagan.

Eventually, she tried to explain to Maria what it had meant to lose her baby, Ishme, her first-born son.

The never-completely articulated loss and rage flowed in a torrent of tears and disconnected phrases. As she told of the loss of her child, she spoke of the loss of her faith. She surprised even herself with the discovery of the searing anger that still remained, with over twenty years gone by.

Maria, a lump forming in her own throat, was not the type to hug or to put an arm around anyone, but she did.

This happened as they sat upon a huge sun-warmed rock near the edges of a waterfall. They had expected to eat their lunch, a California-cuisine-low-fat eggplant dish that Rosie had bought at a famous local deli; she no longer cooked, it seemed, if she could avoid it. But they saved that delicious food. They were too emotional to eat.

Maria did not tell Rosie that years before she had listened to the same disturbing story from the father of the child. And—the memory now stung—at that time, both he and she had continued with the eating of their meal.

*   *   *

Finally, Rosie came to the subject of her impending divorce. It was the unsurprising climax of her day-long revelations. But, for Maria, it turned out to be the most unpredictable revelation of them all. For, what Rosie's rushing words confessed—the reason she left Michael— was not only different from the reason Maria had expected (and what Michael, himself believed), it was, in fact, exactly its opposite.

Yet, all the same, after she heard Rosie out, what came to Maria most sharply was a sense that she had known, all along, that this was exactly the way it was, that this version was the truth. And she saw that she had fooled herself, deceived herself in many ways, for many years.

Stretched out on the beach, tanned legs splashed by sea water, Rosie Dagan explained why it was that she had betrayed her husband of twenty-five years.

"I left Michael," she confided, "because I loved him too much."

Maria, stunned, at first dispassionately wondered if Rosie had borrowed this reasoning somewhere, if some new self-help book had influenced her decision, convinced her that there was such a condition as loving someone "too much."

"I left him, pure and simple," Rosie went on, "because he was the center of my universe. And I finally faced the painful fact that the vice versa was never coming true." Rosie paused, as Maria felt a shudder pass through her.

"Still, though, to be honest," Rosie said, "I have to admit that I have a secret hope; now that I'm gone, maybe Michael will realize how much he really needs me. At least, maybe, he'll see it more clearly than he seemed to before."

But, in the meantime, she continued, she had the chance to be with a man who already, very obviously, did need her, and very much. And who she liked very much. "Besides," she smiled, "Ellis comes with lots of perks."

Maria ran her fingers through the wet sand and stared at Rosie, who was burdening her—even more than she had already—with this new dash of cynicism, a final ingredient to the mix that she had known to be Rosie Hestia Dagan.

"...*comes with lots of perks*"—so Rosie was becoming cynical. But why was that a surprise? Long ago Maria had decided that cynicism was an easy, dead-end path. Even if so many people did seem inexplicably proud to follow it. (Never in West Africa, amongst the most caring and the wisest villagers, they who knew such hardship, had she met a single cynical woman or man.) *Cynicism is exactly*, she thought, *just like every other path—except for the trail we took today—that Rosie ever chose to follow. Like the way she never studied in college. She always preferred to have fun—always the undisciplined way for Rosie Hestia. The only difference now is that it's an easy exit from unhappiness that she's choosing. How simple it's always been*, Maria realized, *for Rosie to believe that complacency means peace.*

Rosie spoke hardly at all about her son Aaron. In one quick run-on sentence she said that he was seventeen, that he hadn't attended graduation with his high school class because of some kind of environmental traffic-disrupting protest, that he liked to skate board, and that he was about to go train-hopping across the country with a friend—neither she nor Michael could dissuade him. Rosie didn't give any more details about Aaron. She was not interested, she said, in looking at the regrets and the pain, which, ever since her separation, thoughts about her son increasingly contained. *You're neither strong enough, nor wise enough to face them,* thought Maria, sadly *and maybe you don't even care.*

＊　　　　　＊　　　　　＊

On the long deadlocked drive back to San Francisco that evening, Rosie still chattered on, but Maria said little. Impressed and shocked, she was silenced by the honesty, the cruelty, and the self-centered sense of survival which Rosie conveyed. That was her first reaction.

But a different response came at night in bed, hours after they had parted, probably forever, though both pretended future visits were only days away. In bed, Maria felt a cold stiffness come through her, a signal that something was very wrong.

A memory, a fresh one, never before recalled, arose in her midnight awareness. It was a fragment of the odd, old connection between herself and Rosie Dagan. She remembered college—her first year in college—those days when life was barely worth living. She had needed, one afternoon, to use her address book. It was necessary to call Marta Diaz, to confirm the appointment she'd finally agreed to make with the elderly dancer, a meeting Marta was insisting upon.

When she'd opened the address book to Marta's number, she discovered that the page was smeared; there seemed to be water stains. She puzzled over them, unable to figure how the marks could possibly have come on that page, though there arose a certain suspicion, at the time. Then she forgot all about it.

Over thirty years later, now, the thought returned that, yes, of course, the stains were made by her roommate Rosie. *She must have called Marta. I remember suspecting that. Rosie called to ask Marta not to give up* on me, I know it. *To tell her I needed help. To beg Marta to make me visit her. The visit which changed my life. And Rosie, who always talks so much, has never mentioned what she did.* She thought of Marta Diaz, thought of Marta's words about inner beauty and self-mastery; she often thought of those words. She'd attempted, ever since, to live by them.

The next morning, still lying in bed, after a night of two nightmares, and unending tossing, she noticed that there was only an empty space inside her, a vacancy of mood. In that space, in what seemed to be clear and logical phrases, a decision was made.

Rosie's always loved him, I know that, she told herself, *And she's still his wife. The mother of his sons. She loves him now; they're part of each other. I can't deny it any longer. She always cared about me, too. The truth is, she saved me from destroying myself.*

And Rosie, who I've always judged and condemned so quickly, who I've never allowed myself to see, is the one who brought me to my teacher, who gave the meaning to my life.

It doesn't even matter if Rosie goes back to Michael. Or not. That isn't the point. There's only one choice, however I look at it: I can't see him again.

After that, in the early morning, she finally went to sleep. Then she dreamt a vivid dream. In her dream she was making love. With a man she adored. But it wasn't Michael. And yet she seemed to love this person deeply.

At once, the two of them reached ecstasy. They were one; she knew it in the dream. Then, lying side by side, upon their backs, contented, they gazed up at the ceiling. After awhile she wanted to leave, to go and bathe. As she left the room she turned to look at her lover one last time, and she saw that the bed he lay upon was not a bed at all; it was a mat. A beautiful, intricately woven, straw mat.

She woke up, feeling sure she knew who the man was, and she knew the place, as well, if only she could remember, but she could not. She went back to sleep and dreamed a second dream: *her great-grandfather was sitting in some kind of a chair, like a throne, on a snowy mountain. The place was beautiful, majestic.*

*   *   *

The letter which Michael Dagan received three days later contained none of Maria's inner lucidity. It was as though it were written by another woman, with another point-of-view. And yet, it too, was from Maria's logic.

She said she knew he had already been betrayed and hurt, hurt profoundly. She saw clearly that if she were to stay with him any longer, he would be hurt again. Though she truly loved him, there were other considerations. She wasn't a woman who could give her life to him. And therefore, it would be better, she believed, not to lead him on. Then she gave her good-bye.

There was something in the cadence as well as in the choice of words which left him with a sense that the letter offered only partial honesty. And also, of course, complete bewilderment and shock.

*   *   *

He lay face upward on the lawn of the plaza in front of Saints Peter and Paul's Cathedral. Thin and unshaven, he looked as if he were homeless, possibly. In fact, his bank account was zero; except for Aaron's college fund, everything was invested in his film. He'd used up all his inheritance from his father. He wouldn't take more. He wasn't even sure how he would pay his next rent.

The weather was warm, the breezes were mild. He was tired, having walked all over North Beach and the waterfront, and Chinatown, rapidly walking, to the point of a sweat. He lay on his back, arms supporting his neck, looking upward at the clouds. They were magnificent cumulus, milky, edged with gray. He hadn't lain on the ground like this, just looking at clouds, in years. He watched their soft slow movements, surprised by the awe and reverence he felt, as though the clouds were mysterious unknowns, as though he had never been given knowledge that clouds were simply gases, evaporated H2O.

As he saw a cloud that resembled a dragon, a silly, childlike fantasy passed through his mind: the clouds were conscious—though very short-lived—creatures, cloud-beings who knew a few things about humankind. They knew exactly what humans are made of, knew how humans go through changes, how they move in their human environment—with extraordinarily lengthy existences. But the cloud experts assumed that heavy human bodies could not possibly contain awareness, "not like us clouds."

He lay on the grass until the milky white forms began to change to pink streamers. He lay there, inwardly singing the haunting Judy Collins tune about not understanding clouds (nor love, nor life) until the breezes turned cold and the grass became uncomfortably damp.

*   *   *

She didn't know what to do at first.

Her body ached. Every night she cried. She passionately cried, cried until she nearly passed out. In that way she would fall asleep.

But she barely slept. For so many nights she wept and didn't sleep. Her eyes had large blue circles, with puffy wrinkled bags.

Yet she kept on. For weeks, for months, it was like that, until one day, for no particular reason, she was done with the crying. There remained only some sporadic headaches, and some dizziness—what her grandmother would have called "spells." By then she had become a plain looking woman; a pretty face had cried itself away.

She retained her grace of movement, however. She could will herself to dance, to inspire her young students. It was necessary in order to survive, and for the sake of the kids, including six daughters of prostitutes, four "crack babies," and dozens of struggling others. All of them idolized her.

She didn't talk about her problems at work; the dance instructors at the rec-center weren't very close to one another. And as usual, for most of her life, her friends were not really her confidantes.

When she went home at night, every night, she developed a habit; she said a prayer at bedtime, for Rosie. *Please make her beautiful, inside, as well as out; please make her wise*, she begged. She directed these requests to Rosie's deceased little boy—now in heaven? in some other dimension? or once again on earth? She firmly trusted that the spirit-child would intercede to help his hapless mother.

Alone, she faced her action, how she must have hurt the one she loved. But she felt certain she had done the right thing. She believed in herself, and she believed in him; she believed in what she'd done.

She became stronger, after awhile. The strength—that one didn't know one had—eventually came. She knew that he was strong, as well, true and good. He would be fine, she told herself. He, too, would overcome desire, would come on through to "the farther shore."

"Someday, when the American civilization is old enough, when the pot's had enough time, enough centuries, for everyone to melt, there'll be a blended people, a race not seen before, spread from coast to coast. And maybe some of them will look a little like me."

"That wouldn't be too bad, I guess,' she laughed, but she felt his longing, the loneliness of a man without a race, without a people.

She remembered that piece of conversation; she didn't know why it was one of the memories that stayed with her, forever in her mind.

*   *   *

Berkeley, 1993

Mei Wong, having just finished her history of graphic arts seminar at the university museum, sat alone in her parked Mercedes, taking a minute to gather her thoughts. As she gazed through the front window up Dwight Avenue, it seemed to her that the inclined street was, at that moment, a watery medium rather than land and air. Students flowed by, crossing back and forth before her, in the patterns and pacing of fishes, while the dark green Berkeley hills, streaked with autumn mid-morning light, appeared at the far horizon like islands of a stream. The sensation was pleasant, she realized with analytical attention. Though it only lasted a few moments, this was the most satisfying interlude she had experienced in a very long time.

It brought to mind the happiness of a certain era of days gone-by. And a completely unexpected desire came upon her.

Instead of thrusting her key into the ignition as she had intended, she took the keys from her lap and returned them to her purse. She slowly, thoughtfully, slid out of the car, glanced at the meter, which still had time, and walked back through the doors of the museum.

She would find a public phone. Her conversation might, she thought, be too long and expensive for the cellular. If she could just place the call. She didn't know if the number would be correct; she hadn't dialed it, after all, for many years.

*   *   *

"What happened was this, Mei—you see, I had a tape that I'd made of her. I was fooling around with her, perfecting her French. For awhile, a few months perhaps, I would just play the cassette sometimes, before I went to bed, for example. Or when I had my morning coffee. Or when I was in a certain mood." Mei was shocked at the familiarity of the voice. She had forgotten how he sounded, his accent, that calm gentle quality, but it was as though they had only spoken yesterday.

"One night when I was doing this, listening to the tape, an idea came to me. It occurred to me that I could study each little inflection of her voice, the rhythm, the pitch, the emphasis—every subtle softness—and that eventually, in my own thoughts, you know, in the imaginary dialogues I have with her, I would be able to actually, perhaps, almost hear her speaking to me. If I practiced a lot. It was similar to an exercise I used to assign to my French classes.

"I had to work with phrases, of course, which I myself had made up. But I found, when I had continued for a few weeks with this, that I was able to allow her 'voice' in my mind to do it's own creating. And her thoughts, eventually, became as real, as unpredictable, that is, and vivid to me as her visual image. Which I have, in the form of many drawings and one painting, and some very revealing photos, which I made one night—of her in ecstasy. All nudes, you understand, quite beautiful. I keep them permanently in my apartment.

"I found that, especially with the aid of just an insignificant modicum of hashish, I could go very far with all of this. That was the beginning of my becoming more of a user, several times a day. And I went on to the other stuff because, after a while I wanted to explore some further concepts which started to come to me.

"It continued satisfactorily for me in this way for almost a year. There was no problem whatsoever with teaching my classes; the one thing had nothing to do with the other. But I can't remember, Mei, exactly, although I have some idea, when it was that her voice began to change. A new voice started to come to me; it took the place of hers. And a few other voices came, too, but mostly it was that one. The new voice isn't Maria, Mei; at least I don't think it is. She calls herself *Circe…*"

As soon as she had managed an awkward conclusion to this terrible conversation, and had hung up the phone, Mei rummaged, shakily, through her purse for her bottle of Tylenol. Not only did she have a spinning, whirlpool sort of sensation, she was also experiencing, undeniably, one of the highest intensity head-aches she could remember ever having had in her entire life.

16

In the Courtyard of the Temple of Inanna

east of the Euphrates, west of Mohenjo-Daro
circa 2700 B.C.

The hour was late and cool, but they sat by a little warming pot and fire, talking quietly in the moonlight. So much came forth this night. Thoughts and memories that each had not studied in many seasons were rising to the surface of mind and overflowing to hearts and speech.

At last the priestess told the priest that she wanted to ask him a question, about a matter which had always puzzled her. But always before she had felt constrained to broach the subject. How was it, she asked, that most of the slaves in Orom had come to the fate of slaves? Did Gudea know this?

He told her that it was because of the past wars, of course.

But she wanted to know about the present, the time after the wars. The wars, since her coming, had for unknown reasons almost immediately ceased. But there were new slaves, how could that be?

He was startled by her question. He tended to forget that she was, by birth, a foreigner, that she knew little of life outside of the temple and little of the everyday laws of Orom. Nor was it correct for her to casually converse with lesser priestesses.

"Those new slaves are our own people, Inannanin. They are the sons and daughters of Orom," he said. "Slavery is the result of certain wrongs. You do know," he exclaimed, "that we Oromi may sell our disobedient children? Or that we sell the children if the family has financial woes?"

When she replied that no, she had not known this, he realized just how truly cloistered her life had been. Although she was united, body and spirit, with the people of Orom, she had joined with no one but himself in authentic conversation. No exchanges of any substance; only the formalities, ritualistic speech, the politeness of greetings and good-byes. The emptiness which was part of such a life as hers suddenly struck him, like a cold wind in his face. No women friends, no acquaintances. No one to confide in; such was her position, such was her life.

It was then that the desire came upon him, as strong as the desire for the body of a woman, to know her mind. To be her closest friend.

She began to tell him, at that moment, how she was taken from her village. The traders had come looking, just for her, she said. They made speeches and then they purchased her from the town. For two pieces of gold, no bigger than figs. No one of her people, not one, had tried to stop them. "No one but my husband. But as he rose to protest, the gods struck him to the ground."

"The stars ordained your coming here, Inannanin," said Gudea when she finished.

"Yes," she answered, "Yes, I suppose I do see that myself. It is true that Heaven has granted me influence," and she thought of the clay images of herself which they sold near the sacred waters. The people—especially the Oromi girls—purchased those little figurines to set on their personal altars. She recalled how, long ago in Fa-Orszag, she had been bothered with strange forebodings of her own great power.

"But," she added softly, "it has been difficult." Her eyes looked so childlike, so innocent, at that moment. Gudea felt a strong warmth, as he waited for her to continue.

"I did not want to come to Orom." And she said no more.

Why did those words surprise him; it was not startling information. How could she know anything but despair in leaving her homeland and her family, in leaving her world? But yet, here she was in beautiful Orom. Where she was the Light of the City. The Holy One, to whom the people prayed, in unfeigned reverence. Intercessor for the Queen of Heaven. Could she truly be dissatisfied with such a destiny?

But she spoke no more again.

It was getting late. Gudea called for no one; he himself dampened the fires and put out the lamps. He walked with the priestess across the courtyard to her quarters. Then he passed through the *cella*, out the temple doorway. Down the stairs and through the rows of date palms, with quick agility for an old man. Seeing clearly in the moonlight, he climbed into his waiting chariot; his driver would return him quickly to the Temple of Enki. Not at all distant, his temple defined the newer, more modern, center of Orom.

17

Old Ties Still Binding

east of San Francisco
1994 A.D.

> "I'll be damned," he said with amazement. "The Universe disposes of its own evil!"
>
> —*Dr. Sax*, by Jack Kerouac

For many weeks after her interview with Michael Dagan, Deborah Anderson, try as she might, could not get the encounter out of her head. She nurtured herself with comforting homilies: "It's just the breaks, kid," "another of life's little lessons," "chalk it up to experience," and, finally "don't cry over spilt milk." But nothing helped. What rankled most was the night-and-day contrast between the elation she'd felt just before that interview, and the frustration that came with its end.

The popular indie filmmaker had been her meal ticket, the first opportunity for establishing a reputation that she had ever known. On the day they gave her the assignment, she felt as if she'd sprouted wings. She saw herself taking off, heading for where she'd always dreamed, always known, she would fly. She noted on that afternoon that her disgruntled co-workers looked like empty-mouthed seagulls losing their skirmish for a crust of bread. And she knew her success was real. ·

Then, too, there was the high she'd experienced, fantasizing about the way it would be when she finally met the guy.

But in the end all that was left was a bad taste. A sense of failure and embarrassment. Regret, humiliation—aborted flight. She could go on, and she did, in fact, to her roommate and a few close friends.

At first, temporarily, she calmed down. She called Michael Dagan the morning after the interview, phoned him as early as seemed acceptable. As it turned out she did wake him up; but she went on, apologetically requesting, begging, in fact, that he come to her professional rescue.

"Please, Michael, just concede to me just a mere skeleton of just an outline of information on Maria Ananin," she pleaded.

What he gave her was exactly that. Ananin, he said, was an old college friend of his wife. She was a talented dancer, he'd felt she was right for *Dance of Life* and *Gilgamesh.* But he only gave her a bit part in his second film, *Aurelius*—her understanding of that script was intelligent, he said, but it seemed more conservative than his own. He had no idea where she was now. No more idea than anyone else. No anecdotes, no personal asides. No story.

It was after that conversation that Deborah began to truly know her defeat, to run her mind over her failure like a tongue over a sore tooth. Finally, weeks after the interview was published, and she still could not recover, she decided to find Maria for herself.

*   *   *

Deborah's source was correct. Maria Ananin was, in fact, employed as an attendant in a mental hospital! Deborah's acquaintance, an accountant at a credit bureau, learned that a Maria Virginia Ananin, social security #556—7777 had indeed been employed in the psychiatric ward of a large public hospital in San Leandro for the past eleven months.

Unfortunately, Deborah learned by calling the hospital, Maria had lately been failing to show up. It was about ten days now, confided the apparently frustrated supervisor. And Maria Ananin was not returning any calls. Deborah was amazed at how easy it had been to get that information. But she felt no remorse in coaxing it from the supervisor, who, she reasoned, should have known better than to give it out.

In the end, it didn't matter, anyway. She got no further with her attempts to locate and interview Maria. After one month of calling the hospital and receiving no news, and of calling Maria's number and hearing only voice mail, she gave up. Then, at last, she moved on with her life, which, coincidentally, was once again beginning to take on some interest. Her brother had introduced her to another new rising star, a telekinetic meteorologist, whose amazingly accurate weather predictions preceded the more traditional forecast of the six o'clock news. And this latest Bay Area phenomenon had told Deborah's brother that he sensed a deep affinity; he was anxious to see Deborah again! Maybe for lunch.

*   *   *

Meanwhile, unbeknownst to the rest of the world, Maria Ananin was having stellar triumphs of her own, at the hospital. On the psychiatric floor—where she was, in fact, showing up every work day, protected by a thoughtful and savvy head nurse.

In the rooms of that chemically scented, post-modern, institutionally adorned island of despair, middle-aged Maria had become the queen of a singular subconscious subdominion of invisible causes and effects.

Dancing inside a phantom-filled domain, her spirit invaded magically, magnanimously, into the private territory of the spirits of the tragically confused. Conquering silently, she entered, to pierce her laser-like beams of subliminal starlight into the dark nights of morbid hallucinatory universes. The longer she remained on the payroll of that hospital, the more often did this occur.

Eventually every one of the patients whose bedpans and sheets she changed, whose barely-sentient hands she held and whose steroid-sweating foreheads she wiped, were lovingly (with hugs and friendly pats) discharged by the professional care-givers. The cheery, saint-like doctors and nurses of that quite mindfully staffed hospital bade their compassionate farewells to their patients as the grateful, formerly-as-good-as-dead neophytes of normal life passed through the hospital doors and headed for the much yearned for Alameda County bus stop and their departures to shining, love filled, unmedicated existences in the great outside, never to return to a mental ward again.

Among these finally-rescued ones was a poor soul, poor at the beginning, that is, by the name of Jean-Marc Romier. He was a lost man when Maria discovered him one rainy afternoon, sitting, sad and alone, on a caramel colored vinyl sofa in the patients' lounge. He clasped a worn, food-stained paperback on his lap (it was a copy of a Dostoyevsky novella, *The Underground Man*, which Jean gripped tightly in his bony white hands).

After discovering Jean-Marc, Maria immediately initiated an exchange of a multitude of kindnesses. She gave to him her sympathetic ear and compassionate facial expressions, while Jean bestowed upon Maria his gentle and still extraordinary smiles, during the anguished tales which poured from his dry and trembling lips.

Jean-Marc quietly described for his new attendant the history of the magical spells and curses which he had long been suffering. Under the power of *Circe*—an unpleasantly loquacious and unmerciful demoness, he explained, who followed him everywhere; he had almost been destroyed. Circe moved beneath the floorboards of rooms and the pavements of cities, wherever he went, in order to metaphysically metamorphosize him from one horrifying dimension of consciousness to another, without pity, without cease.

But fortunately for Jean-Marc, a caring heroine had come along. With the strong muscles of much-exercised kindness, attendant Maria quickly battled and finished off Jean's foe. It was at the moment just after Circe, visibly, audibly, and hideously, disintegrated into a puff of smoke in the underground of Jean-Marc's mind, that he felt himself able to look his angelic exorcist in the eyes, and whisper to her, very simply, "I did you wrong, Maria. Please forgive."

Then Jean Romier went home. To his one remaining friend, his former girlfriend, Mei. She took him in readily, and later, one day, became his wife. For a year or so, it was Mei Wong Romier who supported the two of them. But eventually Jean's newly inspired career as a writer and illustrator of children's books, a charming teller of tales, balanced that score. Mei was able to happily settle then, with Jean, into a Berkeley hills semi-retirement of travel, dining, movies, plays, parties, cafes, Tahoe skiing, and *Trader Joe/Berkeley Bowl* grocery errands, with daily tennis in the mornings.

Eventually, both now in their early seventies, they devoted themselves to a single focus, becoming loving grandparents to a series of perilously bewildered foster children. Several of these children profusely, and effusively, came to love Jean and Mei in return. The children kept forever close to the aging Romiers throughout their remaining, nature-hike and classical music years, greatly empowering that couple's final, fulfilling twenty-first century chapter of belated, but authentic, happy ever-afterward season of life.

18

The Call

"Swans rise and fly toward the sun—What magic!
So do the pure conquer the armies of illusion and rise and fly."
—The *Dhammapada*

Orom
circa 2700 B.C.

The people told one another over their firesides and they gossiped of it in the marketplace, until everyone had heard the latest episode of the city's tragic story—that of all the grief-stricken citizens, even more than the sorrowing king, even more than the women of the temple, it was Gudea, Priest of Enki, who was most fully overcome, most completely devastated by the sudden and mysterious disappearance of Inannanindigur, the Priestess of Orom.

It was said that Gudea's wife and his many grown children were making great effort to comfort him. But even the grandchildren could offer no solace. The old man seemed to find no solace, save in the inscription of his tablets. He had become no longer able to serve the city as its priest.

*   *   *

an apartment in the Fruitvale District, Oakland
1995 A.D.

On a Saturday morning, in early October, 1995, at ten AM on the week-end after Maria Ananin turned fifty years old and six months after she moved in with a new housemate, her telephone rang. Maria did not answer: she screened her calls to avoid her ex-husband and a few other people as well.

But when she listened for a message, none was on the voice mail. And although she received many such messageless calls, she knew, from the shiver which passed through her entire being when the phone rang, that the call could only have come from Michael Dagan.

After she hung up, she stretched out upon the living room sofa, though it was mid-morning at the time. She was overwhelmed with a sense of enervating remorse. The mood was so oppressive that it left her no energy even to sit. And her body was still shivering, as though she might have developed a fever.

There came none of the serenity she usually felt concerning Michael. She knew only regret—regret that she had loved him, and regret that she had left.

She had no vitality and yet she could not fall asleep.

New opposing emotions soon appeared to vie with her remorse as she tossed upon the sofa. Thoughts came of their times together. Especially of their work—the making of his films. Intense memories of the *Gilgamesh* caused more shaking, a feverish excitement, an unreal sense of awe. She thought then of his wife.

Guilt struggled, elation grew. The one balanced the other—a plus, a minus, a nothingness. She remained awake, yet she did not think. A last odd vision: *Alice in Wonderland*, in blue pinafored dress, long hair streaming; she was falling through the rabbit hole. It was a detailed illustration from her childhood book, in vivid colors.

Then a voice, familiar, from long, long ago: "*Now, child. The ascent...*"

Hours later, deliriously hot and fatigued, Maria experienced a final sensation, a detachment. Then, with deep inexplicable satisfaction, her body at last gave in to welcome sleep, an unending sleep, a sleep omnipotent as death…

*   *   *

At six-thirty that evening, Marvin Sugarman returned home from the celebration of his former boyfriend's daughter's *bas mizvah*. Marvin was slightly flushed from four glasses of merlot. He had thoroughly enjoyed himself at the delightful garden party in the Noe Valley district of San Francisco, and was pleasantly thankful that he was not the one to drive himself and his friends across the bridge.

Marvin's return immediately sobered him. For he entered his living room with an inexplicable and terrified clarity that his sweet companionable housemate was lying unconscious, and not merely sleeping, upon the living room sofa. Her Kiri Te Kanawa CD, the Mozart arias she liked so much, was playing, in a continuous program of CD's; the volume was very low. Marvin contacted Mr. and Mrs. Ananin in southern California, after he called 911.

The Ananins flew to the East Bay. They arranged to have the apparently comatose body moved from Kaiser hospital in Oakland to a private hospital near "Cheery Palms," the desert senior community which they now called home. Eventually they closed up all their daughter's affairs, only leaving her voice mail in operation.

Both parents kept, until Maria died nearly eight years later, an unrealistic hope that a miracle would happen. That their only child would one day return to consciousness. The doctors had said, after all, that Maria's condition seemed, at first, to be more like a trance than a coma.

Many hours after she fell asleep, two *double-hours* it was, the sleeping woman did, in fact, awaken. Her resurrection, however, was not into that world, nor that lifetime; not into those lives of Peter nor Helen nor Maria Ananin…

*   *   *

Fa-Orszag
circa 2700 B.C.

I awoke.

Slowly, with trembling and deep aching, I returned from a great journey of long prevailing dreams. Dreams within dreaming. As if I had permitted, and been permitted, far ranging existences. More than one lifetime was given me. A double lifetime, or perhaps there were more. I knew with certainty, for that moment, that my life in my village, the life of Anarisha to which I now awoke, was itself but a dream within another dream. In truth.

As my vision cleared, I could see that an old woman was kneeling down before me. I saw that it was Ma Agghia. The elder's hair was not, as last I'd seen it, golden-hued; it was silver and black, as of old. Behind Agghia, I saw Simbaya and Charis, my good friends, who sat leaning against the wall. Chari was, at that moment, brushing a large safafi bug away from her leg.

They greeted me with quiet subdued delight. Agghia immediately passed me a cup of water, from the earth beside her. When I finished taking fully of the satisfying drink, and when my friends had finished warmly embracing me, all was again silence.

Then Ma Agghia began to speak. Her words came in that flowing, formal manner which the holy ones can sometimes use, as she imparted knowledge to us three.

"Anarisha, Simbaya, and Charis," she began, "take heed, young mothers, and you shall hear a story of a great secret. I speak of times long ago, many, many seasons ago, in our beloved village of Fa-Orszag. There were certain village mothers then—myself, and two others—who were called together. We were called in the evening, from our family fires to the fireside of the elders. We were three young women, as you three this day. On that evening, in the warm and glowing season of the birth of the orange-breasts, we were called and chosen. And there at the sacred fire of our elders we were given a gift of unique and secret teachings. After years of watching and great deliberation, they chose us. We were chosen, by our own village grandmothers, Ushuma and Suen, those legendary women of whom all the people have heard tales. By Ushuma and Suen, we three were anointed to be taught.

"Those two respected ladies sat us down and carefully instructed us in their knowledge. Theirs was the knowledge of a small, but greatly potent plant. It is a plant which was discovered many generations before, time beyond telling, by a woman called Udé. It is a tiny creature, growing beneath tall trees, deep in the center of the forest of Fa-Orszag. The name of this plant is 'the little revealer.' It is the gift of Enki, Himself, the Father of Time.

My sisters, Eduda and Ni, and I were taught to recognize and to locate this holy medicine-giver. And we learned the ceremony of its preparation. The plant is not known to the people of Fa-Orszag, my dears. Not to your husband, Anarisha, nor even to his father, Erishoul. It is an herb," Agghia said softly, "which takes delight in granting the power of flight. To fly, not as a bird, but as a breath."

Agghia declared that when she was told by Charis that I, Anarisha, had taken sick, she immediately inquired about the details of my illness. She soon recognized my condition, the unique disease which only one medicine can cure. And she knew that I was the chosen vessel.

I was to be given the infusion of the powerful little herb. I was to be healed thereby, but also enabled to travel. To other places and to other times.

And now I had returned. I was home, revived.

Simbaya, Charis and I, she declared, were elected, as was herself and as Ushuma and Suen, simple village women, all, to be the keepers of the knowledge of the little revealer. We three for our own generation.

"And I am sure that you have accomplished much, Anarisha," she said, resuming ordinary speech, "though to us in Fa-Orszag, you have merely been sleeping. In truth, for no more than two double-hours.

"We can never know how great is the influence which we beings carry. I am quite certain you have done some good, my daughter, wherever you have gone. For you are one who remembers to keep to kindness. Were that not so, we elders would never have anointed you. Such medicine as this brings nothing but trouble and evil to the worlds of those who are lacking in wisdom, to those who are selfish, thoughtless, or unkind.

"Perhaps you have, in your flying, Anarisha, somehow established that our village will be safe from war—it has caused so much fear and sorrow. But, whatsoever you have accomplished, dear, I pray that you shall think not on that. It is never a good thing for a human creature to think too much on seeming self-power."

We, all of us, were then silent.

Finally I made reply. I said that however it was, I was feeling much better. "Thank you, Ma, for your potent tea," I said, remembering now, the unfamiliar liquid which she had given me before my lengthy sleep. "I have slept a dreaming sleep. Now my joy returns. I have lost all my confusion. I live again in the wisdom that my mother taught. Thanks be to the Anunnaki! I am healed sufficiently, I am certain, for the fetching of my children. I miss my Saraswati and my Endo so! And I am anxious for my husband. In truth, I do ache for Anurei."

Ma Agghia nodded, and Chari and Simbaya smiled.

I went on. "And I have many questions to ask him. Questions about his own journeys...Yes, I have voyaged, Ma Agghia! I, a village woman, have made my distant trips!

"Since childhood I have heard tales of a Land Between the Two Waters; Anurei has told me more. I know that Inanna is She Who protects that land. But my husband will say if he knows of the city named Orom. The city called Oak Land. San Francisco and the East Bay…

"I shall inscribe pictograms for you, clear cuneiform, of all that I have witnessed and all that I have heard. I will remember my flying, Ma, I will tell my tale."

Then I had to laugh, so full was I, with the mystery of life.

"I am so happy you are yourself again, my dearest Anarisha," Simbaya sighed gratefully. Then she patted my hand and joined me in the laughter.

*   *   *

San Francisco
2000 A.D.

He heard the low, numinous vibration of an airplane, and he was somehow comforted. It came like a *shofar* in the heavens, calling earth to solace, giving refuge in the night.

When this endless, sleepless night was finished, he would dial her number. He knew she'd never answer, but he desired almost nothing; he merely sought contentment in the beauty of her voice, as her message gave her name.

But, in the darkness, as he tossed and struck his pillow, "It's foolishness," he muttered. Then, as in verses to the *Dharma*, he breathed in long and fully and, with superhuman effort, turned his life to that great secret, the good bright road which showed now, so clearly there before him, in the darkness deep inside. Its appearance was familiar, it made him feel at home.

He'd always guessed he'd one day see it, the entrance which would lead him out of night.

In the morning, he reached down, and briskly dialed a different number. "Hello, Ellis"—he was full of peaceful sureness—"I'd like to speak to Aaron. Or, if she's up already, you could let me have my wife."

Epilogue

David and Michael

Oakland
some time in the first decade of the twenty-first century A.D.

> "A shepherd was crossing the field. He had the serenity of a man who is quietly performing a labor of joy…
>
> 'Where are you going?' asked the Master.
>
> 'I am going home to my wife and children.'
>
> 'You seem to know pure happiness, shepherd?'
>
> 'I have boiled my rice, I have milked my cows' said the shepherd Dhaniya; 'I live with my family on the banks of the river; my house is well roofed, my fire is lighted; so fall if you will, O rain of the sky.'
>
> 'I am rid of anger, I am rid of stubbornness,' said the Master; 'I bide for a night on the banks of the river; my house has no roof, the fire of passions is quenched in my being; so fall if you will, O rain of the sky.'
>
> —*The Life of the Buddha* by A. Ferdinand, translated from the French by Paul C. Blum

A Final Excerpt from the Journal of David Dagan:

They say he's been an influence. My son's films have been a "profound influence." On the new generation of young filmmakers. I read that just this morning in the Sunday paper. In the pink section; an interview with another young up-start "cinematographer." Michael seems to have earned his place with the movers and shakers of the younger generation, at least in some circles. Well, thank his lucky stars.

To me, it feels like he only just got started himself. It wasn't that long ago. And already he's a has-been. Everything moves so fast these days.

But he's not a has-been; I'm not correct to say that—he's at this very minute working on another film. A Sumerian thing, again! Something he started awhile back, and never finished—from some obscure manuscript he heard of years ago.

And he's a "profound influence," it's in the paper. To be honest, that's not the first time I've heard words to that effect. No, to be completely accurate, my one regret concerning my son is not his career; it's his marriage. Rosie. If only she had listened to him. Or to me. But the girl never did come to her senses. And it's a crying shame.

I'm getting sentimental, I guess, in my golden years, or maybe I always was a bit "cheezy," as my granddaughter Emily puts it.

But the day Michael told me Rosie was divorcing him, I had this damn deluge of clear memories. Of the wedding day. Big Sur. The sea, the sunlit afternoon, the pine trees—everything so romantic. "Flower children." Flowing robes and wreathes of flowers. They grew up watching The Ten Commandments *and* Spartacus, *you see—that's where all that sixties stuff came from. Some of the wedding guests were even barefoot. I was disgusted a little at the time. But now, since she walked out on him, those memories break my heart.*

That generation always took commitment too lightly—so quick to give each other the brush. I've seen their statistics. If you're not sure what a lifetime guarantee implies, then you ain't got no business signing the contract, I say. And I speak from my own experience.

But, nevertheless, I can see that things have fallen somewhat into place for those two. For their son, as well. Or should I say "and their son, therefore?"

My grandson has just published a novel. My twenty-nine-year-old grandson! I have not read the book. They gave Grandpa a copy—but it's not much done to suit me, to speak frankly. I never understood Michael's stuff, either, at least not his take on Gilgamesh; if you ask me, that old king deserved more empathy.

Aaron likes Bukowski, and Chomsky: I don't relate to either, especially not to Chomsky; but they tell me the guy's a genius. That's what Aaron's Chloe says. Aaron's a reader, like his father. Though neither one of them ever did make it to college. Aaron went to sea, you understand. Not with the Navy. Not like Grandpa, no, that's not our boy. He joined up with the seafarers union. After he finished with that train-hopping business. He travels all over the world now, hauling cables and oil and molasses.

One day he came home to Chloe, he opened his suitcase, and there was the masterpiece. "The Evolution of Enkidu: A Man of the Forest Wanders into a Bar" *Now, how's that for a title? It's some kind of utopian neo-leftist science fiction, something about the sudden "spontaneous self combustion of international corporate power" (which occurs, you see, because everybody's turned into wild men and ascetics). The whole thing takes place in a futuristic low-life nightclub, where all the patrons get high on holy water or something. Aaron's generation was brought up on* Star Wars; *other than that, I haven't a clue where he gets his ideas. Maybe all that coffee he drinks, or his East Bay reaction to this century's events.*

They're all charged up over it. Rosie, Chloe, the in-laws, even Ellis, the new stepfather—they can't get enough of that book. And as for my son, my laconic son, he's just like the rest—talks as much as the women do—if his son's the topic, and his son usually is the topic. Well, Aaron's a good kid; I'm proud of him, myself.

Yes, it's all come together for Michael. Without Rosie, as I say, to my own regret. (He's seeing some new gal, they tell me; I need to ask them more about it.) But Rosie seems happy enough with that developer of hers. And she's well off now, which is what she always wanted.

As for Michael, he's never going to get anywhere near to being in the money. In fact, years ago the movie-making ate up his entire inheritance.

And that, by the way, is a done deal, as far as I'm concerned. Everything I have left is for Estelle and Shoshanna.

Oh, he's maybe known a little share of pain, my son, but you can't expect to be alive and not have the rain fall on your parade, sometimes. In any case, the causes of Michael's confusions go way beyond simply not having his Papa there, making direct investments of time, during one short segment of his childhood. Or so it seems to me.

Then again, it's not for me to say—how the pieces of life fit together, I mean. You look back at your life and for every epiphanyl minute when you think you've caught sight of the big picture, there's ten billion other minutes, before and after, when all you see is a pile of meaningless little jig-saw pieces, the way they are when you first dump them out of the box. For example, that young woman, that dancer, where do I fit her into all of it?

I met her once, you know. I was, I confess, quite taken by her. She had an exotic little round, delicate, high cheek-boned look. Which I happen to find irresistible. Like with my own Felipa. Indeed, there was a slight resemblance in the slants and curves of the physiognomy, between the two of them.

Very elegant little fine-shaped nose, too; something else I tend to appreciate. Her eyes were set wide and deep, with long dark lashes. She had beautiful, almond-shaped eyes. The look was almost Indonesian, maybe Eurasian (Ananin; isn't that a Russian name?) or she made one think of some of those ravishing faces you see in Central America occasionally, or other places, West Africa, India, Egypt—women, children; not a common treasure, that type of face, but to be found in various locales, like diamonds or gold. Her skin was quite pale, almost translucent, a difficult coloring to define, since it seemed to change with the light; it could take on a lot of radiance. I wouldn't guess she wore make-up.

Full lips, a lovely childlike seriousness to the mouth. I'm a bit of a lip connoisseur. I had to laugh, for personal reasons, that is, when George the First used to say "read my lips," because I use that expression myself, when I'm talking to myself. I'm always "reading" lips. There's a lot of revelation to be found in the lips, more than in the palms, no doubt, even concerning the future. In that young woman's lips I saw an unusual combination of factors: there was a potent, but much restrained, sensuality; a refinement, also awareness, and shyness, and disciplined character. The kind of lips one sees on some of those Tibetan monks of about age thirty-something— which I believe was her age when we met.

Her more obvious aspects I need hardly go into. The whole world (at least my whole world) knows that her body is lovely. Anyone whoever saw my son's first film is aware of that. She wasn't wearing clothing which made this especially evident, however, on the occasion when I met her— baggy white trousers and a baggy white shirt, I think it was, the morning I visited the set to watch my son, the moviemaker. I saw delicate hands and wrists. And I could see something from "the way she moved," as they say.

Her hair was luxurious, thick and wavy, very long, dark golden brown, responsive to light. Changeable, like her skin.

*The thing I was most struck by, though—anyone who saw her close up would have been, I imagine—was the feeling in her eyes. But I won't search for words to tell you more of her eyes, because of an interesting synchronicity. On the day I met Maria Ananin, I came home filled with thoughts about what it was that I saw in those eyes, and it hit me suddenly, how exactly her eyes seemed to match a description in a book I was currently rereading. It was an old favorite of mine—*Aphrodite,* by Pierre Louÿs. That French novel which caused such a to-do in the nineteenth century. I immediately hurried to my bedside book pile to search for the passage. When I found it, somewhere in one of that novel's incredible chapters about the evening on the quay of Alexandria, I underlined it, both for my own reference, and, to be honest, for the sake of my son, to observe Michael's expression, if ever I were to show it to him. And so I have it, and here it is for you. I couldn't do a more accurate job of describing those eyes, myself (except to add that in Mlle Ananin's case there was a suggestion of kindness, and also, a suggestion of betrayal—whether of the betrayer or of the betrayed, or of both, I could not tell, but I've seen that look often enough to recognize it. It's especially common in good-looking women). So* *this is what Louys had to say about his "Chrysis," and I about Maria Ananin, in Louys' own old-fashioned French, which is, after all, entirely a'propos, since our young friend, Maria, had something about her that was decidedly old-fashioned:*

"Quand elle ne fut plus qu'a dix pas du juene homme, elle tourna son regard vers lui. Demetrios eut un tremblement. C'etaient des yeux extraordinaires; bleus, mais fonces et brillants a la fois, humides, las, en pleurs et en feu, presque fermes sous le poids des cils et des paupieres. Ils regardaient, ces yeux, comme les sirenes chantent. Qui passait dans leur lumiere etait invinciblement pris."

The line about the siren, that truly says it all.

Because everything about Maria Ananin conveyed a certain pretty eroticism, as with some especially mesmerizing dancers—which she was. But the purest essence of that quality could be seen in her eyes. You felt the full strength of it in the eyes, and you also knew, if you contemplated anything in that kind of moment, that you were in the presence of the real thing; I believe that the woman actually did not even have the ability to desist in her perpetual seduction of you, or anyone else, with those eyes.

Oh, I do go on. I only met her once. But it did cross my mind, at the time, that my terrific little daughter-in-law, Rosie, a real favorite of mine, was in competition with this creature. And so I took it into my head to find out what I could. One reason for showing my son the Louys passage. And the paragraph that followed it, which reads thusly (I prefer to give you my English translation, for this one: I own both the English and the French— you see what a Louys fan I am!):

"The navigators who have sailed over the purple seas beyond the Ganges tell that they have seen, under the waters, rocks which are of lodestone. When vessels pass near them, the nails and the ironwork tear themselves away toward the submarine cliff and unite with it forever. And that which was a rapid ship, a dwelling, a living being, becomes no more than a flotilla of planks dispersed by the wind, driven by the tides.

Thus Demetrios himself was lost before two great magnetic eyes and all his strength fled from him."

Well, when I showed those passages to Michael, making the excuse that I had recently come across them and was impressed by the mood of the metaphors, he did something completely unexpected. He took his wallet out of his pocket. For a second there I thought that he was actually preparing to offer me money for my Aphrodite, I thought he wanted to buy my book! But no, of course that wasn't it. He opened his wallet and it was not money that he took out, but an old, folded piece of paper, which he handed to me.

"And I have a quotation for you," he said, somewhat sternly. The lines were in his own rather plain handwriting. I read them to myself:

"Free from desire, you realize the mystery. Caught in desire, you see only the manifestations."—"The Tao Te Ching"

My scrupulous, enigmatic son. I did not then, do not now, and no doubt never will "realize the mystery!" As well he knew.

But I did realize something. Right then, at that very moment. I realized that clearly there was no need to bother myself for the sake of Michael's wife. At that time, you understand, Rosie was still his wife. My son intended, it seemed, to be stronger than lodestone, stronger than Demetrios, stronger than those eyes.

The other result of my showing him my Aphrodite, I might add, was that he never spoke with me after that time about Maria Ananin again. When I made attempts at bringing up her name, he gave me the silent treatment or, without any courtesy or pretense at being subtle, he simply changed the subject. And once he even left the room.

I found him on that occasion out on my veranda.

From behind the living room curtain I observed him. Twilight was ending, and he stood near my potted gardenia plant, gazing up at the earliest star. Or, rather, he was gazing at the planet Venus, that singular celestial which long ago was given the lasting misnomer: the Evening and the Morning "Star."

Those Beautiful Eyes

He gazed at that ancient point of light, and I noted the abiding calm of his expression. That's the thing I do envy in my son; over the years he's become one of those rare individuals—a man who somehow discovered the mystic's secret of keeping at peace with himself. "Knowing the Oneness," he calls it. Of course I must admit, as for the real solid assets, life's more tangible "manifestations," it's me, his compulsive old man, who's been the greater success.

For awhile that night he stood there, looking skyward. Then he turned and bent down. And with his typical inborn chuzpah, he plucked the solitary and long awaited white flower from my oh-so-carefully tended gardenia plant.

He brought the gardenia to his face. I watched him breathe in deeply, while the fresh and blissful fragrance shaped a passing moment in that now distant summer night.

About the Author

Like the "Patriarcha-Dagans" of her novel, Ann Cowart-Lutzky's family is Spanish-Filipino, European-American and Russian-Jewish. Cowart-Lutzky is from Oakland, California, and is married with a son (1974-1998) and a twenty-year-old daughter. She graduated in philosophy from U.C. Berkeley in l967 and has taught and counseled in Africa and the U.S.